Vampire Beach

Vampire Beach

Ritual and *Legacy*

Alex Duval

Simon Pulse
New York • London • Toronto • Sydney

SIMON PULSE

An imprint of Simon & Schuster Children's Publishing Division

1230 Avenue of the Americas, New York, NY 10020

Ritual copyright © 2007 by Working Partners Limited

Legacy copyright © 2007 by Working Partners Limited

All rights reserved, including the right of reproduction in whole or in part in any form.

SIMON PULSE and colophon are registered trademarks of Simon & Schuster, Inc.

Designed by Steve Kennedy

The text of this book was set in Adobe Caslon.

Manufactured in the United States of America

Library of Congress Control Numbers:

Ritual: 2006928112

Legacy: 2006937103

ISBN 978-1-4169-5455-2

These titles were originally published individually by Simon Pulse.

CONTENTS

Vampire Beach

Ritual

For Deborah Rose Bramwell

Special thanks to Laura Burns and Melinda Metz

ONE

"Let's sign up for an angel reading!" Jason Freeman's little sister, Dani, exclaimed from the backseat of his 1975 Volkswagen. "It says here that the psychic is in touch with the angels all around us and passes on information from them."

Jason was chauffeuring Dani and her friend Kristy to the Arcana Psychic Fair since neither of them was quite old enough to have a driver's license. He had agreed to do this only because Dani had promised to do his chores for three weeks in payment.

Their parents were in New York for some business thing of his dad's, so they couldn't take the girls. And Kristy's parents had given a big "no way" when she had asked them to drive. Maria—Dani and Kristy's designated driver, who was a year older and had already taken driver's ed—was sick. That left Jason, who now had three sweet chore-free weeks to look forward to.

"The angel reading sounds good," Kristy told Dani. "But top of my list is one of those pictures where you can see your aura. You can tell which are your strong points—like creativity or a healing nature."

"Yeah, and a picture would be a great souvenir, too," Dani agreed.

"I don't know if the aura picture is a good idea. It looks like you're having a bad-hair day," Jason teased his sister.

"You're being paid to drive, not talk," Dani joked back, her chin-length auburn hair blowing around her face.

"I'm getting paid? All right. Because getting up at six on a Saturday morning is insane. Is there a reason this thing had to be out in the middle of the Mojave instead of right in our own Malibu?"

"The area near Joshua Tree has great spiritual vibrations," Kristy explained.

Jason nodded. "Well, I'm thinking that four weeks of chores isn't really enough to cover the early hour and the almost-three-hour drive, so I'm glad you're throwing in some cash." Not that driving down the highway through the desert was so bad. Jason loved driving the Bug, top down, on a nice, flat stretch of mostly empty road.

"*Three* weeks," Dani protested, just the way Jason knew she would. "Three weeks. That's your pay. That's what you agreed to, and that is what you're getting. No money, no nothing else. And, actually, I think *two* weeks would be a lot more reasonable since you're getting to use Maria's ticket, which cost forty bucks."

"Yeah. You're getting into the fair for free," Kristy agreed. "And the ticket includes one reading of your choice. You should knock off a week of chores for that."

"That's okay," Jason responded. "I already know what the angels would say: 'Jason, you're so hot.' 'Jason, are we going to hook up at the next party?' Stuff like that. I mean, that's what they say at school."

"In your dreams," Dani muttered.

"You two can have the extra reading," Jason said. "I think I'll go get a coffee or something and pick you guys up later."

"He thinks the whole psychic fair is silly," Dani explained to her friend.

"Maria went to London over Thanksgiving and she said everyone there is really into the occult. Girls go get crystal therapy as often as manicures. Not that it's just a girl thing," Kristy added quickly. "We'll find you a good manly reading, Jason."

He glanced in the rearview mirror and saw Kristy and Dani leaning over the brochure for the fair—as if they didn't have it memorized by now.

"Tarot cards?" Dani murmured. "Past-life regression? Channeling? Hmmm. Channeling. I want to try that. Maria said channelers can warn you about bad things that are going to happen to you so that you can be prepared."

Jason wasn't crazy about the sound of that. "Guys, you know a fair like this is going to bring out a lot of people who are just after your money," he said. "I want you to have fun. But don't let anybody convince you to whip out your AmEx and pony up five hundred dollars for a charm of protection or a love potion or something. Just think of the whole thing as entertainment, okay?"

"Don't you believe in *anything,* Jason?" Kristy asked.

"I believe in a lot of things," Jason answered.

"Yeah," Dani put in. "You believe in surfing, and tacos at Eddie's, and your car, and—"

"Wait! Here's the perfect thing for your brother," Kristy interrupted. "It's a total guy thing. It's not a reading, but it says you can use a reading ticket."

"'A lecture that reveals the dark magic of vampires,'" Dani read over her friend's shoulder. She laughed. "Kristy, we've got to start him out small. Maybe the lecture on herbal healing would be good. Jason's head will probably implode if he tries to accept that *vampires* exist."

But the weird thing was that Jason did. He completely accepted it. Because, since moving from Michigan to DeVere Heights, Jason had found the body of a girl killed by a vampire, been attacked by a vampire, and made friends with a vampire. In fact, in

DeVere Heights, Jason had even fallen in love with Sienna Devereux—and she was, quite definitely, a vampire.

"There it is!" Kristy called out. "The Joshua Tree Center for Mind, Body, and Spirit."

There it is, and nothing else, Jason thought as he parked the Bug. He could forget about his plan of escaping for some coffee and downtime. Unless he wanted to drive twenty miles back to that barely-a-town before the turn off.

"You think they have coffee in there anyplace?" he asked the girls. "Soda? A place where I can get caffeine injected directly into my heart?" Why had he agreed to do anything that involved getting up before noon on Saturday? Especially when it didn't even involve any surfing. Now, riding the waves was a rush it might have been worth getting up at dawn for.

"It says in the brochure that they have all kinds of food and stuff," Kristy told him.

"Does that mean you're coming in?" Dani inquired.

"Lead the way," Jason told her.

"I wonder if we'll see anyone from school here," Dani said as they crossed the parking lot.

"Why would we? We're hours away from Malibu," Jason pointed out. He definitely didn't want to be seen at the Arcana Psychic Fair. It's not that he didn't have an open mind. Or believe in *things*. But this was a completely woo-woo, touchy-feely kind of event at which no self-respecting guy should be seen.

"It's not like we're the only ones interested in this stuff," Kristy said. "And this is the biggest psychic fair in Southern California."

"Okay, let's get one thing straight. You see anyone from school, you give me a heads-up, because I'll be struck with the sudden urge to use the bathroom. And no telling anyone I was here, or I'll never drive either of you anywhere again. Got it?" Jason demanded.

Dani pulled the tickets out of her purse and thrust them at him. "Fine," she said. "Like Kristy and I spend our time gossiping about *you*, anyway."

The two girls hurried into the big adobe building ahead of him. Jason handed the tickets to the guy at the door, shoved the stubs into his wallet, and slowly followed the girls. The large cavern of a room was filled with row after row of booths, some with vendors selling stuff like herbs or books—one actually looked like it was selling *broomsticks*—some set up with people doing tarot readings or crystal gazing. Jason was surprised by how normal many of the supposed psychics seemed. A lot of them were wearing jeans and shirts that could have come straight out of the Gap.

And why shouldn't they? he asked himself. *Why should psychics wear turbans and those long, gauzy skirts?* The vampires he knew looked like normal people.

Okay, über-popular, drop-dead-gorgeous normal people, but normal nonetheless. They didn't wear long black capes—at least, not unless they were Versace or Dolce & Gabbana—they didn't have fangs unless they were drinking blood, and they didn't only come out at night, although he had to admit that they were certainly in their element at night, especially when it came to dancing by moonlight at a hot party in full swing. In fact, the vampires he knew didn't fall into any of the vampire clichés.

Jason headed after Dani and Kristy, not bothering to catch up to them. The air in the center seemed weighted down with the scent of candle wax, incense, and old paper. But he could see equipment that looked ultra high-tech, too, and massage tables that looked like they'd been pulled straight from a sports med clinic.

He paused at one vendor's booth that sold jewelry. There was this one thing that grabbed him: a simple, perfectly round crystal, dark and iridescent, hanging from a slender silver chain. He could see Sienna wearing it, but he knew it wasn't something he could buy her. He could maybe get away with giving her some goofy little thing, but that was it as long as she was with another guy. Which she was. Another guy who happened to be a friend of Jason's.

But that won't be forever, will it? Jason wondered. *They—*

"Jason, we thought you'd want to know," Kristy said, appearing beside him and breaking into his thoughts. "We just saw Belle Rémy heading over to talk to the guy who gives instruction on astral projection. That's just one row over."

"And you know that where there's Belle Rémy, there's usually Sienna Devereux," Dani added, her gray eyes sparkling. "Now, are you still sure you don't want to see anyone from school? Because you usually like to see Sienna."

"One row that way, or that way?" Jason asked, not sure if he wanted to know so that he could go find her or so that he could avoid her. On the one hand, he always liked to see her. On the other, he was pretty sure that a psychic fair was not a cool place for a guy to be seen. That sense of indecision was a feeling he often had about Sienna—the girl he was in love with, even though he shouldn't be. He loved to be around her, but being around her was often hard, too.

Dani and Kristy looked at each other and cracked up. And Jason realized he'd been had. By two little sophomores. He rolled his eyes. "Very funny."

"It *was* very funny," Dani agreed. "You should have seen your face." She widened her eyes and let her mouth drop open, and she and Kristy cracked up again.

"Remember who drove you here," Jason mock-threatened. "Remember how far you'd have to walk to get home—through the desert, in your silly little shoes."

They both ignored him. "Oooh, I'm going to sign up for one of those massages," Kristy said, looking over at a booth across the aisle. "They don't even touch you. They just manipulate your energy field. It's supposed to make you feel amazing. You want me to put you down?" she asked Dani. "Look how long the line is already."

"I think I'd feel weird getting massaged in front of everybody like that," Dani said. Jason nodded, glancing at the masseur, who stood over a woman lying on the table in his small booth, plucking the air around her body as if he were playing the bass.

"That won't bother me," Kristy answered. "Be right back." She hurried over to the booth.

"So what is the deal with you and Sienna, anyway?" Dani asked Jason. "I've seen how you are together at parties, and sometimes even just in the hall at school. There's this vibe between you."

"We're friends," Jason told her. "She was one of the first people I met when we moved here."

Dani raised one eyebrow. "And that's it? Friends?"

Jason shook his head. "Dani, you know every detail about every person at DeVere High. That means you have to know that Sienna and Brad Moreau have been—"

"Together practically forever," Dani finished for him. "I know. But I also know what I see. And I see a vibe, and it's definitely not on the *friend* frequency."

Jason knew where Dani was coming from. The fact was that he and Sienna *had* ended up kissing once or twice—hot, passionate kisses that turned him inside out—and that should never have happened.

After the last time, they had promised each other that they would figure out the whole them-slash-Brad thing. But it had been a couple of days and he and Sienna hadn't spoken at all. Jason didn't know what that meant. Maybe it meant Sienna just wanted to pretend the kissing never happened and stick with Brad. The trouble was that if Jason couldn't be with her soon—with no hiding and no pretending necessary—he felt he'd go mad.

"Am I wrong?" Dani asked.

"You're not wrong," Jason said quietly. "But, like I said, Sienna's with somebody else." He felt relieved when Kristy bounded back over to them. He didn't want to discuss the Sienna situation with his sister.

"Hey, Kristy, don't you think Sienna and my brother would make a cute couple?" Dani asked.

Jason's mouth dropped open in shock. How could she just ask something so blatant? "Danielle—" he began.

"Absolutely," Kristy replied. "Couples are all about the contrast. Sienna has black hair and almost black eyes." She turned to Jason. "And you're more Heath Ledger-ish, what with the blond hair. You two would look amazing together."

"And that's all that matters," Jason joked, trying to act as if this subject didn't bother him.

"No, but you guys have the vibe, too," Kristy added.

Did *everyone* see this thing that sparked between him and Sienna? Jason wondered. Did Brad?

"The vibe is more important, really," Kristy went on. "The looks thing is just—"

"Madame Rosa's Palm Reading," Jason said loudly, interrupting her. "You guys have got to do that. Can't miss it."

"Jason, this wasn't on the list we made," Dani said as she followed him over to the blue and purple tent that had been set up between two of the booths.

"But look at it. It's the best thing here," Jason answered. Anything to get them off the Sienna subject. "And, hey, look, no line!" He ducked into the tent and saw the kind of psychic he'd expected to see all over the fair. She wore a long, gauzy skirt of white and gold, a white peasant blouse, and a necklace made of small gold coins. There was no turban, but Madame Rosa did have a scarf covering her wild gray curls.

"Vel-come," she said.

Outstanding, Jason thought. *She's actually going for a Romanian accent. Well, good for her.* Jason would have had an easier time believing a psychic prediction from somebody in regular jeans and a T-shirt than from this lady right out of some old movie, but, whatever, he was here for the distraction, and Madame Rosa was certainly that.

"My sister wants to get her palm read," Jason told Madame Rosa. "I'll pay."

"Can you tell who is going to ask her to the masked ball?" Kristy demanded as Madame Rosa took Dani's hand.

Jason knew Kristy was referring to the Christmas Charity Masked Ball being given by Sienna's parents. They gave the ball every year to raise money for homeless shelters in South Central. Jason couldn't help wondering if he and Sienna would have the them-slash-Brad issue worked out by then.

"Can you tell me if that note I found near my locker was for me or for someone else?" Dani asked.

"Oh, and you have to say if Max likes her or not. She keeps saying he doesn't, but I know he does," Kristy added.

"Oh, thanks, Kristy," Dani said. "That's so gross."

Operation Madame Rosa successful, Jason thought. Dani and Kristy were so interested in what the psychic had to say that they'd forgotten all about him and Sienna.

"Hush," Madame Rosa said. "I need to concentrate."

She stared down at Dani's palm for a long moment, then ran her finger over the deepest line that ran horizontally across the top of Dani's hand. "This is your heart line. Do you see this star, here?"

Jason leaned forward and saw several short lines crossing the main line in a way that looked sort of like a star—in that way that little kids draw stars. "A star means happiness in your marriage," Madame Rosa continued.

"I better not be getting married soon," Dani said. "I'm planning to have some fun first. My Aunt Bianca might let me work in her casting agency."

"Yeah, you need to be available for any of those hot actors who come in wanting to be discovered," Kristy agreed.

"The marriage comes later," Madame Rosa confirmed.

Jason had the feeling she was the kind of fortune-teller who made money by telling people exactly what they wanted to hear. People like Dani made it especially easy by spelling out exactly what Madame Rosa should, quote unquote, predict.

"But the star is also significant now," the old lady was saying. "Stars hold the key for you. Stars will lead you to your heart's desire. They will lead to your true love. Keep your eyes on the stars." Madame Rosa released Dani's hand.

"Is that everything?" Kristy asked, echoing Jason's thoughts. He had read more substantial predictions in newspaper astrology columns.

"I tell people vat they need to know," Madame Rosa said, tossing in a little accent again. "Sometimes zat takes hours. Sometimes a few minutes. Your friend now knows everything she needs to in order to find the love she vants."

At least Madame Rosa's predictions are cheap, Jason thought as he reached for his wallet. The sign outside the tent had said five bucks. He handed her a ten and waited for his change.

"There's zomething you should know," she told him.

Of course there is. That way, you can keep the whole ten, Jason thought.

"What is it?" Dani asked. She nudged Jason. "I want to know."

"Fine." Jason held out his hand. The so-called psychic grabbed it and pulled it right up to her face. She spent about thirty seconds studying his palm in silence. Building up the suspense, Jason figured.

"Your love line is strong and deep. You will experience true love," Madame Rosa announced.

"Si-en-na," Dani and Kristy said together.

And we're back to that. So much for the distraction, Jason thought.

"But vat I am most interested in vith you is your fate line." Madame Rosa ran one long, deep red fingernail up the line that started near the base of Jason's palm and ended about three-quarters of the way to his middle finger. "You see this island where the line breaks?" She tapped the spot, and Jason nodded.

"That vorries me. You come to this point in your life soon. And it is a time of great danger for you. Your fate vill be decided von way or the other," Madame Rosa continued.

"What's going to happen? You have to give him more than that!" Dani burst out, actually sounding anxious now.

"I cannot. That is all I see," Madame Rosa said, tightening her grip on Jason's hand.

"Isn't there something you can do?" Kristy asked. "A talisman you can give him to wear or something?"

Madame Rosa shook her head. "He alone vill determine his fate."

Now, that surprised him. Jason had thought that for, say, fifty bucks, she'd offer him a lifetime of protection with a money-back guarantee—especially since he'd never see her again.

Madame Rosa locked eyes with Jason. "The only varning I can give is bevare of the cold. There is a connection there to the danger. So bevare of the cold!" As she spoke, a shiver seemed to run through her fingers and into Jason: a rush of ice that traveled up his arm and into his heart.

Jason quickly pulled his hand away. "Thanks. I'll, uh, keep that in mind," he said, shoving himself hurriedly to his feet and leading the way out of the tent as the coldness of unease continued to course through his body.

TWO

An ice pick of cold stabbed into the back of Jason's left eye. "Now I know what Madame Rosa's warning meant," he gasped, shoving his mint-chip milk shake away.

"What?" Dani demanded.

"I shouldn't have sucked that down so fast. I've got a killer ice-cream headache now," Jason explained, toying with the half-empty cup.

Dani and Kristy both shot him the Eyes of Death.

"Kidding. Just kidding," Jason said, and took another cautious sip of his shake. He and the girls had decided to make a stop at a 31 Flavors on the way home from the psychic fair. "I completely respect Madame Rosa." He gave the lump of ice cream in his shake a stir. "Look, it's not that I don't believe that psychic ability exists," he explained. "But the fair just seemed more about raking in the big bucks." He smiled at Dani. "Something you will not be doing while taking care of my chores for the next four weeks, since you'll be handling them for free."

"Yeah, yeah. But it's *three* weeks, not four," Dani reminded him. "And maybe some of the stuff at the fair was fake, but I don't think you should assume all of it was. I want you to be careful, like Madame Rosa told you to be."

"But I already survived the ice-cream headache," Jason told her. "If it hadn't been for Rosa, I might have kept on drinking without a break and my eyeballs might have frozen!"

"Just be a little careful, idiot," Dani insisted.

"What about you?" Kristy asked Dani. "What do you think you should be doing? Madame Rosa told you to pay attention to the stars." She popped the last little bite of her sugar cone into her mouth. And then an idea seemed to hit her. She chewed frantically, waving her hand in front of her face. "Ooh! I got it!" she cried as soon as she'd swallowed the cone. "Maybe a movie star is going to take you to the masked ball!"

"Well, there are a few sons of movie stars at our school," Dani reminded Kristy. "Oooh, maybe Madame Rosa meant Zach Lafrenière! He had that part in that movie that time. He's not exactly a star, but—"

"He will be," Kristy said firmly. "You can't look like Zach, ooze charisma like Zach, and not be a star. And I can so see you with him. He's never gone out with a sophomore before, but you weren't in town until this semester!"

"Maybe Madame Rosa meant you should pay more attention to zee 'oroscope," Jason suggested. He so didn't want Dani going after Zach. Jason had nothing against the guy. Actually, he and Zach were . . . well, not friends, exactly, but they had an understanding.

Zach had come through in a big way when Tyler had stolen the vampire artifact from, oh, yeah, Zach's house! The DeVere Heights Vampire Council had been ready to kill Tyler. But Zach went against them—even though he was the newest and youngest member of the Council—to help Jason and Sienna get Tyler out of Malibu and safely back to Michigan.

But helpful as Zach had been, he was also deep in the vampire world. He knew secrets that even Sienna didn't know. And that could end up being dangerous for Dani—especially since she had no idea that the most popular kids at their school were *all* vampires. No idea that their own Aunt Bianca—the one Dani wanted to work for someday—was on the Vampire High Council, an even more powerful organization than the DeVere Heights outfit. And no idea that vampires even existed. She'd been lecturing Jason all day about keeping an open mind, but Jason knew that not even the tiniest bit of her brain considered the possibility that vampires were real.

"I wonder if Mom knows the exact time of my birth," Dani was saying.

"You'll need it to get a really accurate horoscope done," Kristy replied.

The girls were completely wrapped up in a discussion of horoscopes now, Jason noted with relief. He wanted to keep it that way. Horoscopes were safer than vampires. Much safer.

Jason had planned to sleep well into the afternoon on Sunday to make up for the torment of getting up practically predawn the day before to play chauffeur. But the first day of December was so sunny and warm that he was out of the house and trotting down the wooden steps to Surfrider Beach by eleven, his surfboard held over his head.

Maybe other people were used to December days that felt like June. But this Michigan boy wasn't, and he didn't plan to waste any of the sun.

Adam Turnball, whom Dani always called Jason's wingman, followed him, carrying the only thing he planned to surf: a beach towel with a picture of Alfred Hitchcock on it. Alfred Hitchcock in swimming trunks. Not such a pretty sight. In his other hand, Adam carried his video camera.

"You sure you don't want to try surfing?" Jason asked Adam. "We can rent you a board real quick, and I'll pass on all the wisdom I've learned from the Surf Rabbi." Jason had been taking lessons for months from the fifty-something rabbi who'd ridden the waves all over the world.

"First, I'm going to fry my lily-white skin to a shade of tender pink," Adam told him. "Then I'm going to shoot some stuff on the beach. I want to experiment with color, the way Spielberg used red in *Schindler's List,* and I need some footage to—" He stopped abruptly and studied Jason for a moment. "Your eyes have already started looking like doughnuts."

"What?" Jason asked.

"You know, glazed. Try to keep up," Adam explained. "Now make the rabbi proud. Go do your Johnny Utah impression. See you later." He made shooing motions until Jason turned and headed for the ocean.

Even though the day was so warm, Jason was glad he'd decided to wear his wet suit as he jogged into the cold water. *Dani would probably tell me not to go in,* he thought. She was sure Madame Rosa was a true psychic, but Jason suspected that that was because Madame Rosa had told Dani she'd find love. Dani had been wanting a boyfriend since they'd moved here, but so far nobody had come up to her standards. She'd always been like that, refusing to go out with a guy unless he was perfect in every way. But Madame Rosa or no Madame Rosa, Jason wasn't about to avoid the sea.

Enough thinking about the psychic fair, he told himself.

Giving up a whole Saturday to it was enough. Now he was going to recharge his primordial batteries, as the rabbi said. Jason wasn't sure exactly what that meant. But he did feel like surfing recharged *something*. And, besides, it was great swimming training. He was part of the DeVere High swim team now, and his teammates were *good*. Jason knew he was going to have to keep in shape if he wanted to keep up.

He slid onto his board and started to paddle out to the lineup, where all the surfers waited to pick their waves. Not too many surf dogs out today. Things got a little quieter on the beach post-summer.

Jason spotted a wave coming at him that was big enough to push him halfway back to shore. Time to duck dive it. He kept the Surf Rabbi's instructions in mind as he stretched his hands out in front of him and pushed down the nose of his short board. Just before the wave broke, he took a deep breath and kept the pressure on the board until it submerged completely. When the wave passed, he angled the board up, resurfaced, and kept paddling out.

He remembered how, when he'd first started taking lessons, just making it to the lineup had pretty much exhausted him. Now at least he'd gotten good enough that he still had some energy left to actually surf. He kept paddling and duck diving until he was out far enough to take his place with the other surfers, then he pulled himself into a sitting position and stared out at the ocean, looking for the wave he wanted to ride.

He let a couple go by, then spotted the one he wanted. Jason used his hands and feet to turn the board so it was facing the beach. Then he pushed the board back, stretched out on top of it, and started paddling. He felt the water swell underneath him, tensed for a moment, then snapped into the pop-up and rose to his feet.

I'm surfing, he couldn't help thinking. It still felt so completely cool. He was *surfing.* That's all he wanted to do all day: ride in, then paddle out, so he could ride back in again.

At least that's all he wanted to do until he hit the beach after ride five and saw Sienna, with a bunch of other people from school. They were setting up a volleyball net. And suddenly, all Jason wanted to do was play volleyball.

He headed over to Adam. "Volleyball game starting up. Belle, Van Dyke, Brad . . ."

"Sienna," Adam added.

"Wanna head over?" Jason asked, stripping off his wet suit.

"I don't really do volleyball," Adam answered, but he shoved himself to his feet. "But I guess I can suffer through a game where hot girls jump up and down a lot, if it means so much to you."

Jason toweled off, pulled shorts and a T-shirt over his bathing suit, and ran his fingers through his hair. "Okay. Let's go. But with all that jumping up and down, don't get so distracted that you forget Belle has one insanely jealous boyfriend."

"Ah, you mean Dominic. Make that insanely jealous with extremely low impulse control," Adam agreed as they headed across the sand. "I will keep my eyes off Belle. Not that she makes it easy."

True. Today Belle was dressed like Daisy Duke, except Daisy Duke never wore a diamond belly ring. She'd even managed to wrangle her short blonde hair into pigtails.

"You guys playing?" Brad called.

"Yeah," Jason called back, getting the usual hit of guilt he felt whenever he saw Brad. His eyes drifted to Sienna. It wasn't cool to keep kissing each other behind Brad's back. They had to make some kind of decision. *The next time I see Sienna alone, I'm going to talk to her about it,* he decided. *We'll figure it out together.*

"You're both on Zach's team," Brad told them.

"That leaves me with one more player," Zach said, his eyes hidden by a pair of smoky Diesel sunglasses.

"Yeah, but you've also got Van Dyke, so it's all fair," Brad joked. Brad and Michael Van Dyke were always insulting each other in true best-friend style.

As Jason and Adam took their places on Zach's

team, Jason noted that the non-vamps were now evenly divided. Brad had Kyle Priesmeyer and Aaron Harberts from the swim team. And Zach had Jason and Adam.

"Service!" Zach yelled. A second later, the ball went flying over the net. Sienna managed to hit it with one hand. It would have made it back over the net on its own, but Dominic gave it an assist from the front row. He leaped up as the ball flew over his head, and spiked it. Sand flew up like a dry fountain when it hit right in front of Maggie Roy's toes.

Maggie leaned down to pick up the ball. Jason and Adam exchanged a glance. The thing had sunk about a foot in the sand.

"Holy crap," Priesmeyer muttered. He ran both hands over his shaved head.

"You been taking more than the recommended dose of Liquid Mojo?" Brad asked.

"You wanna watch it. It can be dangerous," Scott Challon added.

It wasn't that Jason knew so many of the vampires' secrets, but he knew enough to translate what Brad and Scott were telling Dominic. Hell, he could even translate it into pig Latin: *Ixnay on the upersay engthstray.*

All the vampires were crazy strong, as well as crazy beautiful. They kept their looks toned down to movie star gorgeous, and they usually kept their muscle power in check too. Dominic just wasn't good with the self-control—in any area. Jason had seen him almost annihilate a guy who was built like a meat freezer after the guy had done a body shot off Belle, at Belle's invitation.

"Good one, baby," Belle called to Dominic as Maggie tossed the ball over the net.

"You're on our team," Maggie reminded her.

"Oh. Whoops," Belle said with a laugh. "Go, us!"

"You can cheer for us if you want, Belle," Erin Henry joked.

Sienna moved into the server position. It almost hurt to look at her. Her long black hair picked up sparks from the sun. And even in December, her s kin was golden. Yeah, it almost hurt to look at her—especially when it was impossible to touch her.

Brad was nothing like Dominic in the jealousy department. If he had been, Jason would probably be dead by now. How could Brad miss the way Jason looked at his girlfriend? Hard as Jason tried not to stare, he—

Womp! Sienna slammed the ball across the net, aiming right at Jason. He caught a glimpse of a play-ful smile on her face as the ball whizzed toward the sand at his feet.

Oh, no, Jason thought. *I'm not letting her get away with that!*

He dove for the ball, managing to get his clasped hands underneath it just before it hit the ground. He shot it up into the air, and Scott tapped it easily back over the net.

Jason leaped back onto his feet in time to get the next volley, and they all played on until Adam somehow whacked the ball out-of-bounds on their own side of the net. As they changed positions, Jason shot a look at Sienna.

She was looking back, her dark eyes shining, and Jason felt a flush of pleasure. He hadn't made a complete fool of himself, then, even playing with all these superhero types. Sienna blushed too, the tiniest bit.

She's thinking the same thing I am, Jason thought with complete certainty. *She's thinking that we should be together.*

"You're actually going jogging now? After the surfing and the volleyball?" Adam shook his head.

"I find my life easier to manage if I'm semi-exhausted at all times," Jason told him. "It lowers my stupidity level."

"I think it works in the opposite direction," Adam said. "If you're tired, you're more stupid. Look it up."

"Not me," Jason muttered. "When I'm lacking energy, I'm less likely to do stupid things that I shouldn't do." *Like kiss my friend's girlfriend,* he added silently.

Adam rubbed his arm. "Well, I'm going to have to pull out the BenGay. I got a bruise from Belle. *Belle*. A petite little *girl*!"

"A petite little *vampire*," Jason corrected him. "You know they're super-strong."

"Yeah, well, strong is one thing. But this is ridiculous—my shoulder got in the way of her hand when she was going for the ball. And now, Ben-Gay. Maybe some Epsom salts."

"That's what happens when we mortals try to play with the superheroes," Jason said. "I wouldn't be surprised if I had some black and blue on me, too."

"I doubt it. You're all sporty and impressive, yourself," Adam muttered good-naturedly as he gathered up his beach gear and camera. "Anyway, I'm out. Got to do a weekend's worth of homework in one night." He glanced up at the parking lot at the top of the cliffs. "Not too many cars—and I use the word loosely because I'm including my Vespa—left up there now."

"I'm not going to stay much longer either," Jason told him. "See you in history." Jason gave Adam a half salute and started to jog down the beach toward the pier. The sun would be beginning to set when he turned back and he could catch the view.

Not that the view going in this direction was bad—he hadn't managed to find a bad view in Malibu yet—and he had it mostly to himself. There were a few surfers still at the lineup. A golden retriever who wanted his ball thrown into the water again and again and again. The golden retriever's person, who seemed happy to keep throwing. And a couple making out, mostly covered by their beach blanket.

By the time he decided to turn around, the only other human he could spot was one seal-like surfer out there in his wet suit. That was one of the cool things about December in Malibu: Sometimes it was like you had your own private island—as long as you didn't look over at the Pacific Coast Highway, running along the top of the cliffs.

The sun was an orange-red ball in a crimson sky that was deepening to purple. Excessive.

Jason veered toward his beach towel as a cool wind suddenly blew across the beach, making the hairs on his arms stand up. He shivered, feeling cold in the evening air. *Beware the cold,* a little voice whispered in his head.

Jason ignored it. A cold wind in December was hardly something to worry about. He reached his beach towel and noted that his wet suit was completely dry. He could just stuff it in his backpack. He leaned down to grab the pack—

Thunk! Jason felt something cold and hard slam into his body.

The impact forced him to stagger backward. Red

dots—like a dozen tiny setting suns—filled his vision for a moment. He blinked and looked down to see a thin metal bar sticking out of his chest. His stomach slowly turned over. Metal. In his body. His brain tried to understand.

The metal shone bright silver, reflecting the dying rays of the sun as Jason gently touched the silver shaft. Waves of cold pain radiated from the metal into every part of his body. *How did it get . . . ? Did someone . . . ?*

Jason realized that it didn't matter. He just needed to get out of there—fast!

He took one step before his knees buckled. The sand and the ocean and the red-orange sun all slid away into blackness.

THREE

"Jason. *Jason!*"

The voice came in a whisper. Or else the person speaking was very far away. Jason tried to open his eyes so he could tell which. He managed to crack them about an eighth of an inch. His eyelids felt like they'd been turned to lead.

"Jason, you *are* awake! I thought so."

Dani. It was Dani's voice. Louder now. Jason struggled to open his eyes a little wider, and saw Dani's face, hazy-blurry, hovering above his own. "Why're you . . . in my room?" he complained. "I can sleep. Sunday."

"Jase, you're in the hospital," Dani said slowly.

It was like hearing the word "hospital" brought the pain back. The intense throbbing, high on the left side of his chest, sliced through his fuzzy head, and everything around him came into sharp focus: Dani's face, the plastic pitcher on the nightstand, the thin, white sheets, the yellow curtain around his hospital bed. Hospital bed. He was in the freakin' *hospital*.

"This old surfer guy found you passed out on the beach," Dani continued. "If he hadn't been around . . ."

She shook her head, not finishing the thought. "Do you remember anything? I know the cops are going to want to talk to you."

"Can I get . . . ?" He flopped one hand toward the pitcher.

"Of course. Sure." Dani seemed happy to have something to do. She leaped up, filled a glass with water, then held his head up enough for him to take a few sips. He felt like he'd been eating sand.

"Mom and Dad are trying to get here. All the flights out of Manhattan are snowed in. Mom's in a meltdown, of course," Dani told him, putting the glass back down.

"S'okay. I'm fine," Jason managed to get out.

"Yeah. That's what the doctor said," Dani answered. "She talked to Mom and Dad too. You got hit high enough in the chest that it didn't damage your heart or lungs or anything vital." She sat down, then immediately stood back up again. "Do you want anything else? Another pillow? Or Jell-O? Don't you always have to eat Jell-O in hospital?"

"You know I hate Jell-O," Jason croaked, smiling at her, trying to calm her down.

"Well, *I* could eat it. I love the wiggly," Dani said. She was trying to sound light, but Jason could see that her gray eyes were dark with worry. "Do you remember any of what happened?" she asked again, getting serious.

Jason shook his head. Big mistake. He'd been hit in the chest, but something inside his skull felt like it had shattered. And the shaking just rattled all the pieces around.

"I remember jogging. The beach had emptied out. I was heading back toward the sunset. I remember starting to pick up my beach gear. Then something slammed into me and I felt cold." Jason shrugged. Pain immediately exploded from the hot nugget in his chest. *Note to self: no shrugging and no head shaking.*

"Cold!" Dani's eyes widened. "Jason, Madame Rosa was right! She said 'beware the cold'—remember?"

"I think the word was 'bevare,'" Jason answered. He yawned. He'd only been awake for a few minutes, but he felt exhausted. "And what she should have told me to bevare of . . . was flying . . . pieces of . . . pointed metal."

His eyelids closed. The bed seemed to lift off the floor and spin for a moment. He thought Dani was saying something, but she was sounding really far away again. . . .

Jason slowly opened his eyes. Plastic pitcher. Thin, white sheets. Sienna's face. Yellow curtain. He was still in the hospital.

Back it up. *Sienna's* face? He blinked a few times. Yeah, it was Sienna sitting by his bed and not Dani.

"You're awake," she said.

"People seem to feel the need to tell me that lately," Jason commented. "Since we're playing state-the-obvious, you're gorgeous." He didn't think he'd ever said anything quite so blatant to her before. But he was in the hospital, which basically gave him a get-out-of-jail-free card. And she *was* gorgeous. Even if you made everything else about her ordinary and just kept the lips, all pink and plump, she'd be gorgeous.

"You're medicated, Michigan," Sienna told him, but she smiled. With the lips.

"I do feel a little . . . woozy," Jason admitted. "Like, wasn't Dani here when I went to sleep?"

"Dani spent all of last night here," Sienna told him. "And half of today. I kicked her out. I told her she wasn't allowed back until she'd had at least five hours' sleep."

"Wait. You're saying it's, like, Monday afternoon?" Jason asked.

Sienna glanced at the watch on her slender wrist. "Six-seventeen p.m. on Monday, December second."

Jason used both hands to try to shove himself into a sitting position, ignoring the jolts of pain rocking his body. Sienna was at his side almost instantly. She had him propped up against two pillows effortlessly. It was so easy to forget how strong she was.

Especially when she was so close. Close enough that her tangy-sweet smell filled his nose. Close enough that her long, inky hair was brushing the skin of his bare arms.

"How did you even know I was here?" Jason said, because he had to say something.

Sienna smoothed the sheet gently over his chest and sat back down. "A little thing called gossip. Haven't you figured out yet that the DeVere High grapevine's pretty efficient?"

"Okay, well, I need you to tell me everything you've heard about that Jason Freeman guy. Because all I know is, I ended up with a piece of metal stuck in me. I don't even know how it got there. Did something blow up? Some kind of freak accident? I can't believe I didn't ask Dani any of this. My brain was kind of all over the place."

"You've been in and out of consciousness," Sienna explained. "Are you sure you're ready to hear everything right now?"

"More than ready."

"Jason, you were shot with a crossbow. That piece of metal—it was a crossbow bolt."

"Someone shot me? With a *crossbow bolt*? Weird!" His heart started to pound, and he could feel every beat in his wound. He took a long breath. "Okay, I guess my next question is, did this person mean to shoot me? Or were they just fooling around and aren't too handy with a crossbow?"

"They didn't stay and help you," Sienna answered. "So . . ."

"Yeah. And the whole beach was deserted. You'd have to have some accident to hit the only person out there." A memory flashed through Jason's brain. He had bent down to get his backpack just before the arrow hit.

"Are you okay?" Sienna asked. "You suddenly went pale."

"I was just thinking . . . I bent down right before I was hit," Jason explained. "So the arrow should have gone lower."

"Lower? But then . . . it would have gone right through your heart!" Sienna said in a trembling voice, her eyes suddenly bright with unshed tears. "It would probably have killed you!"

"Yeah," Jason agreed. It was all he could think of to say. The idea that he had come so close to death was almost impossible to take in.

Sienna did a little shimmy in her seat, as if to shake off the morbid thoughts. When she spoke again, her voice was steady. "So, who do we know that would want you dead?" she asked, all business.

Jason knew the answer immediately: vampires. Vampires, because he knew their secret. Vampires, because Jason's friend had stolen one of their most valued relics—even though Jason had been the one to get it back. And vampires, because surely they were the only people in his life strange enough to use a crossbow as their weapon of choice!

"I don't have to ask what you're thinking now." Sienna sighed, leaning back in her chair, away from him. "You're thinking whoever did it has to be one of my kind."

"Gorgeous girls?" Jason could practically hear the words fall flat. "Sienna, I don't want to hurt you. We both know how much you've done for me, how much you've risked. And not just you, but Zach, too. I don't look at all of your kind and think, *bad*. Or, *good*." He rubbed the bridge of his nose with his thumb. "It's just that the only really big, intense stuff I've ever been involved in—the kind of stuff people get killed over—is stuff that also involves . . ." He let the sentence trail off. He wasn't going to use the word "vampire" in the hospital where anyone could walk in. And Sienna knew what he meant.

"What about Adam?" Jason asked urgently, as a new thought struck him. It was Adam's original suspicions that had led him to do some research and discover that vampires were living in Malibu. Jason would never have known about them if Adam hadn't shared his findings. "He knows everything I do. And he helped me get Tyler away from the—from the Council. What if the same person is after him? Did you see Adam at school today? Where's my cell?" Jason scanned the room, looking for his backpack.

"You can't use cells in here," Sienna said. "And I saw Adam at school. I also saw him about an hour ago when he came by to visit you. He's fine, Jason."

"For a second I thought he could be lying somewhere with a crossbow bolt through his heart," Jason admitted.

"I know," Sienna said. "But think about it. Think about who really knows enough to possibly want to hurt you. Only Zach, Brad, and I know that you and Adam found out the truth about us. We also know that it was a friend of yours who stole our chalice, and that you kept him from discovering the truth. Even your Aunt Bianca doesn't know any of that."

"You're right." Jason nodded. "And if I can't trust you, Brad, and Zach at this point, I can't trust anybody." Brad and Sienna had never threatened him, never even seemed to dislike him, not even at the beginning. They'd both been friendly, right from day one. Zach *had* definitely seemed like he'd rather not have Jason around, but not in a wanting-him-dead kind of way. In fact, Zach had saved Jason's life. And Jason had saved Zach's. They were cool with each other.

"I'm glad you've managed to remember that," Sienna said. "And today, the three of us got together to talk about whether any of our special friends could have been involved. We went through every possibility and we're certain that the shooter wasn't one of us, Jason. Believe that."

"I do." He felt a little better just having talked it out with Sienna. "I guess you guys wouldn't need anything like a crossbow, anyway. A volleyball would be enough of a weapon."

Sienna grinned. "You know it."

Sienna and Jason stared at each other for a long moment, then they both laughed, breaking the tension that always grew between them whenever they looked at each other for too long. Jason was relieved; his body wasn't exactly up to that kind of tension right now.

"Speaking of weapons, who walks around with a crossbow, anyway?" Jason demanded. "Think we're dealing with a wacko who wants to get a really great nickname in the papers?" He didn't think getting close to dead was actually funny. But if he had been shot by some passing nutcase and not by a vampire out for vengeance, he had a much greater chance of staying alive for a while.

Sienna looked thoughtful. "Using a crossbow isn't enough to get him the front page, though. The guy needs more of an angle than that. He should get an agent," she commented. "So, you want to hear what else is on the DeVere grapevine? You weren't the only topic today, you know."

"Of course. Lay it on me," Jason replied. He needed a distraction.

"Well, you were the top story. But Heaton West came in a close second. Basically there was a poll of how many people thought she really wanted the 'growth spurt' she had when she was away before Thanksgiving. And how many people thought her mother was the one who really wanted it."

"Are you saying . . . ?"

Sienna raised an eyebrow. "Tell me you didn't notice," she challenged. "We're talking more than a cup size here."

Jason laughed, and pain shot through his chest. He winced. "Ow. You're not good for me. You make me laugh too much."

"Then you really don't want to hear what Van Dyke was up to Saturday night," Sienna said.

And pretty soon he was laughing again. About an hour later he realized that he'd basically been keeping Sienna hostage. "You should take off. Go gather more gossip. Or create some," he told her. "I'm fine until Dani gets back."

"No. I'll stay," she said quickly. "Unless you want to sleep or something and you'd feel weird with me here?"

"I want you to stay," Jason said, thinking, *How could she not know that?* "I just didn't want you to feel like you *had* to stay. To be polite or something."

"I don't do many things just to be polite," Sienna told him. "I heard you were okay, but I had to see for myself," she added in a rush.

Jason noticed that her voice had a tremor in it again. She was freaked. She was truly freaked by the idea that something could have happened to him.

"Thanks." He reached out to squeeze her hand and reassure her, ignoring the protest from his chest wound.

Sienna slid her chair closer, its metal legs squeaking. And it was like the charge of the ions in the air shifted, the way they do after a thunderstorm. Everything felt newer, cleaner, *better*.

"Jason," Sienna murmured, his name sounding like a term of endearment when she said it like that. "If anything had happened to you . . ."

"It's okay," he said, bringing her hand to his lips. "I'm okay."

Sienna leaned closer as he kissed her hand, her expression intense. "We need to figure this out," she said simply.

"I know," Jason agreed. "Because every time I see you, I want to kiss you."

She nodded. "Me too. Like now."

She bent toward him, and the door swung open. Jason turned his head, expecting to see a nurse or a doctor coming to check up on him. But the person who stepped through the door wasn't a doctor or a nurse. . . .

It was Brad.

FOUR

Brad's eyes flicked from Sienna to Jason, then back to Sienna.

It wasn't like he'd actually caught them kissing or anything, but it was a pretty intense moment, and Brad wasn't stupid. Jason knew he had to sense it.

"Am I interrupting something?" Brad said finally, his tone cold and formal.

A wave of guilt washed over Jason. Brad had never been anything but great to him from day one. And how had Jason paid him back? By going after his girl-friend. *No.* That made it sound too calculating. By wanting Brad's girlfriend for his own—which was bad enough.

Neither Jason nor Sienna answered quickly enough for Brad. He turned and left.

Sienna stood up so fast, she knocked over the flimsy plastic chair. She rushed after Brad. Without a word to Jason. Without even a *look*.

"What is your problem?" Jason heard Sienna say. He could hear each word clearly, because she hadn't stopped to shut the door.

"Oh, sorry," Brad snapped. "I don't know what's the

matter with me. It's just fine for my girlfriend to be staring at some other guy like she can't wait to jump into bed with him!"

Jason did not want to be hearing this, but he wanted to know what Sienna would say.

"That's ridiculous," Sienna retorted. "Jason's in the hospital, Brad. I'm worried about him, okay? That's what you saw. You saw me looking like I cared about a friend of ours who almost died yesterday. Is that okay with you?"

She sounded ready to go up in flames. *Should I go out there? Roll my IV out into the hall and . . .* And do what? Jason didn't know exactly. It was hard to think of anything he could say that wouldn't be gasoline to the fire.

"Whatever! If you say so," Brad told Sienna coldly. He sounded like he was trying to get a grip. "Are you still coming over tonight?"

"I told Dani I'd stay here until she got back," Sienna said. Jason could hear tension in her voice now, but not anger. She was trying to control herself, too.

Jason could remind Sienna that he'd be fine by himself. But he thought he'd let her make the call on her own.

"Do you have a problem with that?" Sienna asked, irritation creeping back into her voice.

"Did I say anything?" Brad demanded.

"No. You didn't have to," Sienna shot back. "I cancel one time to—"

"It's not one time," Brad interrupted. "You're always canceling. Or changing our plans into group things. It's like you don't want to be alone with me anymore."

"Like the volleyball? I thought you had fun with everybody," Sienna said.

"I would have had more fun spending the day at the beach alone with you," Brad told her.

So the trouble between Sienna and Brad was bigger than this one incident. Jason didn't know how to feel about that. Part of him was glad. He didn't want to be solely responsible for their relationship issues.

"Brad, having time by ourselves is great, but—"

"Is this Jason Freeman's room?" a new voice interrupted.

"I'm taking off," Brad said coldly. "You stay with Jason as long as you want."

A moment later, two men walked into Jason's room. One was forty-something, in a suit and tie, and looked kind of familiar. Jason squinted at him for a few seconds, trying to place him. Then it hit him: The guy was a detective. Detective Carson. Jason had talked to him after he'd found Carrie Smith's body. The detective had never figured out that Carrie had been killed by a rogue vampire. But why would he?

Your basic sane Malibu PD official didn't believe in vampires. And it had been a pretty way out situation, even *within* the vampire world. Vampires fed on humans because they had to, but one of their most sacred rules was *no killing*. They never drank enough blood to cause damage—unless they got caught up in a kind of madness, called bloodlust, the way Carrie's murderer had.

"Raspberry-drizzled white chocolate popcorn," said the other guy, who was probably half Detective Carson's age, and had longish blond hair and stubble. He had picked up the bag of popcorn from Jason's nightstand and was giving it a shake. "I like the fake butter myself. I wasn't raised right, I guess."

"Actually, me too," Jason agreed. "I can go with cheese flavored. Especially if the cheese is actually cheez with a 'z.' But that's about it. My friend Adam must have left that when I was asleep. He likes weird movies and weird corn."

"This is my partner—"

Before Detective Carson could finish, Sienna ducked into the room. "I think I will go, if you're sure it's okay," she said quietly to Jason.

"Sure. I'm fine," Jason assured her. "Thanks for coming."

Sienna nodded, picked up her purse, and quickly slipped back out again.

"Nice," the scruffy guy said, dropping into one of the chairs and glancing after Sienna.

Nice, as in nice girl who stopped by to visit hurt friend? Jason wondered. *Or nice, as in something Scruffy Guy shouldn't really be thinking about Sienna?*

"Like I was saying, this is my partner Detective Tamburo," Carson said, nodding toward Scruffy. "I'm Detective Carson. We met—"

"After Carrie died. Yeah. I remember," Jason said.

"You're not too lucky, are you, sport?" Tamburo asked.

He needs to wear a nametag or something saying he's a detective, Jason thought. Carson looked the part, pretty much, with his suit and lace-up shoes. But Tamburo had on motorcycle boots, jeans that looked *real* distressed, not two-hundred-dollar-new distressed, and a black shirt that was unbuttoned too far for someone who had a day job that wasn't bartending.

"I guess I'm either not too lucky or incredibly lucky," Jason answered. He touched the bandaged spot on his chest lightly. "A little unluckier, and I wouldn't be alive. But a little luckier, and I'd be doing something a lot more fun right now!"

"With the babe?" Tamburo asked, one corner of his mouth tilting up in a lopsided grin.

"Or with one of my other friends," Jason replied coolly, wondering how it was any of Tamburo's business.

Carson sat down in the other visitor chair. "What can you tell us about what happened, Jason?"

Jason walked them through it. His decision to take a jog after his friends left. What he saw on the way out: the dog and its owner, the couple under the blanket, the surfers. What he saw on the way back: just the one surfer. Then bending down to get his wet suit. The pain. The blackness.

"Our shooter is quite a marksman," Carson remarked. "If you hadn't leaned down, the bolt would have hit you square in the heart."

"Thanks for reminding me," Jason joked weakly.

"And you didn't get anything on him or her?" Carson asked.

"Even a general impression of height or weight? Anything?" Tamburo added, leaning forward, waiting for Jason's answer.

"The sun was right in my face. I didn't see anyone else on the beach," Jason answered.

Carson let out a frustrated sigh. "Could be this was a random attack," he said. "But let's assume for a minute that it wasn't. Who would want to see you dead?"

"No one," Jason replied immediately.

"Slow down," Carson suggested. "Take a little time and think about it. You never know what will motivate some people. Don't try to think of some huge reason.

Just consider whether you've had any arguments with anyone lately. That kind of thing."

"I haven't. . . . There's nothing," Jason said after he'd thought about it for a few minutes.

"What about Mr. All-American?" Tamburo asked. "We could hear him and the babe 'talking' from down at the nurses' station. Didn't sound like he was a big fan of yours, my friend."

"Brad?" Jason shook his head, starting up a headache to add to the pain in his chest. "No way. Brad's, like, the nicest guy in school."

"Yeah, right. Nicest guy in school yelling at his girlfriend for wanting to—"

Jason didn't let Tamburo finish. "Okay, yeah, Brad was pissed. He thought Sienna and I were, I don't know—having a moment?—when he walked in. They were arguing about that in the hall, but other stuff, too. Stuff that had nothing to do with me. She doesn't spend enough time with him or whatever."

Carson and Tamburo exchanged a look that Jason couldn't read. "Brad and I are friends, okay? We're on the swim team together. I go to parties at his house," Jason explained.

"Okay," Carson said. "Let's move on. Was anything stolen when you were shot?"

"I hadn't even thought about that. I don't know what happened to my board. Or my car. I had my keys in my pocket. Whoever shot me could have grabbed them when I was out," Jason answered.

"Your car and board were both still at the beach. Anything else?" Carson asked.

"My wallet, I guess." Jason looked around the room. "I'm not even sure where it would be. I don't even know where my clothes are."

"As a detective, I would say . . ." Tamburo got up and opened the tiny closet across from Jason's bed. "Yep. Clothes"—he quickly went through the pockets—"but no wallet."

Carson used the phone on the nightstand to call the nurse's station. He asked if the wallet was in the bag with Jason's personal effects.

"Cell phone. Keys. Watch. No wallet," Carson announced as he hung up the phone. "What was in it?"

Before Jason could answer, Tamburo tapped his collarbone. "Nice bruise. Where'd you get it? Got one on your arm, too."

For a second, Jason couldn't remember. "Maybe when I fell . . ." he began. Then he remembered. "No, wait. It was playing volleyball."

"Who were you playing with, King Kong?" Tamburo asked.

"And Godzilla," Jason agreed. It was practically true. Vampires with superstrength could probably take on those two.

"What was in the wallet?" Carson asked again.

"Some cash—about sixty dollars," Jason told him. "An AmEx."

Tamburo snorted, but didn't comment.

"And just, you know, wallet stuff: receipts, ticket stubs." *Like the ones for the psychic fair,* Jason thought. But he did not feel the need to tell the detectives that he went to that particular event. "A grocery list my mom gave me, maybe." Make that a list of potential vampires he and Adam had come up with when they first figured out that there were actually vampires at DeVere High and wanted to work out who they all were—but the detectives didn't need to know about that, either.

Carson frowned. "I can't see you getting shot by a crossbow for sixty dollars and a credit card. Remember to call and cancel it, by the way."

"Seems like you just happened to get yourself in the path of a whack job with a lethal weapon," Tamburo told Jason. "I'm thinkin' our sicko isn't going to be happy until he's managed to off somebody with his little toy." He turned his eyes—blue laser beams—on Jason. "You sure you don't remember anything that can help us catch this freak before that happens?"

"I wish I did," Jason answered.

Carson handed him a couple of business cards. "This is where you can reach us if you remember anything later. I want you to call if you remember the slightest little thing—even a piece of trash you saw lying on the sand—okay?"

"Yeah. I will. I definitely will," Jason promised. He didn't want his family, Sienna, or *anybody* walking around Malibu with a deranged crossbow-wielding killer on the loose.

FIVE

"You're awake!" Jason's mother exclaimed as she rushed into his hospital room, followed by Jason's dad and Dani.

Jason glanced at the clock over the door, trying to figure out just how long he'd been asleep. He was finding it hard to keep track of time here, but he thought it had probably been about two hours since the detectives had left.

"I'm going to have the words 'Yep, I'm awake' tattooed on my forehead," Jason answered, trying not to wince as his mom hugged him carefully.

"I'm sorry it took us so long to get here," she told him as she gently let him go. "I called and called, but you were always asleep, and I didn't want anyone to wake you."

"I'm fine, Mom," he told her.

"You're going to have to have that tattooed someplace too," Jason's dad said, elbowing his wife out of the way and giving Jason a hug that brought tears of pain to his eyes. "Your mother's going to have to hear that a dozen times a day for a month. Then she might believe it."

"Doubtful," Dani commented, perching on the windowsill. "Try a dozen times a day for a *year*."

"Your father was just as worried as I was," Mrs. Freeman replied. "You should have heard him yell at those airline people. As if it were their fault we got snowed in."

"I got Detective Carson on the phone before we took off," Mr. Freeman told Jason. "He said he was coming by to talk to you."

"Yeah, he and his partner were here a couple of hours ago. I couldn't tell them much, though," Jason answered.

His father frowned. "I expect them to have some things to tell *us* pretty fast."

There was a light tap on the door, and Jason's doctor walked in. "Ah, the whole family's here," she said pleasantly, pushing her wire-rimmed glasses up into her reddish hair. "I'm Dr. Quazi. I've been treating Jason since they brought him in."

Jason's mother pounced. "How is he?"

"He's fine," Dr. Quazi answered. Jason shot his mom a told-you-so smile. "As I said on the phone, he was very fortunate in the location of the wound. None of his organs were touched."

"Thank God," Mrs. Freeman said.

Dr. Quazi put her glasses back on and studied Jason's chart. "The pain and shock had him in and out of consciousness initially, but the wound itself should heal nicely," she told them. "Jason will need to keep it dry until the stitches come out, and he'll need to limit his activity for a while. I've told him no swimming for two months."

"Are you listening to this, Jason? No swim team until the beginning of February," his mother cautioned.

"And if there is any new swelling around the wound, or redness or drainage, or an increase in the skin temperature, please call me," Dr. Quazi concluded.

"So you're saying I can go home now? Right?" Jason asked.

Dr. Quazi smiled. "Right. After your parents fill out several dozen forms," she answered. "Please don't hesitate to call me if you have any questions or problems, though." She handed Jason her card and left the room, after being thanked a couple of times by Jason and his dad, once by Dani, and about fifty times by Jason's mom. Jason set the card on the nightstand along with Carson's and Tamburo's. He was going to need a new wallet before he left the building, the way he was collecting business cards.

"I'll go and handle the paperwork," Mr. Freeman announced. "I know your mother won't want to let you out of her sight."

Mrs. Freeman sat down in the closest visitor's chair. It did seem like she planned to get some staring time in.

"Uh, how was New York?" Jason asked her.

She used both hands to push her hair away from her face. "Do you know it feels like about a hundred years since I've been anywhere but the airport trying to get back here?" she told him. She reached for her purse and stood up. "I bet you a hundred dollars your father doesn't have his insurance cards with him. I'll take mine down and come right back." She hurried to the doorway, then turned back and looked at Jason again. "It's really good to see you safe," she told him. Then she hurried off.

"I'm glad she's gone for a minute," Dani said. "I didn't want her to hear this. She's already freaked enough."

Jason sat up a little straighter, trying to ignore the electric zaps in his chest. "What?"

"Everybody's looking for Dominic Ames. He's been missing since Sunday afternoon," Dani told him.

"Sienna didn't say anything," Jason said, frowning. He was sure she would have known. The vampire grapevine was way faster than the ordinary school one.

"It took everyone a while to figure it out," Dani explained. "Seems like Dominic's parents were out late on Sunday night and they didn't even realize he hadn't come home. Then, at school, nobody thought it was strange that he missed a day. He's kind of a class optional kind of guy, anyway, right?"

"He shows up just enough to get by," Jason agreed.

"So what I heard is that Belle went over to his place after school. Dominic wasn't there, but his mom was. She checked with the housekeeper, and it turns out Dominic hadn't slept in his bed Sunday night. I guess he's bed-making optional, too. Anyway, his parents are calling everyone he knows. They've called the cops already."

"Are the cops doing much? He hasn't been gone that long in cop time," Jason said.

"Are you kidding? There's a big search happening," Dani answered.

"Oh, right, I always forget how rich everyone in DeVere Heights is. I guess if someone from the Heights calls the police, they move, huh?" Jason observed.

"That's not it," Dani told him. "Or maybe it is, partly." She leaned closer. "But don't you get it, Jason? It's because of what happened to you." Jason's wound gave an extra-strong zap. "Everyone's really scared that Dominic's missing and the guy who shot you with the crossbow is still out there somewhere!"

Jason flipped through the channels—again. Daytime TV sucked. He should have gone to school.

Yeah, because school is so much more amusing, he thought, settling on a rerun of *Friends* he must have already seen ten times.

"Do you want an apple, Jason?" his mother called from the kitchen. "You should see how red and shiny they are."

"No thanks," Jason answered from the living room, trying not to let his impatience show in his voice. His mom turned into a demented, hypercheerful kindergarten teacher whenever he or Dani got hurt or sick. She'd just told him how red and shiny an apple was, for God's sake! And all day she'd been trying to get him to eat stuff. Or trying to find out if he was too hot or too cold. Or trying to check his wound for symptoms of gangrene, or the flesh-eating supervirus, or whatever.

Yeah, school might have a low amusement value. But it also had a lower annoyance value than home right now. There was no mom at school.

And there was Sienna.

Jason had been thinking about her all day. With daytime TV being so bad, his mind kept drifting to what had happened at the hospital. He wondered what she'd done after she left. Had she caught up to Brad? Had they had another fight? Had they made up?

At school, he'd have been able to suss things out. Get a vibe from Sienna just by sitting in class with her.

Jason picked up the remote again. He needed something to distract him. He'd already gone over every permutation of the situation between him,

Sienna, and Brad multiple times. His brains would start to leak out his ears if he kept it up.

Click. Soap opera. That wouldn't do it. Click. *Dr. Phil.* Jason probably needed the guy, but no. Click. One of those home makeover shows. Click. *Dora the Explorer.*

The doorbell rang.

"I got it," Jason yelled, abandoning the television.

"You're supposed to stay still," his mother called.

"No one said motionless," he answered. He pulled open the door and saw Adam standing there with a bag of what he hoped and suspected were cheese fries in one hand and some DVDs in the other.

"At least one of those had better be an action . . . " Jason began, but he let his voice tail off because Adam wasn't talking, he wasn't already munching on whatever food was in the bag, and he wasn't smiling.

"What's going on?" Jason demanded.

"My dad just called on my cell," Adam answered. "Dominic's dead."

SIX

"You could have been killed," Mr. Freeman said to Jason, shaking his head anxiously. "A boy was shot through the heart with a crossbow bolt only about two hours after the attack on you. Clearly that monster wasn't going to be satisfied until somebody was dead. It could have been you."

"Stop saying that," Jason's mother begged. "It's not . . . it's not dinner-table conversation."

Like that's what's really bothering her, Jason thought. *Like she looks ready to cry for the second time in two days because our table manners are bad.*

Dani didn't look close to tears. She did look close to puking, but she hadn't really eaten enough to vomit. Jason hadn't been able to eat much either. Dominic was dead. Just the other day the guy had been playing volleyball—and now he was dead.

"Sorry," Adam told Mrs. Freeman. "My dad talks about stuff like this constantly whatever he's doing: eating, mowing the lawn, probably in his sleep. It's a side effect of being chief of police."

"Don't apologize. We need to know this," Mr. Freeman said. "Did your father give you any feeling about how close they are to catching the guy? What kind of evidence they've got? Anything like that?"

"He mostly keeps that stuff to himself," Adam answered. "But I know they found the body at that car detailing place over on Center. Right now, Dad's got all his people going over every inch of the place. Plus, they're searching the trunk of the El Camino where they found the body."

Jason noticed a little shudder go through Dani at the word "body." His little sister was having a really hard time with this.

"Are the same detectives working on Dominic's case?" Jason asked Adam, hoping to feed Dani some sort of comforting info. "Those guys seemed pretty sharp."

"Yep. And they *are* sharp," Adam confirmed, taking a big bite of chicken. "Carson's been a detective for more than twenty years. And Tamburo's a real hotshot. He just transferred in from Vegas. They called him Tamburo the Terminator down there. That's how good he is at putting people away."

"That's something," Mr. Freeman said.

"You should be expecting another conversation with Carson or Tamburo soon, by the way," Adam informed Jason.

"I already told them everything I remember," Jason protested.

"But now what you remember could help them find Dominic's murderer," Adam pointed out, serving himself some more green beans—at least someone was up for eating. "Unless there were two maniacs with crossbows running around Malibu on Sunday. But that would be movie reality. Not reality reality. Right, Dani?"

Adam must have noticed how freaked Dani was. He probably thought that including her in the conversation would make her feel better.

Dani managed a small smile. "Yeah, and one maniac is definitely enough," she answered.

"I hope the police are planning to put some safety measures in place until they do find the person who did this," Jason's mother added. "It wasn't long ago that that other girl from your school died. Karen Smith."

"Carrie," Adam corrected. He would know. He and Carrie had been kind of on the way to getting something going before she was killed by the rogue vampire.

"At least we know for sure that that had nothing to do with this," Jason's dad said. "That was just a horrible accident."

Carrie's death wasn't an accident, it was murder! Jason thought, but he kept his mouth shut. He was more than happy that his parents didn't know about that.

"I think I'm done," Dani said suddenly. "Can I be excused? I think I want to go watch *Mean Girls* or something."

Jason knew that *Mean Girls* was Dani's comfort movie. And so did his mom and dad. Jason saw them exchange a worried look.

Then Mrs. Freeman stood up. "I'll go with you. I wouldn't mind seeing it again," she said brightly.

"Me too," Mr. Freeman said. "I don't think I've ever managed to stay awake for the ending." He followed Dani and Mrs. Freeman out of the room.

"You've really heard this Tamburo guy is good?" Jason asked Adam when they were alone.

"Yeah. I mean, he's got a wild streak, as my father would put it," Adam replied. "I'd say he's fifty percent Colin Farrell in *The Recruit*. Forty percent Denzel Washington in *Training Day*—think 'King Kong ain't got nothing on me.' And ten percent Brad Pitt in *Thelma & Louise*."

"I thought Brad Pitt was a thief in *Thelma & Louise*," Jason complained.

"Well, yeah, if you want to be all literal about it. Anyway, the point is, Tamburo's thorough and tenacious. He follows his own rules and he's got attitude but he also has a sense of humor and, I guess you'd call it an honor code," Adam explained.

"I guess we can trust him to get this thing solved,

then," Jason said, standing up and stretching gingerly. His whole body still ached from the crossbow wound. "My mom got some Bubbies Mochi to celebrate me being alive and everything," he went on. "I couldn't tell her that I'd rather have regular mint chip or something like that. I mean, rice paste around ice-cream balls? What's with that? I'll tell you what: a way to damage some perfectly good ice cream, that's what." He shook his head. "Anyway, you want some?"

"Lead me to it, brother," Adam said. "I don't know how they even let you live in the Heights," he added as he followed Jason into the kitchen. "Don't you know Bubbies Mochi is *the* ice cream served at Nobu? You used to only be able to get it in Hawaii."

"How do you even know that?" Jason countered. "You're the son of the poor-but-honest chief of police, as you're always reminding me. So, what flavor you want? Papaya? Lychee? Green Tea?"

"Surprise me," Adam answered. "This may be the only time I get my mouth around anything Bubbies. As I am the son of the et cetera et cetera."

Jason laughed as he opened the freezer. "Mom does know me. There's a carton of mint chip in here too." He suddenly felt a little hungry. "You'll have to scoop it for me, because I'm wounded and all. The Mochi's already in balls."

"So I have a question for you," Adam said.

"The ice-cream scooper's in the drawer next to the sink," Jason answered.

"Funny." Adam grabbed the scooper while Jason got down a couple of bowls from the cupboard, trying not to wince. The motion still made the hole in his chest angry. "My question is, what's the connection between you and Dominic? You go to the same school, you both live in the Heights. What else?"

"We hang out with the same people sometimes. We've been seen at some of the same parties," Jason answered automatically as Adam started dishing out the ice cream. Then he got it. "Wait. You think Dominic and I were specifically targeted? You don't think the crossbow killer just shot us because we happened to be in the wrong place at the wrong time?"

Adam shrugged. "Maybe it was random. *Probably* was."

Jason grabbed spoons. "Want to take the ice cream out by the pool?" he asked. He knew it would be chilly out there. The temperature always dropped dramatically at night, no matter how warm it was during the day. But Jason had a little cabin fever.

"It's your party."

Jason flicked on the backyard lights, and the pool light on the way outside. Then he stretched out on one of the lounge chairs. Adam took the one next to him.

"So we've established you and Dominic do have

some things in common," Adam persisted, digging into his first Mochi ball. "I mean, you're not as possessive and paranoid as Dominic, so people like you a little bit more . . ." He frowned. "I guess I shouldn't talk about Dominic like that. I forgot he was dead for a second."

"Yeah. It's hard to believe," Jason agreed grimly. "And even though the guy's dead, it's still true he was a bit of a jackass. But he was a small-time jackass. You have to be big-time to have somebody want to come after you with a crossbow, don't you?"

"Or you have to be a vampire," Adam answered.

"Did I go unconscious for a minute?" Jason asked. "Because I definitely missed something. What are you talking about?"

"When I was first doing all my vampire research, I read this article on the web about how in medieval Europe vampire hunters used crossbows," Adam explained.

Jason closed his eyes for a moment, then opened them and looked at Adam. "Right away, I see three problems with this new theory of yours."

"Hit me," Adam said, slapping his chest with one hand while eating his ice cream with the other.

"Okay. One, we're thousands of miles from Europe. Two, we're hundreds of years on from medieval times. And three—and pay attention because this is a big one—Dominic was a vampire, but, in case you haven't noticed, *I'm not*!"

Adam laughed. "Good points. All of them." The grin slid off his face. "But I want you to keep thinking about possible connections between you and Dominic. If you're a target, we need to know about it, because we need to be prepared in case that maniac makes another run at you."

"Fine. But I still say it's random," Jason answered. "Dominic and I don't have anything in common that someone would be willing to kill for."

A breeze from the ocean rattled the palm fronds of the huge trees at the far end of the backyard, and gooseflesh rose on Jason's arms. He had the sudden urge to look over his shoulder to see if someone was watching him, but he refused to give in to his burst of paranoia.

Because it was just paranoia. Right?

When Jason walked across the high school parking lot on Wednesday morning with Dani, he was still fighting off the creepy sensation that he was being watched. It didn't help that the whole school felt . . . eerie, somehow. People were standing around in the parking lot as if they didn't want to leave the relative safety of their cars. The usual before-school buzz of conversation was subdued, and most of the students looked tense and anxious. Obviously everybody was freaked out by Dominic's death.

But it was more than that, Jason realized. The reason he felt he was being watched was that he *was* being watched. He was getting a lot of curious looks from pretty much everyone else heading into the school.

"Yo, Freeman," Harberts called as Jason and Dani entered the main courtyard. "You're back. Are you supposed to be back?"

"I missed you too much to stay away," Jason joked. Technically, he was supposed to be home taking it easy for a few more days, but he'd managed to convince his parents that he'd be okay sitting around at school.

"I always knew you loved me," Harberts responded. "You going to come to practice? We're having a team meeting."

"Yeah, I'll be there. I can't swim, but I'm still on the team, right?" Jason answered.

Harberts nodded and disappeared through one of the arches leading into the walkway around the main building.

"There's Billy," Dani said. "I need to ask him something. See you after." She gave him a little wave and veered off toward her friend.

Erin fell into step beside him, taking Dani's place.

"I was just reading this article that said undereye circles are the look of choice for the spring runway. You're now completely fashion forward, just so you know."

Jason rolled his eyes. "That's what I've been striving for."

"Seriously, are you okay?"

"I'm fine." Jason figured he'd be saying that a lot today. "The bolt didn't hit anything vital. The wound'll take a little while to heal, but that's it."

"Good. That's good. We were all worried about you." They walked through the arch and into the dim walkway beyond. "I have to go by my locker. You know we're all supposed to go to the auditorium instead of homeroom, right?"

"Dani told me." He took about three steps by himself before Adam caught up to him. Jason definitely wasn't going to have to worry about being lonely today.

"Your dad have any more info about Dominic's killer?" Jason asked.

"Nope. Dominic's body was clean. The car and trunk, too," Adam answered. "Whoever stuffed him in there was very careful. They didn't leave anything behind. And it's not like Malibu doesn't have the money for all the best forensic toys. Believe me, anything that could be tested, scanned, or run through a centrifuge has been. It's like all three *CSI* shows rolled into one."

"My father's not an idiot or anything, but I think he actually believes the world should work like it does on *CSI*," Jason replied. "He's going to expect, I don't know, your dad to uncover a grasshopper egg and a piece of thread and have the shooter locked away—"

"By the end of the hour?" Adam interrupted as they walked into the auditorium.

"He knows we aren't *actually* living in a TV show," Jason responded. "I figure your dad's probably got a few days, maybe a week."

"Before what?" Adam asked.

Jason shrugged. "Before he starts organizing parents' meetings or civilian task forces or something. He's a results-oriented kind of guy." He dropped into a seat near the back of the room. The topic of the special assembly hadn't been announced, but he was sure it would be about Dominic. And Jason just didn't want an up-close-and-personal view of it all.

"Hey, you didn't by any chance think of anything else that you and Dominic might have had in common, did you?" Adam asked.

Jason was about to tell Adam that he really didn't want to talk about that now—and maybe not ever—when Principal Ito stepped out onto the stage.

"Welcome, everyone," he said. "We are here together on a sad day. As I think most of you know, one of our students, Dominic Ames, is no longer with us.

Dominic was killed. Murdered. It's hard to understand. And even harder to accept. We're going to have grief counselors talk to you in smaller groups later in the day. We want you to have a time and place to express your feelings about Dominic and his death."

Principal Ito lowered his head briefly. "But first, we need to take a few moments to consider your safety. The person who murdered Dominic has not been apprehended. It is very likely he—or she— has attacked another student." Heads all over the large room turned toward Jason, then back toward the principal. "That's why we have two detectives with us today," he continued. "Detective Carson and Detective Tamburo. They will be outlining the safety procedures I expect every one of you to follow until further notice. Some of these apply while you're at school, others are town-wide regulations put into place by Sheriff Turnball." A few heads swiveled toward Adam, who pretended not to notice. "So now I'm going to turn things over to the detectives," Principal Ito said. "I expect you all to give them your full attention."

There was an expectant hush as Carson took Principal Ito's place in front of the microphone. Tamburo climbed up onstage too, but he stayed off to one side, leaning one shoulder against the wall. His eyes roved over the crowd, his face expressionless.

"I wouldn't mind Motorcycle Boots arresting me," a girl—Jason thought she was a freshman—murmured nearby.

"God, Ariel," someone else whispered. "Inappropriate much? Somebody died!"

"Okay, this is going to be simple," Carson announced. "Until further notice, we need you all to stay on campus during school hours unless you have a pass from the office. Yes, that includes lunch," he added as several hands went up. "And I've been in your cafeteria, so you're not going to get me feeling sorry for you.

"We're also going to post a guard at the entrance to the parking lot. You all have a school ID, and you're all going to have to show it—students, teachers, support staff, everybody. That means you'll have to get here early tomorrow morning because there's going to be a line to get in," Carson continued. There were mutters from his listeners.

This is going to make a lot of parents happy at least, Jason thought. *Including mine.* He wasn't exactly bummed to hear about it himself.

"Lastly, we're going to have a curfew for everyone under eighteen," Carson told the group. "You'll need to be home by nine p.m. I don't want to see any of you out on the streets after that time." That one got a lot more mutters and some groans. "Any questions?"

A few hands went up. Carson pointed to Kristy. Jason could only imagine what was going to come out of her mouth.

"What about the Christmas Charity Masked Ball? The one the Devereuxs give?" Kristy asked. "Everyone's already bought their tickets and everything. And it goes on past nine."

Carson shot a glance at Tamburo.

"It's a tough question for him," Adam muttered. "It's hard for even the PD to go up against charity *and* the Devereuxs. They give a lot to the Policemen's Ball, too."

"We have some time on that one," Carson said at last. "Hopefully, it won't even be an issue. If it is, we'll make an announcement later. Anything else?"

No hands went up.

"All right. That's it," Carson said. "Detective Tamburo and I will be pulling students out of class throughout the day. Some of you could have information you don't even realize is important that could help us find Dominic's killer. We want to thank you in advance for cooperating." He gave a quick nod and stepped away from the mic.

Principal Ito moved back to the front of the stage. "I'd like to end with a minute's silence for Dominic Ames." He bowed his head.

Jason lowered his head too. He was ultraconscious

of the heat in his chest wound as he thought about Dominic. The silence in the room was so perfect that he could hear his own heart beating.

Then a small sound broke it. A small sniffling sound. Someone was crying.

The soft sounds turned into sobs, the choking kind, where you can hear that the person can hardly breathe. A moment later, Jason heard footsteps rushing up the center aisle. He looked up, and saw Principal Ito hurrying Belle out of the auditorium. Her face was twisted with grief. She looked nothing like the playful, happy girl Jason knew.

With the principal gone, no one knew exactly when the silence should end. Eventually, hesitantly, people began to gather up their books and backpacks. Adam looked at Jason, shrugged, and stood up.

"Jason, wow, I just kept thinking how it could have been you who died!" Sukie Goodman from his chem class said as she walked by.

Before Jason could answer her, Brad moved up next to him.

"Yeah, it could have been you," he said flatly. And Jason saw something cold and hard in Brad's eyes. Something that told him Brad wished it *had* been Jason.

SEVEN

Jason half wanted to ask Adam if he'd seen the look Brad gave him back in the auditorium. But then he figured it was probably better not to draw attention to it. He hoped that whatever was eating Brad—could it still be a hangover from the argument with Sienna in the hospital?—would soon blow over.

"See you on the flip side," Adam said when they parted ways at the end of the hall.

"If by that you mean history, then, yeah," Jason answered.

As he headed toward calc, he spotted Maggie, Van Dyke, and Zach in an intense discussion near one of the trophy cases. Talking about Dominic, he assumed.

"Hey," he called, slowing down as he got close to them.

None of them answered. They all just looked at him. Like they were thinking, *Who the hell are you and why are you talking to us?*

Which was halfway to normal for Zach. He was a loner, even within the vampire clique, and he didn't have a whole lot of time for humans. He didn't seem to dislike them or anything, he just didn't bother with them much. Kind of the way seniors didn't bother with freshmen. He and Jason had actually had a conversation or two, what with the mutual lifesaving and all, but they weren't exactly best mates. Still, the others weren't usually so standoffish.

Jason didn't know Maggie all that well. But they'd talked. They'd hung out at parties a little. Joked around some. Hell, they'd played volleyball on Sunday. As far as he knew, she'd never had a problem with him.

And Van Dyke. Van Dyke swam relay with him on the team. He and Jason were solid mid-level friends.

So what was the deal?

Jason hadn't expected a parade for being back in school. But he did think one of them would cough up the usual "How are you?" to which Jason would respond with the usual "Fine, thanks," before going on his way.

You need to get a grip, he told himself as he passed the three of them. *They're crushed by Dominic's death and you're bent out of shape because they didn't say hi. Come on, Freeman!*

He stopped off at his locker to get his calc book. He was going to have to make a locker stop between every class, since his injury wouldn't allow him to carry more than one textbook at a time.

"Can you believe she's on the market? I never thought I'd get a shot," Gregory Marull, star forward on the basketball team, said from two lockers down.

"What's the deal? She has to have cut him loose, am I right?" a guy whose voice Jason didn't recognize asked. "Moreau's not stupid enough to have bounced her."

Jason could hardly believe what he was hearing. They were talking about Sienna. Well, about Sienna and Brad, who, from the sound of things, had broken up!

Well, that explained a few things—Brad's die-Jason-die look, for one. Brad obviously blamed Jason, at least to some degree, for whatever had gone down between him and Sienna. And Zach, Maggie, and Van Dyke were right there with Brad, going by the freeze-out Jason had just received.

He wondered whether Sienna had actually mentioned him as her reason for wanting to split from Brad. Jason slammed his locker closed. He hated to think that Brad blamed him. He'd never wanted to hurt Brad. The guy was his friend.

Slow down, he warned himself. If Sienna had decided to break it off with Brad because of Jason, nobody had told him about it. Sienna hadn't hurled herself into his arms when he pulled into the parking lot or anything. *Unfortunately!* Jason couldn't help adding in the privacy of his own head.

He knew he needed to talk to her and hoped he'd get the chance at lunch. On the other hand, he realized he'd look like such a vulture sliding up next to her table under the circumstances. And he didn't want to give Brad any more reason to hate him.

Jason left out a frustrated sigh. He'd just have to wait until English. He sat right behind Sienna in that class. They always talked a little before it started. It would only seem normal if they did today.

Yes, it was definitely better to wait. It's not like it would kill him. After all, a crossbow bolt hadn't.

Sienna was already in her seat when Jason walked into English. *Okay, here goes,* Jason thought.

"Hey, how are you feeling?" she asked quickly, before he could even sit down. She put on a smile that looked bright, but also brittle—as if it would shatter into lipstick-coated bits of glass at any second.

"You seem a lot better than you did on Monday. I wanted to stop by and see you yesterday, but then we heard about Dominic, and Belle really needed me," Sienna went on.

"Yeah, of course," Jason answered. "How's she doing?"

"She had to leave school this morning," Sienna answered. "I guess you saw her break down in assembly."

Jason nodded.

"I'm trying to think of something to do for her— something everybody can do," Sienna told him, pushing her long, silky hair back from her face. "Not a sympathy card, something else. Something . . ." She shook her head. "Something that doesn't exist, basically."

"I don't think anything will really take her mind off Dominic right now," Jason agreed.

"Maybe I'll just try to get her really involved in prepping for the masked ball," Sienna murmured thoughtfully. "My mom's determined that it's going to happen, and that means it probably will." Sienna rolled her eyes, looking, for a moment, like her usual teasing self. "Maybe it would be good for Belle and me to bury ourselves in the million and one chores I know Mom will be happy to give us."

"Anything's good if it keeps her from moping around the house," Jason said. "I know when my grandfather died I needed a distraction. If I was alone, I just kept dwelling on things."

"Exactly," Sienna agreed. "I want to try to take Belle out of herself, you know?"

They were interrupted by Ms. Hoffman tapping Jason on the shoulder. "The detectives want to talk to you next," she told him. "They're using the principal's office."

He stood up. "Should I take my book or . . . ?"

"You might as well," Ms. Hoffman said. "Just in case."

"Bye," Sienna mouthed as Jason turned for the door. He tried to get his brain away from Sienna and onto Dominic during his short walk to the principal's office.

"Hey, it's Lucky," Tamburo greeted Jason when he walked through the door. Cason must be on a break, Jason decided. The younger detective was alone in the room.

"I don't feel exactly lucky anymore," Jason said.

"You're alive, another kid's dead. You're lucky in my book." Tamburo gestured for Jason to take a seat on the couch in front of the principal's desk, while he half-sat, half-leaned on the desktop. "So take me through your story one more time."

"I already told you everything I can remember," Jason said. "I haven't thought of anything new."

"Sometimes just talking brings up things you thought you'd forgotten," Tamburo said. "Besides, you were pretty out of it in the hospital."

"Okay. Whatever I can do to help," Jason said. He made sure to describe every second of what had happened on the beach: what he saw on the jog, getting back to his beach junk, the sun in his eyes. Then bending down, feeling the impact of the crossbow bolt, stumbling backward and blacking out.

"You were facing which way when the bolt hit you?" Tamburo asked when Jason had finished the story.

"I don't know. West, I guess," Jason replied.

The detective looked at him for a long moment, his

expression thoughtful. "You really don't remember anything new, do you?"

Jason shrugged. "Sorry I can't be more helpful," he said. "Were there any similarities between my case and Dominic's?"

"Hard to say, Lucky," Tamburo replied. "Since Dominic isn't here to tell us what happened. There weren't any witnesses that we know of. That's why I'm focusing on you. You're our best chance to catch this killer."

Jason didn't answer. If he was their best chance, that didn't seem very promising. He hadn't seen a thing.

"Don't sweat it," Tamburo said. "You're from Michigan, right?"

"Michigan, yeah," Jason agreed.

"I've never been there," Tamburo said. "I heard about these kids in Kansas, though. They moved on from paintball—you ever play paintball?"

"I played once last summer," Jason answered, confused.

"Anyway, these yahoos, they got bored with it. Seemed a little too tame to them. So they moved on to guns—with blanks, of course." Tamburo shoved himself away from the desk and dropped down on the couch next to Jason. "One of them ended up killing his buddy. You can kill someone with a blank if you're close enough. Not everyone knows that."

Jason raised his eyebrows. "Yeah, I never knew that," he admitted.

"I need to ask you something, and you're not going to like it," Tamburo said. "But do you think something like that could be happening around here—with crossbows?"

"I don't think one of my friends shot me with a crossbow in some kind of game. Or that Dominic got killed like that, no," Jason replied.

"You sure?" Tamburo pressed. "I've seen things like this before, where some kind of fraternity prank goes wrong."

"That's not what this is," Jason said, shaking his head.

Tamburo grinned and nodded. "You know what, Lucky? I don't think so either." He put his motorcycle boots up on the coffee table. "So tell me, how well did you know Dominic?"

Jason was surprised at the sudden change of subject. Apparently Detective Tamburo liked to mix things up a bit. "Not very well," he replied. "I'm better friends with his girlfriend, Belle."

"Oh, really?" Tamburo raised his eyebrows.

"Yeah. Well, Dominic is . . . was . . . kinda hard to get along with," Jason said slowly. "He had a temper."

"And what about you? You got a temper?" Tamburo asked.

"Not like that," Jason answered honestly.

"So you didn't like him?" Tamburo pressed.

"I didn't say that," Jason replied. "Does it matter?"

"Maybe," Tamburo said mildly. "I'm just trying to figure you out. I'd like to know if there's anything about you and Dominic that's similar."

"Oh." Jason thought about it for a moment. "Actually, I'd say that Dominic and I were about as different as two people can be," he said finally.

Tamburo nodded. "Well, that's going to make my job harder."

"How?" Jason asked.

"I'm looking for a motive," Tamburo explained. "Most killers follow some kind of pattern. So far, the only pattern I'm finding is his weapon of choice. Otherwise the two attacks are completely different. And so are the two victims."

"Well, we're both guys," Jason said.

A slow smile spread across Tamburo's face. "You got a point there, Lucky. That does narrow things down by about fifty percent. The killer doesn't like girls."

"Or else he *only* likes girls," Jason replied.

"Good point." Tamburo chuckled. "Well, you can go on back to class. You know where to find me if anything else comes into your head."

"You don't think he'll strike again, do you?" Jason

asked, standing up slowly. The wound in his chest had begun to throb.

"I don't know, Lucky," Tamburo said. "Probably. So do me a favor, will you? Remember what I told you about those kids in Kansas."

Jason stared at him blankly. "Why?"

"Because you can never be sure where an attack might come from," Tamburo said. "It could come from your friends. You keep an eye on them and remember that you never know what's going on beneath the surface."

"I know none of my friends are killers," Jason said firmly.

"I hope you're right," the detective replied.

Jason turned to go, wishing he'd had something—anything—to say that would help catch the crossbow killer.

"And Jason," Tamburo said quietly from behind him. "Don't worry. I'll get him."

EIGHT

Jason headed directly to the pool, skipping the locker room altogether, since he didn't have to change out of his street clothes. And, okay, because he didn't want to deal with all the gossip that would be flying around in there. Especially since today there would be two big topics: one, Brad and Sienna, and two, the crossbow killer. Jason didn't want to hear or think about either of them right now.

He stared into the ultrablue water of DeVere's Olympic-standard pool. He wanted to dive in. He didn't know how he was going to survive two months without swimming. He knew he'd miss the adrenaline rush of the relay, and the total *otherness* of even just swimming laps. Swimming was a time-out for him. In the water, Jason became almost another creature—all body, or maybe all soul. There was no thought, no worries. Just movement. Water. And silence.

Priesmeyer and a couple of the other divers were first out of the locker room. "Jason, good to see you breathing, dude," Priesmeyer said as he sat down with his crew.

"Good to *be* breathing," Jason answered.

Priesmeyer was one of the most devoted guys on the team. He not only shaved his legs and his pits for ultimate slide through the water, he shaved his head. He probably didn't care all that much about the Brad and Sienna breakup. He probably cared even less whether or not Jason had any part in the split. It wasn't as if he were one of the vampires, who mostly seemed to have closed ranks against Jason.

"I hope this meeting's short," Priesmeyer said. "My two and a half pike dive was for crap last time. I need to put in some serious time on it today."

"I don't know why we have to be here, anyway," Wes Duffy, another of the divers, complained. "It's all going to be about how the coach handles the medley without you, Freeman. There's no one else who can take on your position. Everyone else is at least six seconds behind your breaststroke time."

"Not everybody," Brad commented as he and Van Dyke joined the group. He wore his typical friendly smile, but he didn't even glance in Jason's direction, and his voice had an undercurrent of coldness to it. *Not enough for anyone else to notice,* Jason thought, *just enough to make it clear to me that I'm on his shit list.*

"Not nearly everybody," Van Dyke agreed cheerfully.

"Meaning you two, right?" Wes said. "Either of you could cover Jason's slot in the medley, sure. But if either of you *did,* that would still leave one leg of the relay empty. So, I'm basically right. There's no one to take his spot."

"It might take a little time," Brad answered. "But we have to look at the big picture. We need a long-term solution. There were a few good swimmers who didn't make the cut. I'm sure we can get one of them up to speed."

Brad didn't even bother to acknowledge Jason as he said this. It was like Jason was off the team permanently—and not even in the room.

"Yeah, Brad pretty much held Freeman's hand from day one," Van Dyke put in. "Anyone who gets that kind of treatment isn't going to have a problem on the medley team. Brad and I do the heavy lifting."

"Uh, Jason and I. Right here!" Harberts reminded him. Harberts was the other member of the four-person relay team.

"No offense, Harberts," Van Dyke said. "You know we wouldn't be number one without you. Those competitions can get pretty intense. We need someone to make us laugh—you know, break the tension."

Everybody laughed, knowing it was just trash talk. The guys on the team liked to insult one another for fun, but they all knew just how good each and every person on the team was when it came time to compete.

Harberts shook his head good-naturedly. "Thanks. Thanks very much. Just let me go get my big rubber nose and my polka-dot fins," he said, but he grinned as he spoke.

Jason forced a smile too. He wasn't going to let anyone on the team see that Brad and Van Dyke giving him the freeze-out bothered him. Even though it did.

Jason remembered that Brad *had* practically held his hand the first day of practice. He'd introduced Jason to everyone. And later he'd invited Jason to his first DeVere Heights party. Brad had been one of Jason's first friends at the new school.

And now Jason had clearly lost him as a friend—for good.

Jason took a pull on his Jones WhoopAss. Like any energy drink was really going to make him feel better about the day he'd had. "Yeah, so Brad definitely doesn't want me back on the team—ever," he told Adam, who sat across the kitchen table with his own WhoopAss. "He kept talking about long-term solutions for the medley team, like I'm never going to heal up." Jason set the drink back on the table, though it was quite hard to find space since Dani had her astrology charts spread out all over the place.

"It's not really up to him, though, right?" Adam asked. "The coach will make the call once you're ready to swim again."

"Yeah," Dani agreed. "Hey, does this look like a

stellium?" She pointed to a spot on her planetary chart.

"If I knew what a stellium was, I'd tell you," Adam answered.

"It's a conjunction of three or more planets. And a conjunction, before you ask, is when the planets are at the same degree or really close. When that happens, it creates a major energy," Dani explained. "If this is a stellium, it changes my whole reading. It means that guy I'm looking for is going to be more of a Johnny Depp than a Brad Pitt. I think."

"It looks like a conjunction to me," Adam told her. Dani scribbled something in her notebook, and Adam turned back to Jason. "As for you, I bet your horoscope couldn't have been all bad for today. Brad and Sienna broke up. Talk about long-term solutions . . ."

Dani's head came up. Jason shot her a you-speak-you-die look, and his sister reluctantly returned her attention to her charts.

"Yeah, but I think right now what Sienna needs most is a friend. Just a friend," Jason told Adam.

"But long-term?" Adam pushed.

"Long-term? I don't even know if I should be thinking about long-term right now," Jason said. "I don't even know why Brad and Sienna—"

"Hey, this is kind of weird," Dani interrupted. "You and Dominic were both attacked on the first evening of a new lunar cycle," she told Jason, shoving a different chart toward the boys.

"Really?" Adam said, eyebrows lifted in surprise. "That's interesting."

"Wait. You two have left me behind. My brain works on the *normal* frequency, remember?" Jason announced.

"In many belief systems the beginning of a new lunar cycle is a time of great ritual significance," Dani explained, just as her cell began to play some Enya song. She pulled the phone out of her purse and checked the screen. "Billy," she told them. "Adam, you finish educating him."

As soon as Dani left the room, Adam started talking, low and fast. "Want to know something else about the lunar cycle?" he muttered. "When I was researching vampires, I found out that the guys who used to hunt them would begin hunting at new moon and end when the moon was full. I think we have to seriously consider that the crossbow killer is hunting down vampires."

"These are the hunters who used to work in medieval Europe, right?" Jason asked.

"Yeah," Adam said. "And if I'm right, they're now working in modern-day Malibu."

"Adam . . ." Jason shook his head. "Why do you have such a hard time remembering that I, probably your closest friend, am not a friend of Dracula?"

"You ever hear that expression 'If it looks like a duck and it quacks like a duck, it's probably a duck'?" Adam asked.

"Yeah. So?"

"Well, you swim with the vampires, you party with the vampires, you make out with one special vampire—so maybe to the hunter you looked like a duck. I mean vampire," Adam said.

"But these vampire hunters of yours, don't they have any Spidey senses? Can't they, like, smell a vampire at a couple of hundred feet or anything?" Jason asked. "I mean, obviously I *am* astonishingly good-looking. But I'm not quite vampiric in that department, you know?"

"Well, riddle me this," Adam replied calmly. "Do you have a better explanation for why somebody shot you with a freakin' crossbow?"

At one o'clock in the morning, Jason was lying in bed, staring up at the ceiling, still trying to come up with an answer to Adam's question: "Do you have a better explanation for why somebody shot you with a freakin' crossbow?"

Jason didn't have a better explanation, but some things didn't *have* explanations. Some things were just random. And evil.

Jason closed his eyes. And something black slid across his eyelids, a deeper darkness that appeared for a second, then was gone. Jason snapped his eyes open. The shadow slipped along the ceiling and back again.

The tree branch, Jason told himself. *It's the shadow of the branch waving in the wind. Get a grip.*

He knew it was just his brain playing tricks on him. Almost getting killed did that to you, set your imagination running in all sorts of nasty directions. But the shadow had reminded him of something real—he just couldn't quite remember what.

Jason closed his eyes again. But just as he was about to slide into sleep, his body gave a jerk, and he was wide awake. And now he remembered. The shadow had reminded him of being back in the alley by the pawn shop. He'd been there to buy back the chalice— the vampire relic that Tyler had stolen—and someone had seen him. A shadowy figure. A man. Jason wondered if that man had been deliberately watching to see who came for the chalice. Because, if so, it would be easy enough to see why he'd have assumed Jason was a vampire—and it suddenly made Adam's "duck" scenario look a lot more credible.

Jason punched Tyler's number into his cell as he pushed his tray down the metal track next to the row of food in the cafeteria. He took a slice of pesto pizza as the phone began to ring and grabbed a bottle of Borba antiaging water—just because he thought that if Sienna saw him drinking it she'd smile, and Jason thought she could use a smile.

Tyler's voice mail picked up as Jason paid for his food. It announced that the mailbox was full. Frowning, Jason pocketed his cell and headed to his usual table on the terrace. Adam was already there.

"What's up, bro?"

"I just tried to get Tyler on the phone," Jason said as he sat down. "No luck. I haven't talked to him since he left for Michigan. I just wanted to make sure he's okay."

"He's got to be a lot more okay there than he was here," Adam answered. "There are no fanged types after him in Michigan."

"True." Jason took a bite of his pizza. "Last night I was thinking about the, you know, the *cup* that Tyler stole. When I went to buy it back from the pawn shop, I thought there was somebody watching me. Then this truck went by, and they were gone, and I decided I must have imagined it. But now, I'm thinking maybe it could have been the crossbow killer. And if it was, then maybe—"

"That's why the killer thinks you're a V!" Adam finished for him excitedly. "Because the killer saw you buying the relic. Do you remember anything about him, anything at all?"

Jason shook his head. "It's practically all I've been thinking about. I spaced out in every class. At least the teachers are cutting me some slack because I almost died and everything." He rubbed some grit out of the corner of one eye. "But I came up with nothing. The guy was in the shadows. I only saw him for a moment. What about your dad and the detectives? Have you heard anything? They getting close at all?"

"No. And my dad's not exactly easy to live with right now," Adam told him. "I wish I could tell him about my V hunter theory, but if I did, I'd be talking to you from a padded cell for the next decade or so."

"If your theory's right, does that mean there will be more killing before the lunar cycle ends?" Jason asked, his eyes immediately seeking out Sienna at her usual table. Her usual table without Brad, today. Or Dominic, ever again.

"From what I've read, the killing goes on between the new moon and the full moon. Then it's closed season," Adam explained. "It's not good karma, or whatever, to hunt during the waning moon, when the full moon is diminishing. The hunt is supposed to be especially powerful if there is a kill on the day of the new moon—which there was—and on the day of the full moon, which is coming up on the fifteenth."

"So you're saying we could be looking at a killing spree lasting ten more days?" Jason asked. His spine felt like it had been turned into a lightning rod, a lightning rod during a massive thunderstorm.

"Yeah." For once, Adam seemed to have run out of words.

What are we going to do? Jason thought. What *could* they do? He had no info to give Tamburo and Carson. He could hardly tell them to go after a shadowy figure who may or may not have been watching him several weeks ago.

"Hey, Freeman," a voice interrupted Jason's thoughts, and he glanced up to see Van Dyke looming over their table.

"Hey," Jason said, surprised the guy was even talking to him. Van Dyke had been ignoring Jason all week. He seemed to think it was his duty as Brad's best friend.

"Listen, man, I was thinking about your wound," Van Dyke said. "You know, and how you can't swim."

"Only until February," Jason replied.

"Yeah, well, if you can't swim, you probably can't dance, either," Van Dyke said.

"That must be my excuse!" Adam put in cheerfully, talking around a curly fry in his mouth. "If only I'd taken more swimming lessons, I'd be like Justin Timberlake on the dance floor."

Van Dyke ignored him, keeping his eyes on Jason. "Dancing might open up your stitches, right?"

"I guess it's possible . . . ," Jason replied cautiously. He had no idea where Van Dyke was going with this, but he had a feeling he wasn't going to like it.

"Right. So you should probably take a pass on the masked ball." He clapped Jason on the shoulder, and Jason winced in pain. "Just to be on the safe side."

Van Dyke ambled away, looking pleased with himself. Jason just shook his head.

"That unfeeling bastard," Adam said. "I think he's threatened by you. You're the first human around here to attract a V girl. Think about it. Our friends only date their own. They might suck on us regular folk, but that's it. In terms of couples, there's Brad and Sienna—well, there was. And Belle and . . ." Adam thought better of mentioning that couple and just went on. "Zach went to the prom with Sienna's sister. Maggie used to go out with Van Dyke. Erin Henry is with Max Vioget. And so it goes. And so it has always gone. Van Dyke and company don't like you shaking up their old world order."

"I know there are rumors going around that Brad and Sienna split because of me. But Sienna and I aren't together. We've hardly even talked since the breakup," Jason told Adam. "I don't know what's going on with us exactly. But it's not romantic. I don't think she's ready for that. I guess we're what we've always been: friends."

Adam grinned. "Maybe for now. But for how long, amigo?"

NINE

"To go to swim practice or not to go to swim practice, that is the question," Adam said, stopping at Jason's locker after school.

Jason had to smile. He'd been standing there staring at his gym bag for about two minutes, trying to decide whether to head to the pool or not. Obviously Adam had noticed his dilemma. "I want to support the team," Jason said. "But I'm not sure the team is interested in my support."

"Brad and Van Dyke are not the whole team," Adam pointed out. "If you want to go, go."

Jason sighed. Another afternoon of sitting on the bleachers and getting ignored by his so-called friends? It was sure to be a major downer. "You know what?" he said. "I've had enough depression for one day. I think I'll blow off practice. You want to hit Eddie's?"

"Can't do it, my man," Adam replied. "My mom is making me help write the Christmas cards this year. She's got this whole thing set up for today—stacks of cards, tons of stamps, a huge list of names. It's like hell. Only with lots of holiday cheer."

Jason grimaced. "Sorry."

"Yeah. She promised I could eat Christmas cookies the whole time, though, so it's not a total loss." Adam yanked his backpack up higher on his shoulder and headed off with a wave.

Jason swung the locker door shut and turned toward the exit. Now that he'd decided not to go to practice, he wasn't sure what to do. Going home wasn't an appetizing option; his mother would be certain he'd skipped practice because his wound was giving him trouble, and she'd send him straight to bed and make sure he stayed there. And going to Eddie's by himself didn't seem like much fun either.

"Christmas shopping," he muttered. "After all, it's got to be done sometime." The idea of wandering around the mall hunting for suitable gifts was kind of daunting, but it beat anything else Jason could think of.

By the time he reached the mall, he was in a better mood. It was nice to get away from school and all the negativity there. The mall wasn't too crowded, and the hallways were all decorated in pinecone-strewn garlands and twinkling white lights, with humongous bushy poinsettias everywhere. Tasteful carols played softly through the PA system—no "Frosty the Snowman" here in Malibu. It was all "Hallelujah Chorus" type stuff. Jason couldn't help himself—he was getting into the spirit. Only a Grinch would be able to resist this idyllic yuletide setting. Smiling, he headed for Tower Records.

"I don't believe it. The Michigan boy actually shops!"

Jason stopped in his tracks. *Sienna.* He steeled himself to meet her eyes, and turned around.

She looked stunning. Tight, dark blue jeans and an adorable pink ski vest—as if it were really cold enough out to need a vest. Still, she made it look perfectly sensible, like she might have to fly off to Aspen on a moment's notice.

Just friends, Jason told himself. *We're just friends.* "Of course I shop," he said.

Sienna smiled. "Guys usually hate the mall. It's generally a female-only zone until about two p.m. on Christmas Eve. Then the men all swoop in to do their typical last-minute gift shopping."

"Well . . ." Jason felt his cheeks heat up.

"I knew it!" Sienna cried, delighted. "That's your usual MO, isn't it?"

"You got me. I hate shopping. I especially hate shopping for presents. How am I supposed to know what my mother wants? Or my sister?" Jason shook his head. "They're so picky about what they wear, what they eat, how they smell. I'm afraid to buy them anything. I'm sure to get it wrong somehow."

"So what are you doing here? Torturing yourself?" Sienna teased.

"If I'd wanted torture, I'd have gone to swim practice," Jason joked. Sienna's smile vanished instantly, and he sighed. Why had he brought up the swim team? Obviously it would make Sienna think of Brad. How could he be so stupid?

Sienna gazed down at her feet for a moment, and there was an awkward silence.

"I figured I'd hit the music store first and grab a couple of CDs for my dad," Jason said. "He's the easy one to buy for in my family. He has this thing for old doo-wop songs from the fifties. It's totally weird, but it makes things simple. There must've been hundreds of doo-wop bands, because I can always find a CD he doesn't have." Jason felt a little stupid. He was babbling, trying to cover up the awkwardness between them, but all he'd managed to do was make things more awkward. It was obviously time for a different tactic.

"Anyway, where's Belle?" he asked, looking around. "I thought she was your constant shopping companion."

"Um, she's in Cabo," Sienna said quietly. "Her mom wanted to get her out of here for a while. She's pretty freaked out about Dominic."

Jason winced. He'd been trying to change the subject to lighten the mood, but instead he'd just made it even worse. "Of course she is." He shook his head. "I'm sorry. I didn't mean to . . ." He let his words trail off, unsure what to say.

Sienna shrugged. "Don't worry about it. Nobody's thinking straight these days."

"It's good that Belle has the chance to get away. Maybe it'll help," Jason suggested.

"Yeah, she and Dominic had been together since seventh grade," Sienna answered. "She doesn't know what to do with herself now that he's gone."

"That's terrible," Jason said. "Poor Belle. I can't even imagine how it must feel to lose someone you've been with for so long."

Sienna didn't answer. Jason wondered if she was thinking about Brad. They'd been together for years too.

"So when is Belle coming back?" he asked. "Is she going to miss Dominic's funeral?"

"No, she'll come back for that," Sienna replied. "I know Belle will want to come home for the funeral." She ran her hand through her long, dark hair. "You know what? I'm sick of this," she announced.

"Sick of what?" Jason asked.

"Feeling this way." Sienna dropped down onto one of the wrought-iron benches that lined the hallway. "I'm sick of being sad and scared, and I'm sick of crying and worrying. I just want everything to go back to normal."

Jason sat down next to her. "I know what you mean."

"Sorry. I don't mean to whine. And I know it hasn't even been for long. But I just feel like my whole life has suddenly changed and it's never going to change back," Sienna said. "How are you doing? Everything healing up okay?"

"So far, so good," Jason assured her. "My chest aches sometimes, but I can handle it."

Sienna leaned back and gazed at the tall pine tree at the end of the hall. It was decorated with red bows and white lights, and a pile of fake presents was artfully arranged around its base. "Christmastime is my favorite part of the year," she said. "I hate that it's been ruined."

"I know what you mean. Usually right around now is when the holiday spirit really kicks in for me," Jason said. "Of course, usually right around now is when the weather starts getting super cold and there's snow. In Michigan."

"We don't do the whole 'White Christmas' thing here," Sienna said. "The closest you're going to get is some fake snow on a movie set."

"It's hard to get used to," he said. "It's not even cold enough to drink hot chocolate. What kind of Christmas spirit can you have without hot chocolate?"

"We are truly pathetic," Sienna agreed. "Tell you what. Let's make it our mission to get ourselves into the Christmas spirit. Today. Here. Now."

"I *was* starting to feel it for a second, with the carols and everything," Jason admitted. "Maybe, if we both wish very, very hard . . ." He clasped his hands together and did his best imitation of a kid from a holiday special.

"Yes! Yes, miracles can happen!" Sienna answered, in a high, childlike voice. "For starters, I can help you with your Christmas shopping," she offered in her usual tone. "I don't claim to even know what doo-wop is, but I can definitely pick out stuff for your mom and Dani."

"Really? You'd do that?" Jason felt his mood lifting already.

"Sure. But we have to make a pact. Nothing depressing," Sienna said. "As long as we're in the mall, we're in a no-reality zone. I don't want to think about Dominic, or Belle, or . . . anything else."

Brad, Jason thought. *That's what she means. She doesn't want to think about their breakup. Well, that's just fine with me.* "It's a deal," he said. "We're all about the unreality."

"Good. Then let's go," Sienna said, standing up.

"Where do we start?" Jason asked.

"Bloomingdale's for your mom. Then Armani Exchange for Dani," Sienna said. "Or maybe Fendi. I haven't decided yet."

"You're already speaking a foreign language, as far as I'm concerned," Jason joked. He stood up too.

"Just pay close attention to me and I'll have you shopping like a pro in no time," she promised.

Pay close attention to Sienna? That shouldn't be a problem, Jason thought as he followed her toward Bloomie's. Shopping with Sienna wasn't actually as easy as Jason had thought it might be. In Bloomingdale's, Sienna decided that perfume was the way to go for his mother. So she made Jason do a bunch of smell tests of different scents—which meant he had to try to stand still while Sienna waved the inside of her slender wrist under his nose, or lifted her hair and offered her delicate neck for him to sniff. All of which tested Jason's resolve to be nothing more than friends with Sienna for the time being, to the limit.

"You like this one?" she asked, spritzing on yet another scent.

He sniffed at her and made a face, pretending to hold his nose.

Sienna laughed and swatted his arm. "Fine. I'll just pick one."

"How can you tell?" he asked. "Your left arm smells of one thing, your right arm smells of another. You're like one of my sister's fashion magazines—every page has some different perfumed card on it, so the whole thing just smells weird."

"I don't know whether I should be more worried that you clearly spend a lot of your time reading fashion magazines, or that you think I smell weird!" Sienna teased.

Jason tried to protest and explain that that wasn't what he'd meant, but she just laughed at him and held out a tiny bottle of perfume.

"This one," she told him.

He took it over to the cashier without bothering to smell it. If Sienna said it was the right one, that was good enough for him.

"Let's do one of your gifts next," he suggested. "Who do you need to buy for?"

"Well, the hardest one is my dad," she told him. "Every year I manage to pick him something he doesn't need or want."

"What are his hobbies?" Jason asked.

"Complaining about how much money my sister and I spend," Sienna replied. "That's about it."

"I've got it!" Jason replied. "The perfect gift: a money clip."

"Michigan!" Sienna cried. "I'm impressed. That's a great idea. There's a Tiffany's in this mall. They've got to have silver money clips."

"You could even get it engraved," Jason suggested.

"Look at you," she cooed. "Thinking like a shopper already. I'm so proud!"

"Yeah, well, just don't tell anyone," Jason said. "I have a reputation to protect."

"Oh, really? What reputation is that?"

"The one where I'm clueless about stores and shopping—like all the other guys," Jason replied.

"Your secret is safe with me," Sienna promised, leading the way to Tiffany's.

Jason wandered around the store while Sienna talked to the clerk about engraving. He couldn't help noticing that there didn't seem to be a single thing in the whole place for less than a hundred bucks.

"Shopping for your girlfriend?" one of the salesladies asked him. "She's lovely."

"Oh, no, she's not my girlfriend," Jason said quickly, shooting a glance at Sienna. "Yet," he added.

The saleslady laughed. "That's the spirit! Well, if you want to win her over, you might think about getting her some jewelry. We have a lovely friendship ring. . . ."

"Friendship?" Jason glanced into the case at the ring she was pointing to. The ring was a delicate band of gold and silver intertwined. It would look perfect on Sienna's hand. "I guess I could get her a *friendship* ring for Christmas," he mused.

"Ready?" Sienna asked, coming up behind him.

Jason jumped, and exchanged a meaningful look with the saleslady. "Sure," he said. "Maybe I'll come back another day," he murmured as Sienna headed for the door.

"I'll keep the ring for you," the saleslady replied quietly with a smile.

"Let's go to Black Cherry for your sister," Sienna said as they left Tiffany's. "It's this great little boutique that has a bunch of different designers."

Half an hour and one beaded evening purse later and Sienna was clearly just getting into her stride. "How about your Aunt Bianca next?" she suggested, looking around for a suitable store. "Did you have anything special in mind for her?"

"I think I need a break from shopping," Jason admitted. "I feel a little overwhelmed."

She gave him one of her long, sideways looks. "I forgot I'm dealing with a virgin," she teased. "You're obviously not ready for a full afternoon of shopping."

"Sorry," Jason said with a grin. "Hey, how about we just refuel?" he suggested. "Food court?" He'd been having such a good time with Sienna that he'd actually managed to forget about his wound for a while. And he hadn't thought about Dominic or the situation at school, either. He was in no hurry to call an end to the whole Christmas shopping experience—just the shopping part.

"Sounds good," Sienna agreed, and led the way, swinging her small purse as she walked. Jason felt happy just watching her. She seemed in a much better mood than she had before. Clearly their mission to get into the Christmas spirit was working. "What do you want to eat? Sushi? Or they have a pretty decent salad place here."

"No. No way," Jason replied firmly. "I've had it with classy things. It's holiday time, and this is a mall. There's supposed to be a guy dressed in a badly fitting Santa suit, and multicolored Christmas lights all over the place, all clashing with one another. And there should be really loud, really cheesy music playing. None of this lovely classical stuff—it should be 'Rudolph' and 'Frosty' and 'Grandma Got Run Over by a Reindeer.'"

Sienna wrinkled her perfect nose, but her dark eyes danced with amusement. "Is that what the holidays are like in the flyover states?" she asked.

"That's what the holidays are like all over America. Don't kid yourself," he said. "You Malibu kids live in a little bubble."

"Probably true," Sienna admitted with a laugh. "So where does that leave us, food-wise?"

"Well, what we need is something really down home to counterbalance all this snootiness," Jason said. He studied all the options in the upscale food court. It wouldn't be easy to find typical mall junk food in this place. "There!" he cried. "Hot Dog on a Stick!"

Sienna's mouth dropped open. "You are kidding, right?"

"Nope. We're having corn dogs," Jason said. "Come on."

"I thought that place was banned for anyone over the age of eight," Sienna told him.

"You've never had a corn dog, have you?" Jason asked.

She shook her head.

"Oh, you are in for a treat." He walked up to the counter and grinned at the guy in the paper hat. "Two corn dogs. Oh, and an American cheese thing. My treat," he added to Sienna.

"It better be," she joked. "I don't think I'm up to paying for food that comes on a stick."

Jason handed her one of the dogs. "You're going to eat those words. Corn dogs are the best things ever."

Sienna stared at it in dismay. "How am I supposed to eat it?"

"However you want. That's half the fun." Jason took a humongous bite right off the top of his, letting the sweet fried corn bread melt in his mouth before chewing up the hot dog inside.

Sienna went another way. She took a tiny taste of the corn bread. "Yum," she purred. "I see what you mean." She began to carefully nibble all the way around the hot dog, taking itty-bitty bites. "That *is* good."

Jason winked at her playfully, as if to say "I told you so!"

"What's that cheese thing?" she asked when she finished her hot dog. "Give me some."

"I thought you disapproved of food on sticks," he teased her as she devoured American cheese on a stick. "That also comes in spicy jack cheese with a saucy jalapeño flavor that I think your palate will love."

"You've converted me. I want everything on a stick from now on." Sienna said, licking her lips. "What else is there? Popsicles . . ."

"Shish kebabs," he added.

"All kinds of satay at the Thai place," Sienna said.

"Then there's the fruit category," Jason put in. "Chocolate-covered bananas on sticks. Caramel apples."

Sienna was laughing. "You've opened my eyes to a whole new world of culinary delights."

"See? Being cheesy has its charms," Jason told her.

"If only there was some 'Rudolph' playing, it would be the perfect cheesy Christmas," Sienna joked. Then her expression grew serious. "Thank you."

"For what?" Jason asked.

"For this—our afternoon away from all the depressing things that have been going on." Sienna sighed. "It's been a hard week. I haven't had anyone to talk to about . . . anything."

Once again, Jason had the feeling that she was talking about Brad. Between their breakup and Belle's going off to Mexico, Sienna was probably more lonely than usual. He found himself reaching for her hand, and forced himself to stop. *It's too soon*, he thought. Touching Sienna at the moment seemed wrong. It had been less than a week since she'd split from Brad; she might think he was making a move on her because she was suddenly single. And he didn't want to be that guy—the guy Brad and Van Dyke and all the other vampires apparently thought he was. He hoped that if he just waited until it was clear that Sienna hadn't broken up with Brad only because of him, they'd all be able to be friends again. And then, when things had calmed down, maybe he and Sienna could think about dating. But for now, everything had to stay as it was.

Sienna was watching him closely. She had to have seen his hesitation about touching her, but she didn't say anything. Instead, she just smiled at him. "Think you're rested enough to hit Armani Exchange for your aunt now? I won't be able to rest until I've got you through your entire Christmas shopping list."

"Let's do it," Jason said with a grin.

As they wandered back out into the hallway, Jason felt as if he'd lost about fifty pounds. Things were still strained with Brad, but at least he and Sienna were getting along well. She still took his breath away, but it didn't matter. They were friends. Just friends.

TEN

"Do you think this skirt is too short for a funeral?" Dani asked on Saturday morning. Her black, flowy skirt skimmed her knees.

"It looks okay to me," Jason replied, straightening the jacket of his one and only suit. "And if we don't leave now, we'll be late."

Dani frowned at her reflection in the hall mirror. "I guess I don't have time to change."

"Why do you want to come, anyway?" Jason said. "It will only make you sad, and you hardly even knew Dominic. You don't have to do this."

"Like you were such great friends with him." Dani rolled her eyes. "You're only going because you want to see Sienna."

"I'm going because it's the right thing to do," Jason replied seriously. "And I doubt anyone's even going to notice what you're wearing."

"Untrue. It'll be like a fashion show," Dani told him, pulling open the front door and heading out to the VW. "There aren't any parties this weekend, so everyone's going to treat this funeral as an excuse to look good."

"That's not funny," Jason replied.

Dani turned to him, her eyes sad. "I know," she said. "I don't mean that people don't care about Dominic's death. But face it, we live in an image-conscious world. And this is Malibu! People will be mourning and primping at the same time."

Jason hoped she was wrong, but it turned out his little sister understood things better than he did this time. Dominic's funeral—which was taking place at an oh-so-sophisticated and elegant funeral mansion—was packed with what appeared to be the entire population of Malibu, and they were all dressed to the nines. The men wore dark suits, but they were well-cut and expensive-looking suits. And most of the women were in beautiful little black dresses. Even Jason could see that they'd all spent a lot of time on their hair and makeup. It was the best-dressed funeral he'd ever attended.

The vampires looked the most splendid of all, of course. They were all decked out in Italian suits and couture dresses, and they kept to themselves, sitting in a group at the front of the funeral hall. A few of the older women were wearing wide-brimmed black hats, and Dominic's mother wore a black silk veil over her face. Belle sat nearby, dark glasses covering her eyes. She twisted her hands together in her lap, her usually smiling mouth turned down, her chin trembling.

Jason spotted Sienna sitting with her parents next to Zach Lafrenière and his family. Brad was in the next row back.

Aaron Harberts walked by with Priesmeyer. He slapped Jason on the back as he passed. "Hey, Freeman!"

"Hey."

"I hear everyone's heading out to the beach after the service. You coming?" Harberts asked.

"Definitely," Dani answered for Jason.

"What up, party people in the place to be?" Adam said, coming up behind them. Dani smirked.

"It's *not* a party," Jason insisted.

"I know. You're right." Adam pulled at his tie, looking uncomfortable. "I'm sorry. I always act inappropriately when I'm nervous."

Jason nodded. "It just seems all wrong that Dominic's dead. You're not supposed to die young. You're supposed to get your whole life to live."

Dani squeezed his arm. "I see Kristy and Billy. Do you mind if I sit with them?"

"Of course not," Jason said. She gave him a little smile and took off to join her friends.

"You think I can change before we hit the beach later?" Adam asked.

"Why? Having trouble with your formalwear?" Jason asked, taking in Adam's suit.

"My dad made me wear it," Adam grumbled. He shot a look at his father, standing in the back of the room with a few uniform cops. Jason was surprised to see Tamburo behind them, leaning against the doorframe. He was the only one in the entire room not dressed in mourning clothes. Instead, he just wore his typical jeans and boots, and he hadn't even bothered to shave.

He's not even pretending that he's here to mourn Dominic, Jason realized. *He's just here to see if anybody acts suspiciously.*

Tamburo's eyes turned to Jason, as if he could feel that Jason was watching him. He gave a casual nod, and Jason nodded back. Then Tamburo returned his gaze to the other funeral-goers, studying each one in turn.

"Wow. This really is a big event, huh?" Jason said to Adam. "Vampires, cops, and everything in between."

"Anyone who's anyone is here," Adam agreed. "Personally I'm wondering about the rituals of a vampire funeral. What do you think they do?"

"I think they mourn," Jason said sharply. "But then again, most of these people look as if they're just here to be seen, so maybe I'm wrong about that."

"That's the way it is in Malibu," Adam said simply. "Everybody wants to show off, no matter what. It doesn't mean they don't care about Dominic."

A tall man in a black suit stepped up to the podium and cleared his throat to signal that the service was about to start.

"We better find seats. I don't think we non–dentally enhanced types are welcome over there," Adam said, nodding at the all-vampire section.

Jason glanced over. It was eerie to see almost all the DeVere Heights families in a block like that. It was kind of like looking at a living sculpture garden. All of them were almost supernaturally beautiful, each in their own individual way. "Sienna told me that vampires can manipulate their appearance," he whispered to Adam. "That their natural appearance is more beautiful than what they show us."

Adam studied the vampire section. "Looks like they're letting their true selves shine through for today."

Jason nodded as he gazed around the place. All the other Malibu people that had come to the funeral, trying so hard to make an impression in their expensive clothes, they simply didn't stand a chance. The vampires were stunning, and they didn't seem to have noticed that anybody else was even there.

As the service went on, Jason found himself staring at Sienna. He'd seen her look this gorgeous once before, when she had first told him that she was a vampire. She'd let him see her true beauty then, and it was just as mesmerizing now. Her black hair glimmered in the dim light, her skin was sheer golden perfection, and, all of a sudden, Jason felt like the biggest idiot in the world.

Why had he ever let himself think that Sienna would want to be with him? Look at her, surrounded by the otherworldly people she belonged to. She was one of them. He wasn't. End of story.

Then she turned. Her dark eyes met his across the sea of faces, and she smiled.

A sizzle raced through Jason's body, and all his doubt disappeared. It didn't matter what *she* was or what *he* wasn't. They were made for each other.

"I cannot wait for the weekend," Dani said from the passenger seat of Jason's Bug on their way to school on Monday. She raked her fingers through her hair, trying to keep the windy convertible from ruining her careful styling.

"It's only Monday," Jason pointed out. "Isn't it a little early to be wanting a weekend?"

"Duh. The charity ball is this weekend," Dani replied. "If the curfew doesn't ruin it. And I *know* you have to be interested in that."

Jason didn't answer. Sienna's family organized the ball every year. It was basically her party. Of course he was interested.

"I finished my star chart yesterday while you were busy working out," Dani went on. "Which you totally shouldn't be doing, by the way."

"I called and checked in with the doctor. She said light exercise would be okay," Jason protested. "And I only used five-pound weights."

"Anyway, the ball is on a great day for me, astrologically speaking," Dani said. "It's a perfect romance day!"

"You know all that stuff has no scientific basis," Jason said. "I don't think you should count on it. You might be disappointed."

Dani ignored him. "Mom said I can go dress shopping with Kristy after school, so I don't need a ride home today," she told him. "In fact, I'm supposed to meet Kristy before first period to figure out what stores to hit, so can you step on it?"

Instead, Jason took his foot off the gas. There was a string of brake lights up ahead, all of them snaking in a line toward the gates of DeVere High. He slowed to a stop behind the car in front of them.

"How long do you think they're going to keep up this new security thing?" Dani asked, squinting into the sunlight to try to get a better look.

"Probably until they find the guy who attacked Dominic," Jason said.

"And you," Dani said. "You got attacked too, remember?"

"How could I forget? Anyway, that's two students attacked. Makes sense they'd want to be careful."

"Neither one of you was attacked at school, though," Dani said doubtfully. "It seems a little extreme."

The buzzing of a small motor cut through the air, and Adam appeared on his Vespa, driving back along the line of cars. When he saw Jason, he stopped.

"You're going the wrong way," Jason told him.

"I know. The Vespa finally comes in handy!" Adam grinned. "I don't have to sit in traffic waiting to make a U-turn. I can just scooch through the cars and take this baby on the shoulder."

"It's still illegal," Dani grumbled.

"We're all waiting to turn around?" Jason asked. "I assumed it was the usual ID check line."

Adam's face grew serious. "I guess you haven't been listening to your radio, then," he said. "School's closed."

"What? Why?" Jason cried.

"There's been another murder. Scott Challon."

"Oh, my God!" Dani gasped, her face paling.

Jason had a sinking feeling that he knew what was coming next. "How did it happen?" he asked.

"Crossbow bolt to the heart," Adam confirmed, shaking his head. "They found his body first thing this morning. And since all the victims so far are DeVere

High students, Detective Tamburo wanted to sweep the school for anything that might lead to a suspect."

"I see Maria's car up ahead," Dani said. "She drives Kristy in to school in the mornings. I'm going to call them." She pulled out her bright yellow cell phone and dialed.

"Going to DeVere isn't the only similarity between the victims," Adam said, lowering his voice as Dani launched into a conversation on her cell. "Dominic and Scott were both V. You know my theory about this."

Jason nodded grimly. Suddenly Adam's vampire-hunter theory didn't seem so off-the-wall. What were the chances that a serial killer had accidentally chosen two vampires as his victims? "Okay, maybe you have a point," Jason said quietly. "But that still doesn't explain the attack on me."

Adam shrugged. "You were a mistake."

Dani flipped her cell phone shut. "I'm gonna go get in Maria's car," she announced, taking off her seat belt. "Kristy says we can all go to her house and study since school is closed."

"Study what? The best fashions for a formal masked ball?" Jason teased her.

"Maybe." Dani shot him a smile and climbed out of the Bug. He watched her run along the line of cars, waving to a few people she knew. Finally she climbed into Maria's Land Rover, which was next in line to make a U-turn in the high school's wide driveway. Jason waved as they turned around and headed the other way on the divided highway, then inched his car up a little bit as the line moved forward.

Adam kept pace with him on the Vespa.

"Does Tamburo have any leads on the Challon case?" Jason asked.

"Not a one," Adam replied. "And my dad says Tamburo was on the scene within minutes of the attack. Between you and me, I think he's getting desperate."

Jason moved the car up farther in the line. "If it's a vampire hunter, that means the other vampires are in danger too," he said thoughtfully.

"Yup, it means Sienna is in danger," Adam agreed.

"I didn't say Sienna," Jason protested.

"But you were thinking it." Adam revved the Vespa like it was a Harley-Davidson. "You're next for the U-turn, my friend. Wanna hit Eddie's for a breakfast burrito?"

"Sure. I'll meet you there." Jason had reached the school gates, where a cop was directing traffic. As he drove the Bug through the circular driveway, he caught a glimpse of a few police officers roaming the grounds. He wondered what they could possibly be looking for. The killer wasn't a student, was he?

Then Jason was back out on the Pacific Coast Highway, heading for Eddie's. And he wasn't the only one. By the time he got there, the small restaurant was packed with kids from school. Jason found a parking spot and headed inside to snag a table while waiting for Adam. He was hoping Sienna might be among the crowd; it wouldn't hurt to give her a heads-up about the possibility of a vampire hunter, and it wouldn't hurt just to see her face, either. Any Sienna time was good Sienna time.

Except when she was surrounded by people who didn't like him.

Like Zach and Van Dyke, who were sitting on either side of Sienna at one of the small tables near the window. Erin sat across from them, completely blocking Jason's access to Sienna. He'd been meaning to pull her aside to tell her Adam's theory, but that was impossible now.

And a quick scan of the room showed him that the only table open was the one right next to the vampires.

"Great," he muttered. Van Dyke had been giving him the cold shoulder for days, and Zach was never particularly friendly. He didn't feel like being anywhere near them right now. But it didn't look as if there were much choice. Squaring his shoulders, Jason went over and sat down. He caught Sienna's eye and nodded hello.

"Hi, guys," Jason said, including the whole table in his greeting. He didn't want to make a big show of singling out Sienna.

"Hey, Jason," Erin said. The guys didn't answer, and Sienna just gave him a little wave.

Mercifully, Adam showed up at that moment, barreling over to join Jason at the table. "Excellent work," he said. "Ocean view and everything."

"Oh, yeah." Jason hadn't even bothered to look out the window. He'd been too busy trying not to stare at Sienna. He flipped open his menu and studied it.

". . . body was still warm when the cops arrived," Van Dyke was saying. "The killer must've just left."

"You'd think they could find him, then," Erin said.

"It's not like he was right there, though," Zach put in. "He shot the crossbow bolt from a distance. He was probably a mile away before the police showed up."

"Funny how I keep hearing the same conversation everywhere I go," Adam said to Jason. "My dad and the other cops, all the kids at this place. Everyone's trying to figure out who this killer is and why they can't find him."

"But you think you know the answer," Jason said.

"Well, not really. I don't know *who* he is. I just think I know *what* he is," Adam replied. "Although I haven't mentioned my theory to Detective Tamburo."

"Maybe you should mention it to *them*," Jason said, gesturing to the vampires' table. "If you're right, they're in danger. And I don't think they have a clue."

"I'm on it." Adam yanked his chair closer to

Erin's, making the metal legs screech against the stone floor. "So, listen, amigos," he said, interrupting the vampires' conversation. "Have you guys considered the fact that this killer might just be after . . . special people?"

Zach, Van Dyke, and Erin stared at him blankly. Sienna smiled a little.

"I'm sorry?" Zach said politely.

"This crossbow-carrying freak might be deliberately hunting certain types of people," Adam said. "You know, beautiful people. *Special* people." When they continued to look confused, he rolled his eyes. "*Dentally enhanced* people."

Erin and Van Dyke exchanged a worried look as Adam's meaning finally got through.

"It's okay," Sienna said quickly. "We've known Adam forever. We can trust him."

Jason was surprised that Adam was being so blunt about the whole thing. He knew that Zach and Sienna were aware that Adam knew their secret, but he didn't think Adam had ever told any of the vampires that he knew the truth about them. And yet, here he was, going head-to-head with Zach himself.

Zach stared at Adam for a long moment. Jason thought he looked as if he was trying not to laugh.

"I'm trying to help you," Adam said. "You need to be careful. I think this killer could be a . . .

hunter." He lowered his voice. "A *vampire* hunter."

Jason searched their faces, expecting to see alarm. Instead, Erin and Van Dyke rolled their eyes and grinned. Sienna chuckled, and even Zach smiled.

"Well, we, er, appreciate your concern," Zach said. "But you've got this one wrong. There's no such thing as a vampire hunter."

Sienna leaned forward. "Er, there's no such thing as Santa, either, Adam. I'm sorry to break it to you," she teased.

"Santa's overrated, anyway," Adam quipped back. "But you know, most people think there's no such thing as vampires. And they're wrong."

"But if the *vampires* say there's no such thing as a vampire hunter, you might want to believe them," Zach pointed out.

"Okay," Adam replied, unconvinced. "But somebody has managed to kill two of you in less than a week. I'm just sayin'."

"Two vampires. Two DeVere Heights students. Two guys who were both into Green Day. Who knows why Dominic and Scott were both targeted?" Van Dyke put in. "But I can tell you it wasn't because of some medieval vampire-hunter guy."

"I don't think they existed even then," Erin said. "I think they were always a myth."

Adam shot Jason a can-you-believe-this look, and

Jason shrugged. One thing he'd learned since moving to Malibu was not to get involved in too much vampire stuff. Every time he'd got pulled in, it had meant only one thing: trouble.

"Relax. You've given them a heads-up. I guess these guys can take care of themselves now," he told Adam.

"True." Zach gave Jason the smallest of smiles. Then he stood up. "Let's go, Van Dyke. We're late to meet Brad."

Immediately a chill fell over the table. Jason felt like everybody was looking at him—and at Sienna—to see how they responded to the mention of Brad. He did his best not to change the expression on his face, but he felt a flush creeping up his neck. Did every single person they knew think that he and Sienna were having a thing?

Van Dyke stood up and made a big show of saying good-bye to everyone except Jason. Once he and Zach were gone, Erin turned to Sienna with her eyebrows raised. "Adam and I can leave too, if you guys want to be alone," she teased.

"No!" Sienna said quickly.

"Nuh-uh," Jason replied at the same time.

Their eyes met, and they both laughed.

"We're friends," Sienna said. "That's all. Right, Jason?"

"Right," he confirmed.

"Right," Erin said, a tinge of sarcasm in her voice. "How's the weather there in Denial Land?" she murmured, but she was smiling.

Adam tried not to laugh.

Jason decided to ignore them. But Sienna was embarrassed. "Actually, I better go too," she said. "I have to pick up the place cards from the calligrapher."

"Place cards?" Jason queried.

"Yes. For the masked ball," Sienna explained.

"That's not still going ahead, is it?" Jason asked in disbelief.

"Are you kidding?" It was Erin's turn to sound incredulous. "Of course it is."

"I just thought with another murder . . ." Jason let his sentence trail off.

"Important people are coming from all over to go to the ball. They've spent a lot of money on the tickets. And it's all for charity. We can't just cancel it," Sienna explained.

"That's true, I guess," Jason said, realizing he still had a lot to learn about the Malibu way of thinking.

"You're still coming, aren't you?" Sienna asked, sounding just the slightest bit anxious.

"Of course I am," Jason replied. "We all need something to cheer us up, and the ball will probably do the trick." *And besides,* Jason thought, *would I miss seeing Sienna in her element? Not a chance.*

ELEVEN

After school on Tuesday, Jason headed straight for the pool. One day off from swim practice was enough. He had to be there to support the team, because, hey, he was on the team, and he wasn't going to let Brad and Van Dyke edge him out.

"Jason!" Dani's voice echoed through the emptying hallway. "Wait up!"

He turned to see his sister jogging toward him, her auburn hair swinging wildly.

"I can't drive you home until later," he told her when she reached him. "I'm going to practice."

"I don't need a ride. I just wanted to ask you a favor," she said breathlessly. "I'm going shopping with Kristy for a dress."

"Okay. So what's the favor?"

"I need you to back me up tonight at dinner," Dani said. "Kristy's parents gave her a budget of seven hundred dollars."

"For what?"

"The *dress*," Dani said impatiently. "And I know Mom and Dad are gonna flip when I ask for that much. So you have to help me convince them."

Jason whistled. "Where are you going to shop? The Diamond-studded Dress Store?"

"I'm not saying I'll spend that much. I'm just saying that if I find the perfect dress and it's as expensive as Kristy's, I want to be able to buy it." Dani crossed her arms over her chest, a sure sign she was going to be stubborn about this. "I mean, Dad makes tons of money now. So what's a few hundred bucks—"

"Seven hundred."

"Okay, seven hundred bucks to him?" Dani went on. "Besides, it's important. Sunday night is a big romance night for me, astrologically speaking. I have to look my best."

"There is absolutely no way Mom will ever let you buy a dress that expensive," Jason said. "Whether I back you up or not."

"Please?" Dani begged. "She listens to you more than me. She thinks you're the responsible one."

"I *am* the responsible one," Jason said.

"So you have to help me." Dani smiled brightly.

"I'll think about it," Jason promised. "But right now I have to get to practice." He gave her a wave and headed off toward the locker room.

As soon as he stepped inside, he could feel the tension in the air. Nobody was worried about how to dress for the charity ball here, they were all too busy worrying about the psycho crossbow killer.

". . . Tamburo obviously thinks it's somebody we know," Harberts was saying. "He interviewed me again today."

"Maybe he suspects you," Priesmeyer said. Jason knew he was joking, but there was an edge to his voice.

"Well, I know I didn't do it." Harberts slammed his locker shut. "But there have to be some clues that are leading to a student at DeVere. Why else would the cops be focusing the investigation here?"

Jason kept quiet. If he didn't say anything, there was less of a chance that his teammates would ignore him. Or at least, if they were ignoring him, he wouldn't have to have it rubbed in his face. Brad wasn't here yet, but Van Dyke was digging through his locker right next to Harberts.

"I think it's TJ Warwick," Van Dyke said. "He always hated Dominic. Remember when Dom beat him up in ninth grade?"

"Dominic beat everybody up," Harberts replied. "That was his favorite thing to do. He even tried to beat up Jason, remember? And even if TJ hated Dominic, why would he go after Scott?"

"Yeah. It doesn't make sense," Priesmeyer said. "There's no point in all of us turning on one another, it will just make everybody paranoid."

The door swung open, and Brad walked in. Jason

made a beeline for him, leaving the other guys to speculate about potential murderers they went to school with.

"Hey, Brad," Jason said, intercepting him near the doorway. "Listen, I wanted to tell you I'm sorry to hear about you and Sienna—"

"Oh, please," Brad interrupted. "You didn't get enough of a kick from going behind my back with Sienna? Now you're going to lie to my face?"

"I'm not lying," Jason protested. "And I didn't go behind your back with Sienna."

"Freeman, you've been after Sienna since the first time you saw her," Brad spat. "You think I'm stupid? Well, now you've got her. Congratulations."

"I don't have her. I'm not with her," Jason insisted. "I'm not denying she's beautiful, but—"

"Curt!" Brad cried suddenly, cutting Jason off midsentence. "You made it!"

Jason turned to see a tall guy, who seemed to be made entirely of muscle, slapping hands with Brad.

"Yeah, and you owe me big-time," Curt said with a grin. "Don't think I like leaving my own school in the middle of the year to help out your sorry butt."

Brad clapped him on the shoulder and turned him toward the other guys on the team, leaving Jason alone by the door. "Everyone, listen up," Brad called. "This is Curt Tungsten, from Santa Monica. He's agreed to come live at my house for the rest of the season so he can go to school here and, more importantly, help us out on relay."

"Teach you the meaning of the word *relay*, you mean," Curt joked.

"He's our new Jason," Brad said loudly. "And he's got an even better record than the old one!"

Jason watched numbly as Brad introduced Curt to the rest of the guys. Clearly, nothing he could do was going to restore his friendship with Brad. He decided he was just going to have to get over it.

After Curt had met everyone, he went over to an empty locker to change.

Jason wandered over to him. "I hear you're the new Jason," he said, extending his hand. "I'm the old Jason."

"Oh. Whoops," Curt said, shaking Jason's hand. "Sorry about that. It's just trash talk. From what I hear, you're pretty irreplaceable."

"I doubt that," Jason said easily. "But thanks for saying so. You're taking over my place on relay. Make me proud."

"Will do." Curt nodded at him and headed through the swinging door to the pool. Jason sighed and wondered whether he was ever going to get his normal life back?

"I'll be the only one there in a stupid fifty-dollar cock-tail dress!" Dani's voice carried up from downstairs as Jason sat down at his computer on Thursday evening.

"You're going to be wearing a mask, aren't you?" their mother replied. "So no one will be able to tell that you're the 'crazy' one who didn't spend a fortune on a dress she would wear for exactly five hours."

"It's not funny," Dani protested.

It is *a little bit funny*, Jason thought. As predicted, his mom refused to let Danielle spend hundreds of dollars on a dress for Sienna's charity ball. And Dani was convinced that if she didn't have an expensive dress, the guy she was hoping to meet wouldn't even notice her. Jason had pointed out that if it were truly in the stars, the guy wouldn't care what she was wear-ing, but Dani had just rolled her eyes.

Jason shut his door to block out the ongoing argu-ment downstairs. He had to get some homework done. He flipped open his history notebook and glanced over the assignment for the next week's cur-rent events essay. Everyone in his class was supposed to write about a local zoning board issue—as if study-ing something so boring would distract them from the fact that a serial killer was picking off their classmates. *That* was the only current event he—or anyone else—really cared about right now.

With a sigh, he opened his Internet browser and

called up the Malibu city council website. Just as he
was clicking on the zoning laws page, his computer
gave a little bell tone and an instant message window
popped up. Jason quickly opened it—maybe it was
Tyler finally checking in. But a glance at the screen
name and message made Jason forget all about Tyler
for the moment.

BadGirlDev: Michigan?

It was Sienna. It had to be. They had never talked
on IM before, but obviously she'd managed to find his
screen name. Jason hit reply and began to type:

MalibuFreeman: I don't know if I should be
answering IMs from a bad girl.
BadGirlDev: Why? Do I scare U?
MalibuFreeman: A little. ☺
BadGirlDev: Intelligent women are intimi-
dating!
MalibuFreeman: Intelligent, beautiful
women are downright terrifying.

There was a pause. Jason stared at the message
window, wondering if he'd gone too far. He wasn't
supposed to be flirting with Sienna. They were just
friends. You didn't go around telling your friends they

were beautiful. Maybe he'd freaked her out. But he didn't want to leave it like that. He quickly typed another message:

MalibuFreeman: How'd U know my screen
name? Were U searching for me?
BadGirlDev: Not many Freemans in Malibu. U
& Dani.
MalibuFreeman: U were totally searching
for me.
BadGirlDev: Maybe I wanted Dani.
MalibuFreeman: 4 what?
BadGirlDev: Umm . . .
MalibuFreeman: :D

Jason sat back, grinning. He'd caught her—she'd been looking for him. Did that mean she sat around thinking about him the way he did about her?

BadGirlDev: School was weird today.
Depressing.
MalibuFreeman: I know. Everyone's paranoid.

As he typed, he couldn't help thinking about the crossbow-killer conversation in the locker room. His friends on the team were certainly getting paranoid—if he could still call them his friends. He wasn't sure anymore, what with the way they'd all welcomed Curt so warmly. Was he being replaced permanently? It was starting to seem like Brad would never forgive him.

He noticed that Sienna had written more while he was thinking.

BadGirlDev: What R U doing?
MalibuFreeman: Homework. U?
BadGirlDev: Shopping for a Venetian mask.
I want a sexy one for the ball.
MalibuFreeman: Like what?
BadGirlDev: A butterfly mask, maybe. Or
one with jewels that hang on my forehead.
Or long feathers.
MalibuFreeman: Go for feathers.
BadGirlDev: Y?
MalibuFreeman: They're good for tickling.
BadGirlDev: Sounds like fun.

Jason sat back, smiling. Somehow the idea of Sienna in a mask made her seem even more mysterious and exotic than usual—and that was saying something. But even with a mask covering her face, Jason was certain that he'd still recognize her lips and her deep brown eyes. . . .

Another soft bell tone woke him from his daydream.

A new IM window had opened on top of Sienna's. This time it was Adam.

CineGeek: Yo, homie, what up?

Jason smiled. Adam had terrible timing, but maybe it was a good thing. If he kept IM-ing with Sienna, things might get out of hand. He was supposed to be playing things cool with her. So maybe taking a break for a few minutes would help. He hit reply to answer Adam.

MalibuFreeman: Not much. Doing research.
CineGeek: Me too. Check it out:

A link popped up in the window, so Jason clicked on it. Immediately a giant picture of a mouth appeared on screen—a mouth with two gleaming, razor-sharp fangs. As he watched, a drop of bright red blood appeared and dripped from one of the fangs, oozing out into a red blob that expanded to fill the whole screen. A word in black appeared over the red: Vampyre!

Jason shook his head. Leave it to Adam!

MalibuFreeman: Cheesy.
CineGeek: Cheesy & password protected.

Luckily I can hack. Only took an hour to
break into the site! Take a look.
MalibuFreeman: I'm looking at zoning laws.
CineGeek: Well, stop it. The vampyre site
is much more interesting, believe me.

Jason clicked back to the vampyre site. The intro
page had been replaced by a menu that appeared to be
written in blood. And at the top of the list of contents
was something called "Hunters of the Undead."
Obviously that was what Adam wanted him to see.
He opened the page.

The first thing he saw were about ten different pictures of crossbows. The article that accompanied the
photos was entitled "Modern Hunters, Traditional
Weapons." A quick scan of it told Jason all he needed
to know—that these days, vampire hunters liked to
track their prey through bank accounts and Internet
research. But apparently they still liked to kill the
vampires the old-fashioned way, with a crossbow bolt
to the heart before the full moon.

Jason's chest ached where the metal arrow had
embedded itself. Just looking at the photos was
enough to remind him of the pain. And suddenly a
new image of Sienna appeared in his mind: Sienna in
her evening gown, lowering her mask and smiling at
him, looking impossibly beautiful, until a metal bolt

flew through the air and impaled her. Piercing her heart.

Killing her.

Fear shot through Jason. He had to convince Sienna that Adam was right about the vampire hunter. He had to make her see that she was in danger. He closed the vampyre page and went back to Sienna's IM window. He was no longer interested in playing it cool.

MalibuFreeman: Sienna, Adam's right.
There's a vampire hunter.

A window popped up in response: *Username BadGirlDev not currently signed on.*

Jason sighed. That was typical of Sienna, he thought, around just long enough to intrigue him, and then gone. But perhaps it was just as well. Things had been getting a little too heated between them, and he had to cool it down.

Besides, he had other things to think about. He was more worried than ever about the possibility of a vampire hunter. Were more vampires going to die before the moon was full? And was there anything he could do to stop it?

TWELVE

"Tell me again why we're voluntarily subjecting ourselves to this?" Adam said on Saturday evening. He
gestured toward the backseat of the VW, where Dani
and Kristy were sitting. They were in high spirits since
it had been announced the previous day at school that
the curfew would indeed be lifted for the night of the
masked ball. The girls had been talking about clothes
nonstop since Jason had pulled out of the driveway in
Malibu.

But that discussion didn't stop Dani from over-
hearing Jason and Adam's conversation. "Because you
two need to get out of the house and live a little," she
replied. "It's the weekend. Time for fun. Whatever fun
we can squeeze in before curfew tonight."

"Shockingly, we don't necessarily think an in-depth
analysis of Eva Longoria's premiere outfit is fun,"
Jason joked.

Dani playfully stuck her tongue out at him. "Fine.
What do you want to talk about?"

"Who cares? We're here," Kristy put in.

Jason pulled the car into the parking lot near the
Santa Monica Pier. Once he'd stopped, the girls

climbed out and rushed toward the brightly lit board-walk. Jason and Adam followed more slowly. Jason had to admit that he was happy Dani had convinced him to come out tonight. He'd been on edge for the last couple of days, wondering if another tragedy was coming and racking his brains for anything he could remember or think of that might help the police catch the killer before he could strike again. Until the vampire-hunting season ended, Jason just wasn't going to feel comfortable. But the pier was always fun, like a permanent carnival on the beach, and he figured it would help to take his mind off things.

"I can name at least ten movies that have been shot here," Adam commented as they all climbed the weathered wooden stairs up to the pier. "Starting with—"

"Ooh! A fortune-telling machine!" Dani cried, interrupting him. She grabbed Kristy's arm and tugged her toward the old-fashioned machine, which had a little model genie in a turban inside.

"Coming, Jason?" Dani called over her shoulder. "Maybe it will tell you whether you've got a Devereux in your future."

Jason was just opening his mouth to protest when Adam nudged him. "You don't need a machine to tell you that," he said. "Look."

Sure enough, Sienna was standing ten feet away,

waiting as Erin and Maggie bought ice-cream cones from a shop along the boardwalk. Jason felt a tingle dance along his spine at the sight of her.

As if she'd felt his eyes on her, Sienna turned around. When she saw him, a slow smile spread across her face.

"Here we go," Adam murmured, mock-hurt. "Sienna shows up and that's it for our guys' night out."

"We weren't having a guys' night out," Jason reminded him.

"Oh. Right. Well, in that case, let's go hang with the three scorching babes," Adam said, trotting cheerfully over to Sienna and her crew. "Ladies! What's the what?" he cried.

"Adam! Just the man I wanted to see," Maggie declared.

"Really?" Adam was so surprised, he stopped walking. Jason chuckled and shoved him forward a few steps.

"Yeah. You must have some inside info on the killer," Maggie said. "Does your father think they're close to arresting anybody? Because my parents are threatening to send me to boarding school if they don't catch the guy soon."

"Seriously. Van Dyke's mom is organizing a big meeting for all the parents on Monday," Erin put in. "They're thinking of hiring a private investigator because the police aren't getting the job done." She glanced at Adam. "Sorry."

"I don't think a PI is going to help," Adam replied. "They won't find anybody better than Tamburo."

"I agree," Jason said. "The guy's relentless. He'll find the killer." Although, secretly, he was beginning to wonder. If Adam's theory was right and the killer was a vampire hunter, then Tamburo was operating without all the relevant information. He didn't understand the link between the victims. Well, between two of the victims. And if the killer had seen Jason buying back the chalice, he would probably have thought that Jason was a vampire too.

"You're looking pensive," Sienna said, stepping up next to him.

Jason jumped, surprised. He hadn't realized how long he'd been standing there, mulling over the vampire-hunter situation. Adam and the other girls had already started walking up the pier, still discussing the case.

"Yeah. I'm worried about this killer," he admitted. "I'm pretty much on board with Adam's theory—"

"I don't want to talk about it," Sienna said quickly, and Jason could see an edgy, uneasy light in her eyes. "I just can't stand any more murder talk. Every single word out of everybody's mouth lately is about this killer, and it's making me crazy."

"But—"

"I'm not going to listen to you if you talk about it," she said seriously, putting her finger to his lips.

Jason nodded. Maybe it was better not to freak Sienna out any more than she already was.

"Good," Sienna said, and gave him a lingering smile. "Let's catch up to the others. They're going to the amusement park."

"Hang on," Jason said. He raced over to Dani and Kristy at the fortune-telling machine. "We ran into some friends, and we're going to head over to the rides with them."

Dani stood on tiptoe to look over his shoulder. "Some friends? Looks more like Sienna to me." She raised an eyebrow and grinned at him.

Jason ignored her skeptical expression. "Anyway, I'll meet you back here in an hour, okay?"

"Have fun," Dani called after him as he jogged back over to Sienna.

"Sorry if I cut you off a minute ago," she said as they walked toward the gateway that led to the small amusement park that ran along one side of the pier. "I'm just so sick of discussing the murders. Do you know I had a reporter ask me about it today?"

"You make a habit of talking to the press?" he teased.

"No." Sienna slapped his arm. "My mom was doing

an interview for the society section in the *Times*, and I was just sitting in. It was supposed to be about the charity ball, but the guy just kept asking me questions about the murders: did I know the victims, how were kids at school dealing with it, all that garbage."

"Hey, lovebirds, hurry up!" Adam called from the ticket booth. "It's time for Whack-a-Mole."

Sienna shot Jason a smile. "I'm really good at Whack-a-Mole," she warned him. "So don't think you're going to be beating me."

"Are you kidding?" he cried. "Girls can't whack with nearly the strength required to be a true Whack-a-Mole master."

"Oh, you are so going down." Sienna walked over to the Whack-a-Mole booth and slapped down a dollar. "I'm going to kick this guy's butt," she told the tattoo-covered guy behind the counter.

"Good for you," he replied with a grin.

Jason laughed and coughed up a buck of his own. Then he and Sienna both grabbed big, padded mallets and waited for the little mechanical moles to begin popping up.

"I have a feeling this is going to get ugly," Adam joked. "I think I'll wait for the next round."

A buzzer sounded, the Moles began to pop, and they both started slamming the mallets down at the little critters.

Jason hit three.

Sienna hit nine.

"The lady wins by a landslide," Tattoo Guy yelled when they'd finished. "You get a stuffed animal," he told Sienna.

She turned to Jason, her face flushed with laughter. "What do you want?" she asked in a teasing voice.

"Ooohhh," Maggie and Erin cried.

"You know, Jason, it's supposed to be the other way around," Adam said. "You win the prize for the girl."

"You think I'm going to turn down a free stuffed toy?" Jason asked. "No way. I want the snake," he told Sienna.

She laughed and turned to Tattoo Guy. "The snake it is." He handed over the silly-looking purple snake, and Sienna presented it to Jason.

"Thanks," he said. "But I'll totally beat you in the fake bowling game."

"Bring it on," she said. "I'm the queen of every stupid amusement park game there is."

"Forget about the game-booth war," Adam put in. "Let's go on the Ferris wheel."

Erin and Maggie immediately set off for the giant wheel, and Adam hurried after them.

Jason caught Sienna's eye, and they both laughed. "I could use a ride on the Ferris wheel," she said. "Whenever I need a little perspective, I come here.

When you're way at the top, the whole world looks tiny and all your problems seem small too."

"Then what are we waiting for?" Jason said. "Let's go ride on the problem-shrinker."

Sienna reached for his hand, then stopped. She blushed and quickly looked away. "Okay, let's go," she murmured, heading for the ticket booth.

She didn't look at him again during the wait to buy tickets, or on the walk through the crowded park. But Jason felt like he was flying the whole time. She'd almost taken his hand! As if they were together, boyfriend and girlfriend, and it had seemed so natural that she hadn't even realized she was doing it until the last second.

Soon it was their turn to board the Ferris wheel. The thing was huge, at least nine stories high, and the cars weren't your usual rinky-dink two-seaters. They were like small tram cars, and each one held six people.

Adam jumped up to the car at the bottom of the wheel, opened the little door, and gestured Maggie and Erin inside. "After you, ladies," he said. Once they were in, he hopped in after them, yanked the door shut, and grinned at Jason. "Sorry, we're full," he lied.

"Yeah, you guys will have to go in the next one," Erin called. She and Maggie giggled as the wheel began to move and their cart was lifted up into the air, leaving Jason and Sienna all alone.

Now she had no choice. She had to look at him.

They gazed at each other in silence for a moment. "They're so rude," Sienna said finally, breaking the tension.

Jason laughed. "That's all right. We're tough. We can handle a ride by ourselves." He opened the door, and they climbed in. Sienna sat on the bench to the right, so he moved to sit across from her.

"Get over here," Sienna ordered playfully. "I can barely even see you all the way on the other side of the car. You're like eight feet away from me."

"It's more like three feet." But he got up and moved to sit beside her. He'd just managed to get his butt in the seat when the ride began to move.

"It will take at least ten minutes to get the whole wheel loaded with people," Sienna said as they jerked to a stop a few seconds later.

"I guess we have some time, then," Jason said, wondering what to do with his hands. He was sitting so close to Sienna now that their thighs were pressed lightly together. The obvious thing to do was to put his arm around her. But he couldn't. They were just friends. And even though Brad wanted nothing to do with him, Jason still considered *him* a friend, as well. It was too soon to make a move on Brad's ex. As long as Brad still had feelings for Sienna, Jason felt that she was off-limits to him.

The ride moved again, pulling them another few feet into the air before it stopped. Neither of them had said anything in a while, and Jason was starting to feel awkward. "So how's Belle doing?" he asked.

"Not too good," Sienna said softly. "I called her cell tonight, but she didn't answer. I doubt she would have felt up to coming out, anyway. She's still really upset about Dominic. It's hard to believe he's gone. You just take things for granted, you know? Like that Belle and Dominic would always be together. They'd go to the prom together, head off to the same college, all that stuff."

She paused, and Jason took a deep breath. He wasn't sure he should say anything about Brad, but he felt he had to. "You probably felt that way about you and Brad, too," he said gently. "That you'd go to the prom, and go to college together."

"Yeah. I guess I did." Sienna turned to face him. "But the truth is, I was just taking that for granted. I didn't necessarily want it anymore. I mean, I love Brad. But I'm not *in* love with him. Not anymore."

Jason didn't answer. What was there to say? He couldn't exactly ask whether she'd stopped loving her boyfriend because of him, and it really wasn't any of his business.

"I think I started having second thoughts about Brad around the time school started this year," Sienna went on, and she looked up at Jason briefly, *meaning-fully*.

Jason leaned back against the seat, his heart racing. He'd first met Sienna at the beginning of the school year. So she'd basically answered the question he'd been wanting to ask. But Jason felt powerless to do anything with that information. Brad was still cut up about Sienna and mad at Jason, and apparently with good reason. Jason hadn't intended to steal the guy's girlfriend, but still . . .

"Brad's a great guy," he said carefully. "He was the first one on the swim team to make friends with me."

"Yeah. He's the best," Sienna agreed. "The last thing I would ever want to do is hurt him."

"Me either." Jason was glad that Sienna seemed to understand what he was saying.

"I think he'll realize I was right about us, that we weren't really in love anymore," Sienna said. "But he needs some time."

"Right. It's not like you could run right out and start dating someone else," Jason replied.

"Exactly," Sienna said, her face lighting up in a huge smile. The ride took them higher still, and then their car jerked to a stop at the very top of the Ferris wheel. "I think I can start seeing someone else one of these days," she went on. "Just not right away."

Jason nodded. "Sure."

They sat quietly for a moment, gazing out at the view—the dark ocean to one side, the brightly lit pier to the other. Jason knew they'd reached an understanding. Without ever really saying so, they'd agreed that they couldn't be together yet. They had to wait for a while, out of respect for Brad.

But that still meant that he and Sienna could be together someday. And that was enough. For now. In fact, Jason thought, that was fantastic!

He grinned. "You're right about the Ferris wheel," he told Sienna. "Problems seem smaller up here."

"And beautiful things seem bigger," Sienna replied with an answering smile. "Look at the moon. Isn't it gorgeous?"

Jason glanced at the full moon, hanging low over the horizon. From where they sat, the moon appeared to take up half the sky. But his eyes immediately returned to Sienna. The silvery light danced over her silky hair, and her face seemed to glow. "You're gorgeous," he said softly.

Sienna gazed into his eyes, and Jason found himself even closer to her. Close enough to brush his lips against hers . . .

The Ferris wheel gave a jerk, and Jason fell away from Sienna. He gave a rueful laugh as the ride began in earnest. Their car whizzed down the other side and began to climb smoothly back up again.

Concentrate on the ride, Jason ordered himself. *No kissing Sienna.*

Not yet.

"You missed a spot," Jason told his sister the next morning. "On the left side of the windshield."

Dani dropped her soapy sponge into the bucket and frowned at him. "You're pushing it, big brother," she replied. "You know I don't think this counts as one of your chores to begin with."

"Well, the car doesn't wash itself," he said, grinning as he took another swig of his Coke and relaxed in the cushy porch swing near the front door. "And you use it too, sort of."

"Yeah, yeah," Dani grumbled. She squeezed out the sponge and soaped up the windshield again. "But I don't know why you have to watch me."

"I'm supervising," Jason said. "You'd never do it right otherwise."

"You're not *supervising,* you're *torturing.*" She flicked some suds at him. "Go away!"

"Oh, all right. I guess you can handle the rinse yourself." Jason stood up and stretched. He was just pulling open the front door when he heard the beeping of a horn. He turned to see Adam pulling into the driveway on his Vespa.

"Freeman!" Adam yelled. He motored past Dani,

hopped off the bike, grabbed Jason's arm, and dragged him inside. "I have news. They haven't released it to the public yet, but I had to come and tell you." He took a deep breath and then spoke in a tone more serious than Jason had ever heard him use before. "There's been another murder."

THIRTEEN

"Who was it?" Jason demanded, his heart pounding with fear. Had one of his friends been killed? Was it Sienna?

"Trinny Dareau," Adam replied. "She was killed this morning. It was another crossbow-bolt murder. You've seen her. She's a cheerleader in your sister's year."

Jason nodded, relaxing a little. It was horrible that a girl had been killed, but he couldn't help feeling relieved that it was nobody he knew. "She's got red hair, right?"

"No."

"Oh. Well, her name sounds familiar, anyway," Jason said

"Yeah." Adam headed for the stairs. "Let's go up to your room."

"Okay." Jason followed him up and closed his bedroom door behind them. "What's up?"

"It's Trinny," Adam said seriously. "She wasn't a vampire."

Jason dropped down into his desk chair. "And they're sure it was the same killer?"

"According to Tamburo, it's the exact same MO." Adam paced up and down the room. "Except for the fact that Trinny was human."

Jason sighed. "But that doesn't make sense," he said.

Adam nodded. "Looks like my vampire-hunter theory was wrong."

"Yeah, I guess," Jason said slowly. He could hardly believe it. Adam's theory had really grown on him. He'd been sure it was true. "So the theory is wrong," Jason repeated, drumming his fingers on the desk thoughtfully. "That means that the killer's just a nutjob, like Tamburo said."

"Yeah. I feel stupid for doing all that research on hunters," Adam said. "Zach told me there was no such thing. I should've believed him."

"You were only trying to help," Jason said. "And at least you had a theory. Does Tamburo have one? Does he have *any* idea who's doing this, or why?"

"I don't think so. He knows it's the same killer, because the bolts from the crossbow are very specific," Adam said. "Tamburo had the forensics guys check out the bolt that killed Trinny. It's got a groove in the same place as the bolts that hit you, Dominic, and Scott. The groove is made by an uneven piece of metal on the crossbow he uses."

"But that's all? He doesn't even have a suspect?" Jason asked.

"Unfortunately, no. But my dad says he's handling the case as well as it can be handled." Adam frowned. "I think it's just that without anything linking the victims, it's impossible to figure out what the motive is."

"I wasn't thrilled to think that all the vampires were in danger. But I'm less thrilled now," Jason said thoughtfully. "Because if the killer isn't targeting vampires, then everyone is in danger. And the guy is also that much harder to catch. If he's after random people, and we have no idea what his motive is, he could go after anyone."

"At any time," Adam agreed. "If it were a vampire hunter, the season would be over after tonight—at least until the next new moon and the next hunting season starts. But now we'll have to keep worrying. There's no end in sight."

Jason sighed. "It's useless to sit around thinking about it. Tamburo's a hotshot. He'll find the killer sooner or later. We just *have* to trust him to do his job."

"I guess so." Adam cracked a smile. "And I trust him more than I trust the regular cops. Around here, the worst they usually have to deal with is credit card fraud. At least Tamburo has actually caught murderers before."

Jason stood up. "I'm going to head out back and do a few exercises in the pool," he said. "I'm not allowed to swim, but I can use the water for resistance training. I need to start getting myself back in shape."

"I'll come along and stick my feet in the water," Adam said. "Those of us without luxurious heated pools have to pounce on any opportunity we get."

Jason led the way downstairs and out to the backyard.

"You're a glutton for punishment," Adam commented. "I saw you driving to the pier last night, wincing every time you had to turn the steering wheel. You're still in pain."

"I need to keep my muscles in shape for when I can actually swim again," Jason told him. "And I'm only in a little pain now."

"Yeah, but if I were in even a little bit of pain, I would use it as an excuse to sit around eating Fritos and channel surfing," Adam said. "But you, Mr. Overachiever, *you* have to get back in shape before your wound is even healed!"

"Oh, please," Danielle said, carrying the car wash bucket over to the storage shed near the pool. "Jason just wants to impress Sienna with his rippling muscles at the charity ball tonight."

Adam laughed.

"Not true," Jason said. "And if you keep saying things like that, I'll tell everyone at the ball that your dress only cost fifty bucks!"

Dani gasped, shooting a mortified look at Adam.

"Hey, don't worry about me," Adam told her. "My tux is rented from Cheap Tuxes R Us."

"It doesn't matter how much it cost, anyway. Billy helped me redesign the dress, so it's really an original couture design piece now," Dani told him. "And if Jason tells anyone else how much I spent on it, I might have to mention a little trip he took out to the desert. Because I don't think Sienna will find him so cool once I tell her about the Arcana Psychic Fair!"

Adam burst out laughing. "I'm sorry. I didn't know I had a friend who's into the occult," he teased. "I thought I was supposed to be the wacky one. But even I draw the line at attending psychic gatherings."

Dani winked at Jason as she put the bucket away.

"So what's your specialty?" Adam went on, mock-seriously. "Astrology? Or are you more of a palm-reading type, dude? No, wait, don't tell me—you divine the future using tea leaves, right?"

Jason decided it was time for a subject change. "I bet the ball isn't even happening tonight, is it?"

Dani paled. "It's not? It has to! I'm supposed to meet the love of my life tonight! Why would the ball be cancelled?"

"Er, no reason. I'm just kidding," Jason said quickly. He'd forgotten that the news about Trinny Dareau wasn't public knowledge yet.

"Don't joke about things like that," Dani said. She disappeared back inside the house, and Jason turned to Adam.

"Is the ball cancelled?" he asked. "I mean, three murders in a row—that's got to have everyone on edge."

"Nope, it's going on as scheduled," Adam said. "My father is getting a lot of pressure from the Devereuxs not to cancel it. They've got all kinds of influential people coming from Bel Air and Beverly Hills."

"Plus, if they cancel it, the charities it benefits won't get the money," Jason said.

"And Tamburo told my dad it would be better to let the ball go ahead, anyway," Adam added. "That's why they're keeping Trinny's murder quiet. Tamburo thinks maybe the killer likes all the attention he's been getting lately. So if we don't give him any public attention for murdering Trinny . . ."

"Like by canceling the big ball," Jason put in.

"Yeah," Adam agreed. "Well, then he might try to strike again in order to get noticed. And if he's acting in haste, he's more likely to mess up and do something stupid. You know, like try to attack someone in a crowded public place. Tamburo is hoping that he'll try to strike again at the ball itself."

"That doesn't sound very good," Jason said, alarmed.

"Don't worry, my dad's got every cop on the force working the ball," Adam assured him. "Some of them will be in uniform, and the rest plainclothes. The killer will avoid the uniforms, but he'll probably think that's all the security there is."

"And the plainclothes cops will catch him before he acts," Jason guessed. "I hope it works. The whole thing sounds risky to me. Innocent people could get hurt."

"Well, Tamburo is a risk-taker. And he figures innocent people are already getting killed, so it's worth the risk if it means we can catch the guy."

"And your father agrees?"

"Not exactly," Adam said. "He's just made sure that he's got enough people working the ball that they'll catch the guy before he can hurt anyone."

"It's probably a good idea either way," Jason said. "Tamburo obviously thinks the killer is somebody local. Even if he's not planning to attack tonight, he might be at the ball." He headed toward the back door. "In which case, I'd better get ready."

"What? Why?" Adam asked, hurrying after him. "I thought you were resistance training."

"No time. I want to get there early," Jason said.

"Why?" Adam asked. "Did Sienna ask you to help set up?"

"No. I'm sure they've hired an army of people to do that," Jason said. "And that's the problem. If Tamburo is right and the killer comes to the ball tonight, it's possible that he may come as a worker, not a guest . . ."

". . . so he could be there already," Adam finished for him.

"Yeah. Which means that Sienna could be in danger," Jason said grimly. "She's already there too."

They went back upstairs to Jason's room. While Jason began putting on the tux his father had bought him for his cousin's wedding last year, Adam scanned Jason's CD collection. Jason grabbed a pair of cuff links, barely stopping to check that they matched. Right now, he just wanted to get to the ball.

"It's weird, don't you think?" Adam asked. "All the violent things that have been happening around here lately? First that rogue vampire. Then the DeVere Heights Vampire Council sentencing your friend Tyler to death. And now somebody killing people, including a couple of vampires."

"Yup. Lots of bad mojo," Jason agreed. "Which is ironic, considering how safe everybody always says Malibu is."

"Hmm," Adam murmured, staring out the window.

Jason could tell his friend wasn't even listening. "All right, Turnball, out with it," he said. "You've got your thoughtful detective look on."

"It just seems like every strange thing that happens is about vampires. So why would this be any different?" Adam replied. "Two of the victims were vampires. One is a vampire sympathizer . . ."

"Is that what I am?" Jason asked, amused.

"Yes. A guy who hangs with vampires and who could have been seen at a pawn shop retrieving vampire property," Adam said. "You're a vamp-esque kinda guy. And Trinny was French. . . ."

"And French in Malibu usually equals vampire," Jason put in, realizing what Adam meant.

"Exactly," Adam agreed. "If somebody was looking for the fangy types around here, they'd assume anybody who happened to be of French descent was probably a vampire. I mean, even *we* thought Trinny was a vampire when we first found out that vampires existed. Remember? We put her on our final list of everybody we thought might possibly be V."

"That's right!" Jason cried. "That's why her name sounded familiar."

"Yeah, we wrote down every single French person in the school," Adam said. "I think I was a little bit vampire-obsessed back then."

"A little bit?" Jason said skeptically. At the start of the school year, Adam had been on a quest to uncover the truth about the existence of vampires in Malibu. He and Jason had started writing down the names of vampire suspects. Then they'd ordered that list into a new, complete and alphabetical list, and then Adam had researched every single person on it.

"You know, I don't think I ever crossed Trinny off

when we realized she wasn't a vampire," Adam said slowly.

Jason felt a sudden jolt of understanding. Judging by Adam's expression, he felt it too. "The list," Jason whispered.

Adam pulled out his wallet and yanked a faded piece of paper from the billfold.

"I kept my copy in the same place," Jason said. "Right in my wallet—which was stolen by the crossbow killer. *He has this list!*"

"And Trinny's name is on it because we suspected she might be a vampire," Adam went on. "Since she's French, and she used to hang with Maggie sometimes."

"So you were right about the killer being a vampire hunter. And we made his job a hell of a lot easier. We gave him a nice alphabetical list of vampires to kill!" Jason exclaimed in horror. "Or at least a list of people you and I *thought* were vampires. Poor Trinny . . . it's our fault she's dead."

"It's our fault they're *all* dead," Adam replied.

"We've got to stop him before he kills again," Jason said. He grabbed his tuxedo jacket off its hanger.

"If only we knew who his next victim was. He's probably stalking someone this very second," Adam said, his fingers trembling as he tried to unfold the list.

"I already know the answer to that," Jason said grimly, making for the door.

"How come?"

"The murderer is just going down the list," Jason said. "Killing vampires in alphabetical order. Think about it . . ." He was running down the stairs now, with Adam racing after him.

"Dominic Ames, Scott Challon," Adam murmured, still clutching the folded list. "Trinny Dareau . . . oh!"

Jason swung the front door open and as his eyes met Adam's, he knew they were both thinking the same thing: Sienna Devereux was next.

FOURTEEN

"Let's go," Jason said.

"Wait. Hold up!" Adam stepped into the doorway, blocking Jason's way. "I know you're losing it at the moment, but you need to calm down. I don't think Sienna's in any danger, at least not immediately."

"She's next on the list. On *our* list—"

"I know," Adam interrupted. "But tonight is the full moon. The vampire-hunting season is over. The guy's already killed today. He's done. We have a few weeks before the next season begins, and we'll find a way to protect Sienna before then. We'll force Zach to believe us, and with him on our side . . ."

But Jason was already shaking his head. "I don't buy it. This guy wants to kill vampires. He must have realized by now that Trinny *wasn't* a vampire. He made a mistake, and he'll want to fix it. He's only got tonight to do that."

"You're jumping to conclusions," Adam said.

"The last time he made a mistake was with me," Jason pointed out. "Then he murdered Dominic that very same day. He attacked a nonvampire, and when he realized his error, he killed an actual vampire only a few hours later." Jason pictured Sienna, saw her with the crossbow bolt in her heart. "He's going to do the same thing today." He gently pushed Adam aside and headed for his car.

"Your mask!" Adam called, running after him with the hand-painted mask Dani had bought for Jason at the mall. "They won't let you in without it."

Jason skidded to a halt. "And my ticket," he muttered, patting his pockets. "Where's the ticket? They really won't let me in without that."

"Check your inside pocket," Adam suggested.

Jason stuck his hand into the inner jacket pocket and felt the thin piece of parchment paper that the ticket was printed on. He was good to go.

"I can't go with you," Adam panted as Jason slipped behind the wheel. "I have to get dressed. They'll kick me out if I show up in jeans. The Sandhurst Castle doesn't allow jeans. Ever."

Jason glanced at Adam's Vespa. "I'll drop you home on my way to the castle," he said. "It will be faster."

"It's true, the Vespa has never been the choice of an action hero," Adam said, climbing into the VW. "And ever since you moved to town, I seem to keep getting involved in crazy action-hero situations."

Jason floored it, speeding toward Adam's house. As he drove, he fished his cell phone out of his pocket and dialed Sienna. "Pick up, pick up, pick up," he chanted as her cell rang. But instead of hearing her voice, he got the automated voice mail message. Jason hung up.

He screeched into Adam's driveway. "Get there as soon as you can," he said as his friend scrambled out of the car.

"I will. And Jason, don't worry," Adam said seriously. "There are cops all over that place, whether you see them or not. Nobody's going to hurt Sienna."

Jason nodded. But his fear only grew as he drove the rest of the way to the Sandhurst Castle. He had to force himself to stop at red lights and not to do 100 mph. Sienna was in danger and she didn't even know it.

When he reached the Sandhurst Castle, which was really just a big old mansion with a single turret, Jason slammed the car into park and leaped out with the engine still running. The valet had to jog after him to give him the ticket. Jason shoved it into his pocket and pushed through the heavy wooden doors of the building.

The place was filled with music. A string quartet dressed in black played at one end of the huge foyer. All four of the musicians wore white masks over their eyes. A swag of sheer golden fabric was draped from two columns on either side of the group, forming a canopy over their heads.

"Welcome and happy holidays," said a woman in a

deep burgundy evening gown. "May I take your ticket, please?"

Jason stared at her, trying to figure out if he knew her or not. But the green feathered mask she wore covered almost her entire face. "Um, sure." He pulled the ticket out of his pocket and handed it to her as he scanned the hallway for Sienna.

"Not your valet ticket, your ticket to the ball," the woman said, sounding vaguely annoyed, and suddenly Jason could place her. It was Sienna's mother. She always seemed a little annoyed by him.

"Mrs. Devereux?" he asked. "Where's Sienna?"

"I haven't seen her in a while," Mrs. Devereux replied. "Your ticket?"

Jason dug out his ball ticket and handed it over. "Have fun," she called after him as he hurried up the marble steps and into the ballroom itself.

The place was huge, and every single inch of it was beautifully decorated. Lush green pine trees lined the walls on either side, all decorated with golden bows and white lights. Some of the lights were large and some as tiny as little pieces of rice. The mixture of the two made the Christmas trees look magical, as if they were covered with a field of stars.

Burgundy velvet ribbons—the same shade as Mrs. Devereux's dress—formed big bows on the back of each gold-upholstered chair. The tablecloths were the same burgundy color, with an overlay of the sheer golden fabric, and each table had a centerpiece of huge, fluffy ostrich feathers dyed to match the burgundy.

Feathers are ticklish, Jason thought, the memory of his IM conversation with Sienna popping into his head. His throat constricted, and he felt a rush of fear. What if something happened to Sienna tonight, something bad? What if something had *already* happened?

Jason wove his way through the ballroom, searching for her. It wasn't very crowded yet, but everyone Jason passed was wearing a mask, making it impossible to see who they were. How was he supposed to find Sienna when the whole point of the evening was to hide your identity?

"Your mask doesn't work when it's in your hand," a girl in a white dress with a deep V-neck called.

Jason stared at her, trying to place her voice. It wasn't Sienna's, but it was familiar. He looked at her eyes, hidden behind a smooth white mask that covered her whole face. The mask was a different kind of face, like a porcelain doll's, with one exquisite sapphire tear on its cheek.

The girl laughed, lifting the mask away from her face with the fancy carved stick that held it. It was Erin.

"You're supposed to wear it," she said, taking Jason's

mask from his hand. She slipped it into place over his eyes and arranged the elastic band around the back of his head to hold it in place. "Perfect," she said, stepping back to admire him.

"Where's Sienna?" he asked, in no mood to make small talk.

"Wow. You really have it bad for her." Erin laughed.

"I just need to find her. Now," Jason said.

"She's off doing hostess stuff," Erin told him with a shrug. "Maybe she's talking to the chef or something."

Jason moved on to the dance area, where multicolored spotlights moved lazily across the wooden floor. There was more sheer drapery here, surrounding the whole dance floor so that it looked like a gypsy's tent. It was spectacular, but there was no sign of Sienna.

"Have you seen Sienna Devereux?" Jason asked Dani's friend Billy, who was wearing a tuxedo and a mask shaped like a swan, its long, graceful neck curving over his head.

"Nope. Where's your sister?" Billy asked.

"I don't know," Jason murmured, and continued on through the stained-glass French doors to the balcony that ran along the outside of the building.

Alabaster lanterns glowed softly in the darkness. A dark figure stood in the shadows. As Jason stepped closer, the man turned, revealing a tuxedo beneath an old-fashioned cape and a white mask that covered only half his face like the Phantom of the Opera's.

The hair on Jason's arms stood up, and a feeling of unease unaccountably swept over him. Was this mysterious loner the killer?

"Can I help you?" the guy asked, and Jason recognized his voice instantly. It was Brad.

Jason didn't feel like getting into it with Brad right now, so he just shook his head and went back inside. The room was beginning to fill up now. People stood in little clusters of two and three, all of them exquisitely dressed with spectacular masks.

But Sienna was nowhere to be seen.

Jason pulled out his cell phone and dialed her number again. Her voice mail picked up immediately, and Jason cursed under his breath. She wasn't answering her phone, and it seemed she wasn't at the ball. Had the hunter found her already?

FIFTEEN

Jason's cell phone rang, the shrill notes interrupting his search. He answered it immediately. "Sienna?"

"Nope," said Adam's voice. "But that answers my question. You haven't found her yet?"

"No. Are you here?" Jason asked.

"I just walked in. I'm in the foyer," Adam replied.

"I'll be right there." Jason hung up and hurried back to the foyer. He figured maybe Adam could point out which of the masked partygoers were undercover cops. Jason could get some of them to help him search.

Except that Sienna was in the foyer already. The second Jason got there, he saw her. There was no mask in the world that could keep him from recognizing Sienna, and his heart flooded with relief at the sight of her. The crepe fabric of Sienna's gold dress clung to her curves, then widened into a frothy, delicate skirt that was cut dramatically to skim the ground at the back, while rising to just below her knees at the front. She stood talking to Adam and another guy.

"Freeman!" Adam called and waved.

Sienna turned to face Jason as he walked over to them. The mask she held up to her face was a stunning combination of antique white lace and gold enamel, the textured fabric braided into the smooth, shiny gold. It covered half her face, from her forehead down to her nose, with a large ruby set in the forehead between her eyes.

"Jason," she said, lifting the mask away from her face. He noticed that the stick it was attached to had a red silk thread twisted around it, with a long feather dangling from the end.

"Feathers," he murmured, smiling at her.

She smiled back. "They're sexy," she replied, her voice husky.

"Well, hello, Captain America," said the guy standing with Adam and Sienna. "Love the red, white, and blue."

Jason gazed at him in surprise. It was Detective Tamburo, all decked out in a tux with his longish hair pulled back into a neat ponytail. He even had a mask, although his was a plain black leather eye mask.

"Huh?" was all Jason could think to say.

"Your mask," the detective replied.

Jason glanced down at the mask. A field of red stars on a blue background, and a white stick to hold it with. "Oh. Yeah. I hadn't noticed," Jason said.

But Tamburo had already forgotten about Jason. "The sooner we go, the sooner you'll be back," he said to Sienna. "You don't want to miss the whole ball after you planned it all, do you?"

"Go?" Jason cut in. "Go where?"

"Detective Tamburo wants me to go to the police station." Sienna sighed. "Right in the middle of everything."

"This killer isn't going to wait for you to finish your little masquerade, princess," Tamburo said. "And think how happy you'll be if you're the one to help put him away."

"Do you have a new lead?" Jason asked.

The cop nodded. "We've got a witness who can put a friend of Dominic's near the scene of his murder. Since his girlfriend's out of town, I'm hoping the divine Ms. D. here can ID the photo for me."

"Why can't I do it in the morning?" Sienna protested. "Jason, tell him I can't leave my own party."

"Actually, I think it's a great idea," Jason told her. *A great idea that will get you out of harm's way,* he added silently. Then he could concentrate on catching the murderer. He'd check the list to see who was next after Sienna, then he and Adam could alert the cops and they'd all be ready to pounce the instant the killer made a move. If he didn't have to worry about Sienna's safety, Jason knew he'd be able to focus a lot better. He shot a look at Adam.

His friend took the hint.

"It's true, Sienna. If you can recognize the guy,

maybe you'll get a killer off the street," Adam put in. "The party can wait."

"I promise, it will be worth it," Tamburo told her.

"If I ID this guy in a photo, how long will it take you to find him?" Sienna asked.

Tamburo shrugged. "Hey, I'm good, but I can't see the future. You got a crystal ball, princess?" He glanced at Jason. "Although I guess that's more your department, isn't it, Freeman?"

The sound of hundreds of tiny bells chiming at once filled the cavernous foyer.

"It's time for dinner to start. Everyone please find your tables!" Sienna's mother called. Jason spotted Dani and Kristy in the throng of people heading toward the ballroom.

"Let's go," Detective Tamburo said, taking Sienna's arm. "I'll have you back by dessert." They walked off toward the valet desk, and Jason turned to Adam. "We need the list," he said. "If the killer can't get to Sienna tonight, he'll go for whoever is next."

"How do you know? Have *you* got a crystal ball?" Adam joked, pulling the list out of his wallet. "Didja pick one up at the psychic fair?" He began reading the names on the list aloud, but Jason wasn't listening, because things were starting to slot into place in his mind. But everything rested on one very important question. . . .

"Wait a minute," he interrupted Adam. "Did you tell anyone about me going to the psychic fair?"

"What? No," Adam said. "Anyway, if not Sienna, then the next vampire—"

"Are you sure?" Jason interrupted again. "You didn't tell your father? Or any of the cops?"

"That you're a New Age, crystal-toting weirdo?" Adam said. "No. Who cares? We've got bigger things to worry about right now than your supercool image, dude."

"I'm not worried about my image!" Jason snapped. He took off after Tamburo and Sienna.

Adam hurried to catch up. "Where are we going?"

Jason didn't answer. His eyes scanned the people drifting in from outside. Tamburo and Sienna were nowhere to be seen, but he had to find them. Jogging out onto the circular driveway, he finally spotted Tamburo—pulling away in his car, Sienna in the passenger seat.

"Damn," Jason muttered. Just as Adam caught up to him, Jason turned and strode back inside. His pulse was hammering in his ears. Tamburo had teased him about having a crystal ball. About that being Jason's "department." But why would he say something like that . . . unless he happened to know that Jason had been to a psychic fair?

"Freeman, what's going on?" Adam cried, following him back inside.

Jason frantically searched the faces, looking for his sister. "I can't recognize anyone with all these masks," he complained. "Where's Dani?"

"You have to look for the mask, not the person," Adam said. "Dani has that green mask with the cat ears . . . there!" He pointed out Danielle, stepping through the ballroom doors with Kristy and Billy.

Jason sprinted over to her, gently pushing masked partygoers out of the way in order to reach his sister.

"Dani," he cried, grabbing her elbow and trying to stay calm enough to ask her the all-important question. "Wait. I need to know if you told anyone about the psychic fair."

"Told anyone what?" she asked, looking over her shoulder as her friends disappeared inside the room.

"That I was there," Jason explained impatiently.

"Oh. No. I wouldn't do that to you." Dani took her arm away from him. "Why are you being so weird?"

"Did Kristy tell anyone?" he asked urgently. "It's important, Danielle. Do you know if she told *anyone at all* that I was there?"

"No. Of course she didn't tell. I'm sure." Dani pulled her mask away from her face and frowned at him. "Seriously, what's up with you?"

"Nothing," Jason told her. "Don't worry about it."

"Well, you're a jerk," Dani said mildly. "Now I have

to find my table on my own. I've totally lost Kristy and Billy in the crowd."

"I can help you find it," said a tall guy with a mask that looked vaguely Egyptian. It covered his entire face. "It would be my pleasure."

Danielle gazed up at him for a moment. "Do I know you?"

"Not yet," the guy said. He offered her his arm, and Dani took it with a smile. They walked off together without a backward glance.

"Okay, spill," Adam said when she was gone. "What's the deal with the psychic fair?"

"No one knows I was there but Dani, Kristy, and you. But Tamburo's joke implied that he knew too," Jason said.

"But if nobody told him, how can he know?" Adam asked.

"There's only one way," Jason said grimly. "He found the ticket stubs—which were in my wallet when the crossbow killer took it!"

"You mean . . ." Adam blanched.

"Tamburo is the crossbow killer," Jason said. "He's the vampire hunter. And he's going to kill Sienna."

SIXTEEN

Jason practically flew out of the castle. "Keys," he snapped at the closest valet. He fumbled in his pocket, pulled out the ticket, and thrust it at the guy in the white jacket. "Just the keys. I see my car. I'll get it." He shoved a twenty into the dude's hand to get him motivated, and the guy quickly turned toward a board full of keys and started looking for Jason's.

The valet threw him his keys just as a hand clapped down on Jason's shoulder. Instinctively, Jason wrenched himself away and spun around to see Brad, without the mask this time.

"Freeman," he said. "We need to talk. I—"

"Later," Jason interrupted, running for his car. He leaped into the Bug, slammed the key into the ignition, and powered out of the lot. At least there didn't seem to be much traffic on the roads.

Which way am I supposed to turn? Jason wondered when he reached the Pacific Coast Highway. *Where is Tamburo taking her?* One thing he was sure of was that they definitely weren't heading for police headquarters. But that's where Sienna thought she was going, so Jason decided to head toward the station. He was betting that Tamburo would at least start out in that direction so that he wouldn't panic Sienna right off.

He floored the gas, taking a yellow light and the very beginning of a red to a chorus of honks. Okay, okay, there it was: Tamburo's anti-subtle, Vegas-baby 1967 Eldorado. The taillights were still quite a way ahead of him, but they were pretty distinctive. He was sure it was the right car. Jason let up on the speed and let the Bug slide in behind an SUV. He didn't want Tamburo to spot him. He was going to need the element of surprise.

Tamburo turned inland at Las Flores Canyon Road. It wasn't exactly the way to get to the station—not the fastest way—but it wasn't exactly the wrong way, either. Jason followed, losing his SUV cover. He slowed down a little more, letting a new-skool Bug in front of him.

Then Tamburo turned east, into the canyon.

Exactly the wrong way.

Jason could feel adrenaline rushing through his body as he followed Tamburo around the sneaky curves, climbing up the canyon. Where exactly was he taking Sienna? How was she doing up there? She had to know something was very wrong by now. Jason sped up a little, hoping for just a glimpse of her.

As *he* put on a little speed, the Eldorado put on a *lot* of speed.

"Crap!" Jason muttered, realizing Tamburo had spotted him. There was only one thing to do. Jason pushed down on the gas as far as he dared with the tight turns taking them higher and higher. Just a little faster, he told himself. Just a little bit faster. The Bug was a good car for taking curves, but Tamburo's boat of a car had a more powerful engine. The hills didn't slow it down at all.

Jason stamped down on the gas, silently urging the VW on, but it was no match for Tamburo's car. On the uphill, Jason fell farther and farther behind. Luckily, they reached a crest a few seconds later.

Now I can catch up, Jason thought.

He sped downhill, getting right on Tamburo's tail. There was no point in hiding now—it was clear Tamburo was onto him.

Tamburo pulled into the left lane on the two-lane road, away from the edge of the cliff, and pushed the Eldorado even harder. Jason raced after him, determined not to lose the bigger car. Tamburo braked to take a curve, and the Bug slid up alongside. Jason shot a quick glance over at Sienna. She was gripping the dashboard with both hands and she was shouting something at the killer, but she was okay.

A pair of headlights came around the corner, heading straight for Tamburo. It was an eighteen-wheeler and it was thundering right at him.

Perfect, Jason thought. *Tamburo will have to slow down now.* Jason dropped back, allowing room for the Eldorado to pull back into the right lane in front of him. But Tamburo was too slow.

The Eldorado's brakes squealed as Tamburo braked and swerved at the last minute.

The eighteen-wheeler's horn let out a long, panicked blast.

Then the Eldorado spun, slid, flipped—and disappeared over the edge of the canyon.

SEVENTEEN

The truck driver either didn't see or didn't care what had happened to the Eldorado, because he carried on down the road, barely even slowing down. But Jason's hands shook on the wheel as he pulled the Bug over to the side of the road and stopped. He didn't bother with the door. He vaulted out of the convertible, ignoring the pain in his chest, and dashed over to the edge of the cliff.

His eyes went immediately to the Eldorado. It lay halfway down the hillside like a dead thing. The top had buckled, and smoke was snaking out from under the hood. Jason realized that he had to get Sienna out of there in case the whole thing blew.

She's going to be okay, Jason told himself as he half-slid, half-scrambled down the cliff. The hillside was covered in the scrubby little bushes that dotted all the cliffs around Malibu, and sharp branches scratched at Jason's legs, but he didn't care. All he cared about was Sienna. *She has to be okay. She can survive anything but a stake through the heart, right?* he reminded himself. *She's going to be fine.*

Jason skidded to a stop next to the Eldorado and

crouched down to peer in through the passenger-side window. Sienna hung suspended by her seat belt, her long hair hiding her face. His gaze slid lower, and that's when he saw the blood—so much blood! He couldn't see where it was coming from, but the front of Sienna's gown was soaked a deep crimson.

He looked past her, trying to see Tamburo. Was he conscious? It was impossible to tell.

"Hang on, Sienna!" Jason shouted, pounding on the window. "I'm getting you out of there!" He thought she might have moved a little at the sound of his voice, but he wasn't sure.

He grabbed the door handle and yanked, bolts of pain shooting out from his chest wound. Then he realized the door was locked. Of course it was locked. What was he thinking?

"Sienna!" he yelled. "You've got to unlock the door!" Sienna didn't move. Jason scanned the ground and grabbed the biggest rock he could find. He slammed it against Sienna's window again and again and again.

The acrid smell of something synthetic burning filled his nose and worked its way down to his lungs. He realized that he didn't have much time. The car could go up like a torch at any second. "Sienna!" Jason yelled again. And, suddenly, Sienna turned her face toward him.

"Unlock the door. I have to get you out of there!" Jason shouted. Her hand reached in the wrong direction. Jason tapped the spot where the lock was. "You're flipped. It's up here."

A few seconds later, Sienna had the door unlocked. Jason grabbed the handle and pulled. The door opened about a foot, then snagged in the dirt. Jason braced his foot against the car and pulled again. He felt the stitches in his chest rip open as he jerked the door inch by inch through the earth.

Finally, he thought he'd pried the door open far enough. The fumes searing his lungs, Jason leaned into the car. "I've got you," he murmured as he carefully unbuckled Sienna's seat belt. She slid into his arms, unconscious, and as carefully, and as quickly, as he could, Jason maneuvered her body out of the car.

Sienna's blood soaked into the front of his shirt as he carried her away from the smoldering wreck. When he was sure that she was a safe distance away, he gently put her down. He let himself look at her for a long moment, then he turned back to the car. Fingers of flame were reaching out from under the hood. If he wanted to get Tamburo out, Jason knew he didn't have much time.

He was moving toward the Eldorado before he'd consciously decided to save the man. Jason didn't even know if Tamburo was alive *to* save, but actually it didn't matter. He had to at least try. The thought of leaving anyone to be burned alive made his stomach heave. If Tamburo survived, Jason figured he'd let the cops deal with him.

Jason had to crawl into the car himself to release the detective from his seat belt. The smoke was thick inside the car now. The fumes felt as if they had replaced every molecule of oxygen. Jason couldn't tell if Tamburo was unconscious or dead as he dragged the man out of the car and away from the wreckage, and he didn't stop to check. All he wanted was to get Tamburo clear and get himself back over to Sienna.

He'd just about decided he'd got Tamburo far enough away from the car to be safe, when there was a *whomp* and a blast of searing air knocked Jason over as the car exploded. "You're on your own," Jason muttered to Tamburo, leaving the cop lying on the hillside behind a large boulder as he ran back to Sienna.

"You're going to be okay now," Jason said as he dropped to his knees beside her. "I'm here." He was worried by the sight of all the blood. It looked as though Sienna's body had lost more blood than it could possibly have held! His eyes darted over her, looking for the source. Then he spotted a ragged cut on the inside of her right elbow. It had caught an artery, and she was losing blood so quickly that even the ability to heal super-fast, which Jason knew all vampires had, couldn't save her. Sienna was bleeding out.

Jason jerked off his shirt and used his teeth to start some tears in the fabric. Then he ripped off a few strips of the cloth. He could feel some of his own blood trickling down his chest from his wound, but he ignored it. He rested Sienna's wrist against his shoulder to elevate her arm while he bandaged it.

The bandage went red with blood almost instantly. Jason wrapped another strip of cloth over the first one. Then, remembering the first aid his old swim coach had taught the team, he wrapped a third strip of cloth around Sienna's arm and pulled it tight, in an attempt to push the artery closed against the bone in her upper arm. He must have been at least partially successful, because the bleeding seemed to lessen considerably. Sienna's eyelids fluttered, and she gave a soft moan, but she didn't regain consciousness.

Jason could see that Sienna needed help. Her face was drained of color, even her lips. And the second bandage was already turning red. He pulled his cell out of his pocket: zero bars—no service. He slid Sienna's cell out of the tiny purse she wore over her shoulder: smashed.

Jason stared at the top of the cliff. He could climb back up there, try to flag down a car. Maybe the driver of the 18-wheeler had even called for help. But he didn't want to leave Sienna.

What am I supposed to do? What in the hell am I supposed to do? Jason wondered desperately. His heartbeat pounded in his ears. And, suddenly, he realized that he had the answer: his heartbeat, his blood! Sienna needed blood, and she had a particularly effective way of getting it.

Immediately, Jason brought his wrist to Sienna's lips. She didn't react.

"Sienna, bite me. Drink my blood. I *want* you to drink it," he pleaded. He nudged her lips with his wrist. Nothing. Was she too far gone? Was she going to die right there in front of him?

Jason wasn't about to let that happen. He pulled his car keys out of his pocket and reached for the little Swiss Army knife key chain. He flipped open the blade and used it to nick his wrist. A few droplets of blood sprang to the surface.

Jason thrust his wrist in front of Sienna's mouth again. This time, her lips twitched. Then she bit into him and began to feed, fast and hard, drawing the blood out of his veins.

It was nothing like the time Erin Henry had fed on him. Jason hadn't been aware of the blood leaving his body then. He'd just felt dizzy and drunk and . . . ecstatically oblivious. This time he was aware of the small sharp pain of Sienna's teeth piercing his skin, of his blood racing through his veins at an accelerated speed. And it was slightly terrifying. *She needs this,* Jason reminded himself. *She has almost nothing left.*

Sienna's dark eyes snapped open. She stared up at Jason blankly and he wasn't sure if she recognized him. Was it shock? Jason wondered whether, in her current condition, Sienna would be able to stop. Maybe she needed so much blood that she would have to keep drinking now. Would she be taken over by the blood-lust? Would she drain him completely?

He thought about pulling away, but he didn't know how to tell if she'd had enough. He had to trust her. *She will stop, won't she?* he thought, starting to feel slightly light-headed himself.

Sienna's sharp teeth didn't release his wrist.

Jason tried to say her name, but a wave of dizziness spun him away. Blackness crept into the edges of his vision, and he felt himself sliding into unconsciousness. . . .

EIGHTEEN

Jason felt Sienna jerk her head away from his wrist. Slowly his vision cleared and he struggled back to full consciousness. He looked anxiously down at Sienna and was relieved to see that pink had seeped back into her lips and cheeks. She brought her fingers to her mouth and held them up in front of her. They were stained with a few drops of his blood. "What did I do?" she whispered, sounding horrified.

"What I wanted you to do," he said quickly. "What you needed to do. You and Tamburo were in a car crash. Do you remember? You'd lost a lot of blood."

"But how much have I drunk?" Sienna asked. "It must have been a lot."

"I've still got plenty," Jason told her. He thought it was true. His head felt like it was slowly bobbing up and down, but he was alive, and she was alive, and that was all that mattered.

He tossed her his shirt. "You might need another bandage on your arm. I need to go check whether Tamburo's still alive. Just rest, okay?"

Jason pushed himself to his feet and cautiously crossed the few feet to the killer. He'd seen a lot of horror movies and he half-expected the man to suddenly leap to his feet and attack. But Tamburo lay motionless.

"Hey!" Jason said, kneeling down and checking the side of Tamburo's neck for a pulse.

"Is he dead?" Sienna called. She was sitting up now, staring over at him, her face expressionless.

Jason kept his fingers pressed to the detective's neck for a few moments more, just to be sure. "Yeah," he answered at last. "He's dead."

Sienna let out a long, shuddering sigh as Jason walked back over to her. "Adam was right about the crossbow killer being a vampire hunter," she said. "But even he didn't figure out that the killer was the detective who was supposedly *looking* for the killer."

"How did you figure it out?" Jason asked.

"I didn't exactly have to," Sienna admitted. "It didn't take me long to realize we weren't going to the police station. When I asked Tamburo why, he just told me. He said I was going to make the perfect kill for the full moon. He wanted to come out here to do it right. I guess there's some kind of ritual or something. The guy was seriously whacked."

"Tell me about it," Jason said, glancing down at his chest wound. It had mostly stopped bleeding.

"What I don't understand is how he knew to come looking for vampires here," Sienna said. "I mean, we've been in Malibu for generations and no one's come after us before. We didn't even know there *were* any hunters."

"I have an idea about that," Jason admitted. "I think maybe Tamburo knew about the chalice. I mean, it's a pretty ancient artifact. I guess a few vampire hunters still exist and they try to trace items like that, hoping they'll lead to vampires. He could have been the guy who bought it, and when the pawnbroker said someone wanted it back, he probably guessed that that someone would be a vampire. I think he was watching me the day I went to get the chalice back from the pawnbroker. I had a feeling at the time that somebody was."

"So that's why Tamburo went after you in the first place," Sienna said. "He thought you were one of us—because you bought the chalice."

"I think so," Jason agreed, suddenly realizing there was something he ought to do. Quickly, he went back over to Tamburo and searched through the detective's pockets for the wallet the killer had taken from him. He soon found it—along with something else. . . .

"Tamburo's receipt for the chalice is right here," Jason told Sienna. "So he obviously *was* the guy who bought the chalice from the pawnbroker originally." He crumpled up the receipt as he walked over to Sienna. "And this is my wallet that Tamburo stole from me," he went on. "And in it is this." He handed her a folded piece of paper. "It's a list of possible vampires that Adam and I made when we first discovered there were vampires living in DeVere Heights." He ran his fingers through his hair. "I'm sorry, Sienna. We practically handed him your names and addresses."

Sienna sighed. "Don't worry, I won't mention it to the others," she said, sounding tired but not angry. "After all, have you forgotten that you got shot too?"

"That's true. I wonder why Tamburo never tried to take another shot at me," Jason said.

Sienna smiled. "The amount of time you've been taking to heal from one little, tiny crossbow wound would have told him not to bother," she answered. "You clearly *aren't* a vampire. But no more lists of people who are, okay?"

Jason nodded. "Of course!" he said. "Now, give me *that* list."

"Why?"

"Just give it."

Sienna handed it to him. Jason took it and the receipt for the chalice and walked as close to the burning car as he could. He stared into the blaze for a moment, then tossed the two pieces of paper in. They were devoured instantly.

He considered adding the ticket stubs from the psychic fair to the fire, but decided not to. If you thought about it a certain way, his going to the psychic fair had saved Sienna's life—not because of Madame Rosa and her "varning" of "great danger," but because if Jason hadn't had those ticket stubs from the fair in his wallet, Tamburo wouldn't have made that comment about a crystal ball, and Jason wouldn't have realized that Tamburo was the killer in time to stop him killing again.

That was not something Jason even wanted to think about. Instead, he decided to keep the stubs right where they were. He felt he could use a good-luck charm. He believed in those, sort of.

"You think you can walk?" he asked Sienna when he returned to her. "Because I'm pretty sure I can't carry you back up to the road."

Sienna nodded. "Maybe I should carry *you*," she said as Jason helped her to her feet. "I definitely think I should drive home. You look a little shaky."

"Me? *You* were unconscious about ten minutes ago," Jason replied as they slowly started to climb. "There's no way I'm letting you drive the Bug."

"But you know I'm superhuman," Sienna countered, with a grin. "I'm mostly healed up already."

"Yeah, but I'm a guy," Jason argued. Unfortunately, at that moment he stumbled and had to grab on to Sienna's arm to keep from falling on his butt.

She laughed. "Yeah, you're a guy—a lifesaving

hero, but also a normal guy, which is why I should drive," she told him as they reached the road.

"How does that make any sense? I don't know what you keep doing to your Spider, but how many times has it broken down since I've—"

Jason broke off abruptly, distracted by a car pulling over to the side of the road behind his VW. The headlights were bright and they were shining right in his eyes.

"You two need a ride?" a familiar voice asked, and Brad stepped into view. His eyes widened with shock when he saw Sienna. "Is that blood? What happened? Are you all right?"

"I'm fine," Sienna told him. "Jason gave me a little . . . transfusion."

"What happened?" Brad repeated.

"The crossbow killer is down there—dead," Jason said. "Sienna was going to be his next victim."

Brad sank down on the hood of his car. They all stared at one another silently for a moment. "Tell me," Brad said simply.

Sienna and Jason sat down next to him and answered as many of his questions as they could.

Finally Jason asked a question of his own. "What are you doing out here, anyway?"

Brad grinned. "I had this speech to make to you. More like an apology, I guess. I tried to talk to you at the ball, but you blew me off, so I decided to follow you. I didn't think I'd be able to have a good time until I'd said what I had to say. I got lost a few times—you were kind of hard to keep track of—but here I am." Brad looked from Jason to Sienna, and then down to the burning Eldorado. "Now it seems like it's maybe not the time for that conversation."

"You don't have anything to apologize to me for," Jason told him. Well, he kind of did, but Jason was willing to let it slide. It wasn't like Brad had tried to kill him or anything.

"Yeah, I do," Brad answered. "Sienna broke up with me because, for a long time, we've been more friends than anything else. We weren't in love like we used to be." He looked down at the ground for a moment, then over at Sienna. "It was true, but I didn't want to hear it. I thought—and I thought everyone else would think—she was dumping me because she'd found somebody she liked better. Basically, you," he told Jason.

"Brad, I really meant it when I said it was about us, about how things were with us," Sienna said softly.

"I know, but it took a while for that to sink in," Brad replied. "And while it was sinking in, I was a jackass." He stuck out his hand. "I'm sorry, Freeman. You have to accept my apology or the whole swim team will be on my back. Curt's missing his girlfriend.

I don't think I can keep him at DeVere the whole semester."

Jason grinned and shook Brad's hand. "Accepted. And thanks."

Brad opened the back door. "You two get in. I'll be the chauffeur."

Jason slid into the car. Sienna gave Brad a quick hug and then slid in beside Jason.

"So, Freeman," Brad said cheerfully as he pulled out onto the road. "You look like crap."

Jason laughed, then groaned. Even laughing hurt. "Yeah, well, you guys aren't the easiest people to hang out with," he said. "What with the extra strength and the high pain threshold and all."

"And don't forget our extreme good looks," Brad joked.

"Luckily for me, I'm naturally gifted in that department," Jason retorted.

"Yeah, that bruised-and-battered look is really working for you," Sienna teased.

She was right about the bruised and battered. Every muscle in Jason's body ached. He was going to have to get new stitches. And he'd probably need to take iron supplements or something for his blood loss. But Jason felt great. His friendship with Brad was back on track, he'd saved Sienna's life, and the crossbow killer could no longer hurt anyone. But what made Jason happiest of all right now was the feeling of Sienna sitting right beside him—and the promise of all the possibilities that lay between them. . . .

Vampire Beach

Legacy

To Peter Sharoff

Special thanks to Laura Burns and Melinda Metz

"There's this juicy French girl I'm trying to seduce," Jason Freeman told his juicy French girlfriend, Sienna Devereux. "I need to have some lines ready to go."

"I'm almost positive Madame Goddard isn't going to have pickup lines on the test." Sienna laughed. She pointed to the French textbook lying open between them on her bed. "I am *also* almost positive that some version of this reading comprehension exercise *will* be. So read this story about Jacques and Pauline at the Tour de France aloud, and then I'll ask you questions."

"Who cares about Jacques and Pauline?" Jason replied. "All I can think about is the French babe."

"Oh, yeah?" Sienna raised one eyebrow. "What's this girl like?"

Jason opened his mouth to answer.

"In French," Sienna added.

"*Très jolie. Et*, um, *très . . .*" Jason struggled to come up with more French words for a moment, then gave it up. "She's way gorgeous. Long black hair. These killer lips. Amazing legs." He slid one arm around Sienna's waist.

He could hardly believe that he and Sienna were

officially together now. And, thankfully, Brad Moreau—Sienna's old boyfriend, and one of Jason's first buddies when he started DeVere High at the beginning of senior year—was actually okay with the whole deal.

"This girl clearly has a lot of depth," Sienna teased, playfully slapping Jason's arm away.

"Oh, I'm just getting started," Jason said quickly. "She's insanely smart. She always knows where the best parties are. And you know what else?"

"What?" Sienna asked, her dark eyes warm as she looked at him.

"She's a vampire, which means she has super-strength. You should see her play beach volleyball."

"Hmmm. And you think you have enough to offer this fabulous French vampire goddess woman? You, a mere mortal?" Sienna asked.

"Well, in the sixth grade I won a hot-dog-eating contest," Jason answered. Sienna snickered. "Plus, when a car breaks down, I can dial AAA with incredible speed. No one's faster. I have also been told— admittedly by my little sister—that I am the less British version of Jude Law. What more could any French vampire goddess woman want?"

Sienna burst into giggles. It was good to see her laugh. Sienna hadn't done much laughing since the crossbow killer started murdering vampires in Malibu right before Christmas. The guy—who had turned out to be a detective with the Malibu PD—had mistaken Jason for a vampire and shot him on the first night of the hunt. If the crossbow bolt had landed an inch or two lower, Jason would be dead.

Dominic Ames, a vampire and longtime boyfriend of Belle Rémy, Sienna's best friend, *was* dead. So was a human girl Detective Tamburo had wrongly assumed was a vampire. Tamburo had planned to kill Sienna on the last night of his vampire-hunting cycle. He'd actually had her in his car while Jason had been right behind in his VW Beetle, trying to get to Sienna before it was too late. An 18-wheeler had been caught up in the middle of their car chase, and Tamburo's El Dorado had shot off one of the cliffs in the Malibu hills. He died. Sienna lived—but only thanks to a transfusion of Jason's blood, straight from his wrist.

"Of course, I can also burp the Pledge of Allegiance," Jason went on. He knew he was being a dumbass, but he just wanted to keep Sienna laughing a little longer. It was the beginning of February, and she still wasn't quite back to her usual self. She was a little quieter. A little more serious. A little less . . . Sienna.

Jason could tell that it was mostly because Belle was so messed up. She was grieving for Dominic in a huge way. Sienna had been going to therapy sessions with Belle because Belle found it impossible to do them by herself, and Sienna's parents had insisted Sienna get some therapy of her own, too. They thought she needed help dealing with the trauma of almost being a victim of the crossbow killer.

"Enough goofing around. Back to the book," Sienna instructed. "You have to pass French or you don't graduate. And I'm telling you one thing right now: There's no way I'm going out with a high school boy once I'm in college." She gave him a teasing smile.

"This French thing is unjust," Jason said. "I already have foreign language credits. I took two years of Spanish back in Michigan."

"In case you haven't noticed, this isn't Michigan," Sienna replied. "That sound you hear? That whooshing? We call that the o-cean. That's one way you can tell you're not in Michigan."

"O-cean," Jason repeated slowly.

"Or, *en Français, la mer,*" Sienna added. "*Répètes, s'il te plait.*"

"*La mer.*"

"*Donne-moi un baiser chaud et mouillé, bébé,*" Sienna said, in flawless French. "*Répètes, s'il te plait.*"

"*Donne-moi un baiser chaud et mou-something, bébé,*" Jason said, attempting to *répètes* what Sienna had just said.

Sienna gave him a slow smile, then leaned over and kissed him.

"What was that for?" Jason asked. "Not that I'm complaining."

"You wanted a line to snag your French girl, so I gave you one. You just said, 'Give me a hot, wet kiss, baby,'" Sienna explained.

"I did?" Jason tried to remember the words he'd mangled. "Well, I always did have a way with the ladies. How do I say it again?"

"*Donne-moi un baiser chaud et mouillé, bébé,*" Sienna told him.

"All right, all right, I'll kiss you. You don't have to beg," Jason teased. He threw the French textbook to the floor, pressed Sienna back against the pillows, and kissed her.

Sienna pushed him away before he'd had nearly enough of her. "Not in front of the children!" she teased, gesturing to the mound of stuffed animals that had come with the parade of get well cards after her "car accident."

Jason's blood had helped Sienna heal from her severe wounds almost instantly. But the vampires of DeVere Heights were very careful about keeping up the appearance of being human, which meant that after a near-fatal car crash, Sienna would have weeks of "recovery," accompanied by weeks of visits by friends with cards and presents, most of the presents being stuffed animals.

"The children like to see Mommy and Daddy getting along," Jason joked, and kissed her again.

"You need to study," Sienna said at last. "I told you, if you don't graduate, I'm going to have to find myself a new guy."

Jason leaned off the bed and picked up the French book. "Fine. But there are a lot of good-looking high school girls. I might just find myself somebody new too."

"Yeah, right." Sienna took the book and flipped back to the page they'd been working on. "Jacques and Pauline at the Tour de France..."

They kept at it for an hour. French, French, more French, nothing but French. "*La classe est terminée*," Sienna finally said, closing the book. "Class dismissed."

Jason let himself flop back on the bed. He loved hanging out in Sienna's room. He wouldn't want it for his own, but there was something about spending a little time in her space—all candles and sheer curtains around the bed, and more pillows than any human could ever use—that just made him feel good.

"I'm kicking you out now," Sienna told him cheerfully. "My mom and I always watch *Project Runway* together, and it's about to start. She'll be miffed if I miss it. Besides, it's kind of fun."

"You vampires and your rituals," Jason mock-complained as he stood up.

It had been an adjustment getting together with a vampire. A big adjustment. For one thing, it meant accepting that Sienna had to feed on other guys. That had felt like a punch in the gut the first few times it had happened, even though she made sure to do it in private, not right in the middle of the dance floor at a party or something, the way a lot of vampires did.

He'd come to terms with that one—basically because he'd *had* to, but there were still times when he felt like a complete outsider. There were a lot of secrets about the way vampire society operated that Sienna wasn't free to tell him. In spite of it all, though, being with a vampire had started to feel surprisingly ordinary.

Sienna walked Jason over to the door and kissed him, her arms wrapped around his neck. "You know what? I want to tell you something," she said when the kiss ended. Her lips were still just a breath away from his.

"What?" Jason asked. She suddenly sounded so serious.

"I just feel . . . safe when you're around. Safe and happy. My parents should be paying you instead of that therapist I see," Sienna told him, her dark eyes intense. "You have made my life a better place to be."

Jason smiled. "So, how much money are we talking here?" he began. "What kind of bucks does your therapist . . ." He let the sentence trail off. What she'd said was too big to joke about. The fact that she trusted him in that way meant everything to him. "I'm always going to be here for you, whenever you need me," he said seriously. "I promise."

TWO

My life just can't get any better, Jason thought.

He couldn't stop smiling as he steered the Bug home. He knew he was being kind of a geek, but what Sienna had said had made his night. That and the fact that she'd been willing to spend hours helping him with his French.

Most of their friends were at the beach, the movies, or the mall, indulging in full-on cases of Senioritis. Their college apps were in. The schools had their transcripts and their SAT scores and their recommendations—everything the admissions officers would use to make their decisions. What Jason and the other seniors did this last semester didn't really matter. Unless they really screwed up, by, say, not passing French, which was a required subject at DeVere High for some insane reason—probably because the money for the DeVere Library and the DeVere Symphony Space and the DeVere Athletic Complex and almost everything else that was cultural in Malibu was funded by the Devereux family, who happened to be French. Just like almost every important family in Malibu.

And all those French-ancestored, very important families, also happened to be vampiric and living in DeVere Heights. Where else? Jason suspected that he and his family were practically the only regular humans who lived in Malibu's most exclusive gated community. And he *knew* he was one of the very few regular humans who'd made it into the über-popular group at DeVere High.

Sienna could have been out having fun with any of those übers tonight, Jason thought as he pulled into his driveway. He knew she could have been indulging in some Senioritis of her own. Instead, she'd chosen to help her French-challenged boyfriend study. He grinned. He was one lucky individual.

As he climbed out of the car he heard the soft purr of his friend Adam Turnball's Vespa pulling in behind him. Turnball—as in, not of French ancestry, not even especially good in French! Adam was mid-level popular at DeVere High, except to the movie nerds—Adam was a god to them—and definitely not a vampire.

"What's up, my brother?" Adam called as he parked the moped. "Is everything copacetic?"

Jason laughed. Who but Adam talked like that? "Ultra copacetic," he answered. "Come on in. Mom hit Malibu Kitchen today. Let's see what she brought home." He led the way into the house and straight to the kitchen. His father sat at the table, brow furrowed, shoulders hunched, surrounded by stacks of papers, forms, and receipts. A calculator was positioned at his elbow.

"Hey, Dad, we're doing a food raid," Jason announced.

"I always fast before I come over," Adam told Mr. Freeman. "I like to have belly room because you guys always have the best chow."

Mr. Freeman answered with a grunt. *Weird!* Jason thought. *He usually talks too much to my friends.*

"What are you in the mood for?" Jason asked Adam, opening the closest cupboard. It was only then that his brain registered what his eyes had just seen: forms, receipts, calculator, cranky and distracted father. Jason knew these could mean only one thing: His dad was in the middle of his usual February pretax family financial review. A financial review that would include Jason's college fund, which happened to be seven thousand dollars light for a reason that Jason absolutely could not explain to his parents. He'd withdrawn the cash to buy back a vampire artifact that his friend Tyler had stolen and pawned. That was the kind of thing parents just didn't understand.

All the saliva in Jason's mouth dried up. His father was going to go ballistic. *Maybe I'm wrong,* Jason told himself. *I could be wrong.* He swallowed hard, then forced out the words, "Whatcha workin' on, Dad?" while peering over at the table to see if statements for his college fund account were in the mess of papers.

"Just going over our financial stuff so I won't go nuts at tax time," his father answered.

Adam's eyes widened. Jason could see he understood that they had walked into a Code Red situation here.

"Hey, you know what? There's a *Godfather* marathon on tonight. It's starting . . . basically now," Adam said. "We all have to watch it. We're men. That's what we do. We watch *The Godfather*, then quote it on all occasions to the bafflement of womankind," he finished in a rush.

"Yeah, Dad. You've got ages to worry about taxes," Jason added, getting on board with Adam's Plan of Distraction. "Let's do *The Godfather*. I'll get snacks."

"'Leave the gun, take the cannoli,'" Adam encouraged, already quoting. "Now that has to be an offer you can't refuse, Mr. Freeman," he added in his best Brando imitation.

Jason's father twisted his neck from side to side, trying to work out the kinks. "I'm almost done here, and it's wiped me out. I'll have to take a pass."

Almost done? Jason thought. Surely that meant that at any minute his dad was going to find out about the missing cash.

"I completely forgot. I didn't do my chem homework for tomorrow. I should take off," Adam said, inching toward the door.

Rat attempting to abandon sinking ship, Jason thought. Well, there was no way he was letting this rat leave. As long as Adam stayed, the extreme badness that was about to rain down on Jason would be delayed. And the delay would give Jason's dad some cool-down time.

"You can use my chem book," Jason told Adam, giving his friend a meaningful glare. "I need to finish up the assignment, anyway."

Adam replied with a reluctant okay-okay-I'll-stay nod, and Jason turned back to the cupboard. "Here, we'll take these wasabi peas," he said, hurling the bag at his friend. "And, um, this black licorice." He tossed the package over his shoulder in Adam's direction and heard it hit the ground. "And now a couple of sodas." He plucked two Dr Peppers out of the fridge. "So let's get upstairs to the Wonderful World of Chemistry." Jason started out of the kitchen, knowing Adam would follow.

"Jason," his father called.

Jason stopped. This was it. His life was over.

He turned around.

"Don't blow up the house," Mr. Freeman joked.

"Just pens and paper, no chemicals," Jason answered,

wondering if his father could possibly have forgotten to look at his account.

Mr. Freeman stood up and started gathering his piles of receipts together. "I think we're in decent shape for April. The—" He was interrupted by his cell. He pulled it out of his pocket and checked the screen. "It's work. I'll take it upstairs. I might need the computer," he said.

Jason felt like the oxygen in the room had turned to helium. That's how relieved he was. As soon as his dad left, Jason rushed over to the table.

"Do you think he could have forgotten how much money you were supposed to have in the account?" Adam asked as Jason scanned the piles of paper for his college account statements.

"By a few hundred bucks, yeah. By several thousand, no way," Jason replied, spotting the statements and snatching them up. The most recent one was on top. And the total . . . was exactly what his father would have been expecting. *Not* minus seven thousand. Jason stared at it, his mind whirling. The account was exactly as it had been pre-pawn shop. The seven thousand dollars had miraculously reappeared.

His dad must have checked only the current total, because down a few statements it was clear that Jason had taken out the cash—right when Tyler had rolled into town from Michigan. Tyler had owed his drug dealer some serious cash, so when he had gone to a party at Zach Lafrenière's place—Lafrenière, as in French ancestry, as in vampire—he hadn't been able to resist picking up a silver chalice that looked like it was worth enough to save his butt.

It was. But the chalice was also an heirloom used in sacred vampire rituals, and the vampires were not at all happy that it was gone. In fact, they had planned to kill Tyler in retribution. Jason had managed to save his friend's life. And then he'd bought back the chalice in a gesture of goodwill. In the end, the only thing that had got hurt was his college fund.

"Somebody put the money back," Jason told Adam. "There's a statement—a statement I'm going to, um, disappear," he added, folding the statement and putting it in his pocket, "that shows me taking seven thousand out. Then, three weeks later, it shows that there was a deposit for seven thousand going back in."

"Hmm. Looks like you were the recipient of a special grant," Adam said. He tore open the bag of wasabi peas he still held and popped a handful in his mouth. "Dr Pepper! Now!" He stuck out his tongue and fanned it with his free hand.

Jason handed him a soda, and Adam drank it down. "I love those things, but I always forget how insanely hot they are," he explained.

"You're not supposed to scarf them." Jason laughed.

Adam coughed a couple of times, then cleared his throat. "As I was saying, it seems like someone made a contribution to the Jason Freeman Needy Boy Foundation."

"Who would do something like that?" Jason asked. "Not that I don't appreciate it, but I can't think of anyone who—"

A car horn cut him off.

"That's for me!" Jason's sister Danielle called from upstairs. "Wave or blink the lights or something to let them know I'm coming."

"Remember when Dani didn't think she'd have any friends at her new school?" Adam asked.

"Yeah, for that whole day and a half," Jason replied as they walked over to the front door. He flipped the porch light on and off.

"Who's out there, anyway?" Adam said, peering through the long, narrow window next to the door.

"Kristy, of course," Jason said, taking a look. "She and Dani start to wither if they are apart for more than eight hours. And that's Maria, Billy . . . and I think Ryan Patrick from down the block is driving." Jason turned to Adam. "So what's our thinking on Ryan? He spent last semester in Paris as an exchange student. He lives in DeVere Heights. But Patrick is not a French last name."

"True. But he's always been a member of the V-crowd, ever since we were kids," Adam answered. "I think odds are that he's a Friend of Dracula."

"Where are you off to?" Jason asked as Dani rushed toward the door. The heels of her leopard-print Stella McCartney shoes—the ones she "love, love, *loved* and could not live without"—were clicking on the tile of the entryway, and her auburn hair was flying around her face.

"Big date?" Adam chimed in.

"No, just the movies. No parties on Wednesday night. Nothing juicy," Dani explained.

"Just the movies," Adam repeated, shaking his head sadly as Dani hurried out to the car. "Even a bad movie is better than pretty much anything else the world has to offer."

"You need to get out more," Jason told Adam as he watched his sister and her friends drive off. He didn't think he'd ever seen Ryan in the mix before. But at this point, Dani had even more friends in Malibu than she'd had in Michigan. And that was saying something. He could only really keep track of the key players.

"So you want to hang by the pool for a while?" Jason asked his friend. "Oh wait. No, you have all that chemistry homework to get to."

"Smart-ass," Adam answered. He headed back through the kitchen and straight out the French doors to the pool. "Although I really do have homework. I've been spending too much time on my extracurricular project."

"Still?" Jason asked.

"Still!" Adam repeated, sitting down on the diving board. "Excuse me for wanting to make sure another vampire hunter doesn't slide into town. I want us to be prepared next time."

"Tamburo *was* the first one since the Renaissance," Jason pointed out. Like he'd pointed out several times before.

"That doesn't mean it will be centuries until another one shows," Adam argued, as he always did. "The bad thing is, I'm having a hard time finding any solid info on the web. It's all Van Helsing and Buffy and Blade and the Belmont clan."

"The who?" Jason asked.

"It's from this Japanese video game series, *Castlevania*," Adam told him. "It's fun, but not useful. I—"

The French doors swung open. "Guys, what, no *Godfather* marathon?" Mr. Freeman called. "I got my second wind. And I made popcorn!"

Adam turned his head to hide his laughter.

"We're there," Jason called back. He glanced at his friend. "It was your idea. Looks like you're stuck watching a Mafia-fest."

"Oh, like I'm going to complain about that," Adam said, getting up. "You really dodged a bullet tonight, you know."

"I know." Jason grinned, still feeling a little heliumed out. "I've got good friends, a truly amazing girlfriend, Dani is happy, the parents are happy, there's an actual swimming pool in the backyard, and since my dad is ignorant of the seven grand I spent on non-college-related expenses, I can live to enjoy it all!"

"And we're about to watch *The Godfather*," Adam added as they headed inside.

"And that," Jason agreed. "Life is good."

THREE

𝕿he life-loving feeling was still there the next day at lunch, when Jason and Adam headed out to the huge balcony overlooking the ocean. Sometimes Jason still had trouble wrapping his head around the fact that this was part of his school cafeteria.

He spotted Sienna and Belle at one of the larger tables, and his pace automatically picked up. He slid onto the bench next to Sienna, put down his tray of food, and gave her a quick hello kind of kiss. As he started to pull away, Sienna wrapped her fingers in his hair and pulled him back, keeping the kiss going. "Not in front of the children," Jason finally said, jerking his chin toward Adam and Belle.

Sienna laughed. Jason couldn't get enough of that laugh!

"We have our own Romeo and Juliet at the table," Belle said to Adam.

"Are we talking the Baz Luhrmann or the Franco Zeffirelli variety?" Adam asked.

Belle looked helplessly at Jason. "Translation?"

"Can't help you," Jason told her. "I'm pretty sure he's slipped into film-speak."

"Okay, I'll forgive you for not knowing Zeffirelli," Adam said. "But Baz? He's one of the greatest directors of our time. *Moulin Rouge!* anyone?"

"Sorry," Belle answered, shaking her head.

"Wasn't there singing in it?" Jason asked. "I don't do movies with singing."

Adam turned to Sienna. "You're my last hope. Tell me you saw *Moulin Rouge!*"

"I think I was, like, twelve, when that came out," Sienna protested.

Adam leaned across the table toward her as if he were imparting a great secret. "There's this new invention. A machine that lets you play movies on your TV screen whenever you want to!" he told her. "The movies come on these cool little discs—they look like crêpes, but smaller, and thinner, and metallic. With this machine, you can watch movies that were made before you were even born!"

"Maybe I'll check it out sometime." Sienna laughed.

"Not with me," Jason teased.

Brad Moreau dropped his tray onto the table and sat down next to Jason. "What's the topic?" he asked. Ryan Patrick and Maggie Roy were with him.

"Please tell me one of you knows who Baz Luhrmann is," Adam pleaded.

"Can't help you," Brad said.

"Didn't he direct those Chanel commercials with Nicole Kidman?" Maggie asked.

"Yes!" Adam cried. "They show some of his trademark Italian operatic influences."

"Like in *Moulin Rouge!*" Ryan added.

"Thank God!" Adam exclaimed. "I thought I'd entered some unholy dimension where I would never be able to communicate with the natives."

"I'll watch anything that's set in Paris," Ryan said. "It's hands down my favorite city. I hated coming back after living there last semester—although it was almost worth leaving just for the going-away party. It was wild; we snuck down into the catacombs. I was having so much fun I lost track of time. Almost missed my flight."

Maggie ran her fingers through Ryan's curly blond hair. "Well, we're all glad to have you back."

"You're going to be extra glad, because I'm throwing a Valentine's Day party that will be extreme," Ryan continued. "It's a week from Friday, and you're all invited to come and make complete fools of yourselves."

"Too bad Zach's still going to be in Australia," Maggie commented.

"Yeah, it's so horrible that he has to be out of school, spending days on the beach, hanging out with all the actors in his mom's movie," Sienna joked.

"My party is going to be wilder than any movie set," Ryan said. He turned to Jason. "Think you can be there?"

Why is Ryan singling me out? Jason thought. *He hardly knows me.* But a Valentine's Day party—with his new Valentine, Sienna? He wasn't going to pass that up. "Absolutely," Jason told Ryan. "Thanks."

"Cool. Bring your sister. If she wants to invite some of her friends, that's cool too," Ryan said.

"Oh. Okay." Jason frowned as he took a swig of his Coke. He had the strangest feeling that Ryan was really just trying to make sure Dani would show.

Sienna pulled him out of his thoughts by leaning close and whispering into his ear. "There are no parties *this* weekend. But I have an idea," she breathed.

The bell rang. Jason stood up, grabbing his tray and Sienna's. "So what is it?" he asked as they walked back inside together.

"Gotta go," Sienna teased. "I'll have to tell you later. Just make sure you have Sunday free. All day."

Jason dumped their trash and stacked the trays on top of the garbage can as Sienna headed off to class. "A hint. I need a hint," he called after her.

"I'll be there," Sienna threw back over her shoulder. "Do you need to know more?"

Actually, he didn't.

It was Sunday morning, and Jason was driving toward the marina with Adam.

"I'm definitely not complaining about an invitation

to spend the day on a yacht," Adam said. "But wouldn't you and Sienna prefer to be alone?"

"Sienna likes to make sure Belle has plans every weekend since she's still so ripped up about Dominic. And she didn't have anything going for today," Jason answered. "Besides, it's not like the yacht is so small that we all have to be on top of each other. "

He pulled into one of the parking spots in the marina's lot. Sienna's Spider was parked a few cars away. "They beat us here."

"Well, I hope they waited for us," Adam joked. "Otherwise I'll have to go home and watch *Titanic* just to console myself."

Jason led the way over to the Devereux berth, slowing as they approached the gigantic boat anchored there. "*That's* the yacht?" he asked, disbelieving. "I mean, it's beautiful, but it looks more like a paper airplane than a yacht."

"I heard that," Sienna called from the top of the gangplank. "I'll have you know this is a WallyPower 118. There are only three of these in existence."

"Wait. This is the yacht from *The Island*? The *Renovatio*!" Adam exclaimed.

"Not this exact one. But one of them, yeah," Sienna told him as they walked up the gangplank toward her.

"Hardcore," Adam said approvingly. "This day is going to be even better than I thought!"

When they reached the top, Sienna took Jason's hand. "This is Lee Osbourne, our captain for the day," she announced, smiling at a tanned, thirty-something guy who'd appeared next to her. His dark hair was pulled back into a ponytail, and he wore an easy grin.

"Call me Oz," he said. "You guys ready for your first Wally ride?"

"Absolutely," Jason replied.

"Head on in to the lounge then, folks," Oz instructed. "Lunch will be served later. Until then, there are some drinks and snacks to hold you."

"Come on, guys," Sienna said. "Belle's already in there."

Sienna led the way into a vast combination lounge/dining area/cockpit. Jason stopped at the top of the stairs and took it all in. Windows wrapped around the whole enormous area, so it felt like you were outside, even though you were inside. The view was breathtaking.

Belle was already in full-on relaxation mode, clad in a tiny bikini and lying on her back on one of the cushy sofas. The diamond of her belly ring sparkled in the morning sunlight. "Do you think Captain Oz has some lemons on board?" she asked. "I want to squeeze some juice into my hair."

"I don't think Oz is in charge of lemons, but I'll

check with the chef," Sienna promised. "Be right back." She disappeared down the stairs.

"The *chef*? This is all a little too much for the child of the poor but humble sheriff," Adam joked. "How am I ever going to be content when you return me to my hovel, now that I've seen how the other half lives?" He stretched out on one of the sofas and gave a sigh of contentment.

Jason took a seat across from his friend. "We'll start a fund for you," he answered.

"I'll contribute," Belle volunteered.

"Really?" Adam asked. "Will you hock that sparkly you've got stuck in your belly button, because that'd go a long way toward—" He stumbled to a stop, and Jason could see why; Belle's eyes had filled with tears.

"Hey, are you okay?" Jason asked.

"Yeah. Sorry," Belle said, wiping away her tears. "It's just that Dominic gave me this." She pointed to her belly ring.

"I didn't . . . Sorry, I didn't mean to remind you of . . ." Adam's voice trailed off. He looked miserable.

"It's okay," Belle told him. "Really. It's not your fault. I think about him all the time, anyway."

She's so torn up, Jason thought. He tried to imagine how he'd feel if anything ever happened to Sienna. But his brain refused to go there.

"Lemons!" Sienna called as she ran back up the

stairs. "I scored a whole bag!" She hesitated on the top step. "What's up?" she asked, clearly sensing the change in mood.

"What's up is that we want our lemons," Jason answered, his voice coming out a little too loud and jolly, like somebody on a low-budget TV commercial.

"Jason decided he needs some highlights," Adam added. "He's going to juice his hair too."

Sienna laughed and tossed one of the lemon halves at Jason. "You should. I think you could use some streaks, don't you, Belle?" She dropped onto the couch next to her friend and put a CD in the player.

"Absolutely," Belle answered, managing a smile. She took one of the lemon halves and squeezed some juice onto her short blond hair, then used her fingers to comb it through.

"How about a game of 'I never' before lunch?" Sienna asked. "Belle rules at that game."

Jason and Adam exchanged a "huh?" look. "Never heard of it," Jason told her.

"I guess it's more of a slumber party thing," Sienna said. "We haven't played it in forever."

"Ooooh, I'm in," Adam said immediately. "I've always wanted to know what goes on at a slumber party."

"Okay, here's how it works. We all start out with, like, ten Tic Tacs each." Sienna pulled a plastic container of the mints from her bag and shook ten out into her palm, then handed the container to Belle. "Then we go around in the circle, and—you know what, it's easier just to start. I'll go first. I never ate an artichoke. Now, if you have eaten an artichoke, you have to give me one of your Tic Tacs," she announced.

"Wait," Adam said. "Are you telling me you've never eaten an artichoke?"

"They smell like feet," Sienna told him, wrinkling her nose. "But if you've eaten them, anyway, you owe me a mint. That's how it works."

"Bor-ing," Belle teased. Everyone gave Sienna a mint. "My turn," Belle said. She glanced from Sienna to Adam to Jason, an actual smile on her face now. "I never made out on a first date."

"You're not supposed to lie in this game, by the way," Sienna pointed out.

"I'm not lying!" Belle protested. "Although maybe it depends on how you define 'date.' Or 'making out.' By my definition, I haven't. Now give me a Tic Tac, wench."

Sienna flicked one of the little mints at Belle. Jason handed one over too. *We definitely made out on our first date,* he thought. *Hell, we made out when Sienna was still with Brad. But was she thinking of me when she gave Belle that Tic Tac, or somebody else?*

Adam sighed loudly and hung on to all of his mints.

Belle winked at him. "Now we know who the hos are," she joked. Then she turned to Jason. "You're up."

"I never went on *Jerry Springer* with my two girl-friends and my chimp," Jason said.

Jason didn't get any Tic Tacs, but everybody laughed, which was all he was going for. Sienna still needed to up her daily laugh quota. And Belle needed a quota, period.

By the time lunch—cajun chicken and a mesclun field greens salad with Champagne dressing—was served up, Adam was ahead by seven or eight mints.

"Time for you to go down," Jason warned his friend, forking a bite of salad into his mouth. "I never saw *Citizen Kane.*"

Adam threw a Tic Tac into Jason's salad. Belle and Sienna didn't have to pay up. They hadn't seen it either.

"What's that movie even about?" Belle asked.

"It's about this man who is tortured by—" Adam began.

"No, don't even tell me," Belle begged. "I had to turn the DVD off in the middle of *Saw III.* The torture scenes were too gross."

"Not that kind of torture," Adam told her. "He was tortured by memories of his past, you know, the choices he'd made."

"Sounds kinda boring," Belle commented.

Jason glanced at Adam's head, looking for signs of imminent explosion.

"I never saw *Apocalypse Now*," Sienna challenged, before Adam could formulate a response to Belle.

Adam squeezed his eyes shut in pain, then handed over a Tic Tac. Jason and Belle didn't.

"I hate those movies about the end of the world. Everything looks so ugly. Especially the clothes. Who wants to watch that?" Belle asked. "Like the one with the people who were hiding out from zombies in a mall—*Dawn of the Dead*. I mean, they were in a mall, and they never bothered to change out of their grungy clothes! And did I say they were in a *mall*, as in *lots of stores*?"

"That actually isn't the kind of apocalypse in—" Adam stopped himself. "You know what? Never mind. It's your turn," he told Belle.

"I never saw . . ." Belle hesitated.

"*Heathers*," Jason stage-whispered.

"I never saw *Heathers*!" Belle exclaimed. "I really never did."

"Unfair. I'm being ganged up on," Adam complained, giving up another mint. "And I can't believe none of you have seen *Heathers*."

"What's it about?" Belle asked.

"This group of girls who torment the less popular—"

"So it's like *Mean Girls*," Belle interrupted. "Grool! You know—'I meant to say cool and then I started to say great'? I just love that!"

Adam groaned. "No comparison. *Heathers* isn't a piece of teen fluff. It's a revolutionary mix of teen comedy, black comedy, absurd comedy, and social commentary on popularity. Plus, there's lots of violence. And croquet."

"As usual, you've lost me," Jason told him.

"You know, I think my sister left a copy of that movie in the cabinet in the stateroom. Not that it ever gets watched—my father practically refuses to remove *The Godfather* from the DVD player," Sienna said.

"'Leave the gun . . .'," Adam began.

"'Take the cannoli,'" Jason finished for him.

Sienna and Belle looked at each other.

"Do you know what they're talking about?" Belle asked.

"No, and I don't care," Sienna answered, shooting a wink at Jason.

Adam shook his head. "I'm giving you that one, because it's not a girl thing. But *Heathers*? Everybody should see *Heathers*."

The chef appeared with plates of Snickers pie.

"I'll watch it with you," Belle volunteered. "We can take our dessert to the stateroom."

"Sounds fun," Sienna said.

"Not you," Belle told her. "You and Romeo stay up here and try to come up with something that's on my 'I never' list." She winked, then grabbed her pie and headed belowdecks. Adam grinned and followed.

"Those are some good friends," Jason commented.

"Very good friends," Sienna agreed. "I'm glad you got Adam to come. He makes Belle laugh. Not many people can do that lately."

"I'm glad he came, and I'm glad he's gone away for a little while," Jason answered.

"Me too." Sienna leaned across the table and kissed him. She tasted like the dessert. But better. Much, much better.

"Let's go out on deck." Sienna took him by the hand and led him out into the salty ocean air. The sound of Louis Armstrong singing "What a Wonderful World" blended with the waves.

"I love this song," Sienna said. "In fact, I'm decreeing this our official song."

"That's how it works? By decree of Sienna?" Jason asked.

"How else?" she replied. "It's now our song, and that means we must dance to it every time we hear it."

Jason wasn't complaining. He'd be happy to dance with Sienna any time, any place, to any music. He pulled her into his arms and began to sway to the rhythm, her body pressed against his.

Now this *is dancing,* Jason thought. The moment was absolutely perfect. Except for the part where his *good* friend Adam was loudly clearing his throat from ten feet away. Reluctantly, Jason pulled away from Sienna.

"Um, sorry to interrupt, but some guys on a speedboat are taking pictures of us," Adam explained.

"They're serious about it too," Belle said from behind him, her voice tinged with panic. "They've got paparazzi-worthy zoom lenses."

"Where?" Jason asked.

"Right side," Adam answered.

Jason immediately started for the railing, Sienna on his heels.

"Why would they want pictures of us?" Belle asked as she and Adam followed. She sounded freaked. Way too freaked for what was actually happening. Jason figured that after Dominic's murder, Belle scared a lot more easily.

He put a reassuring hand on her arm. "I'm sure it's no big deal," he said, trying to sound casual. "They probably just saw you and Sienna and mistook you for Cameron Diaz and Angelina Jolie."

That got a little smile from Belle.

"I'm confused," Sienna said. "Is that them?"

Jason looked where she was pointing. All he saw was a couple of college-age guys in a speedboat, sucking down some beers. He shot a questioning look at Adam.

"That's them. But they got their camera stuff stowed pretty quickly," Adam commented. "Maybe they realized we caught them in the act."

"Ahoy, me beauties!" one of the guys, a redhead with a scruffy goatee, shouted to Belle and Sienna as his buddy powered the boat closer. "Care to board us?" Goatee and his bud laughed like that was the funniest thing they'd ever heard.

"You're drunk!" Sienna yelled back.

"Not too drunk to show you girls a good time," Goatee answered, getting more laughs from his friend.

"My analysis? Obnoxious, but not dangerous," Sienna said, turning her back on the speedboat. "But let's lose them anyway." She led the way to the cockpit. "Captain Oz, how about we make the Wally run? We want to ditch that speedboat."

Oz grinned. "'I feel the need . . . the need for speed,'" he said.

"Finally, somebody else who talks in movie quotes," Adam cheered. "*Top Gun*, baby!"

Oz gave him a thumbs-up and hit the throttle. The yacht shot forward, sprays of white foam in its wake. The wooden floor lurched beneath their feet. Jason instinctively grabbed Sienna by the waist and Belle by the arm, steadying them.

"No, no, don't worry about me," Adam muttered—

from the floor. He'd face-planted when the Wally jumped forward. "I can take care of myself." Adam used both hands to shove himself back to his feet.

"Sorry, guy, I only have two hands and I had to make a choice," Jason said. "Not that it was a difficult one," he added, grinning at Sienna and Belle.

"You were like a rock," Belle said. "You didn't even stumble."

"All that time on the surfboard must have paid off," Jason answered.

"Your boyfriend's useful," Belle told her friend. "I think you should keep him."

Sienna grinned and snuggled closer to Jason, but he was distracted by the speedboat. It had managed to catch up with them and was keeping pace. Goatee and his friend waved and smiled.

"They must have done some serious tinkering with that engine," Oz commented, frowning. "But the Wally has a CODOG propulsion system, and we're nowhere near full power." He let the clutch out. "I'm switching to the jet engines."

The speedboat stayed with them. Goatee raised his beer can in a toast.

Oz's lips tightened. "Okay. Forget tinkering, they must have replaced the engine altogether! But they don't know what they're up against." He flicked a few switches.

The speedboat kept pace for a moment, then began to fall behind.

Jason and Sienna cheered. "Bye, losers!" Belle yelled, even though there was no way the guys could hear her.

Oz grinned, satisfied.

"I'm going to grab a soda," Adam said, unsmiling. "You want one, Jason?" He shot Jason a look that Jason easily interpreted as Adam needing to talk to him—alone.

"Uh, sure," Jason said. "We'll serve you," he told Sienna and Belle.

He and Adam headed down to the lounge, where there was a refrigerator stocked with cold drinks. "What's up?" Jason asked.

Adam pulled a Coke out of the cooler and popped the top. He absently flicked the metal tab back and forth for a moment, trying to decide what to say.

"Come on, what's on your mind?" Jason prompted.

"That speedboat was really tricked out," Adam said.

"And?"

"And it would have taken some serious, serious bucks to do it. That boat shouldn't have been able to keep up with the Wally at all. And the scopes and cameras they were using? I know you didn't see them, but trust me. That stuff is not exactly standard-issue,"

Adam went on. "I think that maybe those guys weren't just . . . guys."

"You mean they were . . . *rich* guys?" Jason joked, but he felt his belly go cold. He was pretty sure he knew where Adam was headed with this.

"I didn't want to say anything in front of Belle, but I think there's a possibility that those guys are hunters. Tamburo-type hunters. The last time I searched 'vampire hunter' on the web, there was this billionaire who was offering a two-million-dollar reward for anyone who bagged a vampire," Adam said.

"Unbelievable," Jason muttered.

"It could be total bull," Adam replied. "The Net is full of trash. But . . ."

"Yeah." Jason leaned close to the huge windows of the lounge and peered out at the stretch of ocean behind them. "They're gone for now, at least."

"But we—"

"Hey, Adam, are we going to watch *Heathers* or not?" Belle called from the cockpit.

"On my way," he called back. He turned to Jason. "Like you said, they're gone now. We'll just have to keep our eyes open, see if they show up again." Jason nodded. "For now, the giant plasma—and Belle—are calling my name," Adam said. He took off for the stateroom. Belle went with him.

Sienna joined Jason in the lounge. "Weren't we in

the middle of something too?" she asked in a throaty voice.

"I think I was in the middle of my Snickers pie," Jason joked.

"Well, if you'd rather eat than dance with—" Sienna began.

"No," Jason interrupted her. "No, no, *no*." He took her hand, and they walked back out on deck, pausing by the CD player for Sienna to get their song playing again. The Wally powered on as they began to dance, the ride smooth even though they were up to almost fifty knots. Glimmering blue-green water all around them. Hot sun on their shoulders. The teakwood deck rocking gently beneath their feet. *Nothing better*, Jason decided as he wrapped his arms around Sienna's waist, pulling her closer, her silky hair brushing against his cheek, the curves of her body warm against him. *Absolutely nothing better.* He'd be happy to stay here, in this moment, for the entire next year.

But the yacht suddenly gave a sharp turn, ruining their dance. A moment later, footsteps sounded on the stairs leading belowdecks. "Did we hit an iceberg or what?" Adam asked as he and Belle emerged on deck.

Sienna frowned, looking around. "We turned back toward shore."

"We're heading home?" Belle asked. "Adam and I

barely started the movie. I thought we were staying out for a few more hours."

"We are. I told Oz we wanted to be on the water for the sunset," Sienna said. "I'll go check with him." She headed for the cockpit. Jason tagged along to see what the deal was.

"Hey, Captain!" Sienna called when they reached Oz. "What's going on? The sun doesn't go down for hours."

Oz gave an apologetic shrug. "Your father just radioed me. He said I had to get you back."

"Why?" Sienna demanded.

"No explanation given," Oz told her. "He just said to return to the marina immediately. And he didn't sound happy."

"Great. Just great!" Sienna fumed, her dark eyes blazing. Jason got the feeling *she* wasn't happy either.

FOUR

"What's the deal?" Belle asked when Sienna and Jason returned to the deck.

"My dad ordered us back in," Sienna explained, her voice filled with anger.

"Why?" Belle exclaimed.

"He didn't give Oz a reason, but . . ." Sienna glanced at Jason.

"Oh," Belle said.

"Oh?" Jason repeated. "What does that mean? Am I missing something?"

Sienna looked away, biting her lip.

"Did he know who we were out here with?" Belle asked.

"I just told him you and a couple of other friends," Sienna admitted. "Which he should have no problem with. Brad and I used the yacht tons of times."

"Oh," Jason said again. He got it now. The difference between him and Brad? Brad was a vampire. Jason, not so much.

"I thought it was supposed to be the other way around," Adam joked. "I thought the *human* parents were supposed to disapprove of their kids dating the undead."

Sienna and Belle stared at him.

"Is 'undead' not the PC term?" Adam asked. "I just meant . . . vampires. They don't even usually have parents around. Angel—no parents. Dracula—no parents. Not that they didn't have parents at some point, but their parents have usually all been dead for . . ." Adam shoved his hands through his shaggy sand-colored hair. "I'm making it so much worse, right?"

"Right," Jason told him.

"I'll shut up now," Adam volunteered.

Belle laughed and patted his arm. "I get the verbal diarrhea sometimes too."

"Who I'm with might not even be the issue," Sienna said. "Maybe Dad got his credit card bill. I did spend a teensy bit more on that Balenciaga bag than my approved clothing allowance for the month."

"Would he really be so pissed about the bill that he'd have the captain turn the boat around?" Jason asked dubiously.

"I don't know. But I'm going to find out," Sienna seethed. "My father's spoiled everything!"

She hardly looked at Jason—or Belle or Adam—on the way back. As soon as the yacht pulled into the marina, she stormed down the gangplank onto the pier. Then she turned and blew Jason a kiss. "Sorry. I know I've been awful," she called. "I just need to get this straightened out."

Sienna turned and headed down the boardwalk, her dark hair whipping in the breeze.

Belle rushed after her. "Bye, guys!" she called over her shoulder.

Jason and Adam stared after them for a moment. Then Adam turned to Jason. "Thanks for inviting me. I had a lovely time," he said solemnly. They both cracked up as they walked down the gangplank.

"I hope Sienna's dad is ticked about the shopping and not about my, you know, being a human," Jason said as they walked past a couple of more ordinary-looking yachts.

"I believe the word you're searching for is 'humanity,'" Adam said. "Or possibly 'humanosity.' Or is it 'humanaliciousness'?"

Jason just looked at him.

"Oh. We're being serious," Adam said. "Okay, well, maybe he just found out Sienna was socializing with somebody from the wrong side of the DeVere Heights gates. You and Belle are acceptable company. But me?"

"Yeah, the slums of Malibu, where you live, are known to produce some pretty dangerous characters," Jason said.

Adam grinned. "But seriously. Really seriously—

your parents would probably not be so happy if they knew you were going out with a V, am I right?"

"You mean after their parental heads exploded?" Jason answered. "It's not so much the going-out part as the vampires-existing part that would, uh, agitate them."

"Good point," Adam agreed. They climbed down the pier steps and started across the beach. "When I first put the whole vampire situation together, I was freaked. Now I spend part of every day researching vampire hunters like it's totally normal adolescent behavior. I mean, I hardly ever get time to even look at MySpace these days. I'm just too busy doing searches on vampire killers."

"It's a good thing you are, though," Jason said. "You're right about us needing to stay watchful. I wanted to think Tamburo was an aberration, but we can't be sure of that."

"So I'll keep doing the research, and we'll both keep our eyes peeled for any weirdness. Any weirdness that isn't our regular DeVere Heights weirdness, that is," Adam clarified.

"Right." Jason pulled out his cell. "How long before I can call Sienna and find out what the deal is?"

"Ten minutes for her to drive home—unless the Spider gets temperamental. Then a parental fight—mine usually last from two minutes to an hour and a half, and girls are more verbal than boys," Adam hesitated, calculating. "I'd say you need to give her at least two hours. More, if you want to factor in some recovery time, which I would."

"Okay, so what are we going to do for the next two hours or so? I need distracting," Jason told his friend.

"Pool table? McGuire's?" Adam suggested. "I could whip your butt a few times?"

"Pool table. McGuire's," Jason agreed. "And maybe I'll let you beat me once."

Three games later—all lost by Jason—Adam replaced his cue in the rack at McGuire's. "Call her already," he told Jason. "You're at an hour fifty-four. And you suck so bad that winning has lost almost all meaning for me."

Jason pulled out his cell and hit speed dial. After three rings, Sienna's voice mail picked up. "Hi, this is Sienna. Do what you've got to do when you hear the beep."

"Hey, it's me," Jason said into the phone. "Just checking in to see if you've been nabbed by the shoe police. Call me."

He tried Sienna again before dinner. Same deal.

And after dinner.

And before he went to bed. Same old, same old.

After he'd lain in bed for an hour, not being able to sleep, he tried her one more time. No Sienna. Just her voice mail message. What was going on?

• • •

"What's going on? What happened yesterday?" Jason asked Sienna when he caught her at her locker between second and third period the next day. This semester they didn't have any classes together except European history—last of the day.

Sienna rolled her eyes. "Parents." She slammed her locker door. "I'm almost eighteen. I'll be in college this year. And they're trying to tell me how I should spend my time!"

"So it wasn't about the clothes?" Jason asked, even though he already knew the answer.

"They didn't like it that you and I were out on the yacht together. They acted like it was some kind of floating motel or something. I mean, yes, it has bedrooms, but we were hardly alone. And it's not like the yacht is the only place we could . . . if we were doing that. We could be doing it in your car, for all they know."

"The Bug is a little small," Jason joked, trying to lighten the mood. "We'll figure something out. Maybe I could talk to them, or you could invite me for family dinner or something."

Sienna smiled. "We'll strategize tonight. We're still going to the movies, right?"

"Definitely," Jason promised as the warning bell rang.

Sienna gave him a quick kiss. "Can't wait," she said.

• • •

Jason couldn't wait until it was time to leave that evening. He had a little more than an hour. He headed to the bathroom for a hair check. He spotted Dani coming down the hall from the opposite direction. "Just give me one second before—"

Too late. Dani had slipped into the bathroom in front of him. "You better go downstairs. I have a lot of girly stuff to do," she told him. "I'm going out."

"I'm going out too," Jason complained. "And it'll take me less than five minutes."

"All my makeup and everything is in here." Dani tossed him his hairbrush and deodorant. "There. You're good to go. Use a different bathroom." She shut the door.

"Guys don't care that much about makeup anyway," Jason advised. "So your hot date or whatever isn't even going to notice."

"Guys like you don't notice," Dani answered. "Other guys do."

"Who is this enlightened guy, anyway?" Jason asked.

"I don't want to talk about it." Dani opened the door a crack and peered at Jason. "I like him . . . a lot. And I'm pretty sure he likes me. I don't want to mess it up by talking about it. It always messes things up if you talk about them too much."

"I doubt this guy has the bathroom bugged. If he does, you have bigger problems to worry about," Jason told her.

"I'm getting in the shower now, so if you keep talking, you're going to be talking to yourself," Dani announced, closing the door again.

"Fine," Jason muttered. He took his brush and deodorant and headed back to his room, wondering about the guy Dani liked so much. He hadn't noticed her hanging around with any one particular guy at school. But she had gone to the movies with Ryan Patrick that time. Well, Ryan and a bunch of her other friends. Was Ryan the guy his sister was falling for?

Ryan did make a point of telling me to invite Dani to his Valentine's Day party, Jason remembered. *So maybe Ryan is falling for Dani, too.*

Jason wasn't crazy about that idea. Not when he was almost positive that Ryan had fangs. Jason didn't have anything against the vampires. How could he? He was totally, insanely in love with one of them. But he knew it could be dangerous to be around them. Hell, it was dangerous just to know they existed! Jason had almost been killed twice since he'd learned the truth about the popular crowd at DeVere High.

But Dani couldn't be in love with a vampire, Jason told himself. Not yet, anyway. Ryan—if Ryan was even the guy she'd been gushing over—had only been back in school for a few months. Surely that wasn't long enough for Dani to get really serious about him.

Yeah, like you didn't fall for Sienna the first time you saw her, a voice in Jason's head mocked. *That first day at school, in the cafeteria line, when she teased you for being clueless about what a green Borba was—you were gone. Do you think Dani is so—*

Jason was pulled out of his thoughts by the sound of a text message arriving on his cell. The message was from Sienna: "Got to go to charity thing with the rents. Sorry, sorry, sorry. Talk in the a.m. XXOO."

Unbelievable.

Or else totally believable and just a continuation of what had happened yesterday on the yacht. *Have Sienna's parents decided to try and keep her from seeing me?* Jason wondered.

Jason took a deep breath. He couldn't let himself get all bent about this until he knew for sure what the deal was. Sienna's parents were really into the local charity scene. Maybe Sienna had just forgotten about one of the million events her parents expected her to attend. Maybe it was just a coincidence that this was happening the day after Mr. Devereux had ordered the yacht back to shore.

Jason flopped down on his bed and kicked off his shoes, then flipped on the TV. He should probably study, but he was so not in the mood. He channel surfed all the way up to the pay-per-view stuff and all the way back down again. Nothing held his attention for more than a few seconds.

Finally, with a growl of frustration, he gave up and snatched his chemistry book off the nightstand. He might as well get something slightly worthwhile out of his evening, even if it was just a few more points on the next chem quiz.

The thing was, four hours later, when he heard Dani coming up the stairs, he couldn't remember a thing that he'd read. He hadn't really been able to stop thinking about Sienna.

Jason couldn't stop himself from grinning, though, when he heard Dani singing as she walked by his room. *At least somebody had a good time,* he thought. He leaned over to switch off his bedside lamp and a twinge of pain vibrated through his chest muscles where the crossbow had wounded him.

The grin slid off his face. If Dani had been hanging with Ryan a few months ago, she could have been the one who'd ended up with a crossbow bolt in her chest. *It's dangerous for her to get involved with any of the vampires,* Jason thought. *Life-and-death dangerous.*

FIVE

Sienna gave a little beep on the Spider's horn as Jason walked through the school parking lot the next morning. He hurried over and swung himself into the passenger seat, leaning in for a kiss before he'd even closed the door.

But Sienna's grave expression stopped him. "What's wrong?" he asked, brushing her long hair away from her face.

"My parents sat me down for a *talk* when we got home from that charity dinner last night," she said. "They don't want me to see you anymore."

"What?" Horror rocked through Jason's body.

"I know." Sienna sounded miserable.

"But I don't get it. What's changed?" Jason asked. "It's not like we've been hiding the fact that we're together. I'm over at your house all the time. Your parents seemed fine with it."

"I know. I thought my parents liked you, even," Sienna answered. "And they do. They kept saying that last night. They think you're a really good person. They are so grateful to you for the way you went after Tamburo when he was going to kill me. They know you saved my life, but . . ." her voice trailed off.

"But I'm not a *vampire!*" The statement came out harder than Jason had meant it to, fueled by frustration and sadness.

"Yeah." Sienna stroked his arm. "Yeah."

"I still don't understand why they suddenly want you to break up with me. It's not like they ever thought I *was* a vampire," Jason pointed out. "It's not new information."

"I know. I said the same thing," Sienna told him. "Basically, they didn't think you and I were ever going to get that serious. They figured that if they just left the situation alone, time would take care of the problem."

Jason ran his hand through his hair. "Problem," he repeated. "And what exactly *is* the problem? Did they say?" Jason asked. "If we knew exactly what they were thinking, maybe we could find a way to change their minds."

Sienna let out a sigh that seemed to come from the very depths of her soul. "They just kept telling me that there were too many risks. They don't think it's safe for me—or for you, either."

Jason took a moment and forced himself to consider things from her parents' point of view. "Okay. I get how there are risks for me," he said. "Like Tamburo coming after me because he thought I was a . . . one of you. But I'm willing to take whatever risks there are. I want to be with you, no matter what." He shook his head. "What I don't understand is why your parents think going out with a human is any kind of risk for you."

"I think they finally realized we're really in love," Sienna told him.

"And that should be a good thing, right?" Jason asked.

"It should be. No it *is*," Sienna said, her voice cracking a little. "But now that they've really accepted that, I think they're afraid that we're going to want to be together forever."

"And what if we do?" Jason demanded.

"Forever. Like *hundreds of years*," Sienna explained. "Which would mean me making you a vampire. Turning you. And that's forbidden. By the DeVere Heights Vampire Council *and* the Vampire High Council."

"What about my aunt? She was turned," Jason argued.

"That was only allowed because her husband was so powerful. He was on the Vampire High Council. No one could stop him." Sienna took Jason's hand. "It's not about you and me. It's about humans and vampires. Transformation brings our two worlds together, and my parents—my parents and everyone else—think that's hugely dangerous for all vampires. And for humans, too."

"So transformation is the big problem. Okay. So we go to your parents and we promise them that that won't happen," Jason said, staring intently into Sienna's eyes. He could see that she wasn't convinced he'd found a solution.

"There's something else," she admitted after a moment's hesitation. "And this is what *they* think. It's not what *I* think. . . ."

Jason nodded.

"They think another vampire is always going to be better at keeping our secrets, because they share the same secrets," Sienna tried to explain.

Jason could feel anger welling up inside him. Sienna's parents thought he couldn't be trusted not to expose them just because he was a human? Even after everything he'd been through in order to protect their vampire secrets.

"I would never do anything that could possibly hurt you. Or your parents. Or any of you. Haven't I proved that?" he demanded. "After stopping Tamburo? After being attacked by Luke Archer when he was consumed by the bloodlust, and *not* going to the cops—or even to my own parents!" He slammed his fist on the dashboard.

Sienna winced.

"Sorry," Jason told her. "I know it's not what *you* think. But your parents are way out of line."

"Jason. My parents think that the DeVere Heights Vampire Council might even decide to take some action—against both of us—if they find out how serious we are about each other. I don't know if they're right or not. No vampire has gotten really involved with a human for as long as I can remember. I'm not sure what the Council would do if they thought ... well, if they thought our whole community was in danger of being exposed."

Jason stared blankly out at the parking lot, trying to absorb this new information. He'd watched the DeVere Heights Vampire Council discuss his friend Tyler Deegan's fate. He'd seen them talking about Tyler as if his life were theirs to take if they wanted to. Half the members had wanted Tyler put to death— even though he didn't have a clue that they were vampires. He was no real threat to them. He'd stolen from them, true, but he couldn't really hurt them.

What would the Council do to Sienna if they thought she was endangering all of her kind?

"So I really am a risk to you," he said slowly. "I don't want you brought before the DeVere Heights Vampire Council because of me. But we need a plan. There has to be some way to prove to your parents— and the Council—that I'm trustworthy."

"My parents aren't going to change their minds," Sienna answered. "And they would have a mutual meltdown if they thought we were going to try to talk to the Council." She fell silent, and suddenly Jason realized what had just happened. She'd said it was over. She'd broken up with him. The truth slammed into him like a killer wave.

Sienna locked eyes with him. "But I'm not giving you up. I'm not."

Jason laughed, relief spiraling through his body. "That's good to hear."

"We'll just have to act like we're going along with my parents," Sienna said thoughtfully. "So, no making out in front of your locker," she went on with a grin.

"Or in my car. Or in the cafeteria line. Or in European history," Jason added.

"Yeah, because I'm always making out with you in the middle of class," Sienna teased.

"You know you want to." Jason laughed. "So, we keep things secret?"

Sienna nodded. "At school we act like we broke up but stayed friends. We only talk to each other if there's at least one other person around. And we don't even do that too much; you know how everyone gossips at this school. Plus, and I hate to say it about my own, but vampires gossip worse than anybody."

"Yeah, I've seen that grapevine in action." Jason laughed.

"Starting now, we go underground," Sienna said with an emphatic nod.

"So after *this*, we go underground," Jason corrected, pressing his lips against hers.

He had meant the kiss to be short, fast, sneaky. But the taste of her, the soft warmth of her lips, made it hard to pull away. Sienna was addictive. No doubt.

"This whole 'not talking to each other too much' thing is going to be tough," he told her at last.

"Complete torture," Sienna agreed. "We have to meet up tonight."

"Where?" Jason asked, already mentally sorting through the possibilities.

"Someplace no one goes," Sienna answered. "But now we have to move. Looks like the first bell already rang." She nodded toward the people suddenly streaming into the mission-style main building of DeVere High. "We'll have to figure it out later."

"Okay. We'll text." Jason took her hand and brought it to his mouth. "And we'll ignore each other."

Sienna's breath quickened as he kissed her palm. "That won't be easy," she murmured.

Jason reluctantly let go of her. When she'd hurried into the school, he climbed out of the car and walked into the building alone. As if they'd broken up. He strode down the crowded hallway, telling himself not to miss Sienna. This was what they had to do to keep the fact that they were still a couple a secret.

He wasn't going to do anything that could bring the Council down on her. He loved her too much.

"5. Under pier. La Costa Beach," Sienna texted him between first and second period.

"Swim practice. Sux. Srry." Jason texted back.

"8. Movie about the math genius? No 1 we know will see that," he suggested in another text message between second and third.

"Auction for some worthy thing. Parents insist. Sux," Sienna instantly answered.

"Mdnght. Ftball field. Bleachers???" Jason offered in his next message as he got in the food line at lunch. Only Brad and two guys from the diving team separated him from Sienna. But Jason didn't want to risk talking to her. Not on day one of Operation Secret Couple.

"If caught sneaking in, grounded 4 life," Sienna answered by text.

"B4 skool a.m. Bad dnut place?" Jason shot back.

"Tomorrow? But it's tomorrow!" Sienna replied. "Can't w8 that long."

Jason laughed and shook his head at his phone. Then he typed, "Skipping swimming. See U under pier."

Sienna glanced over her shoulder and smiled at him by way of reply.

• • •

Jason checked his watch as he sat on the beach waiting for Sienna after school. He'd been waiting for more than an hour under the beat-up fishing pier. Had something gone wrong? Had her parents found out about their plans somehow? The vampire grapevine couldn't be *that* good. Could it?

Sienna's usually late, he reminded himself. She ran on girl time, the same way Dani and his aunt Bianca did.

He looked around and noted with satisfaction that under a half-rotten pier, in February, with the sun about to go down was the perfect choice for an Operation Secret Couple meeting. Other than some fish and some seagulls, Jason seemed to be the only living creature for miles.

He checked his watch again. Sienna was seriously late. Even on girl time.

The sky looked as if it were on fire over to the west as the blazing red ball of the sun got ready to hit the water. *Sienna should be here to witness this,* Jason thought. It was one of the best sunsets he'd seen since he'd moved to Malibu.

He pulled out his cell to text Sienna. Before he'd gotten two letters in, he heard a creaking sound above him.

Jason froze.

Rotten wood creaks, he told himself. But he kept his body motionless, waiting for another sound.

Creak!

Footsteps? Jason wondered. *Sienna?* But they'd agreed to meet under the pier, not on it.

Jason slowly stretched out on his back. He stared up at the warped planks that made up the pier. Shafts of light filtered through each space between the planks. But with the next creak, some of that light was blocked.

The creaks were definitely footsteps. Somebody was up on the pier. And it wasn't Sienna.

Jason felt his heart start to race. He'd been on the beach when Tamburo shot him with a crossbow bolt. On the beach, alone, at sunset. Just like now. And Adam thought there might be more hunters around. Was a vampire-hunter up on the old pier now, looking for him? Or, worse, *looking for Sienna?*

Jason flipped onto his stomach and combat-crawled down the beach toward the surf. When he got to the end of the pier, he put one foot in the V of a support beam and swung himself up to take a quick scan of the pier.

Goatee guy from the speedboat was walking in his direction, looking about him as if searching for someone. He certainly didn't seem to have Sienna. Jason ducked his head, determined to keep out of sight. *You're in the perfect spot,* he told himself, wrapping both arms around the beam. *Even if he looks under the pier, he won't see you unless he circles around and actually stands in the surf.*

Jason held his position until his arms ached and his legs started to cramp, then he allowed himself another quick look over the edge of the pier. It was empty now. Cautiously, he pulled himself up onto the rough planks. In the last bit of light from the sunset, he saw a black Mercedes race away down the Pacific Coast Highway.

When it was out of sight, he pulled out his cell and dialed Sienna.

"Sorry. I couldn't get there," Sienna's voice filled his ear, low and breathless. "I'm helping Mom unload the floral arrangements for the auction. She'll be back any second. I'm stuck here. She insists she needs my help setting up because someone got sick or something."

Jason's galloping heartbeat began to slow. Sienna was okay. If Goatee was a hunter, he hadn't found his prey. "You think your mom knows we were planning to meet?" Jason asked, choosing not to tell Sienna about Goatee; he didn't want to terrify her until he knew what was going on.

"I guess it's possible," Sienna whispered. "But I don't know. She and Dad might just be trying to pack my schedule so full that there's no way we can sneak off somewhere. My father actually signed me up to play in a father-daughter golf tournament this weekend. And I so don't golf!"

"Then when—"

"My mom's coming back. I gotta go," Sienna muttered, and hung up.

Jason slowly folded his phone. Then he sat and stared at the sky until all the color had drained away and the beach and the pier and even the waves were all shades of gray. *Is this how it's going to be?* he couldn't stop himself from wondering. *Is this going to keep happening?*

Is this the end for me and Sienna?

SIX

Jason headed up to his car . . . and sat there, his mind shifting back and forth between the Sienna situation and the strangeness of Goatee showing up at the pier.

Out of the corner of his eye he caught a flash of movement down on the beach. Goatee guy? Had he circled back?

Jason squinted into the shadows by the pier. The figure looked too tall to be either of the guys from the speedboat. The hair looked too dark. . . .

The figure moved out of the shadows. It was Brad.

What was he doing down there? Nobody from school came to La Costa Beach. That was the whole point of Jason and Sienna meeting there. Jason noticed that Brad was carrying fishing gear. The silhouette of the pole was pretty easy to make out. Jason hadn't been fishing since he moved to Malibu. Maybe this was supposed to be a good spot for it. It kind of made sense, with the old pier and everything.

He watched as Brad continued down the beach and then started cutting up the side of the cliff to the highway. Jason realized that Brad's car was parked farther down the road on the opposite side from Jason's. It definitely hadn't been there when Jason arrived.

Jason put his key in the ignition and started the Bug. He wanted to get out of here. If Brad noticed him, he might come over. And Jason didn't want to have to come up with a reason for what he himself was doing there.

He started the car, then impulsively turned right on PCH instead of left. He wasn't ready to go home. He'd only end up staring blankly at the tube or wasting time studying when his retention capacity was a complete zero. He'd drop by Adam's instead.

"Jason, hey," Adam's father said when he opened the front door. "You came on the right night. I just made my ten-alarm chili." The guy was wearing an apron that said BACON IS A VEGETABLE on the front. Jason was starting to feel a little better already. "Adam's eating in his room," Sherriff Turnball continued. "I couldn't pry him away from his computer. Grab yourself a bowlful from the pot on the stove and go on up."

"Cool. Thanks." Jason obediently headed into the kitchen. Just the smell of the chili made his eyes and nose start to water. *What is this stuff gonna do to my stomach lining?* he wondered, serving himself up a big bowlful nonetheless. How could you turn down chow made by somebody with a BACON IS A VEGETABLE apron? Then he made his way to Adam's room.

"Oh, man, you came on the wrong night," Adam told him from his seat in front of the computer. "Ten-alarm chili is dangerous."

Jason flopped down on Adam's unmade bed and caught sight of the image on his computer screen. "Is that a *chicken* drinking that woman's blood?" he sputtered.

"It's one of the Vampire Chickens of Borneo, according to the *believe* website," Adam replied. "Me, I'm inclined not to *believe*. Even I draw the line somewhere, and that somewhere is bloodsucking poultry."

"You haven't seen any more info on that reward for killing vampires, have you?" Jason asked.

"I checked that site again after we got followed by our friends in the speedboat," Adam answered. "A few people had posted messages on the bulletin board: exchanging vampire kill methods, asking if anyone had spotted any of the undead—that kind of thing."

"Anyone mention Malibu?" Jason asked.

His friend spun his desk chair around so he was facing Jason. "Okay, tell Uncle Adam. What's going on?"

"Sienna and I were supposed to meet under that old pier on La Costa Beach this evening."

"Romantic! The smell of mold, the thrilling possibility that you'll die together as the pier collapses on top of you," Adam commented. "So what happened?"

"Sienna didn't show. Her mom made her go early to some charity auction. But I saw the goateed dude from the speedboat."

"Did he see you?" Adam demanded quickly.

Jason shook his head. "I managed to stay out of sight."

"Good." For once, Adam sounded serious. "We don't need you to get shot by another vampire hunter. And Sienna had a close call last time too. I'm kinda glad her mom kept her out of commission tonight."

"Yeah," Jason said. "I'm glad she wasn't there when Goatee came sniffing around. And later I saw Brad. Wouldn't that have been fun—me and Sienna and her ex, watching the sunset together?"

Adam raised one eyebrow. "Brad showed up? That's . . . interesting," he commented.

"I did think it was a little strange that he was there," Jason admitted. "But he had a fishing pole. People fish there, right?"

"People used to fish from the pier all the time, before it started falling apart," Adam answered. "I'm sure people still fish around there, but . . ." He did the one-eyebrow thing again.

"Can you use actual words to say whatever it is you're trying to say? Instead of attempting to communicate with your facial hair?" Jason demanded.

"Okay, okay. But I don't know if I even have anything to say," Adam answered. "Maybe I'm just going all Son-of-a-Cop."

"Spit it out," Jason ordered.

"Well, you might want to consider the possibility that Brad is keeping his eye on you and Sienna. Maybe even feeding intel to Sienna's parents," Adam said.

"I did think that maybe Sienna's parents had found out we were meeting, and that that was why the whole charity thing had come up," Jason admitted. "But Brad? That makes no sense. Brad said he was cool with me and Sienna getting together. He even said he and Sienna were better as friends," Jason protested.

"Again, Son-of-a-Cop here," Adam put in. "But people do this thing sometimes. . . . It's called ly-ing." Adam said the last few words in a whisper.

Jason shook his head. "Why would Brad lie? Why bother?"

"Pride maybe," Adam offered. "It was clear Sienna wanted to be with you, so it was less embarrassing for him to act like he was pretty much done with her, at least in a romantic way."

A fragment of memory flashed through Jason's mind. He and Sienna texting each other at lunch. Brad in the lunch line between them. Could he have read the text messages over Sienna's shoulder?

Still, they were talking about Brad here. Pretty

much the most decent guy Jason knew. "I don't buy it," he told Adam. "But I guess I should keep an eye on him. I'm more worried about Sienna's parents, though. They're the ones who could really mess things up between me and Sienna." Jason started to spoon some chili into his mouth.

"Really. Don't eat it," Adam warned, watching him. "Those wasabi peas I had at your place? Jelly beans compared to that stuff."

Jason felt his eyes begin to water as the chili came closer. He hadn't even put any in his mouth yet. Maybe Adam was right. He put the spoon back and set the bowl down on Adam's nightstand. "So what am I supposed to do?"

Adam pulled an energy bar out of one of his desk drawers. "Eat this. It's not a great dinner, but—"

"What am I supposed to do about *Sienna and her parents*, doofus?" Jason demanded, unwrapping the bar anyway.

"I don't think her parents should be making calls about who she goes out with," Adam said slowly. "That's messed up . . ."

"But?" Jason prompted.

"I didn't say 'but,'" Adam protested.

"Yeah, but it was there anyway. Out with it," Jason urged.

"I've been reading a lot of stuff about vampires,

ever since I started getting suspicious about our, you know, special friends. And now, with trying to find out what other kinds of vampire-hunting freaks we might need to know about . . ."

Jason circled his hands in the air in a come-on, come-on gesture.

"Well, basically, there's a lot of tragic crap that goes down when vampires and humans hook up. Like the whole aging thing. I mean, I'm guessing Sienna and her crowd live a lot longer than we do, if not forever. Am I right?" Adam asked.

"Yeah. From what Sienna told me, they aren't immortal, but they can live for centuries," Jason confirmed.

"So at some point, you'll be this old man, and Sienna will be . . ." Adam let his sentence trail off.

"Still young and hot," Jason finished for him.

"So, hey, you could be like Michael Douglas to her Catherine Zeta-Jones. Not a bad way to go," Adam joked, but his eyes were solemn.

"It's really hard to worry about what's going to happen years from now. I probably should, but right now all I can think about is how I'm going to see her *today*, you know?" Jason took a bite of the energy bar. Stale.

Adam nodded. "And you're already okay with her having to drink blood. That's the other biggie."

"It doesn't thrill me," Jason confessed. "I mean, I understand that she has to do it. But it's a little weird, when you stop and think about it."

"A *little* weird?" Adam grinned. "You've been in Malibu too long, my man. Most people would consider the drinking of the blood a *lot* weird. But what about the bit where she has to make out with other guys to get it?"

"That was hard, at first," Jason confessed. "But I'm used to it now. Hey look, I love Sienna. She needs blood to live. Therefore I want her to drink blood. It's simple. I just have to accept that every few days she's going to have to make out with another guy."

"Would it help if she drank exclusively from a friend, someone you like and admire? Say, Adam Turnball? Because your baby—she's hot."

"Thanks. That was an image I really needed to have in my head," Jason sighed.

Adam laughed. "Sorry. Just pulling your chain."

"Somehow I don't think Dani would be okay with her boyfriend making out with other girls, though," Jason said thoughtfully.

"Whoa. Brain whiplash. Dani? Huh?" Adam asked.

"I think Dani might be into Ryan Patrick. They might even have gone out the other night," Jason explained. "If anyone should be cool with it, it's me.

But it kinda freaks me out. What if someone goes after Dani with a crossbow?" He gave a groan of frustration. "I sound like Sienna's parents."

"No, I can see why you're worried about Dani," Adam said. "It's better if they never get things started. That way they'll never end up in the situation you and Sienna are in."

"But I wouldn't want to go back and warn myself not to fall for Sienna. If time travel were possible and all that," Jason answered. "Whatever the risks, it's worth it. *She's* worth it."

"I think—"

Jason's cell beeped, interrupting Adam. "That's a text. Maybe it's Sienna," Jason said, pulling his cell out of his pocket.

"Is it?" Adam asked.

"Nope. It's my mom, calling me home for dinner," Jason said, deflated.

"Look on the bright side. You're probably not having ten-alarm chili," Adam consoled him.

Jason took a bite of his peach cobbler and tried to focus on what his mother was saying instead of thinking about Sienna.

"I've left three messages for my sister in the last week and a half, and she still hasn't called me back," Mrs. Freeman was complaining.

"Maybe she's out of town," Mr. Freeman suggested.

Yeah, out of town on vampire business, Jason thought. Aunt Bianca was high up in the vampire—he wasn't sure what to call it—the vampire political scene. He'd seen her take charge of the DeVere Heights Vampire Council.

She hadn't seen him, though. Jason still wasn't sure what would have happened to him if she had.

"According to her assistant, she *is* away," Mrs. Freeman agreed. "But how is that any excuse? You know she calls in to the office every day, which means she's got my messages."

"Where's Aunt Bianca this time?" Dani asked eagerly. She was fascinated by her aunt. She'd already decided that she wanted to be a casting agent like Bianca someday. And have a house on each coast. And a huge walk-in closet on both coasts to hold all her fabulous designer wear.

"Who knows?' Mrs. Freeman snapped. "Even her assistant isn't sure. Bianca calls, barks out some orders to Jacinda, and hangs up."

"Maybe she's in Paris," Dani suggested. "Paris is supposed to be awesome."

According to Ryan Patrick, recently returned from a semester in Paris, Jason thought.

"Maybe," Mrs. Freeman said. "Jacinda did say that on one of Bianca's latest calls she insisted that from then on they always answer the phone at the office in French. I think even Jacinda's becoming concerned about her erratic behavior."

"Your sister has never been exactly predictable, Tania," Mr. Freeman reminded her.

"True." Jason's mom stared down at her dessert plate. "True, but predictable isn't the same as weird. The French thing is just weird."

"I don't think it's so weird," Dani said. "Maybe Bianca wants them to speak French because it reminds her of Uncle Stefan."

"But why now?" Mrs. Freeman asked. "Stefan has been dead for almost two years."

"Delayed reaction, maybe," Dani suggested, but even she sounded doubtful. "Maybe it's suddenly hit her that he's gone forever and she just really misses him."

"Maybe." Mrs. Freeman sighed, frowning. "But that doesn't quite ring true to me. I can't shake the feeling that something is wrong with Bianca. Really wrong."

A quick triple knock sounded on the front door.

"That could be Bianca now," Mr. Freeman suggested. "She's got all your messages, she's in L.A., and she decided to drop by. She loves the drop-by, your sister."

"I'll get it," Jason volunteered. If it was his aunt,

he wanted the chance to sound her out in private and find out if she was the one who had restocked his college account.

He swung the door open—and time seemed to stand still. Every thought about his aunt Bianca, his money, everything . . . disappeared.

She stood there. In a strapless crimson dress. Her dark hair cascading over her bare shoulders.

Sienna.

SEVEN

"Wow," Jason breathed. "You look incredible."

Sienna smiled, her lipstick the same crimson as her long dress. "Incredible enough for you to invite me in before someone sees me?"

"Oh yeah, of course." Jason stepped back to let her in. "My parents and Dani are finishing dinner. Let's go upstairs, where we can talk."

Sienna nodded. Jason grabbed her hand and led her up to his bedroom. "Sienna's here, you guys. Somebody finish my dessert," he called down the stairs, realizing he'd forgotten to say who was at the door.

"I'll handle that," his dad called back.

"I can only stay for a minute," Sienna told him once he'd shut the door behind them. "Belle and I got permission to leave the auction early. I'm supposed to be over at her house studying. Her dad's home, and he will definitely report in to my parents if I show up later than he thinks I should. I told Belle not to go straight inside, to buy us a little time."

Sienna started to pace back and forth across the room. "I should have just called. Or texted. But I wanted to see your face. I wanted to tell you in person how sorry I am I stood you up today." Her eyes were bright with unshed tears.

"It's okay. I know you didn't want to." Jason stepped in front of her to stop her agitated pacing. He put his hands on her shoulders. "It's okay, Sienna."

"No, it's not. My parents somehow found out I was planning on meeting you," Sienna burst out.

Brad? Jason couldn't help wondering.

"That's why my mom made me help her set up the auction," Sienna continued. "I don't know how they found out, but they did. And they are so furious with me for going behind their backs." She gave a harsh laugh. "Or, at least, for *trying* to go behind their backs."

Jason felt a tremor run through her body, and he tried to wrap his arms around her. Sienna pulled back, holding him away from her. "Jason . . ." Her voice shook. "They told me since I can't be trusted, they don't want you and I to be alone together. At all. They realize that we have classes together, that we have the same friends and go to the same parties. They aren't saying that we can't be, like, in the same room. But if they hear that we're alone together, anywhere, ever, then . . ."

"Then?" Jason prompted.

"Then they're sending me to boarding school. In France." Sienna's lips tightened into a thin line. "I have an older cousin there. She and her husband will 'keep an eye' on me apparently. And I'd stay at their place when school's out."

Jason was speechless. How had things gotten so insane so fast? Just a few days ago he'd been hanging at Sienna's house, kissing her in her own room.

"Say something," Sienna urged.

"I-I can hardly believe this is happening. I keep trying to think of some way to fix it, but . . . ," Jason replied.

"But there isn't a way." Sienna sighed. "My parents aren't kidding around. And they don't give a lot of second chances. We get caught out one more time, and I'm going to France."

"No," Jason said firmly. "I couldn't take that—not being able to see you at all. We just have to . . . we have to stay away from each other."

Sienna shook her head. "No. I'm not letting them split us up. We'll just be careful. Extra careful. I don't know how they're getting their info on us, so for now let's just be as paranoid as we can possibly be." She glanced at the clock on his DVD player. "I've been here too long. I've got to get to Belle's. We'll talk tomorrow."

"In public," Jason reminded her.

"In public," Sienna agreed. "We'll figure this out."

"Definitely," Jason answered, although he had no clue how. They'd been pretty careful today, and Sienna's parents had still found out about their plans.

He led her downstairs to the front door. "So, I'll see you tomorrow," he said. He wanted to kiss her, but the front door had a long window that ran alongside it. Could someone be watching them even now?

"Tomorrow," Sienna agreed. She slipped out the door and vanished into the darkness.

Jason stared into the night for a long moment, then shut the door. He headed for the kitchen on auto-pilot. He might as well see if there was any cobbler left. Though it was doubtful. His dad loved cobbler.

"I don't know what it is about that girl," he heard his mother saying, just as he was about to step inside the room. "Even though I'm sure she's very nice, there's just something about her that makes me uneasy."

"Overprotective much, Mom?" Dani teased.

Mrs. Freeman laughed. "I expect I am. That's what happens when you love your kids."

If she knew the truth about Sienna, she'd be acting just the way Sienna's parents are, Jason realized. *She'd build a dungeon in the basement, or whatever it took, to keep us apart. What are we going to do?* he asked himself. *What the hell are we going to do?*

Suddenly, he couldn't stand still. Every nerve and muscle in his body was begging for release. He didn't bother to change. He was already wearing his sneakers, that was good enough. "I'm going out for a run," he announced, and was out the front door before either of his parents had time to answer.

As soon as he could, he cut off the quiet streets of DeVere Heights and scrambled down to the beach. He ran at the edge of the shore. Ran until his lungs were burning and his legs were aching. And then he kept on running. He welcomed the pain in his body. If it kept him from thinking, he'd keep running.

But half an hour later, he had to stop. He dropped onto the cool sand, his chest heaving as he gasped for breath.

Slowly, as he stared up at the huge arc of sky above him, his breathing returned to normal and he realized the exertion had cleared his head. There was no way he could deal with his life without Sienna in it. But there was obviously no way they could continue their relationship in the face of all the parental negativity.

He knew what he and Sienna had to do.

And tomorrow, he'd tell her.

"No, turn a little more to the left," Adam told Belle at the cafeteria table the next day. "A little more . . . stop. Perfect."

"This is a little extreme, don't you think?" Belle laughed.

"Not at all, and keep still!" Adam instructed.

Belle sat absolutely still for all of about two seconds

before collapsing into giggles again. Adam shook his head in despair and adjusted himself so that his body blocked Jason's face from the door. "When you've stopped laughing," he said, frowning at Belle, "you're blocking Sienna, and I'm blocking Jason. There will be no lip-reading on our watch."

"You're too funny!" Belle exclaimed, settling into position. "Nobody is here to lip-read, anyway. We're *inside*. No one sits inside for lunch. I didn't even know there was an inside until today."

"Joke all you want," Adam replied. "Just don't move." He shot a sideways glance at Jason. "Okay. You're clear."

"Good. Now tell me what's going on," Sienna said. She started to lean toward Jason, but Adam *tsk-tsk*ed her back into place.

Jason swallowed hard, gazing at her gorgeous face. Adam and Belle could have been on another planet, as far as he was concerned. They were there for camouflage, nothing else.

"I know what we have to do," Jason said. He took a deep breath. "I think we have to . . . We have to go back . . ."

". . . to being just friends," Sienna finished for him. "I know. I was up all night thinking about it. I won't be able to take it if I get sent away from you. At least this way, we can still see each other."

"And talk to each other," Jason said. *Just not ever touch each other*, he added silently.

"It's going to be so hard," Sienna breathed.

"It's going to be killer," Jason agreed. "But we can do it. We *have* to do it. And you know that we can. We did it for most of last semester."

Sienna gave a faint smile. "We did. And it won't be forever. My parents aren't going to have control of me for my whole life or anything. At college, things will be different. I just wish . . ." She glanced over at Belle and Adam, who were doing a good job of pretending that they were deep in conversation themselves, trying to give Sienna and Jason at least the illusion of being alone.

"You just wish what?" Jason prompted.

"I just wish that the last time we kissed, I'd known it was the last time," she told him.

"The last time for a while," he corrected. But he felt exactly the same way.

"Right, the last time *for a while*," Sienna agreed. "I just would have tried to lock the memory away. So I could keep it safe."

All Jason wanted to do right at that moment was kiss her. Give her that memory. Give them both that memory.

But it was too risky.

One kiss, and he could lose her completely.

EIGHT

"Look, I know why you're so upset," Adam said to Jason as they waited for chemistry class to start.

"Really? Because I didn't realize you were sitting a foot away from me when Sienna and I broke up," Jason said, the words slippery with sarcasm.

"Not that. Why you're *really* upset," Adam went on, mock-serious. "You're afraid you're going to flunk out of French without Sienna to help you. And I want you to know that you don't have to worry, because I'm taking over as your tutor."

"Adam, you can't even *say* the word 'croissant'. Forget about spelling it," Jason reminded him.

"Untrue. Okay, it's sort of true," Adam admitted. "I prefer the American term 'crescent roll.' But I can recite most of the lines from *Amélie* flawlessly. I even sound like Audrey Tautou, who played Amélie, which I'm sure you know, since you never miss a film directed by the genius Jean-Pierre Jeunet."

Jason laughed. He hadn't expected that. He hadn't expected to laugh again, well, pretty much ever. "Okay, you're on. You're my new French tutor," he told Adam.

Adam rattled off a whole bunch of what might

have been French, though it didn't sound like anything Madame Goddard had ever uttered.

"I have no idea what you just said," Jason admitted.

"'Amélie has one friend, Blubber. Alas, the home environment has made Blubber suicidal,'" Adam translated. "'It happens right at this point where a goldfish jumps out of the bowl, trying to commit suicide. So fun—'"

"Why don't I think any of that is going to be on Goddard's midterm?" Jason interrupted.

"Don't worry, I know other stuff. Meet me in the parking lot after school and we'll get started," Adam replied.

"Cool," Jason said. But he felt a dull ache roll through his body as he realized he'd never have another French lesson with Sienna. This just-friends thing—it was going to be even harder than he'd thought.

Jason leaned against the Bug, watching Sienna and Belle head across the school parking lot. He knew it would be better not to even look at her. Or easier at least. But looking was pretty much all he had right now, so he was going to look.

Although, maybe he could do a little bit more than look. Sienna was with Belle, after all, so if he went over, he wouldn't be alone with Sienna. And that's what Sienna's parents had forbidden: he and Sienna being alone together.

But Jason had only taken two steps toward her when Brad stepped up beside him, looped one arm over Jason's shoulders, and turned him back toward his car. *What's this about?* Jason thought. *Christ! Is Adam right about Brad?* "What's up?" Jason asked.

"You don't want to go over there right now," Brad said softly. "Sienna's car broke down again, and her dad's come to pick her up. Check it out. At four o'clock."

Jason shot a quick glance in that direction. Mr. Devereux sat behind the wheel of a nearby Bentley. "Thanks," Jason told Brad.

"Not a problem," Brad answered. "I know you and Sienna are getting a lot of flack from her parents."

Man, I've got paranoid, Jason thought. *Brad's my friend. He's Sienna's friend. He just proved that. And he shouldn't have needed to prove anything!*

"Study time!" came a voice from behind him.

Jason turned to face the voice and saw Adam heading toward him, with Michael Van Dyke, Aaron Harberts, and Kyle Priesmeyer from the swim team.

Adam jumped in the shotgun seat of the Bug. Harberts and Priesmeyer took the backseat. And Brad and Van Dyke piled into Brad's Jeep. "Well, get in," Adam called to Jason. "This heap isn't going to drive itself to Venice."

"How does going to Venice help me pass French?" Jason asked as he climbed into the driver's seat.

"It doesn't," Harberts told him. "But it does help you pass Fun, which, from the looks of you, is a subject you also need help in."

Jason got it. The grapevine really did work fast. They all knew what he was going through with Sienna. Harberts and Priesmeyer probably didn't have the whole story, but they still knew something had gone down and that Jason wasn't happy about it. And this trip was their way of showing support.

"Drive," Priesmeyer ordered. "Brad and Van Dyke are already pulling out of the parking lot."

Jason drove. "So where exactly in Venice do you want to go?" he asked as they flew down PCH.

"Is there more than one destination?" Harberts asked. "The boardwalk."

"I actually haven't been there yet," Jason admitted.

"You really do need help," Harberts said. "There are more hot girls on Rollerblades at the Venice boardwalk than anyplace else in the entire world. And they usually wear very little clothing."

Jason didn't care about that. Not unless one of the girls happened to be Sienna Devereux, but he kept his mouth shut. You didn't tell a car full of guys that the only babe you wanted to see was your girlfriend. Your ex-girlfriend. Your very platonic, only-speak-in-public friend.

"This is the exit," Priesmeyer announced. "Go left. Ocean turns into Pacific, and that slams right into the boardwalk."

Jason followed Priesmeyer's instructions and pulled into a medium-size parking lot near one end of the boardwalk. He took the spot next to Brad's Jeep.

"I've got to eat," Van Dyke said. "We're hitting Sausage Kingdom first. No argument."

"You're not getting one from me. My dad actually sent me to school with leftover ten-alarm chili today," Adam answered. "I'm running on empty."

Van Dyke took the lead, weaving through the crowd on the boardwalk, which was really just a sidewalk running right along the beach. Jason tried not to stare at the insanity that bombarded them from all sides. He tried to remind himself that he was a native now. But, good God, that guy had an albino boa constrictor wrapped around his neck! The thing was so big, its tail almost touched the ground. And it definitely wasn't stuffed because its slick black tongue kept flicking out of its mouth, tasting the air. Who did that? Who walked around wearing a killer reptile as a necktie?

"I can't believe the grain of rice stand is still open," Brad said, gesturing to a little sidewalk stand. "Why would anyone want to get their name written on a grain of rice in the first place?"

"Look, it's the roller-skating, guitar-playing dude," Priesmeyer said. "You can't make your first trip to the boardwalk without seeing him," he told Jason. "The guy's a local legend."

"A legendary freak," Van Dyke put in, watching the guy in the flowing robe skate past, strumming away.

"Van Dyke used to be afraid of him," Brad explained. "He literally wet his pants the first time he saw the guy."

"I was four," Van Dyke said. "And I grew up in the Heights. I'd never seen anything like him. I thought he was an evil wizard."

"Oooh. My favorite henna tattoo chick is working the booth today. I've been fantasizing about how it would feel to have her do one of those Hindu designs on my head. I'm all fresh shaved." Priesmeyer ran his hands over his gleaming scalp. "Today is the day to make my fantasy come true. I'll catch up with you." He veered off toward the brightly colored tattoo tent.

Jason and the other four guys kept walking. They paused for a few minutes by an outdoor weightlifting area. "Muscle Beach," Harberts explained. "This is Brad's fantasy. Watching oiled-up musclemen in Speedos."

Brad slapped him on the back of the head. "We stopped for you, Harberts."

Harberts gave a snort and moved on down the boardwalk. Jason and the others fell in beside him.

"Well, here's my fantasy," Van Dyke said. He jerked his chin toward Sausage Kingdom. "Jody Maroni's sausages. And lots of them." He sat down at one of the empty tables outside the food stand.

"Eating some sausage and watching the Rollergirls. Not bad for a Wednesday afternoon," Harberts said.

"Not for you, Harberts. You should stick to a wheatgrass smoothie or something," Brad joked. "Your time in the medley has been for crap. You don't need any extra weight dragging you down. In fact, I've been meaning to suggest you start shaving your head like Priesmeyer to get a little less drag in the water."

"I was thinking of suggesting you shave your legs," Van Dyke added. "Me, I think I should pack on a few pounds. Just to make the competition interesting. It's so dull when I have the best time meet after meet without really trying."

He handed Harberts a fifty. "I want an apple maple, a sweet Italian, and an orange-garlic-cumin."

"Why am I waiting in line for you?" Harberts complained.

"Because I'm holding the table. And I can swim your ass off," Van Dyke said. "And while you're at it, get an assortment of the finest for my friend Freeman here. My treat. The rest of you bozos are on your own, though."

Jason grinned, appreciating the gesture from Van Dyke. Not that it helped get his mind off Sienna. All the sausages on the planet wouldn't help *that*. His name engraved on a grain of rice wouldn't help. A couple of dozen supermodels on skates wouldn't help. It was an impossible task. But still, it was good to know that his friends were there for moral support.

"Thanks for arranging this," Jason told Adam. "But you know you're actually going to have to help me with French at some point, right?" he continued. "Because I will seriously not pass if somebody doesn't help me."

"After school tomorrow. My place," Adam promised. "French will be conjugated and otherwise humiliated. It'll be good for me, too. Get me ready for the ladies. You know how they all go crazy for French, the language of *lurve* and all."

"Please open your French textbook to page 103," Adam instructed the next afternoon. He and Jason sat in the Turnball kitchen, a jumbo bag of sea salt and vinegar chips open in front of them and a couple of Mountain Dews to wash them down.

Jason obediently opened his book and saw the little story about Jacques and Pauline at the Tour de France. "Crap!" he exclaimed. "Everything makes me think of Sienna. Even page 103 of my French book."

"How'd it go today—with the friend thing?" Adam asked.

"She and Belle went someplace off-campus for lunch." Jason said. "So I only really saw her in European history. Cauldwell has us doing these group projects, and I'm not in her group, so . . ."

"Got it," Adam said.

"It's probably better that way. Easier," Jason added.

Adam nodded, but it didn't look like Jason had convinced him. Which made sense. Jason hadn't actually convinced himself.

"Okay, I've decided that we're going to use the same method to study French as I did when I taught myself Klingon in the fourth grade," Adam explained.

"Oh, my God. You have just revealed a whole new level of nerdiness," Jason told his friend.

"I had to learn it to do the voices for the documentary I made with my action figures," Adam explained.

"I don't think you can make a documentary with dolls," Jason said.

"*Action figures*. And I was ahead of my time," Adam answered. "Someday that documentary is going to be recognized as the beginning of Adam Turnball's brilliant directing career."

"How does this have anything to do with French again?" Jason asked.

"Me learning Klingon. Which is a much more

difficult language than French," Adam said. "What I basically did was take part in this Klingon Language Institute project to translate the Bible—Old and New Testaments—into Klingon."

"Uh, I think the Bible has already been translated into French," Jason commented.

"That would be a little beyond the two of us anyway. Although Madame Goddard would probably shell out some bonus points if we gave it a shot," Adam answered. "The thing is, during the project, I e-mailed a lot of people—in Klingon—and that got me pretty proficient." He stood up. "So come on."

"Come on where?" Jason asked.

"To the computer. I found a chat room where everybody writes in French. We're going to hang in there, improve our skills, get some pointers," Adam explained.

Jason snagged his soda and the chips. "Worth a try. Doing some writing and translating can't hurt my French grade."

"Oh, we're definitely going to get you at least a C on the midterm," Adam promised. "Plus, we might hook up with some *très jolie* French babes."

Très jolie. The words sent Jason back to lying on Sienna's bed with her, "studying" French.

"Damn, I got you thinking about her again, didn't I?" Adam asked as they headed toward his room.

"Doesn't matter. Everything does it." Jason hoisted his Mountain Dew. "Even this. I was drinking one of these when I talked to Sienna at my first DeVere Heights party. The one at Brad's. She accused me of bogarting the Dew."

"So are you going to the party at Ryan's? If you want to avoid it—and the hours of Sienna-proximity torture—the two of us could do something else," Adam offered.

"No, I want to go. I can't wait actually," Jason said with a lopsided grin. "All those hours of Sienna-proximity torture."

NINE

"I can't believe Mom and Dad gave me permission to go to Ryan's party," Dani said sarcastically to Jason as they walked down their driveway. "His place is two whole houses away from ours! I might, I don't know, get lost on the way home."

Or you might, I don't know, fall in love with a vampire, Jason thought. *And end up like me.*

"Wow. Look at the Patricks' yard," Dani breathed. Glass hearts—some red, some white—hung from the branches of every tree, glowing with the light of the candles that burned inside. More candles—these as long and thick as Dani's arm—had been staked into the ground on both sides of the walkway leading to the front door. And somehow, Jason couldn't quite figure out the mechanics of how, a second moon was suspended over the house, full and silvery, looking almost as real as the one nature made.

"It's so romantic," Dani said as they cut across the street.

Jason was suddenly struck by the fact that this was a Valentine's party. It was all going to be about couples. He was probably the only guy there without a date. Well, except Adam. Adam didn't do the dating thing much. He claimed he had a rare disease that made him sound like an idiot whenever he was around a girl he liked.

"No offense, but I don't want to walk in with my brother," Dani said. "I'll see you in there." She picked up her pace and, a few moments later, disappeared through the open double doors leading inside.

Jason wasn't ready to go in anyway. He was beginning to feel like this was a big mistake. He spotted a stone bench under one of the trees and headed over. He decided he'd sit there for a while, and then, if he still felt like the party was going to be a torture fest, he'd take off and swing by for Dani later.

He leaned back against the trunk of the tree and watched people drift into the party. Lots of couples, just like he'd thought. *Sienna wouldn't show with someone else, would she?* he wondered suddenly. *We're not trying that hard to fool her parents. Are we?*

No, there she was. Walking slowly through the candlelight. Her hair pulled up, showing off her long neck. God, she was gorgeous. She hadn't seen him, and he didn't call out to her.

"Why didn't I bring my camera?"

Jason smiled, recognizing Adam's voice.

"I could use a few more shots of sad and lonely boy by candlelight," Adam continued, stopping next to the bench.

"And you aren't sad and lonely?" Jason asked with a grin. He looked up at the glimmering glass hearts above their heads. "And also by candlelight. Or is there a girl with you I don't see?"

"Belle is meeting me here," Adam answered.

Wait. Adam and Belle? Wasn't Adam the one who'd spelled out the reasons why a vampire-human combo wasn't all that great? "*Belle's* meeting you here?" Jason repeated, trying to wrap his head around the fact.

"Not like that," Adam told him. "Belle has decided I'm much too groovy to be single. She's making it her mission to find me the perfect girl sometime tonight, at this very party. Her one condition was that I didn't bring the camera along."

"In that case, I'd like to add a condition too," Jason said.

Adam raised his eyebrows.

"Don't mention the Klingon Language Institute until you're . . . until you're married. Maybe have a couple of kids," Jason told him.

Adam shook his head. "Ass. So are you going in? Or are you continuing to brood—or whatever it is you're doing?"

"I'm sticking with the whatever for a while. Sienna's in there. I thought it would be great just to see her. But I'm not sure I can take it."

"I feel you," Adam said. He started to sit down on the bench.

"No way. Get in there. If Belle can't hook you up, no one can," Jason told him.

Adam grinned. "I know. I have the best wingman—wingchick?—going. I cannot help but score."

"As long as you speak English only," Jason reminded him.

Adam shouted something guttural and unintelligible as he started for the house. "That's 'screw you' in Klingon," he called over his shoulder.

So much for hanging with Adam tonight, Jason thought. But he probably shouldn't really do the lonely guy by candlelight thing either. That was just too pathetic. He shoved himself to his feet and walked straight into the party.

Wild! he thought as he looked around. Somehow Jason didn't think Ryan's mom had helped with the decorations—at least not inside. There was another one of those freaky how-do-they-do-that? moons beaming down from the ceiling, and there were go-go girls—that was the only way to describe them—all over the place, shimmying to the music. They wore shiny white vinyl thigh-high boots and shiny white vinyl cupid wings. A few pieces of lacy red material—and a few strategic heart tattoos—completed their outfits.

"How much do I love Ryan Patrick right now?" Van Dyke asked from behind Jason. He held a plate with some lobster, some cinnamon hearts, and some strawberries on it. "He's got to have collected all the red food in the state—and hired every unemployed model in Hollywood," he added with a grin.

"Seems that way," Jason agreed, smiling back.

"Uh-oh. Here comes my date. She'll be pissed if she catches me looking," Van Dyke said. He put his plate down, rushed across the room, and swept Maggie into a deep dip straight out of a chick flick. He kissed her as the go-go cupids boogied around them.

Jason didn't need to be watching this. A drink is what he *did* need. Make that drinks. *Lots* of drinks. He wasn't driving, so no worries on that front. He spotted a goofy fountain of deep red punch on a table to one side of the room. He was sure it would be spiked, but syrupy sweet drinks weren't good for the long haul.

He decided to check out the kitchen for beer. Sure enough, Jason spotted a trashcan full of iced beers as soon as he stepped into the room. But a half a second later, he spotted Sienna. She was sitting on the counter, laughing at some story Lauren Gissinger was telling.

Jason backed out of the room quickly. He knew it was

totally within the just-friends rules to walk over and join the group. But he also knew there was no way he could get that close to Sienna and not want to touch her. And that was too risky. "Punch it is," he muttered.

He strode back out to the fountain, dipped himself a cupful of the red stuff, and downed it. It was definitely spiked. He quickly refilled his cup, then decided to check out the backyard. Who knew what Ryan had going on poolside?

The first thing he saw was Erin Henry feeding on Harberts in the hot tub. Red and pink rose petals swirled around them, matching the dinner plate–size blossoms in the huge vases all around the pool. To non-vampires it would look like the couple were just making out, but Jason knew better. He also knew exactly how radical Harberts was feeling right now. When the vampires drank from you it was like getting a bliss injection. Like getting high on the best drug ever created.

Jason turned away, not wanting to think about anything vampiric. He heard the rhythmic thump of a dribbling basketball and quickly found the source. A lighted outdoor court. Full size. Now *that* he could handle. Jason chugged his punch, grabbed a beer out of the ice-filled garbage can near the diving board, and made his way over to the court.

Brad and Priesmeyer were playing one-on-one. As Jason approached, Brad made a perfect basket from half-court. "And that's it. Priesmeyer goes down!" he cheered. A couple of girls applauded from the sidelines. "Who's next?"

"Me," Jason called.

Brad threw him the ball, and they were on. Jason pounded down the court—but Brad got in front of him, blocking him.

Brad's superstrength and supernatural speed made him a killer opponent. But basketball wasn't all about the physical. Jason feinted left. Brad fell for it, and Jason managed to duck around him and . . . "He shoots, he scores!" Jason cried.

But then Brad shot, and scored—twice. Jason pulled off his sweater and tossed it off the court. Time to get serious.

Even at absolute seriousness, Brad won 11 to 9. But since Jason wasn't supernatural, he felt pretty good about those nine points.

"Good game," Brad said.

"Thanks." Jason used the hem of his T-shirt to wipe the sweat off his face. "I definitely need another beer after that." He snatched up his sweater.

"I'm buying," Brad joked as he led the way back to the garbage can stuffed with beers.

Jason stared at the fake moon above the Patrick house. "Does one of Ryan's parents work at a movie studio or something? That's one hell of a special effect."

"No. His dad's a lawyer. And his mom is a VP at the DeVere Center for Advanced Genetics and Blood Research."

So that made it absolutely clear: Ryan and his family were vampires. There was no way you could get to be a VP at that place with blunt teeth. Sienna's dad was on the board there. Maybe a few non-vampires held some lower-level positions, but quite possibly not even that.

"I don't know Ryan very well," Jason said, doing a little fishing. "It was cool of him to invite me to the party."

"That's Ryan. He'd invite everybody in Malibu if they'd fit in the house," Brad said with a grin. "Belle has this whole system of classifying guys by what kind of dog they'd be if they were dogs, and she says Ryan's a golden retriever: likes everyone, everyone likes him."

I guess if Dani has to date a vampire, it's good that he's also a golden retriever, Jason thought wryly.

"I'm heading back inside. I want to dance with a go-go girl. Those wings—they make me nuts," Brad said. "And I *am* a single guy again. You coming?"

"In a while," Jason answered. He wasn't ready to paste a smile on his face and dive back into the crowd. He headed down to the beach, scrambling down the cliffside to the sand.

It was deserted, which was unusual for a DeVere

Heights party. Generally the beach was the main event. But it was chilly out tonight, and Ryan's house didn't have stairs down to the sand. It was probably just as well that people weren't clambering down the cliff drunk. Jason took a breath of crisp nighttime air and walked down to the sea. A little way farther along the shore a few boulders were scattered at the waterline, the black ocean lapping gently at their bases.

The real moon sailed high in the sky, casting a silver glow over the sand and turning the water to shiny obsidian. Jason had never seen the Pacific so calm before. He walked for a while, making for the boulders. It was nice to be away from the noise and the heat of the party.

He skirted the boulders. And, suddenly, there she was. Waist-deep in the water, the moon glinting softly off her dark hair: Sienna.

She trailed one pale hand through the still ocean, dragging ripples of silver in her wake.

Jason stood still, afraid to move. Afraid to breathe. Afraid to ruin the perfection that was Sienna at that moment.

Then she turned toward him, as if she felt his eyes on her. She started to smile as she took a step closer to shore. Then she froze. He could tell she was remembering the new rules too.

Just friends, a voice whispered in his head. *Friends.*

But the adrenaline coursing through his veins told a different story.

They just stood there. Both staring. Then Sienna moved forward, just a tiny bit, a small step toward Jason.

That's all it took. Jason was moving toward her, running into the ocean. She held out her arms as he reached her, and he pulled her up against him. Her mouth was on his, hot and wet and perfect.

Some small part of Jason's brain was still telling him this shouldn't be happening. That he should stop it. But that was an impossibility. Take his hands off her warm skin? Take his mouth away from her lips? Complete impossibility.

He didn't care what happened. All that mattered was now: this minute, this night. He and Sienna alone on the beach together.

TEN

"I'm sorry." Sienna backed away from Jason, fingers pressed to her lips.

"Don't," he told her. "Don't say you're sorry. Not for that."

Sienna smiled. "You're right. We don't have anything to apologize for. You go to a party, you have some drinks, you end up kissing one of your friends, right?"

"Right," Jason said. "This pretty much falls into the friend category. That punch Ryan's dishing out is lethal. I'm surprised I didn't end up kissing Adam."

Sienna laughed. A completely fake laugh.

"Although I guess I'd have had to wait in line. Belle has made it her mission to find Adam his dream girl," Jason added. *Why am I talking about Adam when I'm finally alone with Sienna?* he thought.

"It's good for her," Sienna answered. "It keeps her mind off Dom." She looked down at the ground, like she was fascinated by the sand at her feet.

"So, we're good, right?" Jason asked, because it didn't feel exactly like they were.

"We're good. We're friends. Everything is . . . it's

okay," Sienna murmured, eyes still on the ground.

He wasn't finding it easy looking at her, either. Not standing so close. Not when he could still feel that kiss.

"Do you think anyone saw?" Jason asked.

Sienna glanced nervously up and down the beach. "I doubt it. There's no cover anywhere. If anyone else was out here, we'd see them, right?"

"Right," Jason said. "We're alone."

They stared at each other for a moment.

"I need to go home," Sienna said in a rush. "I'm going to take the beach route. I'll . . . I'll see you at school, Jason." She turned around and hurried away from him.

"Wait!" Jason called.

Sienna looked over her shoulder.

"Let me walk you," he offered.

Sienna just stared at him.

"Except how stupid would that be? Me walking you to your house—where your parents live," Jason continued.

"Pretty stupid," Sienna said softly. She started away again, her arms wrapped tightly around her body.

"Wait!" Jason called again. He couldn't stop himself. "At least take my sweater. You look like you're freezing." He didn't even know if vampires felt the cold the way humans did, but she looked cold, the way she was rubbing her arms with her hands. Maybe she was just feeling uncomfortable, already regretting what they'd done.

"Here." Jason tossed her the sweater. He didn't trust himself to get close enough to hand it to her. Not without kissing her again.

Sienna wrapped the sweater around her shoulders. "It smells like you," she told him. "And you always look after me—make me feel safe," she added dreamily, almost as if she were talking to herself. "I love that."

Jason smiled. He didn't know what to say.

Sienna shook herself out of the daydream. "It's late," she said. "I'll see you at school."

At school. In a group of people. Where they would never be alone together again.

I'm not doing lonely guy standing on the beach, Jason told himself as he watched Sienna hurry away. He turned and climbed up the cliff, got himself another beer, and reentered party central. Which had turned into make-out central while he'd been gone. It seemed like every available space was taken up by groping couples. He couldn't take it. He was out of there. But first he needed to tell Dani.

He did a pass through the first floor. Didn't see her. Although he definitely noticed Adam. His friend was holding court on the big leather couch, surrounded by about six girls, all of them giggling at something he'd said. Belle sat next to him, grinning.

Jason left him to it and headed upstairs. The first door he opened was a screening room. Of course. What Malibu mansion was complete without one? The credits of what looked like the *Snakes on a Plane* sequel were rolling. A moment later, the lights came up.

"Jason, you missed a great movie!" Dani exclaimed when she spotted him.

It seemed like Dani had missed a great movie too—considering that about half of her lipstick had ended up on Ryan Patrick's mouth.

"I'm heading home," Jason told her. "Are you coming?"

"I guess so," Dani answered. "Ryan's parents are going to be home soon, anyway. They don't want things to run too late."

"Thanks for the invite," Jason said to Ryan.

"Anytime," Ryan answered with a grin. "Don't forget to grab your gift bags. They're laid out in the front hall." He reached over and kissed Dani lightly on the lips. "Good night," he said softly, and Dani smiled.

I guess he definitely is her don't-want-to-talk-about-it-guy, Jason thought. *Well, at least Brad seems to think he's decent. Hell, he even looks like a golden retriever with all that blond hair and the big brown eyes.*

Jason half-turned to give them some privacy while

they said their good-byes. Then Dani joined him. They grabbed their gift bags and headed home.

"Ooooh. Bumble and bumble products. I love Bumble and bumble," Dani cooed, peering into the bag. "And the new Killers CD. It's not supposed to drop for a month and a half. How extreme is that? A toe ring. I guess that's why they divided the bags into girls and guys."

Jason tuned his sister out. He couldn't stop thinking about Dani and Ryan. It was kind of strange that they hadn't even tried to hide the fact that they'd been making out. *Then again,* he thought, *most of the other vampires don't hide their make-out sessions either.* And with that, a sickening thought sliced into Jason's head. *Has Ryan been drinking my sister's blood?*

Jason staggered downstairs around noon the next morning. Head pounding, eyes blurry, stomach churning. He knew he shouldn't have mixed that punch with . . . well, he shouldn't have drunk that punch, period.

"You're up early," Dani teased. She had all kinds of crap for what seemed like a diorama laid out in front of her on the coffee table. *Happy Days* blared from the TV.

"Does that have to be so loud?" Jason asked.

Dani took the volume down a few levels. "Better?"

Jason grunted as he sank down on the couch. "What

are you doing, anyway?" He nodded toward her project.

"Designing a set for one of the scenes in *A Midsummer Night's Dream*. English assignment," she answered.

"You're doing homework? Now?" Just speaking and breathing was all Jason could handle after the party. "Didn't you get dented last night?"

"Nope. Having too much fun with Ryan," Dani replied.

Jason squinted at her, trying to figure out if she'd been fed on or not. If she had, she should still be feeling happy, but not the cheerful, energetic happy she was demonstrating, woozy happy, what-did-I-do-last-night? happy.

"What movie were you guys watching last night, anyway?" Jason asked, to test her memory.

"Some straight-to-DVD spoof of *Snakes on a Plane*," Dani said. "It's so stupid. That movie was practically a spoof to begin with."

So, memory—okay.

Jason watched as Dani carefully glued a tree to the bottom of a cardboard box. Manual dexterity—okay.

"My head feels like a balloon full of whipped cream and rocks," Jason told her. "You're sure you're feeling all right?" Dani looked up at him and smiled. "Jason, if you want to know if Ryan drank my blood last night, just ask."

ELEVEN

"What?" Jason spluttered.

"Ryan didn't feed from me," Dani said calmly. "He would never do that."

Jason gazed at his sister in astonishment.

She stared right back at him. "You might want to close your mouth," she suggested. "You look like a goldfish."

"I can't believe you!" Jason finally burst out. "You *know*? You know about the—"

"Vampires?" Dani finished for him. "Well, I do now. Although I hear *you've* known for ages." She crossed her arms over her chest and raised an eyebrow. "Thanks for clueing me in."

Jason shook his head and gave a little laugh, still reeling. "Sorry."

"Why didn't you tell me?"

"It was a secret," Jason explained. "And it wasn't my secret to tell."

"But you told Adam, right?" Dani demanded. "Ryan says Adam knows all about them."

"Actually, Adam told me," Jason explained. "He'd already done tons of vampire research before I even met him."

"So all this time you knew what was going on and I didn't." Dani took a seat next to him on the sofa, abandoning her project. "No wonder you never backed me up about all the parties Mom and Dad wouldn't let me go to."

"I was afraid somebody would feed on you," Jason admitted. "It happened once, you know, before I knew about the vampires."

Dani's expression grew clouded. "Yeah, I thought so. I mean, not at the time, but once Ryan told me how it all works. I looked back and realized . . ."

"Me too." Jason thought about Erin Henry and how she'd once fed on him at a party. "It's not the worst feeling in the world."

"True," Dani agreed with a grin.

"But afterward, when you know what really went on, it's a little weird."

Dani nodded. "Do you and Sienna . . . ? Do you let her drink your blood?" Dani asked.

"No. Well, I did once," Jason told her. "But only because she needed it. She was dying."

"Wow! Romantic!" Dani exclaimed.

Jason studied her face. She obviously thought the whole dating-a-vampire thing *was* pretty romantic. "I don't know if I'd call it that," Jason said carefully. "I had no choice, and neither did Sienna. It was more about survival than romance. Just hanging out, kissing, holding hands, all the usual stuff—that's romantic. The vampire part is mostly just a complication."

"I guess," Dani said thoughtfully. "But it's also pretty cool, you have to admit. Did you know they can change the way they look? Ryan showed me his real appearance—and he's even more gorgeous than he looks normally!"

"Yeah, I—"

"Plus, he's incredibly strong," Dani went on. "And fast. It's like they're humans, but they're just sort of *better* at it than everyone else."

"I wouldn't put it that way," Jason said. "They're not better, they're just different." He didn't really want his sister getting some kind of starry-eyed idea about the vampires. Dating one of them wasn't the kind of situation she should walk into without some serious consideration.

"Listen, Dani," he said seriously. "I know it probably feels like a TV show or something, dating a wealthy, good-looking vampire, but—"

"A wealthy, good-looking, incredibly *sweet* vampire," Dani cut in.

"Still, this isn't a television series," Jason insisted. "It seems like you're only paying attention to the vampire traits you like. But you can't ignore the fact that there are bad things, too. It's dangerous to date a vampire. It can be life and death."

"You mean the crossbow killer," Dani said. "Ryan

told me that guy who shot you was really a vampire hunter. He said you figured it out—which is incredibly studly of you, by the way."

"Thanks. I think," Jason said dubiously. "But that's not what I meant. Do you want to know how I originally found out about the vampires? Turns out there was a renegade vampire in town. A vampire who was giving in to his bloodlust. Did Ryan even tell you about bloodlust?"

Dani chewed on her lip. "Nooo . . ."

"It's what happens if a vampire lets their hunger get out of control. The need for blood consumes them and they keep on drinking, even if it kills the human. That's what really happened to Carrie Smith the night of Belle's party."

Dani's eyes widened. "Are you serious?"

"Yes."

"Wow." Dani looked thoughtful. "I can't imagine Ryan ever being like that. Or Sienna."

"No, it doesn't happen often," Jason admitted. "And the vampires dealt with it pretty quickly. But I saw the guy's eyes when I fought him—he was off the hook. And vampires are outrageously strong, so if one wants to kill you, well, you're dead."

"Why are you talking like this?" Dani asked. "You're in love with a vampire. You're friends with vampires. You like them."

"That's true." Jason ran a hand through his hair. "I don't know. I just don't want you to get hurt."

"Are you getting hurt?"

"Hell, yeah," Jason said with a rueful laugh. "Emotionally, anyway. Sienna's parents won't let us see each other. And that hurts like you wouldn't believe." Jason took his sister's hand. "Look, I just don't want you to end up feeling like I've been feeling lately. It's not fun. So just . . . don't get in over your head. You've only known Ryan for a few weeks."

"But that's enough," Dani told him. "I know everything about him. I know he loves me. And I know I'm safe with him."

"Okay," Jason said. "Then I'm happy for you."

But as his sister headed upstairs to her room, Jason felt a stab of worry. He had a feeling Dani didn't know as much as she thought she did. Had Ryan really made it clear to her what a big deal it was to have a vampire-human romance? And what about Ryan's parents? Why hadn't they reacted the same way that Sienna's had?

Suddenly Jason realized the truth: Ryan's parents didn't know about the relationship! Dani and Ryan had been keeping it low-key, at least up until the party last night. But now that Dani and Ryan were out of the closet, the Patricks would be sure to find out soon.

And then they would forbid Ryan to see Danielle.

Jason sighed. He didn't want Dani to go through what he was going through. But he had to admit it: He'd be relieved when she and Ryan broke up.

"'Describe in one sentence the theme of William Faulkner's *The Sound and the Fury*,'" Jason read aloud from his English notebook. "Great," he said to himself. "I haven't even finished reading that book."

He let his pen drop onto the notebook, sat back in the deck chair, and stretched. He'd been planning to do his homework out by the pool, but the combination of late afternoon sunshine, birdsong, and the after-effects of last night's party had made him sleepy. And it didn't help that now he was alone in the house. His parents had gone out with Mr. Freeman's boss, to some famous restaurant in Beverly Hills.

Dani was out too, with Ryan. She'd been wearing a huge, dreamy smile when she left. Jason felt a little guilty for wanting her relationship to end. After all, he knew just how it felt to be besotted with a vampire. It was exciting and unexpected and more than a little addictive. He knew he shouldn't have one set of rules for himself and another for Dani. But she was his baby sister. He couldn't help feeling protective.

Besides, she barely knew Ryan. She couldn't really be in love with him already. It was a totally different situation from his own with Sienna. He'd known

Sienna for months, and they'd fought their attraction like crazy before they finally—

Yeah, right, Jason thought. *We fought our attraction because Sienna was going out with Brad. It had nothing to do with the vampire thing. I'd have been with her from day one if she'd crooked her finger. And finding out she was a vampire wouldn't have changed that.*

Jason lurched to his feet, pulled off his shirt, and dove into the pool, letting the chilly water shock him out of his thoughts about Sienna. He couldn't let himself go there, because thinking about Sienna would lead to thinking about last night's events. And just the memory of Sienna's body pressed against his was enough to make him lose his mind.

After a couple of laps he climbed out and headed over to the pool house for a towel. He dried off and walked back to the deck chair, surprised to see that the sun had disappeared. A quick glance up showed dark clouds encroaching on the constant blue of the California sky.

The doorbell rang.

Jason jogged through the house to the front door and yanked it open, expecting to see Adam, or maybe just the mailman with a package or something.

He didn't expect Sienna.

"Hey there, Michigan," she said, a smile playing about her mouth. "Did I catch you in the shower?"

"Excuse me?" Jason asked, still trying to process the fact that she was actually standing on his doorstep. He felt alive and awake, all his senses tingling.

"You're dripping." Sienna reached out and playfully tousled his wet hair.

Jason automatically reached for her hand, then stopped himself at the last second. He wasn't supposed to touch her anymore. They were just friends.

Sienna seemed to realize that at the same moment. She snatched her hand away from him. They stared at each other awkwardly for a few seconds.

"I was in the pool," Jason said finally. "Hence the moisture."

"Oh." Sienna nodded. "Well, I should boogie. I'm supposed to be at Belle's, and she can only cover for me for so long before her dad figures it out. I just came by to give this back." She held out the sweater he'd loaned her the night before. "Thank you."

"No problem."

"Okay. So . . . I'll see you later." Sienna turned away, and Jason's heart gave a lurch. He didn't want her to go.

"Wait!" he called.

She turned back immediately. "Yes?"

"Don't you want to come in?" Jason asked.

Sienna raised one eyebrow. "Is coming in a good idea?" she asked.

Jason grabbed her hand—in a friends way, he told

himself. "Oh, just come have a drink. Friends are allowed to do that. And there's no one else home, so no grapevine potential." He tugged her inside, and he couldn't help noticing that she didn't resist too much.

"One drink," she said.

"Right." Jason reluctantly let go of her hand when they reached the kitchen. "What do you want? Coke? Iced tea? I think Dani's got some health water in here somewhere. . . ."

"Do you have any lemonade?" Sienna asked. "I always like to have lemonade out by the pool."

"Lemonade it is." Jason maneuvered things around so that he could get the big pitcher of lemonade from the back of the refrigerator.

"I'll grab glasses." Sienna immediately pulled open the right cabinet and took out two tall glasses. Jason watched her, remembering when she was allowed to just come hang out at his house because she was his girl-friend. Now even something as simple as having a drink seemed illicit somehow. "Any sparks between Adam and the girls Belle found for him?" Sienna asked.

"I'm not sure. I don't think Adam got to have a say in it." Jason laughed. "I think Belle was planning to decide for him whether there were sparks or not."

"She's got good taste. I wonder if she already has a dinner date set up," Sienna replied. "She'll probably tag along and coach him on what to say, too."

Jason poured the lemonade and led the way out to the pool. "I don't know how nice it will be today. It looks like rain." He peered up at the clouds.

Sienna stood next to him and glanced at the sky. "It never rains in California," she informed him.

A huge wet *splat!* on Jason's arm made him laugh. "Is that so?" he asked.

Sienna grinned. "Yes. It doesn't rain. It pours. Like you wouldn't believe."

Another drop hit his shoulder. Then another.

Sienna was already running for the pool house. "Hesitate and suffer!" she called.

Jason looked up—just as the skies opened. Rain poured down on him as if he were standing under a waterfall. "Gaaahhh!" he cried, sprinting after Sienna.

She was standing just inside the door of the little pool house, laughing. "You baby," she teased. "You were already wet anyway."

"I know, but the water in the pool is heated." Jason shook his head like a dog, spraying water all over Sienna, who squealed and gave him a playful push.

"Welcome to winter in Malibu," Sienna said. "Either it's bright and sunny or it's practically a monsoon."

"I never knew that." Jason reached up and took down one of the extra lounge chairs they kept on a shelf over the pool supplies. He pulled off the dust cover, and he and Sienna sat down together.

"Yup. Winter is rainy season. Sometimes it will rain for two weeks straight. And then there are mudslides."

"That sounds bad," Jason said.

"It is bad. My family did a big charity auction last year for the victims of a mudslide south of here." Sienna sighed, and Jason knew she was thinking of all the charity stuff her parents were making her do lately, just to keep her away from him.

"So all this 'sunny California' stuff is false advertising?" he asked, trying to lighten the mood.

"Hmm. Well, 'sunny California for fifty weeks a year' is not nearly as catchy."

Jason chuckled. They watched the rain pounding the stone patio outside the door. It was a sheet of water, and it made him feel as if they were trapped in their own private little world.

I wish we were, he thought. *Just me and Sienna, alone together. No parents. No rules. Nothing to keep us apart.*

"Why so serious?" Sienna murmured, and Jason realized she'd been staring at him.

"Just thinking. I can't see a thing through the water."

"Me neither." Sienna moved closer, her slender arm brushing against him. "I love the sound of rain. It makes me think of lazy days, just staying inside, lounging around in bed. . . ."

Jason's throat went dry. He knew he should answer her, say something boring and friendlike. But the image of Sienna lounging in bed had driven all other thoughts from his mind. All he could feel was the heat of her body close to his, all he could smell was her perfume, and all he wanted was to press his lips against hers.

"Jason . . ." Sienna turned toward him, and then they were kissing. Her arms slid around his neck, and he clutched her waist and pulled her down on top of him as he lay back on the lounge chair.

The sound of the rain pounded in his ears, keeping time with his galloping heart as he tangled his hands in Sienna's thick hair and deepened their kiss. He felt her fingers slide beneath the waistband of his bathing suit, and his breath caught in his throat. He unzipped her hoodie and eased it down over her shoulders as he kissed his way down her neck and across her collarbone. . . .

We are *alone in our own world,* Jason thought. *No one can see us here. No one will ever know.*

"Should we stop?" he murmured, his mouth on Sienna's throat.

"No," she whispered. "I don't want to stop."

Jason gave himself up to the feel of her lips, her body, her skin, hot and smooth as he slid his hand over her bare stomach.

There was a quiet *click* and the rain seemed louder

suddenly. Jason felt a gust of cold air on his face. He pulled away from Sienna, thinking that the door must have blown free.

"Jason!" Sienna hissed, her eyes wide with fear as she stared at the doorway.

Jason turned his head to see somebody standing there, but it wasn't his parents—or even Dani. It was his aunt Bianca—member of the Vampire High Council—and it was horribly clear that she'd seen everything.

TWELVE

"Aunt Bianca!" Jason cried as he and Sienna scrambled to their feet. Sienna moved as far away as possible in the small pool house, but it was no good. Sienna's hoodie lay in a heap on the floor, and Jason was dressed only in a bathing suit. It was obvious what had been happening.

"Looks like I caught you," Bianca said with a small smile. She was holding an umbrella, but rainwater poured off the edges, landing with little plinking sounds on the tile floor.

Jason sighed. Aunt Bianca had seen them. She knew Sienna's parents. And she was a vampire herself. So even if she wasn't aware of the Devereuxs' ban on their romance, she'd find out soon enough. And she would side with them because she was one of their kind.

"Hello, Sienna," Bianca said. She closed her umbrella and propped it near the door. "I'm assuming your parents don't know where you are."

"I just came to return a sweater I borrowed," Sienna said.

Bianca raised her eyebrows. "Is that what you kids are

calling it nowadays?" Her tone was light and teasing, the way it always was. But Jason thought there was a hint of menace underneath, a menace he'd only caught a glimpse of once before—the day Bianca had decided to execute his friend Tyler for stealing from the vampires.

He hadn't seen Bianca since then. Jason had a feeling he'd never talk to Bianca again without sensing that edge of danger.

"Let's not play games," Bianca went on, briskly. "I know you two aren't supposed to be seeing each other. All I have to do is tell your parents I found you here and they'll send you straight to France, Sienna."

Sienna's dark eyes filled with tears. Jason stood up and reached for her hand. There was no point in pretending now. Sienna's fingers wrapped around his. Jason felt a little better just touching her. "Why would you do that, Aunt Bianca?" he asked. "We love each other. We're not doing anything wrong."

"Love between a vampire and a human is wrong," Bianca replied. "You both know that."

Jason couldn't believe it. She sounded so casual, so normal. But she had basically just admitted that she was aware Jason knew about vampires!

"*You* were a human in love with a vampire once," Sienna pointed out. Her voice shook, and Jason realized she was afraid. As a member of the Vampire High Council, Bianca had a lot of power over Sienna.

"Yes," Bianca acknowledged calmly. "So I think you will agree that I know what I'm talking about. I know how it works. And I know that it *doesn't* work."

"I don't understand," Jason managed. He was still reeling from the shock of Aunt Bianca even being there.

"I *was* a human in love with a vampire," Bianca said. "But I'm not a human now. I haven't been for a long time."

"Right. But you were human when you fell in love with Stefan," Jason said. "And you two made it work. So can we."

"No, you can't. Stefan and I knew we couldn't be together when we were so different," Bianca explained. "So I made a choice. And now I'm giving you the same choice, Jason." Her blue eyes glowed eerily with excitement. "You can do what I did. You can become a vampire."

"What!" Jason exclaimed in shock. Become a vampire? He could barely believe what he was hearing.

"You can transform, like I did." Bianca's voice was filled with wonder. "Oh, Jason, you can't even begin to imagine how incredible it is. No sickness, no aging, nothing can hurt you. You'll be strong, and fast, and beautiful. You think you can swim now? Just think of how it will be when you've got the power and the speed of a vampire! You think your life is charmed here in DeVere Heights? It will be a hundred times better once you've transformed. You'll have wealth beyond your wildest dreams." Bianca's face had been changing as she spoke, and now it was glowing with an otherworldly beauty that astonished Jason. He'd never seen his aunt look so stunning.

That's her real face, he realized. *Her true vampire face.* Sienna had told him that the vampires toned down their natural beauty to fit in among humans. Clearly Aunt Bianca didn't think it mattered if Jason now saw her the way she really was.

She turned her luminous eyes on Sienna. "And once you've made the transformation, Jason, you and Sienna will be free to love each other," she said ecstatically.

"The transformation?" Jason said hesitantly. "What exactly—"

"No!" Sienna cut in. "You shouldn't even think about this, Jason." She turned to Bianca. "What if he doesn't *want* to transform? Anyway, the DeVere Heights Vampire Council would never allow it."

"The DeVere Heights Vampire Council answers to me," Bianca said dismissively. She narrowed her eyes at Sienna. "Why wouldn't Jason want to transform?" she asked, her voice suddenly as cold as the rain outside. "He'll have everything he's ever wanted."

"But he might—"

"That's enough!" Bianca snapped. Her blue eyes

had turned to stone. She turned and looked at Jason as if he were a bug under her shoe. "If you're not willing to transform, I'll simply tell Sienna's parents what I saw here today. They'll send her to France within twenty-four hours," she said flatly.

Jason's mouth dropped open in shock. What had happened to his aunt? One second she was alive with joy, gushing about the joys of being a vampire. The next she was threatening him.

"How can you say that?" he gasped. "Aunt Bianca—"

"It's time for Sienna to leave," she said.

Jason felt a stab of anger. Did she really think she could throw the girl he loved out of his own house? But Sienna's cheeks were pale. *She's scared,* Jason thought. *We were trying to keep the DeVere Heights Vampire Council from finding out about us, and now one of the* High *Council knows everything!*

Sienna let go of his hand. "I'll see you in school," she said quietly.

"Yeah," he replied. He smiled reassuringly, trying to cut through the worry that he saw in her eyes. But Sienna didn't smile back. She just shot a nervous glance at Bianca, turned, and hurried out into the rain.

"I don't like being threatened," Jason told his aunt, trying to control his anger.

Aunt Bianca laughed. "Don't be angry with me,

honey," she said, walking over to him. "I only want what's best for you." When she put her arm around him, Jason's shoulders tensed in spite of himself. She was still his aunt, but the way her personality seemed to flip from sweet to sour was starting to freak him out.

"There's simply no reason to even think twice about undergoing the transformation," Bianca went on conversationally. "I'm talking about money, power, prestige . . . everything that I have. You know I have no children. You and Danielle are my closest family. You're my heirs."

Jason wasn't sure what to say. He'd never thought about this sort of thing before.

"But only a vampire can inherit my estate," Bianca continued. "You understand, don't you? Most of what I have belonged to my husband. He left me his position in the community. All his influence, his wealth—it was his legacy to me. And it will be my legacy to you—but it's a vampire's estate, and that's how it must remain."

"You're not sick or anything, are you?" Jason asked uncertainly. Why was she talking about inheritances?

"No." Bianca waved her hand dismissively. "I'm fine. I'm simply thinking about the future. At some point, you and Danielle will need to undergo the transformation. So why not now? If you became a vampire now, the Devereuxs will have no reason to object to your relationship with Sienna. It seems like perfect timing."

"I guess it does . . . ," Jason murmured, still trying to get his head around the idea.

But Aunt Bianca lit up as if he'd given his whole-hearted agreement. "You can't imagine how happy it will make me to see you join me as a vampire!" she cried, her eyes shining once again with that eerie light.

Jason ran his hand through his hair. "I can't believe you know," he murmured. "All this time, I thought you had no idea that I—"

"That you were aware of the vampires?" Aunt Bianca finished for him. "Well, I didn't know for a while. But once Sienna's parents told me about your heroics with Tamburo, I figured it out pretty quickly. How did you discover us?"

"When we first moved to Malibu, there was a vampire with the bloodlust," Jason said. "I fought with him. That's when I found out about the vampires."

"Hmm. I hadn't heard about that part," Bianca said with a little chuckle. "I knew about Luke Archer, of course, I just didn't know you were involved. But when Tyler stole the Lafrenières' chalice, you knew I was one of the vampires then, didn't you? You knew I was on the High Council."

Jason didn't answer. Just hearing her say Tyler's

name sent chills up his spine. The last time she'd spoken about Tyler, she'd been planning to kill him.

"You tricked me in order to save your friend," Bianca said lightly, reading his face, even though he hadn't said a word. Thankfully, she didn't seem angry.

"Yes." Jason took a deep breath. He was a little afraid to ask his next question, but he had to know. "Is Tyler safe now?"

Aunt Bianca rolled her eyes. "He's fine," she snapped, sounding irritated now. "As long as he minds his own business, he's inconsequential."

Jason frowned. One second Bianca seemed so warm, so much like her usual Aunt Bianca self. The next there was that *edge* again. He'd never seen his aunt so changeable before.

"Tyler never knew that the chalice belonged to vampires," Jason told her. "He had no idea—"

"Yeah, yeah, I heard the whole story." Bianca shook her head. "The stupid kid shouldn't have taken the chalice regardless."

"He was desperate," Jason argued. How dare she call Tyler stupid? "And besides, I got the chalice back."

"Right. Using money from your college fund. As if your parents weren't going to figure that out!" Bianca said harshly. "Luckily I found out in time to put the money back before they noticed."

"You did that?" Jason blurted.

"Who else?" Bianca asked. "I'm your aunt. I'll always be looking out for you."

That was kind of . . . creepy. The idea that Bianca kept such a close watch over him.

"Aren't you going to thank me?" Bianca asked, oozing sarcasm.

"Yes. Of course. Thanks," Jason said in a rush. Except it was hard to feel grateful for her help when she was being such a bitch.

"You're welcome. Now let's talk about something more interesting. Your future. As a vampire." She put her hand on his arm. "Think about it, Jason! You'll have long life, wealth, power. And you'll get to be with Sienna."

Her eyes were shining, and she wore a huge smile like a kid at Christmas. Jason just stared. She'd flipped back to Happy Bianca. This was more like the aunt he'd always known. More like the aunt he loved. Maybe it was just talking about Tyler that made her act strangely. Maybe she felt like she'd handled that situation badly.

Well, she did handle it badly, he thought. *And it makes me wonder how much I can trust her at all.* "I'm not sure," he said aloud. "I'll have to think about it. I mean, it's a pretty major decision."

"I guess it is." Bianca shrugged. "Okay, you take some time and mull it over. I have other things to attend to in the meantime." She grabbed her umbrella.

"Wait," Jason said. "What about Dani? Have you talked to her about this?" *Please say no,* he pleaded silently. Dani was so besotted with Ryan right now, and so in awe of Aunt Bianca all the time, that she'd probably jump at the chance to become a vampire without a second thought.

"Of course not," Bianca said, stepping out into the rain without opening her umbrella. "I think Danielle would find it a little odd, considering that she doesn't even know vampires exist!" She stood there talking to him, seemingly unaware of the rain soaking through her hair and clothes.

"Um, right," Jason answered. "Aunt Bianca, you're getting wet."

Bianca glanced up and seemed to notice the rain for the first time. "Oh, I'd better run inside, then. We'll talk about this again soon." She gave him a little wave and dashed for the main house.

Jason watched her go, frowning. He wasn't sure what to think. At least his aunt didn't know about Dani and Ryan yet, so he could weigh the pros and cons of becoming a vampire without having to worry about his sister.

Wait, Jason said to himself. *Am I actually considering this?* Was he really thinking about becoming a vampire? His heart beat faster at the very thought of it. To be like Sienna or Zach, to have that kind of power—it was an incredible idea.

So why did he have such an uneasy feeling about this? Why did he feel a strange reluctance to go through with it? Why did everything about Bianca and her suggestion make his brain scream, "Danger!"?

THIRTEEN

"Bee!" Jason heard his mother squeal half an hour later. "You didn't tell me you were coming!"

Jason got up and made his way into the house. He'd hung in the pool house until the rain stopped, but that hadn't been nearly enough time to come to any conclusions about Aunt Bianca's suggestion.

In the kitchen, Mrs. Freeman was hugging her sister.

"I only found out this morning that I have a meeting in L.A. this week," Bianca said. "My new assistant keeps messing up my calendar. I never know where I'm supposed to be."

Jason's dad frowned. "I didn't know you had a new assistant."

"What happened to Jacinda?" Mrs. Freeman asked.

Bianca shrugged. "I fired her."

"Why?"

"Because I wanted to," Bianca snapped. She turned toward Jason and smiled. "Here's our swimming sensation!"

"Um . . . hi, Aunt Bianca," he said. Was he supposed to pretend he hadn't seen her already today?

He could see why she'd want to keep their conversation in the pool house private.

"Where is my beautiful niece?" Bianca asked.

"She went out with some friends," Mrs. Freeman said. "Who was it again, Jason? Kristy and Billy?"

He wasn't sure what to say. Dani was with Ryan, but obviously his parents didn't know that. And he didn't want to mention Ryan's name in front of Bianca. She'd know Ryan was a vampire, and it wouldn't take her long to figure out that Dani knew it too. Still, he hated lying to his mom. "I'm not sure," he fudged. "I didn't see her leave."

Mr. Freeman took out his cell phone. "I'll give her a call," he said. "I'm sure she'll want to come right home when she finds out you're here, Bianca."

"It's true. She worships you," Jason's mom said. "Everything *you* do, *she* wants to do."

Bianca shot Jason a secret smile. He pretended not to see. That was exactly what he was afraid of: that Dani would turn herself into a vampire just to be like her aunt. And that was not a good enough reason to make such a drastic decision. *Do I have a good enough reason?* he wondered. He was in love with Sienna. But was that enough?

Dani arrived home about ten minutes later, just as Jason was sitting down to banana splits with his parents and Bianca.

"Aunt Bee?" Danielle called the second she stepped in the front door.

Bianca jumped up and held out her arms as Dani bounded into the dining room and flung herself into the hug. "What are you doing here?" Dani cried happily. "Where have you been lately? I've missed you so much!"

"That's true. You haven't told us why you've been out of touch," Mrs. Freeman put in. "I was starting to get worried, Bee."

"Look at your hair," Bianca gasped, grabbing a lock of Danielle's dark red hair. "You changed the color."

"Yeah, I went a little darker. Do you like it?" Dani asked. "It's almost as dark as yours, now that I look at it. Just with more red highlights."

"I told her I didn't want her coloring her hair," Mrs. Freeman said.

"Oh, Mom, everybody at school does it," Dani retorted. "You should see Kristy—hers is practically black now! This will wash out in a few weeks, though, don't worry."

"But your natural color is so pretty," Jason's mom said wistfully. "But let's get back to you, Bianca. Where have you been?"

"You know. Here and there." Bianca waved her hand dismissively. "Nowhere interesting. I'd much rather hear your gossip. Any new boyfriends, Danielle?"

Jason nearly choked on a piece of banana. "Aunt

Bianca, you're not allowed to ask that!" he said quickly. He didn't want her getting into Ryan territory.

Thankfully, Dani backed him up. "Yeah. Love life gossip is off-limits." She laughed.

"At least while we're around, right?" Mr. Freeman joked.

"And I want to hear about you, Bee," Mrs. Freeman insisted. "I called your apartment in New York a dozen times. And I kept leaving messages with Jacinda."

"I told you Jacinda was hopeless. That's why I fired her," Bianca said breezily. "I'll have to check that the answering machine is working at home, I guess."

"Do you have any new celebrity sightings to tell me about?" Dani asked.

"Tons," Bianca replied. "I've been casting a remake of *Saturday Night Fever*, so I have lots of gorgeous guys coming in to audition."

"They're remaking *Saturday Night Fever*?" Jason asked. "That's a terrible idea!"

Aunt Bianca shrugged. "I don't come up with these ideas, I only cast them. And you wouldn't believe how much bad dancing I've had to sit through."

"That's my cue to leave," Jason said. "Hearing about actors is bad enough. I don't want to know about them trying to dance." He stood up. "I'm going to get some work done on my Faulkner paper."

As he climbed up the stairs, he heard Bianca

continuing her casting story. *Looks like she finally found a way to make Mom stop asking where she's been,* he thought. He couldn't help but wonder why his aunt was so reluctant to talk about herself on this visit. Usually she was more than happy to tell them all about what she'd been up to.

Jason shook his head. Would he ever be able to stop thinking this way: as if everything Aunt Bianca did was suspicious somehow? He doubted it. She'd been willing to kill Tyler—a kid she'd known since he was little.

I'll try to forget about it, Jason promised himself. *I'll try to focus on the future, like Bianca said. She is my aunt, after all, and I know she loves us.* But then he remembered the look in her eyes when he had argued with her about Tyler. *At least, I think she does....*

When Jason arrived at the breakfast table the next morning, his mother was already grilling Bianca.

". . . but I don't understand. You have your cell phone with you all the time. Why haven't you been answering?" Mrs. Freeman asked quietly.

"I'm very busy, Tania." Bianca replied, sounding annoyed. Last night, she'd avoided his mother's questions, but she couldn't keep doing that forever. Jason hovered in the doorway, wondering if he should go back upstairs. He didn't want to interrupt.

"Too busy for your family? Too busy to just let me know you're okay?" Mrs. Freeman pressed.

"Yes!" Bianca snapped, standing up abruptly and going to refill her coffee cup.

"Well, that's not acceptable, Bee," Mrs. Freeman said, sounding annoyed herself. "What could possibly be keeping you so busy that you'd act so inconsiderately?"

Jason turned to go, but the movement caught Bianca's eye. "Jason!" she cried in a relieved voice. "Good morning! Want some coffee? I can make more."

With a grimace, Jason spun back around. "I'm sorry. I didn't mean to barge in on you guys," he said.

"Nonsense. We're not talking about anything important," Aunt Bianca said. But Jason saw his mother's eyes flash, and knew she wasn't thrilled that he'd shown up when he did.

"Okay. Well, I'm just going to grab a granola bar and head back upstairs," Jason said. That way, he could get in and out of the kitchen quickly and leave his mother and Aunt Bianca to talk.

"Absolutely not. That isn't a good breakfast. And besides, I'm not here very often," Bianca said. "I want to see as much as I can of you and Danielle."

"Who's talking about me?" Dani called from the stairs. "You better be saying nice things!"

So much for letting Mom have a private talk with Bianca, Jason thought. He headed for the fridge to see if there was any steak left over from yesterday's lunch. Why have a granola bar if he didn't have to?

"Morning," Dani said, padding into the kitchen in jeans and a T-shirt, with bunny slippers on her feet.

"Hi, sweetie," Aunt Bianca practically sang. "Sleep well?"

"I guess . . ." Dani went straight for the coffee pot. She wasn't a morning person.

"You were telling me what you've been busy doing, Bianca," Mrs. Freeman reminded her. Jason shot his mother a surprised look. Obviously she wasn't going to drop the subject just because Aunt Bianca preferred to talk with him and Dani.

Bianca sighed. "I'm working, all right? Why do you care so much?"

"Because I'm your sister," Mrs. Freeman said. "And I'm worried about you. First you drop out of sight and don't return calls. Then you show up looking tense and exhausted. And, strangest of all, when I spoke to Jacinda before you let her go, she told me you'd been insisting that everyone talk only in French! What is going on, Bee?"

"Nothing. I'm fine. Everything's fine," Bianca said shortly.

"But—"

"Come on, Dani," Bianca suddenly cried, jumping up from the table. "Let's hit Melrose."

Dani's eyes went wide and she put her mug down. "Seriously?" She glanced at her mother to see if it was okay, since they were obviously mid-argument here. Mrs. Freeman sighed loudly and nodded at Dani.

"Yup, let's go," Bianca said. "We'll be there when the stores open and we'll stay all day. There's a new restaurant at the corner of Melrose and La Brea that I want to try, so we can do lunch there. And one of the vintage shops is holding a dress for me."

She was already heading for the door.

"Let me throw on some shoes," Dani said, racing for the stairs.

"Hurry," Bianca said impatiently. She stopped at the table in the foyer and glanced into the mirror on the wall.

"Bianca." Jason thought his mother sounded annoyed, but she forced a smile. "How long are you staying in California this time?"

"I'm not sure yet," Bianca said, running her fingers through her hair. She frowned at her reflection, and ran her fingers through again. Then again. Jason wasn't sure why; her hair looked fine.

"Ready!" Dani clomped down the stairs in a pair of wedge-heeled shoes.

Bianca was still trying to fix her hair. "Do you have a brush, Danielle?"

"Sure." Dani pulled a hairbrush out of her bag and handed it over. "But your hair looks perfect."

Aunt Bianca didn't answer. She took the brush, flipped her head upside down, and brushed out her long dark hair. Then she stood upright, checked the mirror again, and nodded with satisfaction. "Okay, I'm ready. See you later, everyone." She grabbed her keys and headed out the door, Dani on her heels.

Jason looked at his mother. She was staring after her sister with a concerned expression on her face. "Mom?" he said. "You okay?"

"I'm fine," she replied. "But I don't think Bianca is."

"She just has a lot on her mind," Jason assured her. "I'm sure she's okay."

"I hope you're right," Mrs. Freeman said, starting to clear away the breakfast dishes. Jason sat down and finished eating in silence, deep in thought. He knew what Aunt Bianca had on her mind: his transformation. It was preying on his mind too.

All night long he'd had dreams about Sienna. Sometimes they were bad—he and she were being torn apart from each other—sometimes they were good, and, once, he'd been drinking blood. That was the dream that had woken him. He had to admit that it had made him feel kind of nauseated. The thought of drinking blood was sickening. But it was also the only bad thing he could think of about being a vampire.

Otherwise it sounded like a pretty good deal. The vampires in DeVere Heights were rich, powerful, and stronger than any human. Besides which they could heal with incredible speed, change their appearance, and live for hundreds of years. All in all, it was good to be a vampire.

And it's not as if they just sit around thinking about how cool they are, Jason thought. *The vampire families do all kinds of charity work.* It was likely that Jason would be able to do more good in his life if he were a vampire than if he remained an ordinary human.

Aunt Bianca thinks it's the right thing to do, Jason reminded himself. Yeah, his aunt had been acting kind of bitchy lately. But she was the one who had put the money back in Jason's account. That proved that she was looking out for him. And didn't he owe her something for that?

Most important of all was Sienna. If he were a vampire, he could be with Sienna. There would be no more obstacles between them.

"Honey, I'm going to check on your father," Mrs. Freeman said, interrupting Jason's thoughts. "He's been working all morning and he hasn't had his coffee." She carelessly tousled his hair as she walked by, heading upstairs with a steaming coffee mug.

As his mother disappeared up the steps, Jason sighed. He'd just realized the biggest downside to becoming a vampire. It wasn't drinking blood—he could probably get used to that, given enough time. It was his parents. His mom and dad weren't about to turn vampire. He probably wouldn't even be allowed to tell them what he'd become. How could he do something that would set him apart from his own parents in such a drastic way?

It's not as if I've decided yet, he reminded himself. *I have to talk it through with Sienna first anyway.* She hadn't seemed that thrilled with the idea when Bianca had mentioned it yesterday. Was that all about her parents' opposition? Or was there another reason she didn't want him to become like her? Did she just not want him to make such a big change *only* to be with her? And if he decided to do it, would it be mostly for her? Even Jason wasn't sure about that.

The phone rang, making him jump. Jason tipped his chair back on two legs so he could reach the cordless on the counter. "Hello?"

"*Bonjour. C'est Adam,*" said Adam. "Am I interrupting anything?"

"Yes, and thank you," Jason replied. "I was making myself insane."

"Insane about what?"

"Oh . . ." Jason hesitated. "My aunt, who's willing to kill people, wants me to become a vampire like her" wasn't the kind of thing you just blurted out over the phone. "I'll tell you about it later," he said finally.

"Cool. So listen, it's time for more French practice,"

Adam declared. He lowered his voice and added quietly, "If you know what I mean."

"Well, what I think you mean is that it's time for more French practice," Jason replied.

"That's right, my crafty friend," Adam whispered. "Frrrrench practice."

Adam was being unusually cryptic—even by Adam's standards. "What's up?" Jason asked, intrigued.

"Nothing," Adam said in his normal voice. "So meet me at the Getty Center."

"The Getty Center?"

"Yup. At noon," Adam said. "In front of the doors."

"Why are we going to the Getty Center for French tutoring?" Jason asked.

"Because you suck at French," Adam replied. "Duh. See you there." He hung up.

Jason stared at the phone for a few seconds, then hit the off button. Adam was being bizarre. But Adam was always kind of bizarre, and Jason needed a break from his vampire thoughts. It would be good to get out of the house for a while, and he'd never been to the Getty Center.

An hour later, Jason was riding the monorail up the steep hill to the museum. He'd had to leave the Bug down below in the parking garage, and now it felt as if he were riding a futuristic train to some sci-fi city. Everything was made of some kind of beige stone, and the whole place looked as if it had simply grown out of the mountain. When he got off the monorail, he just stood still for a moment, looking around. The Getty Center was a little above him, up a series of wide, shallow steps. Beige steps. He could already see Adam at the top, moonwalking back and forth for Jason's amusement.

Jason shook his head and jogged up the steps. "This place is outrageous," he said.

"Say that in French," Adam replied.

"I don't know how."

"Neither do I," Adam admitted. "But, yeah, it's pretty cool. I always think this is what everything will look like once we colonize the moon. It's very *2001: A Space Odyssey*."

"If you say so," Jason replied. "So is there French art here or something?"

Adam gazed at him blankly.

"Art?" Jason repeated. "Inside the museum? And French, for the French practice?"

"No, are you crazy?" Adam said. "Let's go out to the gardens. The museum is lame. This place is all about two things and two things only: the architecture and the views." He led Jason through a couple of sets of glass doors and out through the other side of the stone building. A green lawn and a huge garden lay spread out before them. There were more stone buildings surrounding it—classrooms or something, Jason assumed. They were beige too.

A quick movement near one of the buildings caught Jason's eye. He squinted into the sun. A door was just closing, but he could swear he'd seen somebody there just a second before. Watching him.

"See? Ocean," Adam said, pointing to the right. "And that way, city." He pointed to the left.

Jason peered at the blue horizon, then at the smoggy gray buildings of Los Angeles. "Wow," he said. "You can see pretty much everything from up here."

"Now you understand, young apprentice," Adam said. "It's a rockin' place, and the café makes a mean mozzarella and tomato sandwich."

"And we're here . . . why?" Jason asked.

"Because it's far from the listening ears of Malibu," Adam informed him. "The listening vampiric, *parental* ears of Malibu."

"Oh," Jason said. *"Oh!"* Now he got it. They weren't here for French lessons—they were here because Adam had a message for him. From Sienna.

"Slow on the uptake, aren't you?" Adam teased. "Here I am being all cryptic and you don't even notice."

"Sorry. I thought you were just being you. I usually only understand about a third of what you say on a good day," Jason said. "So what's up?"

"I got a phone call from the lovely Sienna this

morning," Adam said. "She wants to see you. Tonight. She's seriously nervous about her parents, isn't she?"

"Yeah. Why?"

"She kept going on and on about how I couldn't put anything in writing. No sending you e-mails or text messages or even good old-fashioned notes. She even made me promise not to talk about it on the phone with you."

"So that's why we had to meet somewhere?" Jason guessed.

"Yeah." Adam's hazel eyes were serious. "She doesn't really think her parents have your phone bugged, does she?"

"I don't know," Jason said. "That seems crazy. But . . ."

"But the fact that the toothy ones exist at all is crazy," Adam finished for him. "Right. Better not to take chances."

Jason glanced back over at the door to the classroom building. "Yeah. Listen, did Sienna say what she wants?" Jason asked.

"I kind of assumed you'd know that," Adam said, wiggling his eyebrows suggestively.

Jason ignored that. "Where am I supposed to meet her?"

"At the observatory in Griffith Park," Adam said. "It's far from home and it's in the middle of nowhere. Too bad it's not still closed for renovations—that would have made it an extra good rendezvous point, although the new Leonard Nimoy Event Horizon is awesome. Anyway, you guys should be safe from Sienna's parents there. Plus, it's an excellent make-out spot. Or so I've heard. It's in lots of movies."

"What time?"

"Nine o'clock." Adam's face broke into a grin. "This is so cloak-and-dagger! I should do a movie about it— part thriller, part romance. All good."

The door of the classroom building inched open again, and a guy slid out, his eyes on Jason. But this time, Jason's eyes were on him, too—and Jason recognized him: It was the goateed guy from the speedboat, and the pier.

Jason's blood seemed to freeze in his veins. They stared at each other for a moment, then Goatee slipped quickly back inside the building.

"Time to go," Jason said grimly.

"What? Why?" Adam trailed after him as Jason rushed back through the museum toward the main entrance. "I was only kidding about the movie—"

"We're being hunted," Jason told him quickly. "Remember our friend with the stupid goatee?"

"Who could forget?" Adam replied.

"He's here."

Adam stopped in his tracks. "But there are no toothies here," he said. "There's just you and me. You don't think he could've assumed that we're V, do you?" He sounded frightened. After all, Jason had nearly been killed by the last hunter who'd thought he was a vampire.

"Keep moving. We need to get back down to the parking garage," Jason said. "I'll recognize his car. Maybe we can follow him."

Adam pointed to the monorail stop. "There's a train about to leave. Let's go." They ran for the monorail, squeezing through the doors just as they were closing.

Jason did a quick scan of the car. No Goatee. "I'm confused," he said. "This is twice I've seen the dude when I wasn't with Sienna. Is he looking for her, or looking for me?"

"And if he's found you, why hasn't he taken a shot?" Adam murmured.

Jason didn't know the answer. They rode in silence the rest of the way. The monorail doors slid open in the parking garage, and they hurried out. The museum wasn't too crowded today, and the parking attendants had directed all traffic to park on the same level. Adam kept watch for Goatee while Jason jogged up and down the line of cars, looking for the black Mercedes.

"There!" he said, spotting it behind an enormous Escalade.

Adam ran over and studied the Mercedes. "Are you sure it's this one?" he asked.

"I got a pretty good look at it from the fishing pier," Jason said. "Okay, let's get the Bug. When he comes down to the car, we'll be ready to follow."

But Adam was shaking his head. "Sometimes, my friend, I think I've been gifted with all this brilliance just so I can help you in your quest for . . . What *are* you questing for, anyway?"

Jason just stared at him.

"Right. Sorry. What I mean is, we don't have to follow him. As if he wouldn't notice your silly VW in his rearview anyway!" Adam said.

"What do you mean?" Jason asked.

"If you look closely at the bumper of this car, you'll see a sticker with a D and a circle and a little triangle-type thing," Adam pointed out.

"So?"

"So that is a parking permit for the DeVere Center," Adam said. "Only employees are allowed to park in that lot."

Jason's eyes widened. "Are you telling me that this guy works at the blood research center?"

"I'm telling you he works for Sienna's father— who runs the blood research center," Adam said. "Although I'm guessing that the only research our goateed friend does is research into Sienna's boyfriend and his activities!"

"I can't believe it," Jason said. "They actually have

somebody following me just to make sure I stay away from her! That's insane."

"On the up side, at least now we can keep your meeting with Sienna tonight a secret," Adam said, then raised his eyebrows. "Go ahead, ask me how."

"How?"

"Well, if you'll look back at this lovely Devereux-mobile, you'll note that the license plate has a registration sticker on it."

Jason glanced at the plate. "So what?"

"It's expired," Adam grinned. "See what you learn to look for when your father's a cop? I'll call in the expired registration just as you leave tonight. The police will pull him over to give him a ticket, and you'll have the time you need to lose him."

"Wow!" Jason said. "Maybe you could have a career in espionage movies. Thanks, man."

"Your eternal worship is the only thanks I need," Adam told him, leading the way back to the Bug.

Jason slid behind the wheel, feeling hopeful for the first time in days. Tonight he'd see Sienna.

And nobody would catch them.

FOURTEEN

"The parking lot of the observatory was dark when Jason pulled in. He cut the engine and turned off his headlights, but left the roof of the Bug up. Even though Adam was taking care of Goatee, it didn't hurt to be careful. He didn't want to risk being seen with Sienna, and sitting in a convertible with the top down was a good way to be seen.

There were a few cars scattered around the parking lot. Maybe the other people were here to see the view, which was definitely something to see. The observatory was set up high in the hills near the Hollywood sign, and the city lay spread out beneath it. The lights of the L.A. streets stretched out in front of him like the neon spokes of a giant Ferris wheel. Still, Jason guessed that the people in the other cars were probably too busy making out to look at the view.

By the time he heard the car door open, Sienna was already sitting next to him. He smiled. She could move fast when she wanted to. If he were to become a vampire, he'd be able to do that, too.

"One of your father's security guys followed me,"

he told her. "It was the goateed guy from the speed-boat, remember him?"

Sienna nodded. "So those guys were spies for my dad!" she fumed.

"Don't sweat it. Adam helped me lose him," Jason told her. He grinned. "And probably got him a traffic ticket in the process."

"Good," Sienna laughed. Then she sighed. "We can't get caught, Jason. If I have to go to France, we'll *never* get to see each other."

He took her hand, twining his fingers through hers. "I won't let that happen. Maybe I should just do what my aunt Bianca says. I think she really does want what's best for me. I found out she was the one who put the money back in my college account. She—"

"No, you can't do it!" Sienna cut him off. "That's why I had to see you tonight, to tell you I don't want you to try and become a vampire."

"But if I did, we could be together," he began.

"You don't know what a huge risk it is," Sienna cut in. "Did your aunt tell you what could happen?"

"No. What do you mean?"

"Jason. It's not a simple little thing, for a human to turn into a vampire," Sienna said, her tone serious. "There's a reason the High Council forbids it. And not just because it brings the vampire and human worlds too close together." She drew a deep breath.

"One of the reasons we don't like humans to turn is that they could die."

Her words hit Jason like a splash of ice water. "Die?"

"Yes. The transformation is very difficult. Sometimes humans just can't handle it. Their . . . your genetic structure is different from ours. For some humans, it's fine and they become vampires with no trouble. They have our powers, our long life, everything we have. They become just like us."

"Right," Jason said. "That's what I could be."

"Yes, but not necessarily," Sienna corrected him. "Some humans become . . . well, they become . . .unstable. Physically. Their bodies break down. They die."

Jason took a deep breath. "That doesn't sound good."

"That's not the worst thing," Sienna said. "Believe me, the incompatible ones who die are lucky compared to the ones who live. When a human is unable to handle the transformation, we don't always know right away."

"But you said—"

"I said sometimes they die. But sometimes they go mad."

Jason frowned. "Go mad how?"

"A long, slow descent into insanity," Sienna explained, her voice trembling as she spoke. "It doesn't show for a long time, years even. Everything seems fine. The turned vampire has powers and long life and the whole deal. But then something happens. They start hallucinating sometimes. Or they become violent. Sometimes they even succumb to the bloodlust—and you know what that's like."

Jason nodded, remembering the glowing green eyes of Luke Archer, the bloodlusting vampire he'd fought back when he'd first moved to Malibu. There had been nothing human about Luke. Nothing sane. He'd been a monster.

"It's not just bloodlust," Sienna went on. "Sometimes there's extreme dementia. One turned vampire in France went so crazy that she began feeding off herself. She thought she was drinking the blood of a human, but she was really drinking her own blood. They found her dead of starvation."

Jason swallowed hard. The image was disturbing.

"And there was a vampire in New York with the transformation sickness who had such extreme delusions that they had to put him in a mental institution. Think about that. We live for centuries, Jason, so the High Council had to find a way to kill him, otherwise the doctors would have noticed that he wasn't getting old like he was supposed to."

"So he was murdered?"

"Yes. To protect the other vampires."

"It might have been better that way," Jason said. "He was insane. And he would have had to live that way for *hundreds* of years!"

"Exactly." Sienna clung to his hand. "It's a horrible fate. Not only to go mad, but to descend deeper and deeper into insanity over such a long period. Jason, do you see why I can't let you take that risk?"

He nodded slowly. Dying or going mad. Those were pretty bad side effects. Why hadn't Aunt Bianca mentioned them?

"Anyway, transforming is not something you even have to consider right now," Sienna went on. "I mean, we're young. There's no rush. We have plenty of time to make life choices like that. If we're still together in ten years, you can decide then."

He pulled her closer and kissed her, letting his lips linger on hers. "We'll still be together," he murmured.

Sienna pulled back. "But what are we going to do about Bianca? If you tell her you're not going to undergo the transformation right now, won't she tell my parents about us? She seemed so insistent that it's something you have to do right away. I don't get that."

"She wants Dani to transform right now too," Jason told her. "She was talking about her legacy and how we'd have to be vampires to inherit from her. I guess she just wants it done—so she can be sure that we're her vampire heirs, or something. I mean, once

Dani and I transform, there's no going back, is there?"

"No, that's true," Sienna said thoughtfully. "But what are we going to do? How long do you think she'll give us before she goes to my parents?"

"She's my aunt. She loves me. I'll just tell her I'm considering transforming into a vampire. I think she'll be satisfied with that for a while," Jason answered, hoping it was true.

"Right." Sienna relaxed. "Good. Then it's settled." She pulled her bag onto her lap and dug around inside. "I brought you a treat."

"Just being with you is a treat," Jason said.

She laughed. "Aren't you a smoothie?" she teased. "Look!" She took a Tootsie Pop from her bag and handed it to him, then pulled out another one for herself.

"Candy on a stick," Jason said, chuckling.

"We have a long tradition of foods on sticks," Sienna said, unwrapping her lollipop.

Jason opened his, too, remembering the afternoon they'd spent at the mall. They were Christmas shopping, and he'd introduced Sienna to the concept of the corn dog at the food court. They'd been officially just friends then, and it was one of the best times they'd ever had together. He held up his Tootsie Pop in a toast. "Here's to you and me," he said. "And our friendship."

Sienna ceremoniously tapped her Tootsie Pop against his, then stuck it in her mouth. Jason did the same, and for a moment they just sat silently, looking at the view. "We've been through a lot together," Sienna murmured finally.

He nodded. "And we'll get through this as well. Somehow. Your parents can't keep us apart forever."

"We have to be careful," Sienna said. "I'll stay in touch with you through Adam. But I'd better get going now." She glanced out the car window, her brow furrowed. "I know you weren't followed, but I still can't shake the feeling that they'll find us somehow."

"What did you tell your dad?"

"I said I was going to a club in Hollywood, so I have to put in an appearance there."

Jason nodded thoughtfully. "Hmm, that means that Goatee will probably have gone there when the cops finished ticketing him. He'll be looking for me, but he'll only see you. It's perfect!"

Sienna grinned, reached over, and kissed him lightly on the forehead. "I'll see you in school." Then she was gone, and Jason was alone with the view.

He pulled out his cell and started to dial Adam's number, then stopped. He wanted to get his friend's take on the whole vampire transformation thing. Adam was good at making decisions. He always had lists of pros and cons, and he managed to think of things in a slightly skewed way that helped to give Jason a new perspective. But how could Adam help him here, really? Jason knew there was no real decision to make. Sienna was right: It was too big a risk to take right now. It was too big a decision to rush. There was no harm in waiting.

Except for the part where he couldn't be with Sienna while he was a human. Which made him consider the risks all over again. . . .

FIFTEEN

When the alarm clock went off on Monday morning, Jason was already awake. He'd been tossing and turning all night, thinking about the vampire transformation. It sounded like pretty scary stuff. But how often did the transformation go wrong? What percentage of the time did it work perfectly? He should have asked Sienna those questions.

Jason dragged himself out of bed, exhausted. He figured a nice cold shower would wake him right up, so he padded down the hallway to the bathroom and pushed open the door.

Bianca stood inside, her face about an inch from the mirror. She was concentrating so hard that she didn't notice him behind her. Jason started to leave, but not before he saw what she was doing: plucking her eyebrows. To be more exact, plucking *every single hair* from her eyebrows. One after the other. Already one of her eyebrows was entirely gone.

That was not normal.

Jason slowly backed out of the bathroom. *Whoa,* he thought. *Mom's right after all. Something freaky is going on with Aunt Bianca.*

All through breakfast Jason kept an eye on his aunt. She'd drawn her eyebrows in with some kind of makeup and she was acting normal, just eating and reading the paper. On the drive to school, he glanced over at Dani, who was frantically trying to finish her reading for English.

"Is there some new fad where you pluck out your whole eyebrow?" he asked.

Dani didn't glance up from her book. "Why? You planning to try out a new look?"

"Aunt Bianca was doing it this morning."

That got her attention. "Aunt Bee? Really? Maybe it is a new fad." She thought for a moment. "There were some old-time movie stars who did that. Shaved off their eyebrows and drew in new ones with eyebrow pencil. They got the perfect shape they wanted that way."

She kept reading. But Jason was still worried.

"How was shopping yesterday?" he asked.

Dani dropped her book into her lap. "Well, I got this great new pair of jeans. They're distressed, but not *too* distressed, you know?"

"I *meant*, how was Aunt Bianca?"

"She was fine, Jason. What's this all about?"

"She's just being a little weird, I think," he said. "She's so moody and she doesn't want to tell Mom why."

"Yeah, she was kinda moody yesterday," Danielle said thoughtfully. "At one store, she actually made the salesgirl cry."

"How?"

"Oh, Aunt Bianca wanted these shoes and the only ones they had in her size were scuffed. So she had a little tantrum and she called the girl a wannabe. I felt bad for the girl."

"That really doesn't sound like Aunt Bianca," Jason pointed out.

"I guess not." Dani frowned. "It's pretty typical Hollywood behavior, though. And Aunt Bianca has been working in Hollywood for a while. Maybe it's rubbing off. She does seem very stressed about work."

"That's true," Jason said. "And she's not dating or anything. Between losing Stefan and having this high-pressure career, she's probably at the end of her rope. She needs a vacation."

"I know! I'll tell Mom to invite Bianca to a spa week. That's totally relaxing. They could just drive out to Palm Springs or something. It's perfect!" Dani picked up her book, a big grin on her face. "I'm such a genius."

Jason let her read for the rest of the drive. His mind went back to the question of becoming a vampire or not. He couldn't really think about anything else. What would it be like, to know you were going to live for a couple of hundred years? To not worry about sickness or injury?

He turned the VW into the parking lot at DeVere High and found a spot next to Brad's Jeep.

"There's Belle," Dani said, peering at the vintage Beemer two spaces away. She slammed her book shut, stuffed it in her bag, and jumped out of the car without a glance at Jason. "Belle!" she yelled. "What up, homegirl?"

Belle laughed. "Come here. I found the ideal shade of brown lipstick for you yesterday. As soon as I saw it, I thought of you. . . ."

Jason climbed out of the car as Dani and Belle walked off toward the school.

"When did they become such good friends?" Adam asked, coming up behind him.

"Since Ryan Patrick," Jason replied. "And palling around with Dani helps take Belle's mind off of Dom."

Adam nodded. "So, what are you up to tonight?"

"Why?"

"Because, *mon ami*, I have something to show you. Something you really want to see."

"ParanormalPI.com?" Jason asked later that evening.

"That's what I said," Adam replied, tossing Jason's Nerf basketball at the hoop attached to the bedroom door.

Jason typed the web address into his computer and watched as a serious-looking site appeared. "It looks like a college information page or something."

"Well, yeah, it *looks* all scholarly. And it is compared to most of the vampire websites. But there's still a lot of trash. Check out the titles of the articles in the archive," Adam told him.

Jason took a closer look. "'Ghost gives accurate information on Mississippi shootings'."

"Oh, that one was cool," Adam said, tossing the ball again. "This ghost communicated with the homicide detective through his iPod."

"'Woman gives birth to flying fish'," Jason read dubiously.

"Like I said—a lot of trash." Adam threw himself down on Jason's bed. "But it's a pretty good site even so. They investigate every paranormal story they find in the tabloids, and a lot of them are really hilarious. One or two even turn out to be true—in one way or another."

"Okay. So why am I interested in this?"

"Um . . . because you're dating a vampire?" Adam said.

"We're just friends," Jason corrected him.

"Yes. And I'm a world-champion bodybuilder," Adam replied, deadpan. "So do you want to see the vampire-interest story or not?"

"I guess so."

"Search for 'vampire' in the database."

Jason typed in "vampire" and hit enter. The first link that popped up was entitled "Priceless Vampire Artifact for Sale." He clicked on it.

"'A Malibu, California pawnshop is offering an antique chalice for sale to the highest bidder,'" he read aloud. "'This is no worthless trophy cup. This is a valuable piece of art that is linked with several legendary vampire rituals. Blood sacrifices, undead wedding ceremonies, and vampire initiation are only a few of the sacraments rumored to have been performed with this beautiful chalice.'"

Jason stopped reading. "Well, they got *one* of the rituals right." The chalice had definitely been used to initiate Zach Lafrenière into the DeVere Heights Vampire Council.

"I'm thinking this is where our not-so-friendly neighborhood vampire-hunter got his lead on the DeVere Heights toothies," Adam said. "Tamburo probably lurked on sites like this all the time. He saw the notice about the chalice, he came straight to Malibu to find out whether it was a real vampire artifact or not. Because where there's an ancient vampire chalice, there are likely to be vampires to kill."

Jason nodded, his face grim. "I wonder how many other vampire hunters do the same thing."

"And I wonder how the website even heard about the chalice," Adam replied.

"That pawnbroker probably put it on this site to advertise it," Jason said. "It's a site for supernatural enthusiasts, after all." He closed the page, and the "vampire" search results filled the screen again.

"Yeah, I guess saying that it was mysterious and all that would get some publicity and drive the price higher," Adam agreed.

But Jason barely heard him. His attention was on another link down toward the bottom of the search page: "Blood Research Center Creates Top Secret Vampire Test." Jason clicked on it.

He'd only read about three sentences before he knew he had to call Sienna. Immediately. He reached for the phone, then stopped. Sienna had been worried about his calls being monitored. "Can I borrow your cell?" he asked Adam.

Adam handed it to him, then came to read the web page over Jason's shoulder. Jason dialed Sienna's number.

"Hello?" she answered. "Adam?"

"No, it's me," Jason said. "Can you talk? It's important."

"Yes. My parents are out at a meeting. Are you okay?"

"I'm reading an article online. It mentions the DeVere Center for Advanced Genetics and Blood

Research. Your father is on the board of that place, right?"

"Right," Sienna said. "Why?"

"This article says that research scientists there have devised a DNA test to determine whether a human could secretly be a vampire without knowing it," Jason told her.

"That's ridiculous," Adam said.

"That *is* ridiculous," Sienna put in.

"Well, yeah, obviously it's been exaggerated," Jason agreed. "I think it would be pretty hard not to notice yourself drinking blood. But a few of the other articles on this site have a grain of truth to them. It's possible that this one does too."

"Okay . . . ," Sienna said slowly.

"We were talking about genetics yesterday," Jason reminded her. "If the DeVere Center is doing any research on vampire genetics, it might be useful to us."

"The center e-mails my father every week with progress reports," Sienna said. "Just to keep him up to date on their latest research."

"Can you find those e-mails?"

"I'll try. But it has to be fast. My parents will be home any minute." Jason heard Sienna moving around as she spoke. "Dad's computer is downstairs, in his study."

"Put it on speaker. I can't tell what's happening," Adam complained.

Jason set the cell phone on his desk and hit the speaker button.

"Okay, I'm at the computer," Sienna's voice came through the tiny speaker. "I just have to log on as my dad."

"Do you know his password?" Adam asked.

"Yup. It's my middle name," Sienna replied. "Genevieve." Jason heard the keys tapping as she typed. A little bell sound announced that she was logged in. "I'm going to his e-mail," she narrated. Then she groaned.

"What?" Jason and Adam asked together.

"There are hundreds of them," Sienna explained.

"How many from the DeVere Center?" Adam said.

Jason quickly scanned his computer screen for the date of the article on ParanormalPI.com. "This piece is from last week, so check the last couple of months."

"This is weird. I don't see any e-mail from the DeVere Center, but there should be a bunch," Sienna told him.

"Go Dumpster diving," Adam suggested.

"What?" Sienna asked.

"I think I can translate," Jason offered. "Check the recycle bin for deleted messages."

Sienna was silent for a moment, then Jason heard her gasp.

"What?" he asked.

"Yeah, the suspense is killing me," Adam agreed. "Especially since I don't know what we're talking about."

"Okay, this is an e-mail from a couple of weeks ago," Sienna said. "Apparently there was an accidental discovery at the research center. They're always trying to find a way to manipulate our genes to allow us to drink synthetic blood. That's the whole point of the DeVere Center."

"Why, thank you for that generous thought," Adam cracked. "Synthetic blood means no more human blood, right?"

"Right. So apparently they were working with vampire DNA and human DNA together and they were building some sort of hybrid blood, but in the course of doing that they discovered the location of the human gene that causes the transformation sickness."

"The what what?" Adam asked.

"There's a specific gene?" Jason asked.

"Yes. And knowing where the gene is means they can develop a test to find out in advance whether a human has the proper genetic makeup to become a vampire with no ill effects. This e-mail is a request for funding to develop that test."

"And?" Jason demanded.

"'This is of course not the breakthrough we were hoping for, but it is an interesting and potentially useful side effect nonetheless,'" Sienna read. "'The test would match human mtDNA against—'"

"Why did you stop?" Adam asked. "It was just getting good."

"I heard a car." Sienna sounded far away, and Jason figured she'd walked away from the phone. "Damn! My parents just pulled into the driveway. I have to go."

"No! This is important," Jason cried.

"Print out that e-mail," Adam said.

"And we need the answer to it. Did they get funding? Does the test exist?" Jason added. "Sienna?"

"I'm looking," she answered, her voice tense. "Here it is. My father deleted his reply too. I'm opening it now. . . ."

"You should print a copy. We might need to reference it," Adam instructed her.

"Yeah, and Dad might empty the recycle bin and delete everything before I can get another look at this," Sienna agreed. "Okay. It's going to the printer. If my father catches me doing this, he'll freak."

"Is it printing?" Jason demanded.

"Crap! They're inside," Sienna whispered.

"But did it print?" Adam asked.

"Not yet."

"Sienna—" Jason began.

But the line went dead.

SIXTEEN

Jason stared at the cell phone as if he could will it to bring back Sienna.

Adam reached over, picked up the phone, and hit end. "I'll get her back," he said, starting to redial.

"No!" Jason snatched the phone away from him. "If she's hiding in her father's study and the phone rings, it could give her away. We don't want her to get caught."

"Right. Sorry. Let's just hope she hasn't been caught already," Adam said darkly.

"I don't think there's anything we can do now except wait to hear from her." Jason ran his hand through his hair, frustrated. He hated not knowing whether Sienna had managed to get away with it or not.

"Out with it," Adam said.

"Huh?"

"Why do you care so much about the transformer whoosie-whatsit?"

"Transformation sickness."

"Yeah, that. Are you planning something I should know about? Like, oh, transforming into a vampire?" Adam demanded.

"My aunt Bianca caught me with Sienna the other

day," Jason explained. "She gave me a choice: Become a vampire, or she tells Sienna's parents about us."

"And Sienna gets sent away," Adam said thoughtfully. "Got it. But you're not actually considering transforming, are you?"

"Wouldn't you?"

Adam thought about it. "Would I want to become a vampire and have looks, money, power, and long life? Seems like a no-brainer."

"But?" Jason prompted.

"But if I were a vampire, then I wouldn't be . . . human," Adam said. "I'm not sure that's a good thing. Plus, there's the having to drink blood issue."

"You see my problem," Jason said, shaking his head. "I keep going over and over it in my mind, but I can't decide."

"And then there's some kind of sickness?" Adam asked.

"Transformation sickness is what happens to some humans when they transform into vampires," Jason explained. "Basically there are three possibilities: You're totally fine, you die instantly, or you slowly go insane."

Adam whistled. "Seems like pretty bad odds. Two of those possibilities bite. Hard. No pun intended."

"That's probably why their scientists suggested developing a test for it. The vampires aren't thrilled when one of them dies or goes crazy, either."

"So that's what the test is about," Adam said thoughtfully. "If you could find out in advance that you would be okay—not, you know, dead or crazy—at least you'd know what you were getting into."

"Exactly," Jason agreed.

"Then your course of action is clear," Adam declared. "If that test exists, you have to take it!"

The next morning, Jason got to school so early that he was the first car into the parking lot. He'd left Dani to fend for herself—he was so eager to find out if Sienna was okay that he didn't have the patience to wait for his sister.

Adam pulled in on his Vespa half a minute later. "Is she here yet?" he asked.

"Nope." Jason peered at the line of cars waiting to get into the school. He shaded his eyes against the sunshine. "There she is!" he cried, relieved. Sienna's Spider was almost hidden between Van Dyke's huge Hummer and Erin Henry's Escalade. Jason's heart-beat slowed, and he relaxed a little. He'd been afraid he would show up at school only to find out that Sienna had already been packed off to France.

He and Adam jogged over to her as she parked. "What happened?" Jason called.

Sienna rolled her eyes. "I felt like Sydney on *Alias*," she joked. "Doing computer espionage . . ."

"Lookin' hot," Adam joked along, leering. Sienna gave him a light—vampire light—shove, and he almost fell over.

"Anyway, I got what we needed. It finished printing about two seconds before my father walked through the door," Sienna told them.

"Well?" Jason asked.

"He funded the research," Sienna said. "They were supposed to have a prototype of the test ready by Christmas."

"So it will definitely be ready by now," Adam said. "What are we going to do about it?"

"We?" Sienna asked.

"Yeah. I'm in." Adam frowned. "What, you think I'm only good for the go-between mushy romance stuff?"

"I want to take the test," Jason told Sienna. "I want to know if I can become a vampire."

"Even if you can, that doesn't mean you should," Sienna said quietly.

"But at least I'll have all the facts."

Sienna nodded. "So what do we do?"

"We need recon," Adam said. "Can you get into the lab?"

"Sure," Sienna said. "I'll just say I'm there to visit my father."

"But you can't go when he's there," Jason pointed out. "Otherwise he'll find out what you're doing."

"So I'll wait for a day when I know he's *not* going in to the center," Sienna agreed.

"Cool. Then you just have to sweet talk one of the scientists into showing you the new test," Adam said. "They'll probably be psyched to demonstrate it, anyway, and then you'll know how it works."

"And we can do it on me," Jason said.

Sienna smiled. "It's a plan!"

When Jason got home that afternoon, Dani was already in the kitchen eating Häagen-Dazs straight from the carton.

"Hey," he greeted her. "I haven't seen you all day. Did you catch a ride home with Ryan?"

"No." Dani's lower lip began to tremble, and she swatted at a tear in her eye.

"Are you crying?" he asked, concerned.

"No," she said again. She stuck a spoonful of Dulce de Leche in her mouth.

"Yes you are," Jason told her. "Is it Ryan?"

"No."

"Can you say anything but no?" Jason teased gently.

She dropped the ice-cream carton onto the counter and turned to face him. "It's not Ryan, it's his parents. They suck."

Ah, the vampire parents make their appearance, Jason thought. *I knew it was only a matter of time.* "They told

Ryan he couldn't date a non-vampire," he said aloud.

"Yeah," Dani sniffled. "It's so unfair! I'm not going to spill their secret."

"I know. But they don't like human-vampire relationships," Jason told her.

Dani narrowed her eyes at him. "Wait a minute," she said. "Is that why you and Sienna—" Her cell rang, singing out the theme from *Grey's Anatomy*. Dani grabbed it and hit talk. "Ryan? Oh hey, Belle. It's true. He told me at lunch today."

She covered the phone with her hand and glanced at Jason. "Can you put the ice cream away for me?"

He nodded. *Belle has an even bigger project to keep her mind off Dom, now,* he thought, as his sister headed out to the pool, detailing her conversation with Ryan. *A broken-hearted Dani.*

Jason grabbed the ice cream and stuck it back in the freezer. He knew it was hypocritical of him, but he was relieved that Dani and Ryan had had to break up. Sure, he was thinking of becoming a vampire himself, but somehow he still didn't like to think of Dani getting involved with one.

Thank God Bianca never talked to Dani about the possibility of transforming, he thought. He knew his sister was impulsive enough to do it without thinking it through, if it meant she could stay with Ryan.

Jason headed upstairs, feeling like a jerk. He wasn't

sure why he had such a double standard for Danielle dating a vampire. *Once we figure out how to do the test, I'll talk to Dani about the transformation situation,* he thought. *I just need to get all the information first.*

By the time Friday came, Jason was exhausted. The weeks he'd had to sit out of swim practice while the crossbow wound had healed had taken it out of him, and he'd been training hard lately, trying to get back to optimum speed. But he knew that wasn't why he was so tired. It was the waiting that was getting to him. Waiting for Sienna to find time to get to the DeVere Center. Waiting to find a few stolen moments with her when they could actually talk. Waiting to find out if he could become a vampire, if he could change his life forever without dying or going insane.

He came home from school and dropped facedown onto his bed. "Thank God it's the weekend," he muttered to himself. He was definitely sleeping late tomorrow.

The phone rang. When Jason picked it up, he was shocked to hear Sienna's voice on the other end of the line. "What are you doing?" he cried. "You said we couldn't use the phone!"

"I couldn't help it, I just had to talk to you," she said in a rush. "I'm on a pay phone, so I think it will be okay."

"All right, but hurry," Jason said nervously.

"I went to the lab, it was no problem," Sienna said.

"The guy showed me the whole thing, how to do the test and everything. It's really simple. It tests DNA, so we need a strand of your hair or a mouth swab or something."

"Okay," Jason said. "That's easy enough."

"Yeah, but here's the thing," Sienna said. "We need the equipment at the lab to do the test. We need to physically be there."

Jason thought fast. "They're closed for the weekend now, right? Is everybody out of the building?"

"Everybody leaves by eight or eight thirty," Sienna replied. "Why?"

"We'll go at eleven. That should give us enough of a buffer—all the workers will be gone by then."

"Eleven o'clock tonight?" Sienna sounded surprised.

"Sienna, if I have to wait for one more day to take this test, I'm going to explode," Jason said.

"Okay," Sienna began.

"And besides," Jason rushed on. "It's my life we're talking about. It's my future. I have to know what the possibilities are. Otherwise I'm just thinking about it over and over with no way to make a decision. It's driving me crazy."

"Then we'll do it tonight," she agreed. "But Jason, you know there are guards, right? There's a whole security system."

"I know," Jason said. "We'll just have to break in!"

SEVENTEEN

Jason grabbed his keys from the dresser, jogged downstairs, and headed out the door. He had to see Adam. His friend's father was the sheriff, which meant that Adam had read practically every police report ever filed. Who better to plan a break-in with?

When he got outside, Jason saw Bianca just getting out of her car. "Hi, Aunt Bianca," he called, pulling open the door of the Bug.

"Jason, wait." Bianca strode over to him. "You haven't given me an answer yet. Are you going to undergo the transformation?"

"I'm still thinking," he said truthfully.

"What's to think about?" Bianca replied quickly. "You know what you would gain: power, prestige!"

"I don't care about that," Jason told her.

Bianca gave a wry smile. "I forget how young you are. Of course you don't care about that now. But you will. Trust me," she replied. "I'm your aunt. I just want what's best for you. I want you to have health and long life. That's something your mother would want for you too. Anyone who loves you would."

She put her hand on his arm. "Accept the gift. There's no end to the wonderful things you can have if you become one of us."

Jason looked at her hand. The nails were bitten to the quick, and her red nail polish was chipped. He pulled away, startled. Aunt Bianca was all about appearances. Her nails were always perfectly manicured.

"Aunt Bee . . . are you okay?" he asked. "You seem really stressed out lately."

"I have a lot of things on my mind," she replied. "A lot of people to deal with."

Jason frowned. Was she saying there were bad people to deal with? Or bad vampires? Jason had no real sense of just how many vampire communities there were in the world like DeVere Heights. Were there turf wars? Political differences? Had Bianca become involved in some sort of vampire struggle she couldn't handle?

That's unlikely, Jason thought. *She's too powerful.* "Listen, I'm still thinking about transforming. I really am," he assured her. "But I have to go now."

Bianca stared at him, her eyes suddenly cold. She pulled her hand away. "Don't think for too long!" she snapped. "I'm not going to keep your secret about Sienna forever."

"I won't. Just . . . just keep this between us for a little longer," he said. "Please."

"Maybe I should talk to Danielle," Bianca said, her eyes narrowing. "She might be more willing to make a change than you are."

"No!" Jason cried. "Just give me another day or two. I promise I'll give you an answer then."

"Fine," Aunt Bianca sighed, and suddenly she threw her arms around him and hugged him tightly. "You know how much I love you, don't you? You and Dani both."

"Of course," Jason said, surprised at her sudden warmth. "We love you, too."

Bianca released him and turned away abruptly. "See you later," she called, walking into the house.

Jason climbed into his Bug. He wasn't sure he'd ever get used to Aunt Bianca's sudden mood changes, but he was very relieved that he'd managed to convince her not to tell Dani about the transformation. Or at least he hoped he had. The way Bianca was acting lately, he was a little worried she might just change her mind and tell Dani all about it anyway.

"Dani," he murmured thoughtfully. He was going to the lab tonight. He'd find out for sure whether he could become a vampire or not. Why not find out for his sister at the same time?

Jason jumped out of the car and ran back inside. Dani was still out by the pool, on her cell. But her bag sat on the table in the hall where she always left it. He grabbed it and began rummaging around inside.

"What on earth are you doing?" Bianca asked, peering at him from the kitchen table.

"Oh. I, uh, forgot to get this DVD from Dani. She said I could lend it to Adam." Jason turned so that his body blocked the bag, then he pulled out Dani's hairbrush and stuck it in the inside pocket of his jacket. "Bye, Aunt Bee!" he called. Then he was out the door.

"Let me get this right. You want me to help you break into a top-secret vampire laboratory monitored by security guards and a high-tech alarm system so that you can use outrageously expensive scientific equipment to test your own DNA," Adam said an hour later.

"Is that a problem?" Jason asked.

"No, not at all," Adam replied with a grin. He jumped up and grabbed a backpack from his closet. "Just wanted to be sure I had it straight. So, let's see . . . we'll need a couple of lock-picks, probably a smoke bomb or two, in case we get caught. . . ." He rummaged around in the messy closet, pulling things from boxes and shelves. "Flashlights for all of us, walkie-talkies. Ooh, a taser! We better bring that—"

"Are you insane?" Jason began to laugh. "We're not infiltrating the CIA."

"But we could, my friend, as long as we had the proper tools."

"Where did you get all this stuff?" Jason asked.

"Shh. If I told you that, I'd have to kill you."

"From your dad's office, huh?" Jason guessed.

"I never reveal my sources," Adam said, stuffing his equipment into the backpack. "How about a dog whistle? There are probably German shepherds. In the movies, whenever you break in somewhere, there are German shepherds. Or Dobermans. Do you think they'll have Dobermans?"

"I told Sienna we'd meet her at eleven," Jason said. "I'll drive."

"Okay." Adam followed him toward the door. "Maybe they'll have pit bulls instead. Pit bulls are trendy. . . ."

When they got to the DeVere Center, Sienna's Spider was already parked along the street outside the ivy-covered wall of the property. Jason pulled up behind her and cut the engine. He got out of the Bug as Sienna climbed out of her Spider.

"Hey there," Sienna called softly.

"Hi. I brought Adam along to help." Jason gestured to his friend, who was wrangling the overstuffed backpack out of the car.

"I didn't bring anything to deal with the gates," Adam called. "Should I go back and get some dynamite?"

"Just ignore him," Jason told her. "He's a little overexcited."

"But look at those gates," Adam said. "They're huge!"

Jason glanced up at the wrought iron gates. They stood at least twelve feet tall and had sharp spikes on the top. "How *are* we going to get through those?"

"Relax, spy boys," Sienna said. "We don't need the nitro and detonators tonight. I borrowed Dad's key card. The gates are no problem." She led the way over to the edge of the stone wall that surrounded the center. "We have to stay out of sight of the gates until the security guy goes by. Then I'll open them."

"How did you get the key card without your dad noticing?" Jason asked in a whisper.

"Same way I always used to 'borrow' his credit cards without him noticing," Sienna said with a wink. "I'm crafty."

"How often does the security dude go by?" Adam asked, slipping into a camouflage jacket.

"Every ten minutes. I've been watching him," Sienna replied. "We have to stay far away—he's got a dog with him."

"I told you!" Adam said, nudging Jason.

"*Shh!* Here he comes," Sienna said. They all fell silent as the guard slowly walked to the gates, his boots crunching on the gravel of the driveway. He came straight up to the gates and peered through the iron bars onto the street.

Did we park far enough away? Jason wondered, suddenly paranoid. Their cars were to the side of the gates, so he hoped the guard couldn't see them from where he stood. His dog gave a soft whine, and he said something to it. Then they heard him crunch away again. None of them spoke for a minute or two.

"I think he's far enough away now," Sienna whispered. "Let's go." She pulled the key card from the pocket of her jeans and held it up to the electronic pad mounted on the stone wall. Her eyes met Jason's. "Ready?"

He nodded. "Let's do it."

Sienna swiped the card through the slot. The gates gave a loud *clang* and began to swing outward.

"That was loud," Adam whispered.

"It only seemed loud to us," Jason assured him, hoping he was right.

Sienna led the way past the gates as soon as they had opened wide enough to squeeze through. On the other side was another electronic pad, and she swiped the card again. The gates halted, then began to swing closed. "No reason to let them open all the way," she whispered. "Someone might notice that."

Jason nodded. "Where do we go now?"

Sienna pointed across a wide lawn. A two-story building loomed on the other side. Jason couldn't tell how big the place was; all the windows were dark, and there was no real light but the moon.

"There's a door near those bottlebrush trees. You see it?" Sienna asked.

Jason squinted into the darkness. He thought he could make out a faint blue light near the black blobs of the trees.

"Is that a light over it?" Adam asked. "A safety light or something?"

Sienna nodded. "Yes. It's the closest entrance. We need to get in before the security guy comes around again."

"Come on," Jason said. He took off running for the blue light, moving as quietly as he could. The others followed. As he got closer, Jason could see that the blue light was just a dim bulb next to a plain door. No windows, no signs—just a door with a tiny night-light illuminating the keypad next to it.

"This is a back door," Sienna said breathlessly. She swiped her key card. "It has double security. I need to enter a code, as well."

"Do you know the code?" Jason asked.

"I memorized it. My father keeps the codes written on his calendar. They change every week."

"It's been seven and a half minutes since the security guy passed," Adam said, jogging up to them. "Hurry!"

Sienna punched five numbers into the keypad. Nothing happened.

"When do they change the codes?" Jason asked. "Is it before the weekends?"

"I don't know," Sienna replied, biting her lip.

"I hear the guard," Adam whispered frantically.

"Try again," Jason told Sienna.

She took a deep breath and slowly punched in the numbers again. There was a soft *click* as the door unlocked. Jason yanked it open and ushered his friends inside. He pulled it closed again just as the security guard came into view on the lawn outside. They all held their breath, waiting to see if he had spotted them.

"I don't think he saw us," Jason whispered after a minute.

"I put the wrong number in the first time," Sienna murmured. "I hit the three instead of the six."

"It doesn't matter now, we're in." Jason squeezed her arm. "Nice job."

She smiled at him, her expression playful now that the danger had passed. "Thanks. Let's get to the lab. We've got to do this quickly and quietly and just hope none of the security guys hear us."

Inside the building, the hallways were lit with faint green lights every ten feet. Once Jason's eyes had adjusted, he found it pretty easy to see where they were going. The part of the building they were in looked just like the science wing at DeVere High: lots of rooms filled with lab tables and standard equipment like microscopes and test tubes. But Sienna led the way past all that, and into another wing.

This area was different. The lighting was the same, but here there was a faint humming sound that pulsed through the air. Jason thought he could actually feel it like a vibration in his body. "What is that?" he asked.

"Machinery," Adam answered, keeping his voice quiet. "I had to get an MRI once when I hurt my wrist, and the room it was in felt like this—all magnetized."

"He's right," Sienna said. "There's a lot of high-tech stuff down here. All the testing equipment. MRIs, CT scans, PET scans, X-rays . . . plus a few things I don't even know the names of. We have some toys that other labs don't have."

They reached the end of the hallway and went down a flight of stairs. "We're below ground now," Sienna whispered. "They keep the most sensitive machinery down here because it stays cooler. And here's the test room we're looking for." She pushed open a heavy door and stepped inside. Jason and Adam followed.

Once the door had closed behind them, it was pitch black. "I got this!" Adam said. Jason heard him fumbling around, then a flashlight beam cut through the darkness. "Bet you're glad I brought these," he said, handing a flashlight to Jason and another to Sienna.

"I am," Jason agreed. "I don't think we can risk turning on the lights."

"No, but we do have to turn on all the equipment," Sienna said. She began punching power buttons, and various sleek black machines sprang to life with low beeping noises.

Jason examined them, baffled. "I've never seen anything like this before," he said, peering at a two-foot-square box. It had a single opening on the top that looked like a shallow bowl. "Is it a centrifuge?"

"Kind of," Sienna replied.

"Then what's this?" Adam asked. He was staring at a tall, thin machine with a slot in the side. "Am I supposed to stick a dollar bill in here?"

Sienna laughed. "We're going to stick a DNA sample in there. I don't think a dollar bill will help much!"

Adam shook his head, impressed. "This is truly beyond. I mean, I've been in the police CSI lab, and let me tell you, the Malibu police have serious money compared to most cops. But they have nothing like this stuff."

"I'm not sure *anyone* has stuff like this," Jason said slowly. "Regular research labs . . . do they know about this technology?"

"Not all of it, no," Sienna admitted. "The whole point of this center is to work on vampire research. We've had a lot of time to develop new technology, and we . . . uh . . . have pretty good funding. It's a very high-tech place."

"High-tech? It's astronomical-tech!" Adam exclaimed. "I don't even know what these machines are."

"Honestly? Neither do I," Sienna told him. "But the lab technician was more than happy to show me how they work. He explained all the science, but I was too nervous to pay much attention. I doubt I would've understood most of it, anyway. I remember which buttons to push and that's about it."

"How did you get him to talk so much?" Jason asked.

"Well, first I told him who my father was. And then I flirted with him," Sienna said matter-of-factly.

Jason raised an eyebrow.

"I smiled at him and acted impressed," Sienna clarified. "The guy spends half his life in an underground lab with a bunch of computers. It doesn't take much to make him talk. I think he was just psyched to speak to someone other than himself."

"I know just how he feels," Adam cracked.

"Let's get on with this," Jason said. "Before we get caught."

"Okay. I have everything turned on, and I'm telling the main computer to set up the human genetic test for one subject." She typed a command into a keyboard set up beneath a flat screen monitor on the wall.

"Make it two subjects," Jason corrected her. "I

brought some of my sister's hair. I figure we may as well test her, too. Aunt Bianca will want her to undergo the transformation at some point."

"Okay, let's see . . . here it is, multiple subjects," Sienna said, clicking on a box onscreen. "We're set. We need to get the samples on slides and put them in the slot."

"I am the slide master," Adam announced, rummaging in one of the cabinets. He pulled out a box of glass slides and began to lay them out on the counter. "Slides, I understand. This DNA-reader-thingie I do *not* understand. Does it have a name?"

"Not that I know of," Sienna said.

"Then I hereby christen it the DNAbilizer," Adam announced. "Jason. Hair."

Jason reached up to pull a strand of his hair out.

"Wait!" Adam said. "Make sure you get some skin on the end of it. The DNA is in the skin, not the hair."

Jason obediently pinched his scalp and yanked out some hair. Adam slipped on a plastic glove, took the hair, and began preparing a slide.

Jason reached into his pocket and pulled out Dani's brush. "Can you hold the light for me?" he asked Sienna. She aimed her flashlight at the brush while Jason pulled out a few strands of hair. He studied the ends. "I can't see well enough to tell if there's any skin on the ends," he said.

Sienna leaned in close to him and examined the hair. "Neither can I," she finally said. "Let's make slides for a couple of pieces of hair. Hopefully the DNAbilizer will be able to find DNA to read on one of them."

Jason chose a few strands and handed them to Adam, who put each hair on its own slide.

Then Sienna took the slides and fed them into the slot in the DNAbilizer. Each slide disappeared soundlessly into the machine. Then a series of knocking sounds began, growing faster, then slower, and then starting the entire process again.

"What's it doing?" Adam asked.

"Performing the test," Sienna said. The knocking cycle stopped, the machine now whirring softly.

"All in that one machine? We don't have to do anything else?" Jason asked.

"The DNAbilizer is actually about five machines in one, based on what the technician told me," Sienna said. "They like to streamline everything here."

"Well, what's taking so long?" Adam demanded.

Sienna gaped at him. "It's isolating a single strand of DNA for detailed analysis. How fast do you think that can happen?"

He shrugged. "It would probably take a week to get DNA results at the CSI lab. So I'm thinking it should take about three seconds here."

"We have advanced technology, not a magic wand," Sienna said. "It takes a while."

"*Shh!*" Jason hissed. "I hear something."

They fell silent. From out in the hallway came the unmistakable sound of footsteps.

"Turn off the flashlights," Sienna whispered frantically. They all shut off their lights. The computer monitor glowed in the darkness, casting an eerie bluish light over all the black machines.

The door opened.

Wordlessly, Jason grabbed Sienna's arm and pulled her back into the shadows behind the DNAbilizer. Adam crouched below the counter he'd prepared the slides on.

A security guard stepped into the room, propping the door open with his foot. Some of the green light from the hallway leaked into the darkness. The eerie glow backlit the guard, making him much easier to see—Jason hoped—than he, Sienna, and Adam were in the shadows.

Jason felt Sienna's hand grasp his, her fingers cold. He looked at her, and she gestured with her head toward the monitor. Data had begun scrolling quickly down the screen, numbers changing faster than the eye could follow.

In the doorway, the guard frowned. He reached for the light switches. Jason's breath caught in his throat: If the lights went on, they'd be discovered for sure!

EIGHTEEN

*B*eeeeep!

The DNAbilizer let out a loud final sound and turned itself off. On the monitor, the numbers vanished and a message flashed up: DIAGNOSTIC COMPLETE.

In the doorway, the guard chuckled to himself. "Damn machines!" he muttered, stepping back outside. The door swung shut behind him, and the room returned to darkness. Jason held still, his heart slamming against his ribs. Sienna waited beside him, not moving.

Across the room, Adam slowly crumpled to the floor. "Oh, thank God," he whispered. "I totally froze in the wrong position and got a leg cramp!"

Jason bit back a laugh. He could see Sienna and Adam also struggling not to crack up. The relief of not getting caught was making them all giddy.

"That was close," Sienna said finally. "It's a good thing the DNAbilizer is fast." She clicked on her flashlight and crossed over to the keyboard. She typed in a command: display results. The monitor went blank. A green light clicked on over the slot in the machine, and one of the slides slid back out. Jason took it. It was his hair, short and blond.

On screen, a report appeared: SUBJECT #1. COMPATIBLE.

A tingly feeling shot up Jason's spine. He locked eyes with Sienna. *Compatible.* He could do it. He could become a vampire if he wanted to. He could be with Sienna. Forever.

The green light went on again, and another slide popped out.

Adam grabbed it. "Uh-oh," he said.

Jason pulled his gaze away from Sienna. "What?"

"Subject number two, incompatible," Adam said, gesturing at the monitor, where Jason could read the words for himself.

"Oh, no," Sienna murmured. "Dani . . ."

The green light came on again, and a third slide shot out. The monitor added a new line: SUBJECT #3. INCOMPATIBLE.

"Wait. What?" Jason said. "What does it mean, subject number three?"

"We did two slides from the hair on the brush, remember?" Sienna reminded him. "It probably thinks each slide was for a separate person. Here, I can make it give more detailed info. We can check." She typed in another command: Display details. Immediately a long list of numbers appeared under the heading SUBJECT #1.

"See? That's everything about you," Sienna told him. "The mtDNA markers are displayed in red."

"Maybe I should print it out for future reference," he murmured.

"Now here's Dani," she said, as the monitor displayed the detailed results for subject number two. "And here's the mysterious subject number three. It will all be the same data. . . ." Sienna's voice trailed off. The numbers appearing underneath subject number three were *not* the same. They could all see that. The numbers displayed in red were different numbers. Not all of them, but enough to prove that this was not the same person.

"That's not Dani," Jason said slowly. "And it's not me. The numbers are different."

"Maybe somebody else's hair was in Dani's brush," Sienna suggested. "Kristy's?"

Jason grabbed the hairbrush and began pulling out individual strands. Some were only seven or eight inches long, some were more than a foot long, and all were dark.

"Is there a way to tell if the subjects are related to one another?" Jason asked Sienna. His stomach was cramping. He had an idea who subject number three was, but he really, really wanted to be wrong.

"I think the number of shared DNA markers indicates that," Adam told him.

Sienna toggled back and forth between the results. "Well, all three subjects have a lot of markers in common," she pointed out.

"I'm pretty sure that means all three subjects are related," Adam said.

Now Jason knew exactly who those hairs belonged to. He knew exactly who the incompatible subject number three was. He ran his hand through his hair in agitation.

"Jason?" Sienna asked. "What is it?"

"Subject number three," he whispered. "It's not Kristy. It's my Aunt Bianca."

NINETEEN

"But it can't be!" Sienna exclaimed.

Suddenly a whole lot of things were starting to make sense to Jason. "I'm pretty sure it can, actually," Jason replied. "She's been acting totally weird. She plucked out all her eyebrows the other day."

"Dang," Adam muttered.

"That doesn't mean—" Sienna began.

"It's not just that," Jason interrupted. "It's the way she's acting. You saw a little bit of it in the pool house, Sienna. Aunt Bianca has a different personality every thirty seconds."

Sienna shook her head in disbelief. "I don't want to believe it, but she certainly was acting weird that day."

"Bianca's been acting crazy, but it never occurred to me that she really *was* crazy," Jason said, his head spinning. Aunt Bianca was incompatible with the vampires, but now she *was* a vampire. And she was going mad. She had the transformation sickness.

"Jason." Adam's voice cut through his thoughts. "We have to get out of here."

"You're right." Jason tried to shake off his worry.

"I'll figure out how to deal with this once we're safely away from the lab."

Adam pulled the remaining slides from the machine and shoved them in his overstuffed backpack. Sienna typed "Delete Diagnostic" into the keyboard, then turned off all the machinery.

Adam shut off his flashlight, pulled open the door, and led the way out.

"There's a closer exit," Sienna whispered. "It's that way." She pushed Jason in front of her and brought up the rear. Jason appreciated her concern—he knew he wasn't thinking too clearly at the moment. What was going to happen to Aunt Bianca? How was he going to break the news to her?

"Crap!" Adam muttered. He held up his hand, signaling for them to stop. "Look."

Jason glanced up—and froze. A camera was mounted in the ceiling, its red light focused like a laser as it swept slowly across the hallway. "Two more seconds and it'll be right on us," Jason said. He turned to Adam. "Take off your jacket."

Adam whipped it off and tossed it to Jason. "Get close together," Jason ordered. Then he flung the camouflage jacket over their heads.

"Now run!" Adam cried. Huddled together, they raced for the nearest door. Adam elbowed it open, and they all hurried inside.

"Damn! I was so busy thinking about the key codes, I completely forgot about the cameras," Sienna cried. "Did they see us?"

"I think Jason got my coat over us in time to block our faces," Adam replied. "But they definitely saw a bunch of idiots running around under a camouflage jacket."

"My father will murder me if I get caught breaking into the center with a couple of humans," Sienna said. "This is so far beyond what's acceptable to the Council."

"Are you kidding?" Adam cried. "My father will murder me if I get caught breaking into anything, anywhere, with anyone. He's a cop! He's the *sheriff*! His son is not, repeat *not*, allowed to commit crimes."

"Everybody calm down," Jason ordered them. "The longer we stay near that camera, the faster they'll find us." He took off down the hall and pushed open the first door he came to, holding it open until Sienna and Adam got inside.

Jason scanned the room. It was another lab, this one without any super-secret vampire machinery. There were windows in the far wall. "Quick. Out the window!"

In one fluid motion, Sienna moved across the room and unlocked the window, sliding it open and peering outside. "Okay, I know where we are," she said, as the two guys joined her. "But the gates are way on the other side of the building. We'll have to climb the wall and then walk back to the cars once we're outside."

"The wall is covered in ivy," Adam said. "It shouldn't be too hard to climb. Unless, you know, there are dogs nipping at our heels—although that might be quite the motivator. How do we know where the guards are?"

"I think we just have to chance it," Jason said. "They must've seen us on the camera. They'll be looking in the building first."

"Then let's go." Sienna climbed out the window and took off toward the wall.

"No fair," Adam muttered. "She has super-human speed."

"So let's not hang around," Jason said. He swung his legs through the window, jumped down, and sprinted after Sienna. He heard Adam running behind him.

By the time Jason reached the wall, Sienna was halfway up, climbing the vines like a rope. He grabbed on to one of the leafy branches and pulled himself off the ground. Any second he expected to hear the barking of dogs. Or to see a spotlight go on and catch him, like in a prison-escape movie.

But suddenly he was at the top of the wall. He straddled it, then reached down a hand and hauled Adam up beside him. "I don't see anyone following us," Jason said.

"That's no reason to stay here talking," Adam replied. He swung his legs over and climbed down the other side. Jason followed more slowly.

Sienna was waiting at the bottom, her expression serious.

"What's wrong?" Jason asked.

"I turned my cell back on and there was a message from Belle," she said. "It's bad."

Jason's throat went dry. Had the security guards called Sienna's father already? Were they caught after all?

"It's about Dani," Sienna went on.

"Dani?" Jason repeated, surprised. "What about her?"

"She took off with Ryan," Sienna said. "She told Belle they were going to Le Fleur."

"The hotel?" Adam asked, frowning.

"What hotel?" Jason demanded.

"It's mostly for honeymooners. It's a very private inn on the beach," Sienna said. "That's the thing. Belle is worried. She thinks Dani and Ryan are so upset about having to break up that they might have gone there to do something drastic."

"Drastic like turning Dani into a vampire?" Jason asked.

Sienna nodded.

"But they can't!" Adam cried. "The test showed that Dani is genetically incompatible with the vampire genes. If she undergoes the transformation, she could go insane. She could die!"

"All true," Jason said grimly, already running for his car. "But Dani doesn't know that, does she?"

TWENTY

Jason headed for his car at a dead run. He had to get to Dani. If he was too late, if she'd already undergone the transformation. . . .

He couldn't even think about it.

When they got back to where the cars were, Jason didn't hesitate. He jumped into the Bug and started it up. Adam squeezed himself into the tiny backseat, and Sienna took shotgun. "Where is this hotel?" Jason demanded.

"It's just up the coast a few miles," Sienna said. "Ryan's family owns it. That must be why they went there."

Jason hit the gas and screeched out onto the road, heading for Pacific Coast Highway. As he drove, he fished his cell out of the glove compartment where he'd left it when they broke in to the lab. He hit speed dial for Dani's number.

"We're sorry," said an electronic voice. "The wireless customer you have reached is unavailable or has traveled out of range—"

"Dammit," Jason muttered. He hung up and dialed again.

The same message greeted him.

"Her phone's not working," he told his friends.

"If she's really planning to do this, she probably doesn't want to be reached," Adam pointed out.

Jason slammed his fist against the steering wheel. "I knew she would do this if she found out about transforming! She doesn't think before she does things."

"You never told her?" Sienna asked. "About your aunt wanting the two of you to become vampires?"

"No. I wanted to get all the information first," Jason said. "I wanted to prevent Danielle from doing something like this. I didn't want her to even know it was possible to turn into a vampire."

"Well, if you didn't tell her, who did?" Adam asked.

"Ryan must have," Jason said. "If he's done it, if he's turned her, I'll kill him."

"Slow down," Sienna said, putting her hand on his arm. "There's no way Ryan would do this on his own. He would never in a million years try to talk Dani into transforming. None of us would. We all know how dangerous it is." She paused, then went on carefully. "Do you think it could have been Bianca's idea?"

"She told me she wouldn't say anything to Dani," Jason said, not wanting to believe that his aunt would do such a thing. "She promised."

"But she's not herself, Jason," Sienna said gently.

"Bianca has the transformation sickness. We know that now. There's no telling what she might do."

Jason whipped the Bug down the ramp onto PCH. He floored it, picking up speed. How long had Dani been gone? How long did it even take to complete the transformation? Was he too late already?

Frantic, he grabbed his cell and dialed again. The same message answered him. He hung up and dialed Aunt Bianca's number. The phone rang, and then her voice mail picked up. "Aunt Bianca!" Jason yelled into the phone. "I need to talk to you! Dani's in danger. If she transforms, she'll get sick. You have to help me stop her." He hung up. PCH was only two lanes here, with sheer bluffs on one side and a steep drop down to the beach on the other.

"There!" Sienna pointed to a sign. "That's our exit. Go slow, the road isn't paved."

Jason hit the brakes as he made the turn onto a dark, narrow lane. He wouldn't have even noticed it was there if Sienna hadn't told him. The Bug skidded on the loose gravel as they went downhill toward the Pacific.

"Here." Jason shoved his cell at Adam. "Keep trying Dani." Adam turned on the speaker and hit redial, but Dani's phone didn't pick up.

"Doesn't matter. We're here," Sienna said.

Jason turned the Bug into a small parking lot near

a white Cape Cod–style inn with an antique gas lamp glowing outside the front door. He shut off the engine, grabbed his cell phone, and leaped out of the car, running for the entrance. The lobby was tiny—just a wooden desk and a big fireplace with a couple of overstuffed chairs in front of it.

The woman at the desk jumped when she saw Jason racing in. "Can I help you?" she asked, frowning.

"Ryan Patrick. Is he here?" Jason demanded.

"We need to see him. It's urgent," Sienna explained.

The receptionist checked her computer. "Yes, he has cabin six," she said. "I'll call over for you."

"Never mind," Jason said. He was already out the door.

"I saw a sign for the cabins this way," Adam told him. "Down the stairs."

Jason veered to the right and hurried down the steps that led toward the beach. Several private cabins lay spread throughout the dunes, each with a cabin number lit by a tiny lantern. He spotted cabin six right away.

"Dani!" Jason yelled, racing toward the cabin. "Dani!" He pounded on the door, but there was no answer. Jason tried the knob. The door swung open, unlocked. The cabin was empty.

A wave of panic washed over him. Where was his sister? What had happened to her?

"We'll search the whole place," Sienna said, sensing

his terror. "Don't worry. We'll find them. We'll stop them."

"I'll check the bar," Adam called, sprinting back up the steps.

"I'll check the hot tub," Sienna said, disappearing in the other direction.

Jason wasn't sure where to check. While he thought about it, he pulled out his cell and hit redial.

The phone rang, and then Dani's voice answered. "Jason," she hissed. "What is going on? You've called me about twenty times. This better be an emergency!"

"Oh, thank God," he cried. "Are you okay? Where are you?"

"Jason—"

"I'm already at the hotel. Now tell me exactly where you are," he said sternly.

"On the beach. Down by the water," Danielle answered, confusion in her voice now. "What are you—"

"Stay there. Don't do a thing," Jason instructed. He hung up and rushed to the stairs that led from the dunes down to the sea. As he reached them, he almost crashed into Adam, who was on his way back from the bar.

"She's down on the beach," Jason told him. "Go get Sienna."

Jason kept running, down through the dunes and onto the flat stretch of beach. He dreaded what he might find there. What if Dani had already transformed?

Four tall tiki torches had been set up on the sand near the sea, with a thick blanket spread between them. Jason could see Dani and Ryan sitting there, a bottle of Champagne in a bucket and a picnic dinner laid out in front of them.

Dani scrambled to her feet when she saw him. "Jason," she cried angrily. "I can't believe—"

"Have you done the transformation yet?" he demanded.

Both Dani and Ryan just stared at him.

"Have you?"

"No," Dani said, a tinge of worry creeping into her voice. "We're just having dinner."

"Look, Jason . . . ," Ryan began, just as Sienna and Adam raced up.

Danielle gaped at the new arrivals. "What on earth—"

Jason took his sister's arm and drew her to one side while Sienna and Adam went to talk to Ryan.

"Let go," Dani said, shaking him off. "I can't believe you—barging in on my date! What's wrong with you?"

"You're not supposed to be with Ryan," Jason said.

"You're not supposed to be with Sienna," she pointed out.

"Okay, point taken," Jason agreed, running his hand through his hair. "You're okay?"

"Yes." Dani's voice softened. "Why?"

"Dani, you can't become a vampire," he said. "Not ever."

"Aunt Bianca said I could," she replied. "She told me—"

"I know what she said, but she's wrong," Jason interrupted. "She didn't tell you about the risks, did she? She didn't tell you about transformation sickness."

"No," Dani said slowly, suddenly seeming very small and unsure.

Jason took her hand and pulled her down onto the sand, then sat down next to her. "Aunt Bianca isn't really . . . she's not herself lately," he said. "She has something the vampires call transformation sickness. It's what happens to some humans who turn into vampires. The thing is, some humans can't handle the change, and they die."

Danielle gasped.

"Others don't die, but they get sick," Jason continued. "Mentally, I mean. They go insane. There's a test for it, and I took the test tonight. I took a sample of your DNA, and I tested that as well. It said you were incompatible, Dani. Your body couldn't handle the transformation."

Dani pulled back, tears in her eyes. "You're lying," she said. "Aunt Bianca turned into a vampire years ago. Nothing happened to her. She's not sick." But Jason could tell that Dani was already doubtful.

"Think about it, Dani. Think of how weird she's been acting lately," he pressed. "And when Tyler was in town, he stole something from the Lafrenières. Now, I'm not saying it was right. Far from it. But Aunt Bianca wanted to have him killed because of it!"

Danielle covered her mouth in horror. "I can't believe it," she murmured. "Poor Aunt Bee." Dani stared down at her toes, buried in the cool sand. "And that's what would happen to me?" she asked at last.

"Yes. I'm sorry," Jason said simply.

"Thank you, Jason," she whispered. "Thank you for finding me. We were planning to . . . later. We figured since we had Bianca's blessing, it would be okay. Ryan's parents couldn't be mad with Bianca on our side."

"Ryan!" a voice cut through the air. "Where are you?"

Jason jerked his head toward the sound. A tall, broad-shouldered man was striding down the beach toward them, his brown eyes blazing. He had blond hair cut military short, but Jason suspected that if it was a little longer it would be curly—like Ryan's. The man had to be Ryan's father. He stalked across the sand, practically mowing down a couple taking a romantic moonlit walk. They stopped in their tracks, took in the group by the blanket, and turned back toward the cabins.

"Dad? What are you doing here?" Ryan asked.

Yep. The man was a lot more guard dog than puppy dog, but Jason had been right.

"I got a call from the manager. She saw you checking in with a girl, a human, and thought I should know about it!" Mr. Patrick snapped. "I knew it would be Dani." His eyes swept over Jason's sister, and Jason moved closer to her, protectively.

"You were planning to transform her, weren't you?" Mr. Patrick continued. "Because your mother and I forbade you to see her."

"It didn't happen," Jason put in quickly.

"Yeah, Dad, we didn't do anything," Ryan added.

"Who are you?" Mr. Patrick demanded, ignoring his son and staring at Jason.

"I'm Dani's brother. I . . . we . . ." He gestured to Sienna and Adam. "We found out what was going on in time to stop them."

"The important thing is that nothing happened, Mr. Patrick," Sienna said coolly.

He nodded.

"And right now, there's something even more important that you need to know," Sienna went on. "Something about Bianca." She quickly filled him in.

Mr. Patrick sighed and shook his head. "I'll inform the Council. They'll need to hear about this right away," he said. "Come on, Ryan." He turned and marched away without a backward glance, clearly expecting Ryan to follow—which Ryan did, with an apologetic look over his shoulder at Dani.

"Why don't we all get out of here?" Adam asked. "I feel we may be spoiling the vibe for the actual honey-mooners."

"I just want to be home," Dani answered miserably.

Jason pulled her into a quick hug. "You'll be there in a few minutes," he promised. Sienna wrapped her arm around Dani's shoulders, and they all walked toward the car.

"She only told me how great it would be," Dani said, her voice so soft, it was almost as if she were talking to herself. "She kept saying it would be her legacy to me. That I'd live a really long time, and that I'd be totally rich because I'd inherit everything from her, and that everyone would be okay with Ryan and me being together."

"Bianca's ill, Dani," Sienna reminded her. "I know she wasn't trying to hurt you."

Jason looked at Sienna across the top of Dani's head. "Speaking of Bianca," he said grimly, "we have to find a way to help her—before she goes completely insane."

TWENTY-ONE

"Okay, showtime," Jason said as he pulled the Bug into his driveway after dropping Adam off at his house. "Are you ready to go in there and show our parents what happy, normal, non-acquainted-with-vampire teens we are?"

Dani nodded, her eyes glassy with shock.

"Hey, Dani . . ." Jason hesitated, not knowing exactly what to say. "It'll be all right. You're all right. You had a close call tonight, but you're okay."

She nodded again, then forced a smile. "Thanks for riding to my rescue."

"Yeah, you looked real happy to see me when I showed up," Jason teased gently.

His sister smiled again. A little more convincingly this time. "Look at me. I'm a happy normal teen! And I don't believe in vampires!" she exclaimed. "How was that?"

"Oscar-worthy," Jason told her.

Dani opened the car door. "Let's do it."

Jason followed her up to the house, and they walked inside together. They found their parents in the living room. The TV was on, but neither of them was watching it. Mr. Freeman sat on the couch, frowning, and Mrs. Freeman paced up and down the length of the room.

"Hey, we're home," Jason told them. "What's up?" Because something definitely was.

"Did either of you talk to your Aunt Bianca tonight, by any chance?" Mr. Freeman asked.

"Nuh-uh," Jason answered for both of them. He'd *tried* to talk to Bianca, but she hadn't answered her cell.

"She just packed up and left," Mrs. Freeman burst out. "No note, no good-bye, nothing! I just don't understand what's going on with her."

Could she be feeling guilty about what almost happened to Dani tonight? Jason wondered. But when he thought about it, it seemed more likely that his aunt's disappearance was just another sign of her mental deterioration.

"She'll probably call you in a few days to say she's jetted off to Italy to buy shoes or something," Mr. Freeman said reassuringly.

"Yeah, that sounds like Aunt Bianca," Dani agreed, her voice shaking just the tiniest bit. Enough that Jason knew she was thinking about what was happening to Bianca's mind. And what had almost happened to Dani herself.

But then Dani sat down next to her mother and

took her hand. "Really. Don't worry, Mom," she said, her voice strong now. "Aunt Bianca will be fine. I know it."

And Jason believed her.

She's okay, he thought, relieved. *We got to her in time. Dani is truly okay.*

"How's Dani doing?" Sienna asked the next day at lunch with Belle and Adam.

"She's still a little shaken up," Jason admitted.

"Poor baby," Belle said sympathetically.

"She's going to be fine, though. Dani always has a fast recovery time. She's a bounce-backer," Jason added.

"I found out from my parents that Ryan's dad called an emergency session of the Council last night," Sienna informed them. "I thought my parents would freak when they heard about us breaking into the center. But instead the whole Council is thanking their lucky stars that we figured out what would happen if Ryan transformed Dani. If she underwent the transformation and got sick, it would've been a huge tragedy. They're all thrilled that we prevented it." She smiled at Jason. "We actually sort of ended up looking like heroes."

"I *am* extremely heroic," Adam commented. "It's the chin. I have a strong chin, the chin of a hero." He put his hands on his hips, mock-superhero style. "Do not fear. My chin and I will always be here to protect you. We are available for any mission. And we will fearlessly continue to search the web for news of vampire hunters and other dangers to our special friends." He winked at Sienna and Belle.

"I feel very safe now," Jason told Adam, as Belle and Sienna laughed. "What'd the Council say about my aunt?" he asked Sienna.

"That the center is trying to find a cure for transformation sickness," Sienna explained. "Until they do, the Council will keep tabs on Bianca—if she ever shows up again. They've got people out looking for her, but it seems as if she's just vanished. I hope she's all right."

"I hope so too," Jason thought, his mother's worried face flashing into his mind. "I wonder if she knew she was getting sick. Maybe that's why she was so worried about her 'legacy.' It might explain why she was in such a rush to get Dani and me to transform."

"I think she must have known deep down, on a subconscious level," Sienna answered. "The mood swings she got from the transformation sickness definitely upped her intensity too."

"I hope we'll hear from her again soon," Jason said. "Nobody can help her while we don't know where she is." He, Sienna, Belle, and Adam considered this in silence for a long moment.

"My parents gave me some other interesting news," Sienna said, finally, an unexpected smile tugging at her lips.

"Well, lay it on us," Adam demanded.

Sienna leaned across the table, took Jason's face in her hands, looked him in the eye for a long moment, then kissed him. And kissed him, and kissed him, and kissed him.

"Woo-hoo!" Jason heard Adam whoop.

"So is the news that it's okay with your parents if you're with Jason? Or is it something else?" Belle asked, deadpan.

Sienna grinned, breaking the kiss. "They said that as long as I promise faithfully not to transform Jason, they give us their permission to get back together. And the Council is cool with that too."

"I wasn't expecting that," Jason said. "Not that I'm complaining."

"Like I said, we ended up looking like heroes for the way we handled the Dani and Ryan sitch. That's a big reason my parents and the Council are willing for us to be together. You've given them a big reason to trust you—*another* big reason, that is. Also ..." Sienna hesitated.

"Also?" Jason prompted.

"I think that everybody's a little afraid that if they don't give us permission to be together, I'll just transform you right now whether they approve or not. They know that we know it's safe for you," Sienna explained.

"*C'est bon!*" Adam exclaimed. "And . . . I'm out of French."

"I'm so happy for you guys," Belle told them.

"Me too," Sienna said, her eyes on Jason. "And if we're still together, say, after college, then my parents agreed they'd feel differently about you becoming one of us—if that's what you want—since we know for sure that the transformation sickness won't affect you."

"We'll still be together," Jason promised her. "I know it."

Jason bounded into the house after swim practice on Wednesday. Life was good. He had Sienna. He'd just beaten his best time in the medley. And, oh yeah . . . he had Sienna!

"You look happy," his mom commented.

"I am. How about you?" he asked, realizing that his mother actually looked happier than she had lately.

"I'm a lot better now that I've heard from your aunt. Bianca called this afternoon from the office. All la-di-da, like I had no reason to have been worried. She'd just had to fly back to New York to see a hot new up-and-comer in a play." Mrs. Freeman shook her head. "I figured my little sister would have got a bit more mature by now, but I guess not. I'm just relieved that she's okay."

"Me too," Jason said. And he hoped she stayed okay for a long time.

"What do you say we make some of Dani's favorite jam thumbprint cookies?" his mom asked. "She seems blue-ish to me these past few days. I expect it's boy trouble—not that she talks to me, I'm only her mother."

"Sure. Why not?" Jason answered. He hadn't helped his mother make cookies since he was a little kid. But it could be fun. And his mom was right: Dani definitely did seem like she needed cheering up. She hadn't said anything to him about what was going on with her and Ryan, but he had the feeling she was having a hard time.

"Great. Go wash your hands and we'll get started," Mrs. Freeman said.

"Why do I have to wash my hands?" Jason mock-whined. "I was just at swim practice. My hands were submerged in water for hours."

She laughed. And Jason was struck by the thought of just how hard it would be if he did let Sienna transform him someday. He'd never be able to tell his mom or his dad the truth. There'd always be this *thing* between them. This huge secret.

Jason headed into the kitchen with his mother. *It isn't even something Dani and I could both do, even though she knows the truth about the vampires*, he thought as he started to wash his hands. His sister had no choice but to remain human. And maybe he should too. It's what he was. It's what his family was.

But now that Sienna knew Jason could safely undergo the transformation, how would she feel if he decided not to? Would she think that meant he didn't love her? Or didn't love her enough to want to be with her for her whole life?

"I think you're probably clean enough," Mrs. Freeman commented, pulling him away from his thoughts. "We're baking, not performing surgery."

Sienna and I will work it out together when it's time, Jason decided as he dried his hands on a paper towel. *We always do.*

"Don't eat the last of the cookies," Dani warned him on Friday night. "Those are mine. They were made for me."

"They were made *by* me," Jason countered. "I should get a couple more."

"Nope. All mine!" Dani told him. She looked down at her skirt. "I don't know if I should go with the Diesel. Maybe I should change. What do you think?"

"When you start talking about clothes—and I assume you are, since you were looking at your skirt when you asked the question—it's like Adam talking about movies. I pretty much have no idea what you're saying," Jason confessed.

Dani ran her hands down her short—way too short, Jason thought—brown skirt. "Just, do you think it looks good?"

Looks good for Ryan? Jason wondered. "Well, it's longer in the back than the front," Jason told her. "Is it supposed to do that?"

"Yes," Dani said, all *duh*. "It's called a fishtail."

"And are those straps doing anything?" There were these two thin strips of webbed material that ran from the waist of the skirt to the hem. They were like luggage straps or something. "Are they supposed to show?"

"I really shouldn't have asked you," Dani commented.

"You really shouldn't have," Jason agreed.

"Maybe I'll go try on my new—" The doorbell interrupted her. "That's for me!" Dani exclaimed.

Jason followed her to the hall. He had to admit that he was a little curious to see if it was Ryan picking her up. Although it was hard to imagine Ryan's dad being okay with that—after the hotel fiasco.

Dani pulled open the door and Jason saw Kristy and Maria standing on the porch. But, more importantly, he also saw Sienna pulling her car into the driveway behind them. Jason smiled. He couldn't help himself. When he saw Sienna, he smiled.

"Love the Diesel," Sienna told Dani as she came in.

"Thank you!" Dani replied. "I was trying to get an opinion from my brother and it was hopeless."

"He's fashion illiterate," Sienna agreed.

"No more mocking of the guy," Jason ordered. "Where are you three off to?"

"We're going to Thai Town," Maria told him. "Dani needs to see Kevin, the Thai Elvis, do his thing. And also, we need coconut rice."

"Have fun," Sienna called as they hurried out.

"We will, don't worry," Kristy called back. "We're going to make sure Miss Dani has lots and lots and lots of fun."

"Why do I have the feeling that they're trying to take Dani's mind off something—like when the guys took me to Venice Beach after our sort-of breakup?" Jason asked as he closed the door behind them.

"Because you're right. I was talking to Belle before I came over, and she told me Dani broke up with Ryan," Sienna answered.

"Weird that I have to figure out what's going on with my sister through the best friend of my girl-friend," Jason told her.

"Belle and Dani have gotten really close. She's been like a big sister to Dani through the Ryan romance. It's been good for Belle, having something to think about other than all the bad stuff. She's starting to get over Dominic's death, I think."

"It's been good for Dani, too. It's not like she could talk to Kristy or my mom about the difficulties of dating a vampire," Jason pointed out. "Did Belle say anything else?"

"Just that Ryan's hurting right now," Sienna told him.

"Dani, too," Jason said.

"She'll recover. They both will," Sienna promised. "In fact, word on the grapevine is that there's a very cute boy who is going head over heels for Dani. A *human* cute boy," Sienna added before Jason could ask.

Jason grinned. "Now that that's settled," he said happily, "what should we do tonight? What are you in the mood for? Anything you want . . ."

"Well, we never got to really dance to our song," Sienna answered. "How about we go back to the yacht and finish what we started? It'll be even better under the stars."

"And that's okay with your father?" Jason asked doubtfully. "The place *is* a floating motel, so I hear."

"He trusts us," Sienna replied. She pulled a key ring out of her pocket. "He gave me the keys himself."

"So should I call Adam and Belle?" Jason teased. "Since we're trying to finish what we started. They were there the first time and all."

Sienna gave an exaggerated frown. "Sadly, Belle and Adam are on their way to the Cinerama Dome. Belle thinks the bar at the theater is the perfect place for Adam to meet some simpatico, movie-loving chicks."

Jason grinned and opened the door for her.

"Should we take my car or yours to the marina?" Sienna asked.

"Yours. Definitely," Jason answered.

"You know the Spider is temperamental," Sienna warned. "We could end up breaking down."

"That's what I'm hoping for," Jason confessed. "Nothing better than breaking down with you and getting stuck somewhere." He leaned close and whispered in her ear. "All alone."

Sienna gave him that slow, sexy smile of hers and grabbed his hand. "My car it is."